OH MAN,
OH WOMAN . . .

HOUSTON, HOUSTON DO YOU READ?
It was a bad trip, a really bad trip for the crew of the *Sunbird*. Somehow they had lost radio contact with Houston . . . and just to make things worse, they had lost several hundred years too.

HER SMOKE ROSE UP FOREVER
Some things are wonderful, and guys like Peter never forgot them. But there were other things, too —agonizing things—and no matter how you died, they lived on forever . . .

A MOMENTARY TASTE OF BEING
Dr. Lory Kaye wasn't lying. She had been interrogated as if she were an enemy by members of her own crew on the *Centaur*. The planet she and the Gamma scout crew had found was a paradise, ideal for human habitation . . . even though opening certain doors to it meant death!

Star Songs
OF AN
Old Primate

James Tiptree, Jr.

A Del Rey Book

BALLANTINE BOOKS • NEW YORK

ACKNOWLEDGMENTS

"Your Haploid Heart," copyright © 1969 by the Condé Nast Publications, Inc., for *Analog Science Fiction,* September 1969.

"And So On, And So On," copyright © 1971 by James Tiptree, Jr., for *Phantasmicon 6.*

"Her Smoke Rose Up Forever," copyright © 1974 by Edward L. Ferman and Barry N. Malzberg for *Final Stage.*

"A Momentary Taste of Being," copyright © 1975 by Robert Silverberg for *The New Atlantis.*

"Houston, Houston, Do You Read?" copyright © 1976 by Fawcett Publications, Inc., for *Aurora: Beyond Equality.*

"The Psychologist Who Wouldn't Do Awful Things to Rats," copyright © 1976 by Robert Silverberg for *New Dimensions 6.*

"She Waits for All Men Born," copyright © 1976 by Gene Wolfe for *Future Power.*

Library of Congress Catalog Card Number: 77-6129

ISBN 0-345-25417-1

Manufactured in the United States of America

First Edition: January 1978
Second Printing: February 1979

First Canadian Printing: January 1978
Second Canadian Printing: February 1979

CONTENTS

INTRODUCTION

by Ursula K. Le Guin

> *Abominations, that's what they are: afterwords,
> introductions, all the dribble around the story.*
> —J. Tiptree, Jr., 1971

When the author of this book requested me to write an
introduction for it, I was honored, delighted, and appalled. Omitting the civilities and apologies customary
between old primates, and which went on for about a
week, the request appeared in these terms, and I quote:
"Write a two-line introduction saying, Here are some
stories."

I have been trying to obey these instructions ever
since. Various versions have been tested; for example:

1) Here
   Are some stories.

2) Here are
   Some stories.

3) Here are some
   Stories.

Since none of these efforts seemed entirely satisfactory, I took the liberty of expanding upon the basic instructions, at the risk of offending the profound and authentic modesty of the author, and arrived at this:

4) Here are some superbly strong sad funny and very beautiful Stories.

That seems a little more like it. I may return to this problem later, with renewed vigor. There must be some way to do it.

I have known James Tiptree, Jr., for several years now; known him well, and with ever-increasing trust and pleasure, and to the profit of my soul. He is a rather slight, fragile man of about sixty, shy in manner, courteous; wears a straw hat; has lived in, and still vacations in, some of the more exotic parts of the world; has been through the Army, the Government, and the University; an introvert, but active; a warm friend, a man of candor, wit, and style. He always types with a blue typewriter ribbon, and the only question I have asked him which he has always evaded is, "Where do you get so many blue typewriter ribbons?" When he himself is blue, he has told me so, and I've tried to cheer him up, and when I have been blue I've been turned right round into the sunlight simply by getting one of Tiptree's preposterous, magnificent letters. Tiptree has introduced me to the Clerihew; Tiptree has pulled me from the slough of despond by means of a single squid drawn (in blue ink) on a postcard. The only thing better than Tiptree's letters is his stories. He is a man whose friendship is an honor and a joy.

The most wonderful thing about him is that he is also Alice Sheldon.

Recently I've been hearing from people who have friends who say, "I knew all along that Tiptree was a woman. I could tell it from the prose style," or "from the male characters," or "from the female characters," or "from the Vibrations." I don't know any of these people who knew all along; they didn't say much about it; never even happened to mention that they knew, for some reason, until all the rest of us knew. We (the rest of us) knew rather suddenly and utterly unexpectedly. I don't think I have ever been so completely surprised in my life—or so happily. All I can say is I'm glad I didn't know all along, because I would have missed that joyous shock of revelation, recognition—that beautiful Jill-in-the-box.

Quite a lot of us did, however, suspect the short-story writer Raccoona Sheldon of being either an invention of Tiptree's or his natural daughter, and we were quite right; only what is right? What does it mean to say that "Tiptree is Sheldon," or that "James Tiptree, Jr., is a woman"? I am not sure at all, except that it's a fine example of the pitfalls built into the English verb *to be*. You turn it around and say, "A woman is James Tiptree, Jr.," and you see you have said something quite different.

As for *why* Alice is James and James is Alice, that is still another matter, and one where speculation very soon becomes prying and invasion of privacy. But there are fascinating precedents. Mary Ann Evans was a Victorian woman living with a Victorian man to whom she wasn't married; she took a pen-name to protect her work from censure. But why a male pen-name? She could, after all, have called herself Sara Jane Williams. It appears that she needed to be George Eliot, or George Eliot needed to be her, for a while. She and he together got past certain creative and spiritual deadends and morasses that the woman Mary Ann alone was in danger of getting stuck in. As soon as she felt herself free, she admitted and announced the George Eliot/Mary Ann Evans identity. George's name continued to appear on the title pages of the great novels: as a practical matter, of course—the name was a bestseller—but also, I should guess, in gratitude, and in sheer, and characteristic, integrity.

Dr. Alice Sheldon isn't a Victorian, nor are we, and her reasons for using pen-names may be assumed to be personal rather than social; and that's really all we have any right to assume about the matter. But since she did use a male persona, and kept it up publicly with perfect success for years, there are some assumptions that we ought to be examining, gazing at with fascinated horror, revising with loud cries and dramatic gestures of contrition and dismay: and these are our assumptions—all of us, readers, writers, critics, feminists, masculinists, sexists, nonsexists, straights, gays—concerning "the way men write" and "the way women write." The kind of psychic bias that led one of the keenest, subtlest minds in science fiction to state, "It has been suggested that Tiptree is female, a theory that I find absurd, for there is to me something ineluctably masculine about Tiptree's writing. I don't think the novels of Jane Austen could have been written by a man nor the stories of Ernest Hemingway by a woman. . . ." The error was completely honest, and we all made it: but the justification and the generalisation—even with such supposedly extreme examples as Austen and Hemingway . . . that bears some thinking about. We ought to think about it. And about all our arguments concerning Women In Fiction, and why we have them; and all the panels on Women In Science Fiction (omitting, of course, James Tiptree, Jr.) And all the stuff that has been written about "feminine style," about its inferiority or superiority to "masculine style," about the necessary, obligatory difference of the two. All the closed shop attitudes of radical feminism, which invited Tiptree out of certain inner sanctums because, although his stories were so very good and so extraordinary in their understanding of women, still, he was a man. All the ineffable patronization and put-down Sheldon is going to receive now from various male reviewers because, although her stories are so very good and so extraordinary in their understanding of man, still, she is a woman. All that. All that kipple, gubbish, garble and abomination which Alice James Raccoona Tiptree Sheldon, Jr., showed for what it is when she appeared, smiling a little uncertainly, from her postbox in McLean, Virginia. She fooled us. She fooled us good and proper. And we can only thank her for it.

For though she stood us all on our heads, isn't it true

that she played her game without actually lying—without deceit?

The Army, the Government, the University, the jungles, all that is true. Mr. Tiptree's biography is Dr. Sheldon's.

The beautiful story "The Women Men Don't See" (oh—now that we know—what a gorgeously ironic title!) got a flood of nominations for the Nebula Award in 1974. So much of the praise of the story concerned the evidence it gave that a man could write with full sympathy about women, that Tiptree felt a prize for it would involve deceit, false pretenses. She withdrew the story from the competition, muttering about not wanting to cut younger writers out of all the prizes. I don't think this cover-up was false, either: the truth, if not the whole truth. She had had a Nebula in 1973 for "Love Is the Plan the Plan is Death," and a Hugo in the same year for "The Girl Who Was Plugged In." These prizes sneaked up on her and caught her by surprise, I think. Her 1976 Nebula for the powerful "Houston, Houston, Do You Read," in this volume, came so soon after the disclosure of her name that she didn't have time to think up a good excuse for withdrawing it; so she went off and hid in a jungle instead. She practices that "low profile" which Carlos Castaneda, standing in high profile on the rooftops, preaches. The cult of personality, prevalent in art as in politics, is simply not her game.

Yet she did fool us; and the fact is important, because it makes a point which no amount of argument could have made. Not only does it imperil all theories concerning the woman as writer and the writer as woman, but it might make us question some of our assumptions concerning the existence of the writer, per se. It's idiotic to say, "There is no such person as James Tiptree, Jr." There is. The proof that there is, which will incidentally outlast us all, is these stories. But, because James wrote them, is Alice now to be besieged by people asking impertinent questions about her family life, where she gets her ideas from, and what she eats for breakfast—which is what we do to writers? Can anyone explain to her, or to me, or to themself, what all that has to do with the stories, and which is more real: the old primate or the star songs?

Again, there are lovely precedents; this time the one I'd choose is Woolf's novel *Orlando*. Alice Sheldon has quite a lot in common with Orlando, and, like Orlando, is an unanswerable criticism of the rational and moral fallacies of sexism, simply by being what and who she is. She also provides an exhilarating criticism of what real life, or reality, is, by being a fictional character who writes real stories; here she surpasses Orlando. On the edge of the impenetrable jungles of Yucatan, on the beach, the straw-hatted figure stands, dapper, fragile, smiling; just before vanishing into the shadows of the trees he murmurs, "Are you real?" and Alice, in a house in far Virginia, replacing the blue ribbon in her typewriter, smiles also and replies, "Oh, yes, certainly." And I, who have never met either of them, agree. They are real. Both of them. But not so real, perhaps, as their stories. This book you hold now in your hand, this is the genuine article. No fooling.

5) Here are
    Some real stories.

Your Haploid Heart

This very early story is collected here for the first time because you may enjoy the genuine sexual—biological "mystery" in it. It's an example of what the software sciences can contribute to hardware-oriented sf, and it's still being reprinted here and there around the world.

And those of you who write may enjoy comparing it with "A Momentary Taste of Being." The difference between the two stories represents what seven years of sweat do to the presentation of a similar psychosexual theme.

ESTHAA (Aurigae Epsilon V) *Type:* Solterran .98
Dom. race: Human to undet. degree
Fed. status: Pending certification
Extraplanetary delegs., embs., missions: None

Esthaa is sole inhabited planet of system, first contact from Aurigae Phi, 3010 ST. Native cultural level then approx. Terran Greek city-states, grouped around inland sea on single continental mass. Navigation, wheel, money, protoalphabetic script, numbers incl. zero, geometry; smelting, weaving, agriculture. Space trade route estab. 3100 ST. Esthaan students to Gal.

1

Fed., no perm. emigration. Progress rapid in light metals extraction, machine tooling, assembly. Exports: Electronic and mechanical components. Imports: Tool, vehicle and generator prototypes, scientific instruments. Esthaan workers noted for ability to copy complex devices.

Sociological: Since contact, pop. concentration in urban complex around spaceport, becoming one-city planet. Political structure thought to be oligarchy, or council of family heads. Religion unreported. Language one, agglutinative. No known wars except sporadic police actions against nomadic tribes of hinterland known as the Flenn peoples. The Esthaan temperament reported as peaceful and friendly but remarkably reserved.

MacDorra's landsled brings us down fast; Marscots don't waste fuel. Pax lunges across to peer out my port. I see the color on his high cheekbones and the light in his eyes. His first big job. He has a severe, luminous eye like a certain Chesapeake retriever I recall too well.

Reeling past below is as charming a great garden city as you could wish for. Miles on miles of honey and cream-colored villas in a froth of pinky-green flower trees with here and there an administrative center or industrial park like plates of pastel pastry. On the far horizon, gently glittering sea. A one-city world.

The spaceport shows beyond a line of wooded hills, and the pilot slams us into a wallowing stall. Suddenly there's a blaze of color in the hills below—red, purple, orange—a carnival? No—a warren of twisted streets alive with people. A hidden village.

Then we're back over spacious suburbs and braking into the field. When the ports clear we see a human-looking figure in a dull gold uniform getting out of a rollercar.

The human-looking part is why I am here.

MacDorra's pilot has us and our equipment out into the dust before you can say parsimony. Three clipboards to sign, a handshake that breaks my pencil—"See you in six months, Doc, good luck!"—and we're fleeing for the roller with the field lab while the sled's turbines howl up. The Esthaan comes to help. He's big, and seems amused by MacDorra's operation.

We sort ourselves out in Inter-human while the roller trundles through tree-lined avenues. Reshvid Ovancha has a cultivated Gal Fed University accent.

Very human, is my snap reaction. He has the same number of fingers and features, his joints work like ours, and his skin texture—a feature on which I place great hunch reliance—is a cream-yellow version of my own brown. Eyes round, with laugh lines, and his smile shows human teeth with an extra pair of frontals. All quite standard except that his torso looks a trifle thick or blocky. Like me, he's beardless. I see nothing to explain why as of that minute I would bet my tour pay that MacDorra's return will find me with a negative report to file.

Wait till we see the women, I tell myself.

Pax is pointing his Scouts of the Galaxy profile as we roll through endless avenues bright with suburban shrubbery. Possibly he has much the same idea. It always strikes the younger ISB agents as grossly unfair that middle-aged, monogamous noncharismatic types like me should be charged with investigating the question of alien sex.

Bureau Personnel learned that the hard way. The first ISB agent sent to Esthaa, over a century back, was a lad called Harkness. Among other idiosyncrasies, Harkness had a weakness for laboratory-fermented brew. The sensitive, reserved Esthaans were very unfavorably impressed when a wing of their new university went up with him. After the investigation and reparations Esthaa had been dropped to the bottom of the sector list to cool off. A hundred years later Auriga Sector had only Esthaa left to check and the Esthaans were persuaded to accept another Interplanetary Survey team, guaranteed nonexplosive. Which is now arriving as one Pax Patton, mineralogist-stratigrapher, and one Ian Suitlov, middle-aged ecologist in public and Certifying Officer in fact—as Harkness had tried to be before me.

"What's this 'mystery man' bit they give you COs?" Pax asked me while we were getting acquainted on the ship. I looked at his eager face and cursed Bureau security.

"Well, there is the Mystery, you know. Silly name, to your generation. When I started work people were still ready to fight about it. The True Blood Crusade was active—in fact, two of my graduating class got kidnapped and given the conversion treatment. One forgets how much energy and money and blood got spent over the fact that human races are scattered through the galaxy. Religions, sciences, whole planets were in turmoil. Many people wouldn't believe it. Nowadays we've settled down to the job of counting and describing and we don't encourage talk. But it's still a mystery. Where *do* we come from? Are we a statistical peak, a most-probable-bridge-hand of evolution? Or are we one crop out of one seed pod that was spilled through the stars? People got pretty excited over it. I know one or two who still are."

"But why the Security angle, Ian?"

"Didn't anybody brief you? Use your head, look at the human position in the galaxy. A new race can get all lathered up over whether or not they're certified Human. We know it doesn't mean anything—you have Hrattli in top Gal Fed jobs and they look like poached eggs. But try explaining that to a newly-contacted, proud, scared humanoid race! They take Noncertification as inferiority. That's why COs aren't called COs out loud. We try to get in and get the data quietly before any uproar can start. Ninety percent of the time there's no problem anyway and CO work is the dullest kind of routine. But when you hit one of the emotional ten percent—well, that's why the Bureau pays our insurance. I'm telling you this so you'll remember to keep your mouth very carefully shut about my work. You do your rocks, I do my biology—but nothing about humans, humanity, mystery—right?"

"Aye aye, sir!" Pax grinned. "But, Ian, I don't get the problem. I mean, isn't being human basically a matter of culture, like sharing the same values?"

"Great green orcs. What do they teach you rock hounds these days? Look: Shared culture is shared cul-

ture. Psychic congeniality. It is not humanity. Are you
so arrogant as to label any general ethical value a crite-
rion of humanity? Being human is nothing so vast. It
reduces to one nitty gritty little point: *Mutual fertility!*"

"A damn limited concept of humanity!"

"Limited? Crucial! Look at the practical conse-
quences. When we meet and mingle with a nonhuman
race, no matter if they're totally sympatico and look like
the girl next door, the two groups stay separable to the
end of time. No problem. But when we meet a human
race, even if they look like alligators—and some of 'em
do—those genes are going to flow into the human gene
pool despite any laws or taboos they can set up. Q.E.D.
every time—with all the social, religious, political fall-
out the fusion entails. Now do you see why that's the
one fact the Bureau *has* to know?"

Pax subsided, giving me his Chesapeake stare. I wondered if I'd been out too long. Auriga Sector had caught
me a month short of Long Leave and talked me into
helping close out the Sector survey. "A piece of cake,"
the chief had called it.

Well, I have to admit that it looks like a piece of cake
as we roll up to the palatial Esthaan guest villa. Reshvid
Ovancha's horn brings a squad of servants for our bags,
and he personally shows us about. It's amazingly like a
deluxe version of a Gal Fed faculty residence. Even the
plumbing works the same. The only alien feature I notice is a diffuser emitting a rather pleasing floral scent.

"This is the home of my cousin who is away at sea,"
Ovancha informs us. "I trust you will be comfortable,
Reshvidi."

"We will be more than comfortable, Reshvid Ovancha. We did not expect such luxury!"

"Why not?" he smiles. "Civilized men enjoy the same
things!" He makes a minute adjustment to the scent
dispenser. "When you are ready I will take you to lunch
at the University where you will meet our Senior Councillor."

As we roll through the University gates Pax mutters,

"Looks just like Gal Fed campus before the Flower Dance."

"Ah, the Flower Dance!" says Ovancha gaily. "Delightful! Did you encounter Professor Flennery? And Dr. Groot? Such fine men. But that was long before your time, I fear. We live long on Esthaa, you know. A most healthy world!"

Pax's face grows longer. I personally wonder what has happened to the famous Esthaan reserve.

We meet it at lunch. Our hosts are gracious but formal, smiling gently when Ovancha laughs, and gravely observant while he chatters. Some wear faculty robes; a few like Ovancha are in uniform. The atmosphere is that of a staid gentleman's club.

"We hope you will feel at home, Reshvidi," intones the councillor, who has turned out to be Ovancha's uncle.

"Why not?" Ovancha beams. "Now come, you must see your laboratories."

The laboratories are very adequate, and by evening we have our schedules and contacts set.

"Do we have to go to all those dinners?" Pax is prowling the patio, his eyes on the line of distant mountains where two pink moons are rising. Fountains tinkle, and a bird sings.

"One of us must. You can start some field work."

"While you look into the fertility. Say, Ian, how do you—"

"With a culture tank," I tell him, "and a great deal of caution. *And* it's a ticklish business until you know what the taboos are. How would Victorian England, say, have reacted to a couple of aliens who demanded a look at people's sex organs and a fresh slice of someone's ovary? I'd like to get it through your head that this is a very good subject to shut up about."

"Aren't you too tight up, Ian? These people are very enlightened types."

"One of my friends had both feet cut off by some supposedly enlightened types."

Pax grunts. Maybe I have been out too long. This place gives me the feeling of a stage set, it's so insistently human-norm. Well, I'll know more after I see the women.

Three weeks later I am still looking. Not that I haven't seen Esthaan ladies—at dinners, at lunches, at merry family picnics, even a field trip with two lady marine biologists. Or rather, with what passes for biologists on Esthaa. It soon appears that for all the shiny instruments, science on Esthaa is more an upper-class hobby than a discipline. People collect oddities and study what amuses them, without system. It's an occasion for wearing a lab coat, just as their army seems to be merely a game of wearing uniforms. My Esthaan ladies are like everything else here, charming, large, and wholesome. And decorously mammalian to outward view. But have I seen *women?*

Well, why not, as Ovancha would say. . . . I need a closer look.

The usual approach on an advanced planet is through the schools of medicine. But Ovancha is correct; Esthaans are healthy. Aside from injuries and a couple of imported infections now controlled by antibiotics, sickness doesn't seem to exist here. *Medicine,* I find, refers to the pathology of aging; arthritis, atherosclerosis and the like. When I ask about internal medicine, gynecology, obstetrics, I get stopped cold.

One chubby little orthopedist allows me to take a few measures and blood samples from his child patients. When I ask to see adult females he begins to dither. Finally he sends me to a colleague who reluctantly produces the cadaver of an aged female worker, a cardiac-arrest case. She has evidently been operated on for hernia in middle life.

"Who did this operation, Reshvid Korsada?" I ask. He blinks.

"This is not the work of a doctor," he replies slowly.

"Well, I would like to meet the person who did this work," I persist. "Also I would like to meet one of your doctors who assist in delivering new life."

Embarrassed laughter. He licks his lips.

"But—there is no need for doctors! There are certain women—"

He runs down there, and I see the sweat on his forehead and talk of other matters. I have not lived twenty years in this job by poking sticks into sore places and I want to make that Long Leave back to Molly and the kids.

"These people are touchy as a pregnant warthog," I tell Pax that night. "Apparently birth is so taboo they can't mention it, and so easy they don't need doctors. I doubt these medicos ever see a woman naked. Like Medieval Europe where they diagnosed with dolls. This is going to be very ticklish indeed."

"Can't you count chromosomes or something?"

"To determine *fertility?* The interior of the cell is not called the last fortress or neg entropy for nothing, Pax. Quantitative DNA analyses plus the few gene loci we know tell us little. The only reliable index we have is the oldest one of all—you bring a male and female gamete together and see if the zygote grows. But how in Mordor am I going to get an ovum?"

Pax guffawed. "I hope you don't expect me to—"

"No. I do not. I'll put in time cataloging and figure something out. How are your rocks coming along?"

"That reminds me, Ian, I think I've hit a taboo myself. You remember that village we saw, coming in? I asked Ovancha's wife about it last night, and she sent the kids out of the room. It's where the Flenni live. She said they were *silly* people, or *little* people. I asked her if she meant *childish*—at least I think that's what I said. That's when she sent the kids out. Why don't they hurry up and invent that telepathic translator the videos show?"

"Maybe it's some tie-up with child . . . baby . . . birth?"

"No, I think it's the Flenni. Because of what happened today. I was out on that geosyncline back of the port and I heard music from the village. I started over and suddenly here comes Ovancha in the university roller and tells me to go back. He said there was sickness there. He almost hauled me into the roller."

"Sickness? And Ovancha was right there? Indeed I do agree with you, Pax. I'm very glad that you thought of telling me about this. And as head of this mission," I continue in a tone that turns his stare around to me, "I want you to stay away from the Flenni and any other sensitive subjects you happen across. I'm responsible for getting us out of here in one piece and there's something about this place that worries me. Call me what you like, but *stick to rocks*. Right?"

For the next two weeks we are model agents. Pax does a coastal profile and I bury myself in routine taxonomy. One of my chores is to compile a phylogenetic survey of native life forms based on the Esthaan's own data. Their archives are a jumble of literary bestiaries and morphological botany, topped off by a surprisingly large collection of microscopic specimens all abominably muddled and dispersed. To my astonishment, in a packet of miserable student mounts of rotifers I come upon what I realize must be Harkness' work.

Back at the base they told me that all Harkness' data vanished with him. I went to the trouble to look up the old report of the ISB inquiry. There seemed to be no doubt that Harkness had been running a still, and that there had been a big fire. The only note the ISB team found was on a scrap of paper in a drain. In a large and wavery script were the words, "MUSCI! They are BEAUTIFUL!!!"

Musci are, of course Terrestrial mosses, unless Harkness had been abbreviating Muscidae, or flies. Beautiful mosses? Beautiful flies? Clearly, Harkness was a rumhead. But he was also a first-rate xeno-biologist when sober, and his elegant mounts, still clear after a century, are saving me a lot of work. His neat marginal chromosome counts are accurate. There are other brief notations, too, which get me very excited as my data piles up. Harkness had been finding something—and so am I. The problem of getting human gametes recedes while I chase down the animal specimens needed to fill in the startling picture.

In our free evenings Pax and I cheer ourselves with

song. It turns out we are both old ballad buffs and we work up a repertory including "Lobachevsky," "Beethoven's Birthday Calypso," and "The Name of Roger Brown." When we add an Esthaan mouth organ and a lute I notice that our Esthaan house-factor is wearing small earmuffs.

Our reward for all this virtue arrives one morning in the form of Ovancha with a picnic hamper.

"Reshvidi!" he beams. "Perhaps today you would like to visit the Flenn village?"

We trundle out across the spaceport and over a range of low hills in bloom. Then the roller lurches into a gorge under a shower of flowers, and jolts up a stony pass in which there are suddenly adobe walls brilliantly colored in hot pink, greens, electric blue, purple, dry-blood color and mustard. I catch the start of an amazing smell as we burst over the hilltop and into the village square. It is empty.

"They are timid," Ovancha apologizes. "The sickness also has been hard."

"But I thought you didn't have—" said Pax, and glares at me for the jab.

"*We* do not," replies Ovancha. "They do, because of their way of life. They have a bad way of life, bad and silly. They do not live long. We try to help them, but—"

He makes a weary gesture and then toots melodiously on the roller's horn. We get out. Shrill orange flowers are blowing across the cobbles. The smell is remarkable. From somewhere a flute blares brilliantly and stops. Across the square a door opens and a figure limps toward us.

It is an old man robed in blue. As he comes near I see he is very delicate—or rather, Ovancha suddenly becomes an oversized rubber truncheon. I stare; something about the old man is sending strongly to my hunch-sense.

I miss Ovancha's introduction.

We walk down a side street. It too is empty. An overpowering feel of hidden eyes watching, ears listening. A gate snicks shut like a clam shell. The houses are interspersed with tents, pavilions, shanties, dark recesses which rustle.

We come to a courtyard covered with a torn green canopy where a dozen frail old people recline silently against the curb. Their faces are turned away. I see skeleton hips and ribs under the bright, soiled cloaks. Is this the sickness of which Ovancha had warned Pax? But he has led us right to it.

Suddenly a side door creaks and out into the silence bursts a flock of children. The old ones rouse, hold out shaking arms, smiling and murmuring. Voices call urgently from the doorway, but the little ones run wild—incredibly tiny and active, fluttering gay silks, shouting high and sweet. Then a robed figure herds them inside and the old ones sink back.

Beside me Ovancha is making a strange sound. His mouth works and his face is green as he marshals us back toward the roller.

But Pax has other ideas. He strides smartly on around a corner. Ovancha throws me a distraught look and goes after him. I follow with the limping old man. We proceed thus around a second corner, and I am about to shout after Pax when a flurry of silk comes shooting out of the wall beside me.

My hand is clutched by something tiny and electric. An impossibly small girl is scurrying alongside, her face turned up to mine. Our eyes meet joltingly. Something is being pushed into my fist. Her head goes down—soft, fierce lips press my hand—and then she's gone.

Twenty years of discipline tells me to open my fingers. The old man is gazing straight ahead.

We catch up to Pax and Ovancha in the square. Pax's back is rigid. As we say our farewells he grips both the old man's hands in his. Ovancha is still pale. The roller starts, the unseen flute peals out again and is joined by a drum. A trumpet answers from across the square. We drive away in a skirl of sound.

"They are fond of music," I remark inanely. My hand feels on fire. Pax's eyes look dangerous.

"Yes"—Ovancha speaks with effort—"some do not

call it music. It is very harsh, very wild. But I find . . .
I find it has some charm."

Pax snorts.

There is going to be a blowup.

"In my home," I say, "we have also an animal like
your *Rupo* which we use for hunting. They have a very
strong character and think only of hunting. Once my
friends and I took a certain *Rupo* on a hunting trip and,
as is also your custom, we often drank wine with our
lunch and did not hunt in the afternoon. The *Rupo* re-
garded this as a sin. So one night when we were many
days from base he carried all the wine bottles to a deep
swamp and buried them."

They both stare at me. Ovancha finally smiles.

Back at the villa I see Pax's mouth opening and pull
him over by a fountain.

"Keep it low."

"Ian, those people are human! They're the only *human* Esthaans I've seen. These owl-eyed marshmal-
lows—Ian, the Flenni are the people you should be
looking at!"

"I know. I felt it, too."

"Who are they? Could they be the survivors of some
wreck?"

"They were here before First Contact."

"They're terrified of the Esthaans. I saw them run
for cover as we came up. They're in trouble, Ian. It isn't
right. You've got to do something!"

He is flushed and frowning. Just like that Chesapeake the night before he imposed Prohibition. I sigh.

"You, Dr. Patton, are a professional mineralogist
sent here at enormous cost to do a specific job your
Federation wants done. So am I. And our jobs do not
include mixing into native political or social conflicts. I
feel as you do, that the Flenni are an appealing native
group who are being oppressed or exploited in some way
by the civilized Esthaans. We have no idea what the
history of the situation is. But the point is, we are not
free to endanger our mission by intruding into what is
clearly a very tense position. This is something you will
have to face on planet after planet in order to do your

job. It's a big galaxy, and you'll see worse things before you're through."

He blows out his lips. This is not like the videos.

"I thought your job was to find humans."

"It is. And I'll check the Flenni out, later. And I'll report their condition, for what good it'll do. . . . Now let me tell you something I suspect. Did you ever hear of polyploidy?"

"Something about big cells—what has that got to do with the Flenni?"

"Bear with me. I can't be sure until I get a few more specimens, but I think we've come on something unique: Recurrent tetraploidy in the higher animals. I've found it in eighteen species so far, including rodents, ungulates, and carnivores. In each case you find two closely similar animals, one of which is bigger, stronger and more vigorous. And tetraploid—that means, by the way, not big cells but an extra set of chromosomes. A mutation. Tetraploid and higher polyploid forms of food plants are used on many planets but it's almost unknown among animals. Here you have it all over the place—and often in the tame domestic form. That big cowlike creature they milk has twice the number of chromosomes the little wild cow has. Same with their wool-bearing beast versus the wild sheep. Their common rodent has twenty-two chromosomes, but I trapped a king rat—a gigantic brute—with forty-five. Harkness was working on it before me. Now do you see what the possibility is?"

"You mean these Esthaan jumbos are tetraploid Flenn?"

"That's exactly what I expect to find. And if so, what?"

"Well, what?"

"A case where nature has set the stage for genocide, Pax. The two forms compete and the bigger, stronger, more vital form wins. The Flenni are weak, short-lived, defect-prone and they're up against people who are simply more of everything they are. Shocking as it sounds, you have here almost a quantitative measure of humanity—if they're human. Under the circumstances it's a

credit to the big Esthaans that the little race has survived so far. Remember, *our* species exterminated all
our close relatives."

"But they could be given a place of their own."

"Provided the mutation isn't a recurrent one. If it is
recurrent, the situation will only repeat. And it looks as
if it is. . . . Why does each species have a tetraploid
companion? If there'd been only one mutation 'way
back, the separate evolutions would have diverged. Now
I suggest we quit talking and play something. How
about 'Hold That Tiger'?"

Our hearts aren't in it. When we turn in I look at the
note which has been burning a hole in my pocket.

*"Doctor from the stars come to us! Help us dying we
pray."*

I sleep poorly. In the morning we find a sheaf of the
vivid orange flowers has been thrown over the wall by
our table.

Ovancha joins us at breakfast. With him is a muscular young Esthaan wearing high boots and imported
dark glasses.

"Reshvid Goffafa!" Ovancha announces. "He is
ready to guide Reshvid Pax to the volcanic mountains.
Perhaps this is too short notice? But Reshvid Goffafa
has classes beginning just after the rest days and he has
returned specially for you!"

With Pax gone I concentrate better and in a few
days' steady drudging I turn up three Harkness slides
marked *"Fl."* in a collection of waterplant tissues. One
firmly stained section labeled *"Fl. Inf., vascular marrow"* gives me what I need. There are karyokinetic
anomalies but the chromosome count is clearly half of
that on my Esthaan samples.

My involuntary satisfaction gives me a pang. The
thing is a tragic trap for the Flenni. And mixed with the
pang something like a faint voice is saying "Tilt" about
the whole beautiful structure. But surely Harkness—

"You study in a trance!" Ovancha has entered quietly.

"It is our way," I reply. It has just struck me that
Ovancha is unusual in another way. He has gray eyes,

the norm is olive-brown. And the old Flenn also had gray eyes.

"I wonder what you see?" There's a hint of seriousness under his light tone. Is it possible that Ovancha is different enough to be of use to me?

"I see something of great scientific interest on your delightful planet," I begin hopefully. He listens politely, but when I try to show him a chromosome his aristocratic eyelids droop, and he barely glances through the scope. I speak cautiously of a possible genetic difference between himself and unnamed "others." His mouth twists.

"But one can see the difference, Reshvid Ian!" he reproves me. "There is no need to go further. We are not interested in such things in our science."

No help here. I go back to chewing on the problem of obtaining Esthaan gametes while Ovancha chats on about a Reshvid doctor who perhaps has some slides, and a Reshvid somebody else who will be delighted to show me his preserving technique—after the rest days, of course. Meanwhile, since no one is really working now, why not come to dinner and view the museum president's collection of luminous sea bats?

The next day the university blimp-flier goes out to pick up Pax and Goffafa, but they're not there. Nobody's concerned, since they had ample supplies. It's decided to try again in three days. The second try is also unsuccessful, and the third. Ovancha reminds me that Goffafa is now late for classes.

The orange flowers come over the wall again that night. At noon next day a uniformed Esthaan appears in my lab to tell me I'm wanted at the councillor's office.

Ovancha is standing outside. He acknowledges me with a curt nod and goes in, leaving me to stare at the antiseptic and cylindrical maiden behind the desk.

Finally I am ushered into the presence of the whitehaired Senior Councillor. Ovancha is looking at a wall map. No one offers me a chair.

"Reshvid Ian, your colleague Reshvid Pax is a criminal. He has committed murder. What have you to say?"

I stammer my bewilderment. Ovancha wheels around.

"Reshvid Goffafa is dead. His body was found buried in an obvious attempt at concealment. He died by strangulation. Your colleague Pax has fled."

"But why should Pax do such a thing? Why do you believe he was the murderer? He admires and respects your people, Reshvid Ovancha!"

"The murderer was large and strong. Your friend is strong—and he is excitable, uncontrollable. Disgustingly *silly!*"

"No—"

"He quarreled with Reshvid Goffafa, killed him and fled."

"When Reshvid Pax returns," I say firmly, "I hope you will listen to his explanation of the sad death of Goffafa."

"He will not return!" Ovancha fairly shouts. "He has sneaked into a camp of Flenni and is hiding there. Do you dare to suggest he is not guilty?"

The councillor clears his throat sharply and Ovancha's mouth snaps shut.

"That is all. You will be so good as to stay in your quarters until transportation is arranged. I regret that your laboratory here is closed."

The next days pass in that agony of boredom and worry known only to those who have been alone and in jail on an alien planet. My field kit is returned to me; I set it up and force myself to study the garden flora. There is now a sentry outside the gates. I hear a nocturnal scuffle, and no more flowers come over the wall.

On the fifth night the almost-cat has kittens.

I am pacing the terrace. Senior ISB biologists are not supposed to get the shakes, the *horror alieni.* Certainly on the surface I'm in no danger. Pax is in a serious mess, but all I face is grief from the Sector over a fouled-up mission. And yet I can't get rid of the notion that an invisible set of jaws are about to go crunch. Something here is *wrong;* something that kills biologists. Harkness was a biologist, and he is dead.

I become aware of action by my feet under the amber

ferns. The big pet we call the almost-cat is rolling on the ground among a heap of small, scuffling, squeaking things. I focus my pocket light. The "cat" sits up, yawns in my face and saunters off leaving me gaping at the wiggling heap on the ground. Kits! But how many? A dozen tiny faces turn up to the light—two dozen—four dozen—and how tiny! Still more are struggling or still among the fern roots.

I pick up a handful and head for my lab.

In my head all the puzzle pieces which had fitted themselves so neatly into that damned wrong pattern are again in motion, coming together in a larger, frightening pattern. One of the items in the new pattern is the great likelihood that I will be killed. As Harkness had been when he stumbled on the truth.

Can I conceal it? No chance; two sleepy servants saw me with the kits. And I've said far too much to Ovancha.

I work carefully. It's gray dawn when the microscope abolishes all possible doubts. Outside, a sweeper-boy with a box is scrabbling under the amber ferns. He has trouble—the kits four hours old are running and biting—but he gets them all. He takes the box to the back gate and passes it to the sentry.

Even unto the least, I muse dismally. More pieces fall into place. Why didn't I consider the city more? And the fact that no Esthaans stay long off-planet?

A rustle. Ovancha is behind me, his pale gaze on my bench.

"Good morning, Reshvid Ovancha. Has there been word from Pax?" He doesn't bother to reply. His mask has sagged, showing me a face grave and full of human trouble. Human! How desperately they must want the meaningless certification. How intricately they have built. Ovancha must be one of the leaders—exceptional Ovancha, able to dare, to cope with us. He speaks with obvious pain.

"Reshvid Ian, why do you— We . . . I have welcomed you as a friend—"

"We, too, wish to be friends."

"Then why do you occupy yourself with *revolting, unspeakable things?*"

He is asking in all seriousness. It is not a plot then. It is a real and terrible delusion. They have somehow come to hate what they are so unbearably that they must live a myth of denial, a psychotic fantasy. Harkness—what had he told them? No matter. We have punctured it now and there is no hope for us. But I must answer his question.

"I am a scientist, Reshvid Ovancha," I say carefully. "In my world I was trained to study all living things. To understand. To us, life of any sort is neither good nor bad. We study all that lives, all life."

"All life," Ovancha repeats desolately, his eyes on mine. "Life—"

Pitying, I make my greatest blunder.

"Reshvid Ovancha, perhaps you might be interested to know that in my home world we had once a very great problem because our people were not all alike. We had not two but many different people who hated and feared each other. But we came to live together as one family, as brothers—"

I see his eyes dilate and his nostrils flare. His lips roll back from his teeth, the face of one hearing the ultimate insult. One hand twitches toward his ornamental side arm. Then his lids fall, he turns on his heel and is gone.

The least likely male can move with unexpected agility if he is sufficiently motivated and if his employers have insisted on regular training courses. As Ovancha goes downstairs, I go out the lab window with a bundle and over the kitchen roof to the wall, which turns out to be set with broken glass.

I land in the alley on an ankle that feels severed. One cheek and arm are full of glass. I pull on the Esthaan cloak and hobble up the alley. Each block has a walled center alley that conceals me from the sides, but I have to cross the wide avenues between blocks. Luckily it's just dawn. I make three crossings before a big roller full of uniforms whooshes by the end of the block I'm in.

Four more blocks; my face and arm are on fire, and my ankle gives out. A trash recess in the wall. I dodge in—how quickly fugitives connect with garbage!—and listen to the Esthaan police bell clanging from the direction of our house.

Suddenly a mustard-colored roller-van comes swishing into my alley and stops fifty feet away. The driver gets out. A gate bell tinkles; the gate opens and closes. Silence.

I make it to the roller, pull open the tailgate and scramble in. Inside is dark with a piercing odor. I crawl behind some crates next to the canvas that closes off the driver's compartment.

The tailgate reopens and a crate slams in. We're off.

Sounds are coming from the crate. Dear God. If my luck holds—if the driver doesn't take all the crates out—if I can hold out against what is now clearly poison in my cuts—if . . .

Hours of agony while the truck starts and stops, opens to receive more crates, slams and jolts on. The noise inside would cover a trumpet solo and the smell is a stench. Finally comes the steady drumming of a highway, and when I have lost almost all hope, we stop.

The driver gets out and comes around to open up. This is bad. I have done some knife work on the canvas curtain, but I'm not sure I can move. Frantically I hack the last threads and push and roll myself through to the front floorboards. The pain is shocking.

There's a crowd outside the van but no one hears me over the uproar. The tailgate crashes—the driver is coming back. I yell and pitch myself out.

I black out as I hit. The next thing I hear is the crunch of the roller's tires by my head. Something filmy is over my face, someone's quick hands push me. Voices hissing, "Down!"

I stay down, all right. The world goes away and doesn't come back except as hot clouds of pain and confusion for several days.

My first really clear moment comes in the form of an endless plain of grass lurching across my view. I focus interestedly and it stays put. I am doing the lurching, tied into the saddle of a pack beast.

Ahead of me is another rider. I gaze contentedly at the slight, hooded figure in saffron robes, reveling in no-pain. We have, it seems to me, been traveling thus for some time.

The rider ahead looks about, and suddenly yanks my beast into violent flight across a stream bed. Then we are under trees and my guide is off and racing up the bank in a whirl of silk. This, too, seemed to have happened many times before. And there have been nights and stars, and hot days in thickets, and pain, and soft hands.

My guide returns slowly, throwing back the hood. The face I see is the flower face of the child who put the note in my hand. She lifts one foot to my stirrup and vaults up beside me, leaning on my breast.

Her body is no more than a bird's wing and mine is a half-dead hulk. Something like a solar flare sweeps through my flesh. The universe contracts to the contact of our bodies, her eyes, the night-cloud of her hair. I breathe her perfume.

Then I remember what I know.

"Friends come now," she smiles.

She lays a frail, violently alive hand over my heart and we stay thus until the hoofbeats arrive. Three bright-robed Flenni and a larger rider—

"Pax!" My voice is a croak.

"Ian, man!"

"Where are we?"

"You're coming to the mountains. To the camp."

But my little guide is already riding away. *Of course.* My knowledge is a cold sadness. The men have stayed hooded too, I see. Taboo. How else to survive?

My mount is taken in tow and we lurch off. I twist round against the pain to watch her dwindle across the savannah. Pax is talking.

"What happened to Goffafa?" I finally ask.

"That *kralik*. We came to a party of Flenn women. He was going to shoot them down."

"Shoot them?"

"He got wild. I had to take his gun away. Like fighting a rubber octopus. He was raving and foaming and believe it or not he threw up his lunch. Agh! I got him in the roller and he tried to brain me with the Geiger."

"So you strangled him?"

"I only choked him a little. Last I saw of him he was crawling. I was going to come back for him when he cooled off."

"He's dead. The Esthaan Council has you booked for murder."

Pac growls.

"Some Flenni found him during the night. They told me he shot two of them when they offered him water, and they finished him. I believe it."

He smite his boot and his mount curvets.

"Those swine, Ian! I can't begin to tell you what I've learned. The Esthaans won't let them raise food! The Flenni start farms and the Esthaans come out here in those gasbag fliers and spray poison. They poison waterholes. Ian, they're forcing the Flenn into those shantytowns where they can keep them under their thumbs. And I believe they *spread* that sickness, they don't cure it. They're trying to kill them off. Ian, it's what you said. Genocide!"

Our guides hear the word "Esthaan" and turn their now unveiled heads to us. It's my first look at young Flenni males.

Handsome? No word for the intensity of life in these proud beaked faces. The brilliant eyes, the archaic arch of nostril, the fierce and passionate lips.

Total virility. And total vulnerability. I am seeing human males of a quality none have seen before.

Involuntarily I bow my head to acknowledge their gaze. They return my bow and look away, their profiles pure and grave against the mountains.

"Pax, it's not—" I begin, when my mount careens forward under a Flenn whip and we're racing pell-mell for a clump of scrub. Behind us rises a soft unearthly hooting. I get a glimpse of a golden contraption about fifty feet up and coming fast. We hurtle on, Pax fighting his mount. A black smoke is belching from the flier's nose.

Pax flings himself to the ground and I am swept into

the copse. There's a roar and a confused crashing as the Flenni drag me off and cover my head. For several heartbeats nothing happens.

I get an eye free. The black stuff is blowing past us. The gasbag flier is down on its side and the pilot struggles out with a gun in one hand. Pax is somewhere in the smoke.

The gas is making me slightly dizzy, but the Flenni are out cold. I fumble around in my swaddling and find the pistol still in my pocket. My second shot gets the pilot's wrist and then Pax stumbles out of the smoke and falls on him.

We have the pilot nicely trussed up when our Flenni revive. There's a little difficulty in making them understand that I want him alive and they throw him behind my saddle with the controlled disdain one shows to a dog who rolls in dead fish. But they're enthusiastic about helping Pax rip out the flier's transmitter and load it on.

We ride on in silence. My captive's face is in rictus and his eyes are rolled up. I reflect on the curious difference in the hate shown by Esthaan and Flenni. Why is it the big, victorious Esthaans who panic like cornered rats? In twenty years of strange and often pitiable cases I have seen nothing sadder.

Pax outlines his plan. He has, it seems, worked up his field kit into a transmitter which, with the flier's power packs, should be able to contact MacDorra when the freighter comes near.

"What makes you think MacDorra will rescue us?" I ask him. "We're both under criminal charges now. MacDorra won't offend a planetary customer. And he'd let his mother drown rather than pay for cleaning his dress uniform, you know that. The most he will do is slow-signal the Sector HQ—collect—for instructions ... the very most."

"It's not a question of rescuing *us!*" Pax says indignantly. "I'm going to see the Flenni get justice. I want MacDorra to send an emergency message to Gal Fed charging the Esthaans with genocide and asking for intervention. The Flenni are human beings, Ian! I don't know what the Esthaans are, but I'm not going to stand by and watch humans wiped out by some kind of *things!*"

"Justice?" I ask weakly. "Genocide?" It's all my fault, but I am suddenly too tired.

"Not genocide, Pax," I mutter and pass out in my saddle. The image of the girl who guided me keeps me company in the dark.

I wake to find myself in the Flenn camp. An enormous cavern sparkling with camp fires, rustling with silk and loud with song. The voices, naturally, are all masculine; only males are here. I am fed and put to rest against my saddle amidst the quick feet, the soft fiery voices. The air is pungent with smoke and Flenn.

During the night I find that the pilot has been dumped near me, still trussed like a sausage. He is the fattest Esthaan I have ever seen. When I clean his wrist he writhes and turns purple and presently, like Goffafa, he foams. I give him water, which he vomits. Finally he lies with eyes wide and glaring, breathing loudly and sweating rivers. I check his circulation and lie down again to sleep.

Pax is conferring with a group of young Flenni when I wake. He towers among them, bronzed and eager. Every inch the guerrilla leader of the oppressed. There will have to be explanations . . . but my head aches very much, and I take some fruit and go to sit outside the cave.

"You are a doctor?" He uses a noun meaning also
An old man quietly joins me.
wise man.
"Yes."
"Your friend is not."
"He is young. He does not understand. It is only recently that I myself have understood."
"Can you help us?"
"I do not know, my friend. There is nothing like this on other worlds I have seen."
He is silent.
"About the sickness," I ask. "How is it done?"

"With music." His voice is bleak.

"Can you not block the hearing?"

"Not enough. Not enough. I myself survived three times, but then—"

He grimaces, looks at his hands. Frail, parched, the hands of great age.

"I will die soon," he observes. "Yet only this spring I helped open the Great Cave."

"Where are the women?" I ask after a bit.

"To the north, half a night's ride. Your friend knows the way."

We look at each other in silence. I now recall Pax's figure against the cave mouth during the night.

"You live long," he muses. "Like the others, the Esthaans. Yet you are like us, not like them. We knew at once. How is this possible?"

"It is thus with all the worlds we know. Only here it is different."

"It is a bitter thing," he says at last. "My friend from the stars, it is a bitter thing."

"Explain to me a little more, if you will," I ask. "Explain how it is with the sickness."

I go to find Pax, jubilant amidst a tangle of wiring.

"I've made contact!" he announces. "MacDorra's in the system! They acknowledged my Mayday and the Federation Emergency appeal."

I groan.

"The genocide part, too?"

"Right. I requested emergency transport and asylum for the Flenni."

"Have you checked this with the Flenni?"

"Why, it's obvious."

I hold my head.

"Pax, it's all my fault. Listen. Have you ever heard of the general class of plants called Bryophytes, chief of which are the mosses, or Musci? Or the Terran animals called Hydrae?"

"Ian, I'm a geologist!"

"I'm trying to tell you, the Esthaans are not committing *genocide,* Pax. It's parricide, filicide . . . perhaps suicide—"

There's a high-pitched commotion behind us. A racing figure that streams pale gold rounds the transmitter and materializes before me into the loveliest girl I've ever seen. I gape at her. Honey and pale flame, high-arched breasts, tiny waist, full oval haunches, an elf's hands and feet, and the face of a beautiful child in love—unfortunately, turned on Pax.

Then she's in his arms, her luminous face eclipsed in his chest, her little hands clutching and caressing him.

Having no hope of being included in this communication, I turn and see that the camp is in motion. Saddles and bundles are being hoisted, fires stamped out. Angry voices echo. My friend the elder is standing with other old ones.

"What's happening?"

"They have captured the women. The young Flanya was with your friend. When she returned to her camp the soldiers were there. She rode to warn us."

"What can be done?"

"There is nothing to do but flee. They will come here—they will drive them here with the music. Against the music we can do nothing. The young men must be gone. As for myself and these, we will wait. We will see our women once more before they kill us. If only . . . if only they do not harm the women."

"Do they dare?"

"Never before. But in recent lives I think they grow mad. They hate without end. I fear that when they find the men gone they will drive the women after them and on—"

His voice fails. Pax has somewhat disentangled himself and the girl is veiling her face.

"How many Esthaans are there?"

"About thirty, Ian; it was too dark to see well. I'm sure we can take them. I've got eight pretty fair marksmen with handguns, plus the converted ditcher and our two heavy guns. The damnable part is that they intend to use the women as cover."

"Pax." I take a deep breath. "I cannot allow you to

shoot Esthaans, and the boys you have trained cannot stay here. They must get out. What's coming here is nothing you can fight with guns. All you'll see will be the Flenn girls, plus some mobile sound equipment. You've got to know. The Esthaans and the Flenni are one—"

An ear-splitting screech erupts under our legs. The Esthaan pilot had been huddled puffy and fasting; now he's on his back kicking like a frog. Flenni who were moving outward turn at his screams.

"Look here, Pax!" I shout above the din. I rip the pilot's clothes, exposing his swollen body. Two great angry scars run from each pubic ligament to above the crest of the pelvis.

"He's a woman!" Pax exclaims.

"No, he's not. He's a sporozoön—an asexual form that reproduces by budding. Watch."

The pilot moans, his body racked by wavelike contractions. Flenni are bringing large baskets stuffed with silk.

"I think most Esthaans are not informed of their true nature," I tell Pax. "This one probably believes he is dying."

A supreme convulsion sweeps the Esthaan and the two gashes in his flanks swell, pulse, and slowly evert themselves like giant pea pods turning inside out. A mass of wriggling blobs of flesh tumbles down his sides. He screams. I pinion his flailing legs, and the girl Flanya rushes up with the baskets. A high wailing— with which I'm very familiar—rises from the mites as we gather them. I hold one up to Pax.

"It's . . . It's a Flenn child!" Unmistakable— barely an ounce of male life with bright gold eyes, clutching, kicking and keening. I lay it on the silk and show him another, an even smaller female with coordinated eyes and the start of a smile reflex. And a withered leg. There are others with defects, or lying still.

The Flenni are running with the baskets to mount and go. I throw the pilot's tunic over his empty belly; he has fainted. We're alone now, the old men, Flanya and Pax.

"You see, Pax? A case of alternate generations, with both the sexual and asexual generations fully developed and complete. Unheard of in mammals. It only lasted as far as the mosses and hydrae on Terra, and then the sporogenetic form took over the gametes—that's you and I. We're somatic sporozoöns, our gametes are reduced to cells. The Esthaans are not tetraploids, Pax—they're normal diploids. But the Flenni are haploid. Living gametes with a half-set of chromosomes each. They mate and produce Esthaans—who have no sex but bud out Flenni, alternately and forever."

"You mean the Esthaans and Flenni are *each other's children?* But we saw Esthaan families!"

"No. Their Flenn offspring are carried secretly out to the Flenni village, along with newborn haploid dogs, cats and everything else, and the Esthaan offspring of the Flenni are brought in for Esthaans to raise. Pseudo-families roles. It's literally insane—they may have built it up after Harkness told them they weren't human.

"Listen!"

The air is throbbing. One of the elders plucks my sleeve.

"Pax, barricade this transmitter and get the power leads out of sight. I'm going to try a forlorn hope."

He races off, Flanya behind him. I turn to my old friend who speaks Esthaan.

"This machine will carry your voice to men like me on other stars. First I will speak, and then you must say what I will now tell you."

As I coach him, the throbbing strengthens and is joined by a rippling, wailing moan which drives into my ears—no, into my viscera. The other elders drift toward the cave mouth, staring blindly. A flash of silk catches my eye.

"Pax! Grab her!"

He is deep in wires. I force my legs into a sprint and tackle Flanya fifty feet from the door. Her eyes come round on me staring-wild, and her body plasters itself against me like an electric eel. The drum note pulses through her like a resonator. I finally find a spot on her neck which puts out the crazy life in her eyes.

"Take her back and tie her up!" I howl over the rising hurricane of music. "Do you understand? Tie her tight if you want her alive!"

We make it behind the barricade as the first women falter into sight outside the cave.

I grab the mike and begin sending to the only source I know which might get action from the gray remoteness of the Federation. If only Pax's lash-up works! If only the electronic bedlam outside isn't jamming us! I repeat and pass the mike to the elder. That tragic whisper should pierce stone—if MacDorra has his recorder on.

"What's that about the Flenni being human and the Esthaans not?" Pax hisses. "I thought you said—"

"Pragmatic definition. How can you fertilize something that doesn't have gametes? Ergo, the Esthaans are non-human, right? By the same token, whose child is Flanya carrying? Ergo— Quick, find us something for ear plugs!"

The cave is clanging and sirening with sound. We crawl to the top of the barrier.

The driven women come like a sea of flowers, limping, stumbling, holding one another as they fan out into the great cave. Here and there one walks alone with blind ecstatic eyes. They fall, crawl, rise again, magically beautiful even in exhaustion. Around them the music is a punishing bray.

They reach the camp fires and begin to run, searching among the rocks, seizing the men's garments to their breasts and faces. Some weave in trance, others push on, picking up and dropping even the sand itself as if seeking trace of a particular man. The music is a pounding ache, relentless slow crescendo of sirens, bagpipes, drums.

Beside me I hear the old men gasp, their eyes aflame. Suddenly one tears the stoppers from his ears and dashes over the barricade to the nearest women. They turn to meet him, arms wide and faces wild and he goes down under a wave of silk. Pax grips my shoulder.

"My boys! My marksmen!"

On the far side of the wall there's an explosion of

motion. Three—no, five young Flenn, their weapons
flung on the rocks, their heads thrown back as they call.
Then they are leaping down to the women, the women
flying to them. But these do not fall as the wave of bodies meets—they gather the women in armfuls, spinning
on the crest of the terrible music. Five burning whirl-
pools in a sea of girls.

Behind us Flanya cries savagely, arched and writhing.

An old man points to the entrance. Three dark
hulks—the Esthaans come to view their handiwork, not
yet aware that the main body of the men has escaped.
Then they see. A signal flares and the music dies in
reverberating discords. An Esthaan shouts, tiny and
hoarse.

All over the cave the women have fallen in heaps.
The Esthaans start down among them, kicking, as they
converge on the pile of bodies around the Flenni boys.

The sight of those beautiful naked ones tumbled amid
each other's limbs and the bright silks affects the Esthaans most horribly. Two turn aside, and retch. The
third marches upon them, unhooking a heavy whip
from his belt, and booting at the nearest women.

The whip slams down on the helpless bodies. The
Flenni can scarcely rouse even under the pain; they
whimper and hold each other. The Esthaan grabs the
nearest boy by the hair and drags him to his knees.

"Where are the men? Where did they go?" he roars
into the boy's face. The boy is silent, his eyes ringed
with white. The Esthaan kicks him.

"Where did they go? Tell me!"

The other Esthaans join him. One of them bends the
boy back across his knee and uses his knife.

"Where are they?" the Esthaan thunders as the boy
screams.

It seems important to what is left of my ISB indoctri-
nation that Pax not be charged with murder. I make
sure each of the Esthaans goes down with two holes
apiece. As the echoes ricochet we race for the boy. Too
late.

"Cover them, quick!"

We yank silken stuff across the uniformed hulks and ourselves.

"They're coming! Keep down!"

We cower, hearing the distant tramp above the soft breathing of the Flenni all around us. My field of vision includes part of our rock barrier and a Flenn lad, fallen between two girls with another's red gold hair across his legs.

We can do nothing but wait. I watch the faint heavy pulse in the boy's eyelids. Then I see he is not only asleep, but also changing. Luster is going from his skin, his hair. Under my eyes the firm young flesh pales, withers on his arms and hands.

His hands. I remember the leaf-thin hands of the old man who said, "Only this spring I helped open the Great Cave." The kits, the babies, grow like hungry flames. In months the little child is a nubile girl. Do they die as fast too, once mated? So it is with the gamete-bearers among our plants. This then, was the Esthaan weapon. To force them to ever-earlier mating and death. I shudder, seeing the boy's temples now sunken and blue. He will waken as an old man waiting to die.

Boots come into my view. Two Esthaans by the rock barrier. I have set the old man to tapping out a signal which might serve as a beacon in the unlikely event that anyone cares. But the Esthaans will hear—

They have. As they start up the rocks, the old man appears at the top, straightens and calls out. Then he is falling on the Esthaans' guns.

"He said *safe*," I hiss, grabbing Pax. "She's safe— Stay down!"

Pax nearly throws me as the Esthaans disappear over the barrier. We hear crashing sounds. They reappear, following the power-lead.

"If they fool with the pack, they'll blow us all."

But a new Esthaan shouts from the cave mouth, and the others turn back.

"They've sighted the men."

We have to watch while the whips are unlimbered and the women rounded up. The awful music crashes upon us. All over the cave, the exhausted women are rising painfully, beautifully, faltering to the cave door before their herders. A swaying river of bright flowers, upheld only by the dreadful stimulation of the sound. A girl falls to her knees before a soldier, who picks up a rock and crushes her skull.

It is as the old man had feared: Madness, among those Esthaans who knew the truth. The soldier probably does not know what he killed, but his orders come from those who know—and can not bear it.

We're up and scuttling for the rock barrier. The transmitter is a wreck, but Flanya is safe where the old man hid her. Pax carries her out. I pause to straighten the old body by the barrier. At the cave mouth we watch the stream of colored silk passing from sight in the gorge below. Somewhere among them is my little guide. The throbbing dies to silence.

"I'm going after them," Pax grits.

"No. That's an order. There's no cover and that flier will pick you off the minute you show."

I point. There is a rear-guard of Esthaans with a blimp and even Pax can read the odds.

"We've got to do something!" he rages.

Flanya's eyes follow him like compasses.

"We will. We will sit here and have something to eat and wait. And we might pray to a god named Baal."

"Baal?"

"Or Moloch, if you prefer. An old god of greed. We pray him to inflame the lust of gain in the guts of an old codger a hundred light-years from here—if he's still alive. If it flames up hot enough, we and the Flenni possibly may survive."

"You mean the Federation Council?" Pax demands. "Or the Bureau?"

"The Interplanetary Survey Bureau," I tell him, "may respond to our plea in time to help anyone who happens to be alive five years from now. The Galactic Federation Council is quite likely to respond in time to compose a documentary on an extinct race. Neither one can possibly move fast enough to help us mortal flesh now. The only agent who can do that is Captain Mac-

Dorra and the only agent which can move MacDorra is cash. Golden Interstellar credits. And the only source from which such is possibly forthcoming is a human fossil, who if he is still breathing, is squatting on the ninety-fifth terrace of his private empire on Solvenus. And the only motive which will move *him* is sheer cupidity and mad lust to beat out another creaking reprobate basking by his private ocean on Sweetheart, Procyon. Hence, we pray to Baal.

"Luckily," I add as Pax's jaw sets, "MacDorra knows I have enough credits in my account to defray an ultrapho signal to Solvenus. Now, how about some chow? And you might rig out a beacon."

It takes a little persuasion to make Flanya stay beside me when he goes away. She nestles down like a little silken dove, and when he climbs out of sight she puts her hand on my arm and looks up worriedly. I see she has a slight deformity of one finger. A defective gene, expressed because there is no companion chromosome to mask it. It is of course the existence of the haploid Flenni generation which makes the diploid Esthaans so healthy—each time the pairs of Esthaan chromosomes break apart to form a Flenn individual, every sort of recessive defect emerges without an allele to temper it. Those dead kits and babies are filters which take out defective genes between every Esthaan generation. Cruel and beautiful mechanism. . . . The quivering under my arm tells me Pax is on his way with provisions.

When we finish I produce an item I have carefully preserved: My mouth organ.

"Can you find us a horn, or a banjo, anything at all to play on?"

He looks at me, and then becomes very restrained. Our search turns up no horn or lute, so I show him what a melodious banging can be made with a cookpot and a broken stirrup. He assents distantly and we take up our watch by the cave mouth, me with my mouth organ and he with the kettle.

We play softly, and Flanya seems to like parts of it, which helps. I refresh us on suitable parts of our repertoire, and begin teaching him a stirring old item called "Roll me over in the Clover."

But I have no hope that anything will happen. For a long time it does not.

It's a shock when the cutting flash finally comes—the KABOOM-OOM! of MacDorra's emergency sled braking into air. MacDorra's a pioneer at heart if his tightness would let him and his emergency kit is First Landing T/E and then some. It sets down daintily on the mesa overhead while Pax and I scramble up, he carrying Flanya and me carrying the pots.

MacDorra's mate Duncannon and four husky assistants pour out, guns ready.

"Where's the warr?" burrs Duncannon. I could kiss him, red beard, bazooka and all.

"They've captured the women and are marching them to their deaths." I point. "Over there."

This has its effect on the mate. Once it's settled who pays, there are no more gallant fighters in the galaxy.

"We saw something that could be that as we came over. Get in, boys."

"Have you a loud hailer?"

"I do."

"Then fly gently just before them and set down as close as you can."

We come on top of the pathetic army as they're struggling up the rocks toward another cave. It is nearly too late.

"That thing over there in the yellow suit is the enemy," I tell Duncannon. "That gasbag is armed and also shoots a gas that doesn't bother much. The game is to find the noise maker they have and silence it. Fire a flare when you have it stopped, I won't be able to hear you. Stay here, Pax. We have work to do."

I hand him the kettle and turned every dial on the hailer to output max.

I don't know what the Esthaans make of it—those who aren't too busy with Duncannon's boys to hear us. I hate to think what we're doing to delicate Flenn ears. Pax gets the idea as I crash into "Sol-Sol-Solidarity", and comes in with a thunderous beat—a walloping

polka beat that has no more sex than a pig in clogs—a
Donnybrook jig that can bounce a "Liebestodt" to
shreds—a ragtime blast to meet and break that mes-
meric Esthaan horror. We give them "Interplanetary
Heroes" and "Stars I'm Coming" and "My Buddy was
a Bemmy." We blow and bang ourselves silly while
Flanya cowers.

Our counterbarrage hits just as the first wave of
women meets and mingles with the men streaming helpless from the cave. The uproar clashes with the mad
Esthaan hooting. As we take precarious control of the
air, the Flenn mass shudders. Couples cling, thrust
apart, race wildly, hands over ears. The women begin
to drop. Finally only the men stand upright, their heads
wrapped in their arms.

When the flare finally goes up I slap Pax's arm and
we hear the last toot-bang of our "music" thunder
across the hills.

"The only race in history ever saved with a kettle and
a mouth organ!" Pax looks horrified.

We shake hands hysterically and hug Flanya. The
hideous death of the Flenn boy mingles with Irish jigs in
my brain, and I am not much help to Duncannon for
the next half hour. We find him systematically hog-
tying Esthaans beside the gasbag. Most of them are in
rather poor shape. His crew has only a few nicks apiece;
ordinary ground-side armament can't do much against
First Landing equipment in trained hands.

We send Duncannon back to comb the line of march
for survivors. MacDorra himself comes down to oversee
the setting up of a relief camp. It is a wonderful camp,
with the ship's medicos and a plasma-synth and a nurse,
and they work like good devils. I notice MacDorra has
a little notebook in which he enters such items as the
sled's fuel supply, the rounds of cartridge, and the number of disposable shrouds. He feeds and ministers lav-
ishly, his face a splendid blend of compassion and business enterprise.

The pitiful burdens Duncannon is bringing in upset
the Captain.

"Gurrrl children," he growls, motioning the doctor to open universal serum. He sniffs and turns away to make a notebook entry. I can see the Esthaans will be having trouble with their freight rates.

The last load brings in the small shrouded figure I feared to see. After a bit I carry my sleeping bag up to the mesa where the pink moons are rising over the floodlights below. Somewhere beyond the empty plain the Esthaan Council waits. Frozen in their pitiable masks. Somebody else will have to be assigned to unwind their madness; I cannot.

Pax climbs to join me. The nurse has taken Flanya away from him. He stretches, scowls happily.

"All right, Ian. Who is Santa Claus?"

"Did you ever hear of the Morgenstern Theory of Human Evolution?"

"*That* Morgenstern? But is he still alive?"

"And he still wants his theory proved in the worst way. I ran into him last leave on Eros with his dearest enemy, old man Villeneuve. Villeneuve thinks Morgenstern is a lunatic; he's heart and soul for the diffusion theory. Between them they're rich enough to buy the Coalsack, and they've been arguing this for years, financing expeditions, and betting fantastic sums. Well, Morgenstern took me aside and told me exactly the kind of evidence he wants. Instances of human development which cannot possibly be interpreted as diffusion in Villeneuve's terms. He gave me a code word—*Eureka*. If I ran across the right case he told me to U.P. him collect at once.

"It occurred to me that the alternating generation setup here, shared by lower mammals and man, is about as close as Morgenstern can get to the proof he wants. It's not a hundred percent; there may be discontinuous mutation. But it's enough to give Villeneuve a very hot time. So I flashed him 'Eureka repeat Eureka' and added that the evidence would be wiped out within hours by intertribal war unless he chartered MacDorra for immediate intervention and rescue. He may have

bought the ship or the whole freight line. You've seen
the result. Sheer orneriness and ego—that's what saved
us, son, not altruism or love of science."

We share a companionable silence. It's just dawning
on me that I can take Molly's name out of the file
marked Widows.

"What about the Bureau?"

"Well, that's where I get reclassified to assistant
slide-cleaner. There's a thing called an Irreplaceable
Datum of Human Science. You may have run into
IDHS areas somewhere—I believe there's one on Terra.
In the old training regs it says that any officer of the
Service can declare an area or species to be an IDHS
and this automatically puts it under Federation protec-
tion until the case is reviewed and confirmed, or dis-
allowed. The declaring officer has to present a formal
justifying brief. It's a long business and it costs plenty.
Almost never done any more; I think there's been only
one in my time.

"I signaled the Bureau declaring the Flenni as an
IDHS in danger. This should eventually produce a Bureau relief team to take over from MacDorra. But it's
going to be a merry dust-up. Old Morgenstern is surely
on his way right now with the idea that the Flenni are
his personal pets. In the Bureau's eyes he'll be just a
meddling private citizen. And I'm going to have a time
seeing that the Flenni come out of this right side up and
that I'm not thrown out of the Service for exceeding my
authority, engaging in local warfare and native homi-
cide, endangering Bureau relations, conveying Federation authority to private citizens, and general knavery.
Not to mention a formal Declaration Brief to draft."

Pax frowns.

"What do you call right side up for the Flenni?"

I sigh. Pax does not really understand yet.

"Well, tentatively, they should be protected in their
efforts to maintain their own cultural identity, to extend
their life span by deferring ma"—I catch myself—"and
to build an economy. It won't be easy. There's probably
always been a hostile tension between the two forms,

since they are ecological competitors. The long-lived Esthaans had apparently shut the Flenni out of their urban technology by the time of First Contact. I suspect Harkness of having precipitated the acute stage. The Esthaans got the idea that the Flenni cycle was a dreadful defect which barred them from human status. They started out to conceal and minimize it, to ape human ways, and to reduce the Flenni to the status of breeding animals. Maybe the hate is deeper. The Esthaans have all the Flenn genes. They may have a primordial, unconscious sex-drive which they can never fulfill—and which is incarnated in the Flenni. At any rate they're now acting out a full-blown social psychosis, and the social engineers are going to have one sweet job. But of course, biologically—" I pause.

"Go on, Ian."

"Well, you know it. The Flenni genes combine with ours. It's possible the alternating system is carried by recessives and could in the long run be bred out."

Pax is silent. I hear him catch his breath. For the first time he has considered what his child by Flanya might be. Is it possible that this dove of a girl will give birth to a neuter sausage—an Esthaan?

"Time to turn in."

"Yes." His voice is dull.

I lie gazing at the pink moons, thinking *Poor Pax, poor good retriever boy*. Interbreeding may eventually solve the planet's dilemma—but meanwhile, how many human hearts will go out to the Flenn beauty, the Flenn sexual impact? Only in dreams do we ever see beings who are literally all male or all female. The most virile human man, the most seductive woman is, in fact, a blend. But the Flenni are the pure expression of one sex alone—overwhelming, irresistible. How many of us will give ourselves to them, only to find the beauty dying in our arms?

Whatever Pax's first-born will be, the arms that hold it will be those of a dying crone—who only weeks before had been his blooming love.

The pink moons sail the zenith, sweet as the gift of

Flenni love. The image of Molly's face comes finally to comfort me. Molly who can love and live, who will greet me among our children. I must remember, I think drowsily, to tell her how good it is to be a diploid sporozoön. . . .

And So On, And So On

In a nook of the ship's lounge the child had managed to activate a viewscreen.

"Rovy! They *asked* you not to play with the screen while we're Jumping. We've told you and told you there isn't anything there. It's just pretty lights, dear. Now come back and we'll all play—"

As the young clanwife coaxed him back to their cocoons something happened. It was a .very slight something, just enough to make the drowsy passengers glance up. Immediately a calm voice spoke, accompanied by the blur of multiple translation.

"This is your captain. The momentary discontinuity we just experienced is quite normal in this mode of paraspace. We will encounter one or two more before reaching the Orion complex, which will be in about two units of ship's time."

The tiny episode stimulated talk.

"Declare I feel sorry for the youngers today." The large being in mercantile robes tapped his Galnews scanner, blew out his ear sacs comfortably. "We had all the fun. Why, when I first came out this was all wild frontier. Took courage to go beyond the Coalsack. They had you make your will. I can even remember the first cross-Gal Jump."

"How fast it has all changed!" admired his talking minor. Daringly it augmented: "The youngers are so

39

apathetic. They accept all these marvels as natural, they mock the idea of heroism."

"Heroes!" the merchant snorted. "Not them!" He gazed challengingly around the luxe cabin, eliciting a few polite nods. Suddenly a cocoon swivelled around to face him, revealing an Earth-typer in Pathman grey.

"Heroism," said the Pathman softly, eyeing the merchant from under shadowed brows. "Heroism is essentially a spatial concept. No more free space, no more heroes." He turned away as if regretting having spoken, like a man trying to sustain some personal pain.

"Ooh, what about Ser Orpheian?" asked a bright young reproducer. "Crossing the Arm alone in a single pod, I think that's heroic!" It giggled flirtatiously.

"Not really," drawled a cultivated Galfad voice. The lutroid who had been using the reference station removed his input leads and smiled distantly at the reproducer. "Such exploits are merely an expiring gasp, a gleaning after the harvest if you will. Was Orpheian launching into the unknown? Not so. He faced merely the problem of whether he himself could do it. Playing at frontiers. No," the lutroid's voice took on a practiced Recorder's clarity. "The primitive phase is finished. The true frontier is within now. Inner space." He adjusted his academic fourragère.

The merchant had returned to his scanner.

"Now here's a nice little offering," he grunted. "Ringsun for sale, Eridani sector. That sector's long overdue for development, somebody'll make a sweet thing. If some of these young malcontents would just blow out their gills and pitch in!—" He thumped his aquaminor on the snout, causing it to mew piteously.

"But that's too much like work," echoed his talker soothingly.

The Pathman had been watching in haggard silence. Now he leaned over to the lutroid.

"Your remark about inner space. I take it you mean psychics? Purely subjective explorations?"

"Not at all," said the lutroid, gratified. "The psychic cults I regard as mere sensationalism. I refer to reality, to that simpler and deeper reality that lies beyond the reach of the trivial methodologies of science, the reality which we can only approach through what is called aesthetic or religious experience, god-immanent if you will—"

"I'd like to see art or religion get you to Orion," remarked a grizzed spacedog in the next cocoon. "If it wasn't for science you wouldn't be end-running the parsecs in an aleph Jumpship."

"Perhaps we end-run too much," the lutroid smiled. "Perhaps our technological capabilities are end-running, as you call it, our—"

"What about the Arm wars?" cried the young reproducer. "Ooh, science is *horrible*. I cry every time I think of the poor Armers." Its large eyes steamed and it hugged itself seductively.

"Well, now, you can't blame science for what some power-hounds do with it," the spacedog chuckled, hitching his cocoon over toward the reproducer's stay.

"That's right," said another voice, and the conversation group drifted away.

The Pathman's haunted eyes were still on the lutroid.

"If you are so certain of this deeper reality, this inner space," he said quietly, "why is your left hand almost without nails?"

The lutroid's left hand clenched and then uncurled slowly to reveal the gnawed nails; he was not undisciplined.

"I recognise the right of your order to unduly personal speech," he said stiffly. Then he sighed and smiled. "Ah, of course; I admit I am not immune to the universal *angst*, the failure of nerve. The haunting fear of stagnation and decline, now that life has reached to the limits of this galaxy. But I regard this as a challenge to transcendence, which we must, we will meet, through our inner resources. We will find our *true* frontier." He nodded. "Life has never failed the ultimate challenge."

"Life has never before met the ultimate challenge," the Pathman rejoined somberly. "In the history of every race, society, planet or system or federation or swarm, whenever they had expanded to their *spatial limits* they commenced to decline. First stasis, then increasing entropy, degradation of structure, disorganisation, death. In every case, the process was only halted by breaking out into new space, or by new peoples breaking in on them from outside. Crude, simple outer space. Inner space? Consider the Vegans—"

"Exactly!" interrupted the lutroid. "That refutes you. The Vegans were approaching the most fruitful concepts of transphysical reality, concepts we must certainly reopen. If only the Myrmidi invasion had not destroyed so much."

"It is not generally known," the Pathman's voice was very low, "when the Myrmidi landed the Vegans were eating their own larvae and using the sacred dream-fabrics for ornaments. Very few could even sing."

"No!"

"By the Path."

The lutroid's nictating membranes filmed his eyes. After a moment he said formally, "You carry despair as your gift."

The Pathman was whispering as if to himself. "Who will come to open our skies? For the first time all life is closed in a finite space. Who can rescue a galaxy? The Clouds are barren and the realms beyond we know cannot be crossed even by matter, let alone life. For the first time we have truly reached the end."

"But the young," said the lutroid in quiet anguish.

"The young sense this. They seek to invent pseudo-frontiers, subjective escapes. Perhaps your inner space can beguile some for a while. But the despair will grow. Life is not mocked. We have come to the end of infinity, the end of hope."

The lutroid stared into the Pathman's hooded eyes, his hand involuntarily raising his academic surplice like a shield.

"You believe that there is nothing, no way?"

"Ahead lies only the irreversible long decline. For the first time *we know there is nothing beyond ourselves.*"

After a moment the lutroid's gaze dropped and the two beings let silence enshroud them. Outside the Galaxy was twisting by unseen, enormous, glittering: a finite prison. No way out.

In the aisle behind them something moved.

The child Rovy was creeping stealthily toward the screens that looked on no-space, his eyes intent and bright.

Her Smoke Rose Up Forever

Deliverance quickens, catapults him into his boots on mountain gravel, his mittened hand on the rusty 1935 International truck. Cold rushes into his young lungs, his eyelashes are knots of ice as he peers down at the lake below the pass. He is in a bare bleak bowl of mountains just showing rusty in the dawn; not one scrap of cover anywhere, not a tree, not a rock.

The lake below shines emptily, its wide rim of ice silvered by the setting moon. It looks small, everything looks small from up here. Is that scar on the edge his boat? Yes—it's there, it's all okay! The black path snaking out from the boat to the patch of tulegrass is the waterway he broke last night. Joy rises in him, hammers his heart. This is it. This—is—*it*.

He squints his lashes, can just make out the black threads of the tules. Black knots among them—sleeping ducks. Just you wait! His grin crackles the ice in his nose. The tules will be his cover—that perfect patch out there. About eighty yards, too far to hit from shore. That's where he'll be when the dawn flight comes over. Old Tom said he was loco. Loco Petey. Just you wait. Loco Tom.

The pickup's motor clanks, cooling, in the huge silence. No echo here, too dry. No wind. Petey listens intently: a thin wailing in the peaks overhead, a tiny croak from the lake below. Waking up. He scrapes back

44

his frozen canvas cuff over the birthday watch, is oddly, fleetingly puzzled by his own knobby fourteen-year-old wrist. Twenty-five—no, twenty-four minutes to the duck season. Opening day! Excitement ripples down his stomach, jumps his dick against his scratchy longjohns. Gentlemen don't beat the gun. He reaches into the pickup, reverently lifts out the brand-new Fox CE double-barrel twelve-gauge.

The barrels strike cold right through his mitts. He'll have to take one off to shoot, too: It'll be fierce. Petey wipes his nose with his cuff, pokes three fingers through his cut mitten and breaks the gun. Ice in the sight. He checks his impulse to blow it out, dabs clumsily. Shouldn't have taken it in his sleeping bag. He fumbles two heavy sixes from his shell pocket, loads the sweet blue bores, is hardly able to breathe for joy. He is holding a zillion dumb bags of the *Albuquerque Herald,* a whole summer of laying adobe for Mr. Noff—all transmuted into this: his perfect, agonizingly chosen OWN GUN. No more borrowing old Tom's stinky over-and-under with the busted sight. His own gun with his *initials* on the silver stock-plate.

Exaltation floods him, rises perilously. Holding his gun Petey takes one more look around at the enormous barren slopes. Empty, only himself and his boat and the ducks. The sky has gone cold gas-pink. He is standing on a cusp of the Great Divide at ten thousand feet, the main pass of the western flyway. At dawn on opening day . . . What if Apaches came around now? Mescalero Apaches own these mountains but he's never seen one out here. His father says they all have TB or something. In the old days, did they come here on horses? They'd look tiny; the other side is ten miles at least.

Petey squints at a fuzzy place on the far shore, decides it's only sagebrush, but gets the keys and the axe out of the pickup just in case. Holding the axe away from his gun he starts down to the lake. His chest is banging, his knees wobble, he can barely feel his feet skidding down the rocks. The whole world seems to be brimming up with tension.

He tells himself to calm down, blinking to get rid of a

funny blackness behind his eyes. He stumbles, catches himself, has to stop to rub at his eyes. As he does so everything flashes black-white—the moon jumps out of a black sky like a locomotive headlight, he is sliding on darkness with a weird humming all around. Oh, Jeeze—mustn't get an altitude blackout, not now! And he makes himself breathe deeply, goes on down with his boots crunching hard like rhythmic ski turns, the heavy shell pockets banging his legs, down, going quicker now, down to the waiting boat.

As he gets closer he sees the open water-path has iced over a little during the night. Good job he has the axe. Some ducks are swimming slow circles right by the ice. One of them rears up and quack-flaps, showing the big raked head: canvasback!

"Ah, you beauty," Petey says aloud, starting to run now, skidding, his heart pumping love, on fire for that first boom and rush. "I wouldn't shoot a sitting duck." His nose-drip has frozen, he is seeing himself hidden in those tules when the flights come over the pass, thinking of old Tom squatting in the rocks back by camp. Knocking back his brandy with his old gums slobbering, dreaming of dawns on World War I airdromes, dreaming of shooting a goose, dying of TB. Crazy old fool. Just you wait. Petey sees his plywood boat heaped with the great pearly breasts and red-black Roman noses of the canvasbacks bloodied and stiff, the virgin twelve-gauge lying across them, fulfilled.

And suddenly he's beside the boat, still blinking away a curious unreal feeling. Mysterious to see his own footprints here. The midget boat and the four frosted decoys are okay, but there's ice in the waterway, all right. He lays the gun and axe inside and pushes the boat out from the shore. It sticks, bangs, rides up over the new ice.

Jeeze, it's really thick! Last night he'd kicked through it easily and poled free by gouging in the paddle. Now he stamps out a couple of yards, pulling the boat. The ice doesn't give. Darn! He takes a few more cautious steps—and suddenly hears the *whew-whew, whew-whew* of ducks coming in. Coming in—and he's out here in the open! He drops beside the boat, peers into the bright white sky over the pass.

Oh *Jeeze*—there they are! Ninety miles an hour, coming downwind, a big flight! And he hugs his gun to hide the glitter, seeing the hurtling birds set their wings, become bloodcurdling black crescent-shapes, webs dangling, dropping like dive-bombers—but they've seen him, they veer in a great circle out beyond the tules, all quacking now, away and down. He hears the far rip of water and stands up aching toward them. You wait. Just wait till I get this dumb boat out there!

He starts yanking the boat out over the creaking ice in the brightening light, cold biting at his face and neck. The ice snaps, shivers, is still hard. Better push the boat around ahead of him so he can fall in it when it goes. He does so, makes another two yards, three—and then the whole sheet tilts and slides under with him floundering, and grounds on gravel. Water slops over his boot tops, burns inside his three pair of socks.

But it's shallow. He stamps forward, bashing ice, slipping and staggering. A yard, a yard, a yard more—he can't feel his feet, he can't get purchase. Crap darn, this is too slow! He grabs the boat, squats, throws himself in and ahead with all his might. The boat rams forward like an ice-breaker. Again! He'll be out of the ice soon now. Another lunge! And again!

But this time the boat recoils, doesn't ram. Darn *shit*, the crappy ice is so thick! How could it get this thick when it was open water last night?

'Cause the wind stopped, that's why, and it's ten above zero. Old Tom knew, darn him to hell. But there's only about thirty yards left to go to open water, only a few yards between him and the promised land. Get there. Get over it or under it or through it, go!

He grabs the axe, wades out ahead of the boat, and starts hitting ice, trying to make cracks. A piece breaks, he hits harder. But it doesn't want to crack, the axe-head keeps going in, *thunk*. He has to work it out of the black holes. And it's getting deep, he's way over his boots now. So what? *Thunk!* Work it loose. *Thunk!*

But some remaining sanity reminds him he really

will freeze out here if he gets his clothes soaked. Shee-it! He stops, stands panting, staring at the ducks, which are now tipping up, feeding peacefully well out of range, chuckling *paducah, paducah* at him and his rage.

Twenty more yards, shit darn, *God*-darn. He utters a caw of fury and hunger and at that moment hears a tiny distant crack. Old Tom, firing. Crack!

Petey jumps into the boat, jerking off his canvas coat, peeling off the two sweaters, pants, the grey longjohns. His fingers can barely open the icy knots of his boot-laces but his body is radiant with heat, it sizzles the air, only his balls are trying to climb back inside as he stands up naked. Twenty yards!

He yanks the sodden boots back on and crashes out into the ice, whacking with the axe-handle, butting whole sheets aside. He's making it! Ten more feet, twenty! He rams with the boat, bangs it up and down like a sledge-hammer. Another yard! Another! His teeth are clattering, his shins are bleeding, and it's cutting his thighs now, but he feels nothing, only joy, joy!—until suddenly he is slewing full-length under wa-ter with the incredible cold going up his ass and into his armpits like skewers and ice cutting his nose.

His hands find the edge and he hauls himself up on the side of the boat. The bottom has gone completely. His axe—his axe is gone.

The ice is still there.

A black hand grabs him inside, he can't breathe. He kicks and flails, dragging himself up into the boat to kneel bleeding, trying to make his ribs work and his jaws stop banging. The first sunray slicks him with ice and incredible goosebumps; he gets a breath and can see ahead, see the gleaming ducks. So close!

The paddle. He seizes it and stabs at the ice in front of the boat. It clatters, rebounds, the boat goes back-ward. With all his force he flails the ice, but it's too thick, the paddle stem is cracking. No bottom to brace on. *Crack!* And the paddle blade skitters away across the ice. He has nothing left.

He can't make it.

Rage, helpless rage yomits through him, his eyes are

crying hot ice down his face. So close! *So close!* And
sick with fury he sees them come—*whew-whew! whew-
whew-whew-whew!*—a torrent of whistling wings in the
bright air, the ducks are pouring over the pass. Ten
thousand noble canvasbacks hurtling down the sky at
him silver and black, the sky is wings beating above
him, but too high, too high—they know the range, oh
yes!

He has never seen so many, he will never see it
again—and he is standing up in the boat now, a naked
bleeding loco ice-boy, raging, sweeping the virgin
twelve-gauge, firing—BAM-BAM! both barrels at
nothing, at the ice, at the sky, spilling out the shells,
ramming them in with tearing frozen hands. A drake
bullets toward him, nearer—it *has* to be near enough!
BAM! BAM!

But it isn't, it isn't, and the air-riders, the magic bodies of his love beat over him yelling—canvasback, teal,
widgeon, pintails, redheads, every duck in the world rising now, he is in a ten-mile swirl of birds, firing, firing,
a weeping maniac under the flashing wings, white-
black, black-white. And among the flashing he sees not
only ducks but geese, cranes, every great bird that ever
rode this wind: hawks, eagles, condors, pterodactyls—
BAM-BAM! BAM-BAM!! in the crazy air, in the
gale of rage and tears exploding in great black pulses—
black! light! black!—whirling unbearably, rushing him
up . . .

. . . And he surfaces suddenly into total calm and
dimness, another self with all fury shrunk to a tiny knot
below his mind and his eyes feasting in the open throat
of a girl's white shirt. He is in a room, a cool cave humming with secret promise. Behind the girl the windows
are curtained with sheer white stuff against the glare outside.

"Your mother said you went to Santa Fe." He hears
his throat threaten soprano and digs his fists into the
pockets of his Levis.

The girl Pilar—Pee-lar, crazy-name-Pilar—bends to

pick at her tanned ankle, feathery brown bob swinging across her cheek and throat.

"Um-m." She is totally absorbed in a thin gold chain around her ankle, crouching on a big red leather thing her parents got in where, Morocco—Pilar of the urgently slender waist curving into her white Levis, the shirt so softly holding swelling softness; everything so white against her golden tan, smelling of soap and flowers and girl. So *clean*. She has to be a virgin, his heart knows it; a marvellous slow-motion happiness is brimming up in the room. She likes me. She's so shy, even if she's a year older, nearly seventeen, she's like a baby. The pathos of her vulnerable body swells in him, he balls his fists to hide the bulge by his fly. Oh Jeeze, I mean Jesus, let her not look, Pilar. But she does look up then, brushing her misty hair back, smiling dreamily up at him.

"I was at the La Fonda, I had a dinner date with René."

"Who's René?"

"I told you, Pe-ter." Not looking at him, she uncurls from the hassock, drifts like a child to the window, one hand rubbing her arm. "He's my cousin. He's old, he's twenty-five or thirty. He's a lieute*nant* now."

"Oh."

"An *older man*." She makes a face, grins secretly, peeking out through the white curtains.

His heart fizzes with relief, with the exultance rising in the room. She's a virgin, all right. From the bright hot world outside comes the sound of a car starting. A horse whickers faintly down at the club stables, answered by the double wheeze of a donkey. They both giggle. Peter flexes his shoulder, opens and grips his hand around an imaginary mallet.

"Does your father know you were out with him?"

"Oh yes." She's cuddling her cheek against her shoulder, pushing the immaculate collar, letting him see the creamy mounds. She wants me, Peter thinks. His guts jump. *She's going to let me do it to her*. And all at once he is calm, richly calm like that first morning at the corral, watching his mare come to him; knowing.

"Pa-*pa* doesn't care, it's nineteen forty-four. René is my cousin."

Her parents are so terribly sophisticated; he knows her father is some kind of secret war scientist: they are all here because of the war, something over at Los Alamos. And her mother talking French, talking about weird places like Dee-jon and Tan-jay. His own mother doesn't know French, his father teaches high school, he never would be going around with these sophisticated strangers except they need him for their sandlot polo. And he can play rings around them all, too, Peter thinks, grinning, all those smooth sweating old young men—even with his one mare for four chukkers and her tendons like big hot balloons, even with his spliced mallet he can cut it over their heads! If he could only get an official rating. Three goals, sure. Maybe four, he muses, seeing himself riding through that twerp Drexel with his four remounts, seeing Pilar smile, not looking at him. She's shy. That time he let her ride the mare she was really frightened, incredibly awkward; he could feel her thighs tremble when he boosted her up.

His own thighs tremble, remembering the weak tenderness of her in his hands. *Always before your voice my soul is as some smooth and awkward foal*— it doesn't sound so wet now, his mother's nutty line. His foal, his velvety vulnerable baby mare. Compared to her he's a gorilla, even if he's technically a virgin too, men are different. And he understands suddenly that weird Havelock Ellis book in her father's den. Gentle. He must be gentle. Not like—a what?—a baboon playing a violin.

"You shouldn't fool around with older men," he says and is gratified by the gruffness. "You don't know."

She's watching him now under the fall of her hair, coming close, still hugging herself with her hand going slowly up and down her arm, caressing it. A warm soap smell fills his nose, a sharp muskiness under it. She doesn't know what she's doing, he thinks choking, she doesn't know about men. And he grunts something like "Don't," or "Can it," trying to hold down the leaping heat between them, but is confused by her voice whispering.

"It *hurts,* Pe-ter."

"What, your arm?"

"Here, do-pee," and his hand is suddenly taken hold of by cool small fingers pulling it not to her arm but in wonder to her side, pressed in the rustling shirt under which he feels at first nothing and then shockingly too far in not his own wide ribs but the warm stem of her, and as his paralyzed hand fumbles, clasps, she half turns around so that his ignited hand rides onto a searing soft unnatural swelling—her *breast*—and the room blanks out, whirls up on a brimming, drumming tide as if all the dead buffalo were pounding back. And the window blinks once with lemon light shooting around their two bodies where her hip is butting into his thigh making it wholly impossible to continue standing there with his hands gentle on her tits.

"You don't know what you're doing, Pilar. Don't be a dope, your mother—"

"She's a-way now." And there is a confused interval of mouths and hands trying to be gentle, trying to hold her away from his fly, trying to stuff her into himself in total joy, if he had six hands he couldn't cope with electric all of her—until suddenly she pulls back, is asking inanely, "Pe-ter, don't you have a friend?"

The subtle difference in her voice makes him blink, answering stupidly, "Sure, Tom Ring," while her small nose wrinkles.

"Dopee Pe-ter, I mean a boy friend. Somebody smooth."

He stands trying to pant dignifiedly, thinking Jeeze, I mean Christ, she knows I don't have any smooth friends; if it's for a picnic maybe Diego Martine? But before he can suggest this she has leaned into the window bay, cuddling the silky curtain around her, peeking at him so that his hands go pawing in the cloth.

"René has a friend."

"Uh."

"He's older too, he's twen-tee," she breathes teasingly. "Lieute*nant* Shar-lo. That's Charles to you, see?"

And she turns around full into his arms curtain and all and from the press of silk and giggles comes a small voice saying forever, "And Re-*né* and Shar-*lo* and Pee-*lar* all went to bed together and they played with me, Oh, for hours and hours Pe-ter, it was too marvellous. I will ne-ver do it with just one boy again."

Everything drops then except her face before him horribly heavy and exalted and alien, and just as his heart knows it's dead and an evil so generalized he can hardly recognise it as fury starts tearing emptily at him inside, her hand comes up over her mouth and she is running doubled over past him.

"I'm going to be sick, Peter help me!"

And he stumbles after down the dim cool hall to find her crumpled down, her brown hair flowing into the toilet as she retches, retches, whimpering, convulses unbearably. The white shirt has ridden up to expose her pathetically narrow back, soft knobs of her spine curving down into her pants, her tender buttocks bumping his knees as he stands helplessly strangling a sopping towel instead of her neck, trying to swab at her hidden forehead. His own gullet is retching too, his face feels doughy, and water is running down into his open mouth while one of her hands grips his, shaking him with her spasms there in the dim hospital-like bathroom. The world is groaning, he is seeing not her father's bay rum bottle but the big tiled La Fonda bedroom, the three bodies writhing on the bed, performing unknown horrors. *Playing with her . . .*

His stomach heaves, only what it is, he is coming in his Levis in a dreadful slow unrelieving ooze like a red-hot wire dragging through his crotch, while he stands by her uselessly as he will stand helplessly by in some near future he can't imagine or remember—and the tension keeps building, pounding, the light flickers—a storm is coming or maybe his eyes are going bad, but he can see below him her pure profile resting spent on the edge of the toilet, oblivious to his furious towel; in the flashing dimness sees the incomprehensible letters *S-E-P-T-I-C A-B-O-R-T-I-O-N* snaking shadowy down the spine of his virgin love, while the universe beats black—Flash!

Black! Drumming with hooves harsher than any storm—hurling him through lightning-claps of blinding darkness to a thrumming stasis in which what exists of him senses—something—but is instantly shot away on unimaginable energies—

—And achieves condensement, blooms into the green and open sunlight of another world, into a mellow springtime self—in which a quite different girl is jostling his hip.

"Molly," he hears his older voice say vaguely, seeing with joy how the willow fronds trail in the friendly, dirty Potomac. The bars and caduceus on his collar are pricking his neck.

"Yes sir, Doctor sir." She spins around, kneels down in the scruffy grass to open Howard Johnson boxes. "Oh god, the coffee." Handing him up a hot dog, swinging back her fair hair. Her arm is so female with its tender pale armpit, her whole body is edible, even her dress is like lemonade so fresh and clean—no, radiant, he corrects himself. That's the word, radiant. His radiant woman. He shrugs away a tiny darkness, thinking of her hair sliding on his body in the Roger Smith hotel bedroom.

"C'mon sit, Pete. It's only a little dirty."

"Nothing's dirty any more." He flops down beside her, one arm finding its natural way around the opulence of her buttocks on the grass. She chuckles down at him, shaking her head.

"You're a hard case, Pete." She takes a big bite of hot dog with such lips that he considers flinging himself upon her then and there, barely remembers the cars tearing by above them. "I swear," she says, chewing, "I don't think you ever screwed anybody you were friends with before."

"Something like that." He puts his hot dog down to loosen his GI tie.

"Thirty days to civvies, you'll be in Baltimore." She licks her fingers happily. "Oh wow, Pete, I'm so glad you got your fellowship. Try the cole slaw, it's all right. Will you remember us poor slaves when you're a big old pathologist?"

"I'll remember." To distract himself he pokes in the boxes, spills cole slaw on a book. "What you reading?"

"Oh, Whately Carington."

"Whatly what?"

"No, *Whate*-ly. Carington. A Limey. Psychical research man, they do that veddy seddiously, the Limies."

"Uh?" He beams at the river, blinks to get rid of a flicker back of his eyes. Amphetamine withdrawal, after six months?

"He has this theory, about K-objects. Whatever thing you feel most intense about, part of you lives on—Pete, what's wrong?"

"Nothing."

But the flicker won't quit, it is suddenly worse; through it he can just make out her face turned nurse-wary, coming close, and he tries to hang on through a world flashing black—green—BLACK!—is trapped for unbreathing timelessness in dark nowhere, a phantom landscape of grey tumbled ash under a hard black sky, seeing without eyes a distant tangle of wreckage on the plain so menacing that his unbodied voice screams at the shadow of a metal scrap beside him in the ashes, 2004 the ghostly unmeaning numbers—*STOP IT!*—And he is back by the river under Molly's springtime eyes, his hands gripping into the bones of her body.

"Hey-y-y, honey, the war's over." Sweet sensual pixie-smile now watchful, her nurse's hand inside his shirt. "Korea's ten thousand miles away, you're in good old D.C., Doctor."

"I know. I saw a license plate." He laughs unconvincingly, makes his hands relax. Will the ghosts of Seoul never let him go? And his body guiltily intact, no piece of him in the stained waste cans into which he has—Stop it! Think of Molly. I like Ike. Johns Hopkins research fellowship. Some men simply aren't cut out for surgical practice.

"I'm a gutless wonder, Molly. Research."

"Oh for Christ's sake, Pete," she says with total warmth, nurse-hand satisfied, changing to lover's on his chest. "We've been *over* all that."

And of course they have, he knows it and only mutters, "My Dad wanted me to be an Indian doctor," which they have been over too; and the brimming gladness is back now, buoyantly he seizes the cole slaw, demands entertainment, demonstrating reality-grasp.

"So what about Whately?"

"It's serious-s-s," she protests, snickering, and is mercurially almost serious too. "I mean, I'm an atheist, Pete, I don't believe there's anything afterwards, but this theory . . ." And she rattles on about K-objects and the pool of time, intense energic structures of the mind undying—sweet beddable girl in the springtime who has taught him unclaiming love. His friend. Liberated him.

He stretches luxuriously, relishes a cole slaw belch. Free male beside a willing woman. No problems. *What is it man in woman doth require? The lineaments of gratified desire.* The radiance of her. He has gratified her. Will gratify her again . . .

"It's kind of spooky, though." She flings the box at the river with tremendous effort, it flies twenty feet. "Damn! But think of parts of yourself whirling around forever sticking to whatever you loved!" She settles against the willow, watching the box float away. "I wonder if part of me is going to spend eternity hanging around a dumb cat. I loved that old cat. Henry. He died, though."

The ghost of a twelve-gauge fires soundlessly across his mind, a mare whickers. He sneezes and rolls over onto her lap with his nose in her warm scented thighs. She peers dreamily down at him over her breasts, is almost beautiful.

"Whatever you love, forever. Be careful what you love." She squints wickedly. "Only with you I think it'd be whatever you were maddest at—no, that's a horrible thought. Love *has* to be the most intense."

He doubts it but is willing to be convinced, rooting in her lap while she pretends to pound on him and then squirms, stretching up her arms, giving herself to the air, to him, to life.

"I want to spend eternity whirling around you." He heaves up to capture her, no longer giving a damn about the cars, and as the sweet familiar body comes pliantly under him he realizes it's true, he's known it for some time. Not friendship at all, or rather, the best of friendships. The real one. "I love you, Molly. We love."

"Ooh, Pete."

"You're coming to Baltimore with me. We'll get married," he tells her warm neck, feeling the flesh under her skirt heavy in his hand, feeling also an odd stillness that makes him draw back to where he can see her face, see her lips whispering.

"I was afraid of that."

"Afraid?" His heart jumps with relief, jumps so hard that the flicker comes back in the air, through which he sees her lying too composed under his urgency. "Don't be afraid, Molly. I *love* you."

But she is saying softly, "Oh, damn, damn, Pete, I'm so sorry, it's a lousy thing women do. I was just so happy, because . . ." She swallows, goes on in an absurd voice. "Because someone very dear to me is coming home. He called me this morning from Honolulu."

This he cannot, will not understand among the flashing pulses, but repeats patiently, "You love me, Molly. I love you. We'll get married in Baltimore," while she fights gently away from him saying, "Oh I do, Pete, I *do*, but it's not the same."

"You'll be happy with me. You love me."

They are both up crouching now in the blinking, pounding sunlight.

"No, Pete, I never *said*. I didn't—" Her hands are out seeking him like knives.

"I *can't* marry you, honey. I'm going to marry a man called Charlie McMahon."

McMahon—Maaa—honn—aa—on-n-n the idiot sound flaps through the universe, his carotids are hammering, the air is drumming with his hurt and rage as he stands foolishly wounded, unable to believe the treachery of everything—which is now strobing in great blows of blackness as his voice shouts "Whore!" shouts "Bitch-bitch-bitch . . ." into a dwindling, flashing chaos—

—And explodes silently into a nonbeing which is almost familiar, is happening this time more slowly as if huge energy is tiding to its crest so slowly that some structure of himself endures to form in what is no longer a brain the fear that he is indeed dead and damned to live forever in furious fragments. And against this horror his essence strains to protest *But I did love!* at a horizon of desolation—a plain of endless, lifeless rubble under a cold black sky, in which he or some pattern of energies senses once more that distant presence: wreckage, machines, huge structures incomprehensibly operative, radiating dark force in the nightmare world, the force which now surges—

—To incorporate him anew within familiar walls, with the words "But I did love" meaninglessly on his lips. He leans back in his familiarly unoiled swivel chair, savoring content. Somewhere within him weak darkness stirs, has power only to send his gaze to the three-di portraits behind the pile of print-outs on his desk.

Molly smiles back at him over the computer sheets, her arm around their eldest daughter. For the first time in years the thought of poor Charlie McMahon crosses his mind, triggers the automatic incantation: Molly-never-would-have-been-happy-with-him. They had a bad time around there, but it worked out. Funny how vividly he recalls that day by the river, in spite of all the good years since. *But I did love,* his mind murmurs uneasily, as his eyes go lovingly to the computer print-outs.

The lovely, elegant results. All confirmed eight ways now, the variance all pinned down. Even better than he'd hoped. The journal paper can go in the mail tomorrow. Of course the pub-lag is nearly three years now; never mind: the AAAS panel comes next week. That's the important thing. Lucky timing, couldn't be neater. The press is bound to play it up . . . Going to be hard not to watch Gilliam's face, Peter muses, his own face ten years younger, sparkling, all lines upturned.

"I do love it, that's what counts," he thinks, a jumble of the years of off-hours drudgery in his mind . . . Coffee-ringed clipboards, the new centrifuge, the animal mess, a girl's open lab coat, arguments with Ferris in Analysis, arguments about space, about equipment, about costs—and arching over it like a laser-grid the luminous order of his hypothesis. His proven—no, mustn't say it—his meticulously *tested* hypothesis. The lucky lifetime break. The beauty one. Never do it again, he hasn't another one like this left in him; no matter! This is it, the peak. Just in time. Don't think of what Nathan said, don't think the word. (Nobel)—That's stupid. (Nobel) Think of the work itself, the explanatory power, the clarity.

His hand has been wandering toward the in-basket under the print-outs where his mail has been growing moss (he'll get a secretary out of this, that's for sure!) but the idea of light turns him to the window. The room feels tense, brimming with a tide of energy. Too much coffee, he thinks, too much joy. I'm not used to it. Too much of a loner. From here in I share. Spread it around, encourage younger men. Herds of assistants now . . .

Across his view of tired Bethesda suburbs around the NIH Annex floats the train of multiple-author papers, his name as senior, a genial myth; sponsoring everybody's maiden publication. A fixture in the mainstream . . . Kids playing down there, he sees, shooting baskets by a garage, will some of them live to have a myeloma cured by the implications of his grubby years up here? If the crystallization can be made easier. Bound to come. But not by me, he thinks, trying to focus on the running figures through a faint stroboscopic blink which seems to arise from the streets below although he knows it must be in his retinae.

Really too much caffeine, he warns himself. Let's not have a hypertensive episode, not *now* for God's sake. Exultation is almost tangible in the room, it's not distracting but integrative; as if he were achieving some higher level of vitality, a norepi-nephrine-like effect. Maybe I really will live on a higher level, he muses, rubbing the bridge of his nose between two fingers to get rid of a black after-image which seems almost like an Apollo moonscape behind his eyes, a trifle unpleasant.

Too much doom, he tells himself, vigorously polishing his glasses, too much bomb-scare, ecology-scare, fascism-scare, race-war-scare, death-of-everything scare. He jerks his jaw to stop the tinnitis thrumming in his inner ear, glancing at the big 1984 desk calendar with its scrawled joke: *If everything's okay why are we whispering*? Right. Let's get at it and get home. To Molly and Sue and little Pete, their late-born.

He grins, thinking of the kid running to him, and thrusts his hand under the print-outs to his packet of stale mail—and as his hand touches it an icicle rams into his heart.

For an instant he thinks he really is having a coronary, but it isn't his real heart, it's a horrible cold current of knowledge striking from his fingers to his soul, from that hideous sleazy tan-covered foreign journal which he now pulls slowly out to see the pencilled note clipped to the cover, the personally delivered damned journal which has been lying under there like a time-bomb for how long? Weeks?

Pete, you better look at this. Sorry as hell.

But he doesn't need to look, riffling through the wretchedly printed pages with fingers grown big and cold as clubs; he already knows what he'll find inside there published so neatly, so sweetly, and completely, with the confirmation even stronger and more elegant, the implication he hadn't thought of—and all so modest and terse. So young. Despair takes him as the page opens. *Djakarta University* for Jesus Christ's sake? And some Hindu's bloody paradigm . . .

Sick fury fulminates, bile and ashes rain through his soul as his hands fumble the pages, the grey unreal unreadable pages which are now strobing—Flash! Black! Flash! Black!—swallowing the world, roaring him in or up or out on a phantom whirlwind . . .

. . . till unsensation crescendoes past all limit, bursts

finally into the silence of pure energy, where he—or what is left of him, or momentarily reconstituted of him—integrates to terrified insight, achieves actual deathly awareness of its extinct self immaterially spinning in the dust of an aeons-gone NIH Annex on a destroyed planet. And comprehends with agonized lucidity the real death of everything that lived—excepting only that in himself which he would most desperately wish to be dead.

What happened? He does not know, can never know which of the dooms or some other had finally overtaken them, nor when; only that he is registering eternity, not time, that all that lived here has been gone so long that even time is still. Gone, all gone; centuries or millennia gone, all gone to ashes under pulseless stars in the icy dark, gone forever. Saving him alone and his trivial pain.

He alone . . . But as the mercilessly reifying force floods higher there wakes in him a dim uncomforting sense of presence; a bodiless disquiet in the dust tells him he is companioned, is but a node in a ghostly film of dead life shrouding the cold rock-ball. Unreachable, isolate—he strains for contact and is incorporeally stricken by new dread. *Are they too in pain?* Was pain indeed the fiercest fire in our nerves, alone able to sustain its flame through death? What of love, of joy? . . . There are none here.

He wails voicelessly as conviction invades him, he who had believed in nothing before. All the agonies of earth, uncancelled? Are broken ghosts limping forever from Stalingrad and Salamis, from Gettysburg and Thebes and Dunkirk and Khartoum? Do the butchers' blows still fall at Ravensbruck and Wounded Knee? Are the dead of Carthage and Hiroshima and Cuzco burning yet? Have ghostly women waked again only to resuffer violation, only to watch again their babies slain? Is every nameless slave still feeling the iron bite, is every bomb, every bullet and arrow and stone that ever flew still finding its screaming mark—atrocity without end or comfort, forever?

Molly. The name forms in his cancelled heart. She who was love. He tries to know that she or some fragment of her is warm among her children, but can summon only the image of her crawling forever through wreckage to Charlie McMahon's bloody head.

Let it not be! He would shriek defiance at the wastes, finding himself more real as the strange energy densens; he struggles bodilessly, flails perished non-limbs to conjure love out of extinction to shield him against hell, calling with all his obliterated soul on the ultimate talisman: the sound of his little son's laugh, the child running to him, clasping his leg in welcome home.

For an instant he thinks he has it—he can see the small face turn up, the mouth open—but as he tries to grasp, the ghost-child fades, frays out, leaving in his destroyed heart only another echo of hurt—*I want Mommy, Mommy, my Mommy.* And he perceives that what he had taken for its head are forms. Presences intrusive, alien as the smooth, bleak regard of sharks met under water.

They move, precess obscurely—they *exist* here on this time-lost plain! And he understands with loathing that it is from *them* or *those*—machines or beings, he cannot tell—that the sustaining energy flows. It is *their* dark potency which has raised him from the patterns of the dust.

Hating them he hungers, would sway after them to suck his death-life, as a billion other remnants are yearning, dead sunflowers thirsting toward their black sun—but finds he cannot, can only crave helplessly as they recede.

They move, he perceives, toward those black distant cenotaphs, skeletal and alien, which alone break the dead horizon. What these can be, engines or edifices, is beyond his knowing. He strains sightlessly, sensing now a convergence, an inflowing as of departure like ants into no earthly nest. And at this he understands that the energy upbuoying him is sinking, is starting to ebb. The alien radiance that raised him is going and he is guttering out. *Do you know?* he voicelessly cries after them,

Do you know? Do you move oblivious among our agonies?

But he receives no answer, will never receive one; and as his tenuous structure fails he has consciousness only to wonder briefly what unimaginable errand brought such beings here to his dead cinder. Emissaries, he wonders, dwindling; explorers, engineers? Or is it possible that they are only sightseers? Idling among our ruins, perhaps even cognizant of the ghosts they raise to wail—turning us on, recreating our dead-show for their entertainment?

Shrivelling, he watches them go in, taking with them his lacerating life, returning him to the void. Will they return? Or—his waning self forms one last desolation—have they returned already on their millennial tours? Has this recurred, to recur and recur again? Must he and all dead life be borne back each time helplessly to suffer, to jerk anew on the same knives and die again until another energy exhumes him for the next performance?

Let us die! But his decaying identity can no longer sustain protest, knows only that it is true, is unbearably all true, has all been done to him before and is all to do again and again and again without mercy forever.

And as he sinks back through the collapsing levels he can keep hold only of despair, touching again the deadly limp brown journal—*Djakarta University?* Flash—and he no longer knows the cause of the terror in his soul as he crumbles through lost springtime—*I don't love you that way, Pete*—and is betrayed to aching joy as his hand closes over the young breast within her white shirt—*Pe-ter, don't you have a friend?*— while his being shreds out, disperses among a myriad draining ghosts of anguish as the alien life deserts them, strands them lower and lower toward the final dark— until with uncomprehending grief he finds himself, or a configuration that was himself, for a last instant real— his boots on gravel in the dawn, his hand on a rusty pickup truck.

A joy he cannot bear rises in his fourteen-year-old

heart as he peers down at the magic ducks, sees his boat safe by the path he's cut; not understanding why the wind shrieks pain through the peaks above as he starts leaping down the rocks holding his axe and his first own gun, down to the dark lake under the cold stars, forever.

. . . A momentary taste
Of Being from the Well amid the Waste—
             —Khayyam/Fitzgerald

A Momentary Taste of Being

*. . . It floats there visibly engorged, blue-green against
the blackness. He stares: It swells, pulsing to a terrifying dim beat, slowly extrudes a great ghostly bulge
which extends, solidifies . . . it is a planet-testicle
pushing a monster penis toward the stars. Its blood-beat
reverberates through weeping immensities; cold, cold.
The parsecs-long phallus throbs, probes blindly under
intolerable pressure from within; its tip is a huge cloudy
glans lit by a spark: Centaur. In grief it bulges, lengthens,
seeking release—stars toll unbearable crescendo . . .*

It is a minute or two before Dr. Aaron Kaye is sure
that he is awake in his temporary bunk in *Centaur's*
quarantine ward. His own throat is sobbing reflexively,
his eyes are weeping, not the stars. Another of the damn
dreams. Aaron lies still, blinking, willing the icy grief to
let go of his mind.

It lets go. Aaron sits up still cold with meaningless
bereavement. What the hell is it, what's tearing at him?
"Great Pan is dead," he mutters stumbling to the nar-

65

row wash-stall. The lament that echoed round the world . . . He sluices his head, wishing for his own quarters and Solange. He really should work on these anxiety symptoms. Later, no time now. "Physician, screw thyself," he jeers at the undistinguished, worried face in the mirror.

Oh Jesus—the time! He has overslept while they are doing god knows what to Lory. Why hasn't Coby waked him? Because Lory is his sister, of course; Aaron should have foreseen that.

He hustles out into Isolation's tiny corridor. At one end is a vitrex wall; beyond it his assistant Coby looks up, takes off his headset. Was he listening to music, or what? No matter. Aaron glances into Tighe's cubicle. Tighe's face is still lax, sedated; he has been in sleep-therapy since his episode a week ago. Aaron goes to the speaker grille in the vitrex, draws a cup of hot brew. The liquid falls sluggishly; Isolation is at three-fourths gee in the rotating ship.

"Where's Dr. Kaye—my sister?"

"They've started the interrogation, boss. I thought you needed your sleep." Coby's doubtless meaning to be friendly but his voice has too many sly habits.

"Oh, god." Aaron starts to cycle the cup out, forces himself to drink it. He has a persistent feeling that Lory's alien is now located down below his right heel.

"Doc."

"What?"

"Bruce and Åhlstrom came in while you were asleep. They complain they saw Tighe running around loose this morning."

Aaron frowns. "He hasn't been out, has he?"

"No way. They each saw him separately. I talked them into seeing you, later."

"Yeah. Right." Aaron cycles his cup and heads back up the hall, past a door marked *Interview*. The next is *Observation*. He goes in to a dim closet with view-screens on two walls. The screen in front of him is already activated two-way. It shows four men seated in a small room outside Isolation's wall.

The gray-haired classic Anglo profile is Captain Yellaston, acknowledging Aaron's presence with a neutral nod. Beside him the two scout commanders go on watching their own screen. The fourth man is young Frank Foy, *Centaur's* security officer. He is pursing his mouth over a wad of printout tape.

Reluctantly, Aaron activates his other screen one-way, knowing he will see something unpleasant. There she is—his sister Lory, a thin young red-haired woman wired to a sensor bank. Her eyes have turned to him although Aaron knows she's seeing a blank screen. Hypersensitive as usual. Behind her is Solange in a de-contamination suit.

"We will go over the questions once more, Miss Kaye," Frank Foy says in a preposterously impersonal tone.

"Dr. Kaye, please." Lory sounds tired.

"Dr. Kaye, of course." Why is young Frank so dislikable? Be fair, Aaron tells himself, it's the man's job. Necessary for the safety of the tribe. And he isn't "young" Frank any more. Christ, none of us are, twenty-six trillion miles from home. Ten years.

"Dr. Kaye, you were primarily qualified as a biologist on the Gamma scout mission, is that right?"

"Yes, but I was also qualified in astrogation. We all were."

"Please answer yes or no."

"Yes."

Foy loops the printout, makes a mark. "And in your capacity as biologist you investigated the planetary surface both from orbit and on the ground from the landing site?"

"Yes."

"In your judgment, is the planet suitable for human colonization?"

"Yes."

"Did you observe anything harmful to human health or well-being?"

"No. No, it's ideal—I told you."

Foy coughs reprovingly. Aaron frowns too; Lory doesn't usually call things ideal.

"Nothing potentially capable of harming human beings?"

"No. Wait—even water is potentially capable of harming people, you know."

Foy's mouth tightens. "Very well, I rephrase. Did you observe any life-forms that attacked or harmed humans?"

"No."

"But—" Foy pounces—"when Lieutenant Tighe approached the specimen you brought back, he was harmed, was he not?"

"No, I don't believe it harmed him."

"As a biologist, you consider Lieutenant Tighe's condition unimpaired?"

"No—I mean yes. He was impaired to begin with, poor man."

"In view of the fact that Lieutenant Tighe has been hospitalized since his approach to this alien, do you still maintain it did not harm him?"

"Yes, it did not. Your grammar sort of confuses me. Please, may we move the sensor cuff to my other arm? I'm getting a little capillary breakage." She looks up at the blank screen hiding the command staff.

Foy starts to object but Captain Yellaston clears his throat warningly, nods. When Solange unhooks the big cuff Lory stands up and stretches her slim, almost breastless body; with that pleasant, snub-nosed face she could pass for a boy.

Aaron watches her as he has all his life with a peculiar mixture of love and dread. That body, he knows, strikes most men as sexless, an impression confirmed by her task-oriented manner. *Centaur's* selection board must have been composed of such men, one of the mission criteria was low sex-drive. Aaron sighs, watching Solange reattach the cuff. The board had been perfectly right, of course; as far as Lory herself was concerned she would have been happy in a nunnery. Aaron wishes she was in one. Not here.

Foy coughs primly into the microphone. "I will repeat, Dr. Kaye. Do you consider the effect of the alien specimen on Lieutenant Tighe was injurious to his health?"

"No," says Lory patiently. It's a disgusting scene, Aaron thinks; the helpless, wired-up woman, the hidden probing men. Psychic rape. Do them justice, only Foy seems to be enjoying it.

"On the planet surface, did Commander Kuh have contact with these life-forms?"

"Yes."

"And was he affected similarly to Lieutenant Tighe?"

"No—I mean, yes, the contact wasn't injurious to him either."

"I repeat. Was Commander Kuh or his men harmed in any way by the life-forms on that planet?"

"No."

"I repeat. Were Commander Kuh or his men harmed in any way by the life-forms on that planet?"

"No." Lory shakes her head at the blank screen.

"You state that the scoutship's computer ceased to record input from the sensors and cameras after the first day on the surface. Did you destroy those records?"

"No."

"Was the computer tampered with by you or anyone?"

"No. I told you, we thought it was recording, no one knew the dump cycle had cut in. We lost all that data."

"Dr. Kaye, I repeat: Did you dump those records?"

"No."

"Dr. Kaye, I will go back once more. When you returned alone, navigating Commander Kuh's scoutship, you stated that Commander Kuh and his crew had remained on the planet because they desired to begin colonization. You stated that the planet was, I quote, a paradise and that nothing on it was harmful to man. Despite the totally inadequate record of surface conditions you claim that Commander Kuh recommends that we immediately send the green signal to Earth to begin full-scale emigration. And yet when Lieutenant Tighe opened the port to the alien specimen in your ship he suffered a critical collapse. Dr. Kaye, I put it to you that what really happened on that planet was that Commander Kuh and his crew were injured or taken captive by beings on that planet and you are concealing this fact."

Lory has been shaking her short red hair vigorously during this speech. "No! They weren't injured or taken captive, that's silly! I tell you, they wanted to stay. I volunteered to take the message back. I was the logical choice, I mean I was non-Chinese, you know—"

"Please answer yes or no, Dr. Kaye. Did Commander Kuh or any of his people suffer a shock similar to Lieutenant Tighe?"

"No!"

Foy is frowning at his tapes, making tick-marks. Aaron's liver has been getting chilly; he doesn't need wiring to detect that extra sincerity in Lory's voice.

"I repeat, Dr. Kaye. Did—"

But Captain Yellaston stirs authoritatively behind him.

"Thank you, Lieutenant Foy."

Foy's mouth closes. On the blind side of the screen Lory says gamely, "I'm not really tired, sir."

"Nevertheless, I think we will complete this later," Yellaston says in his good gray voice. He catches Aaron's eye, and they all sit silent while Solange releases Lory from the cuff and body wires. Through Solange's visor Aaron can see her lovely French-Arab face projecting worried compassion. Empathy is Solange's specialty; a wire slips and Aaron sees her lips go "Ooh." He smiles, feels briefly better.

As the women leave, the two scout commanders in the other cubicle stand up and stretch. Both brown-haired, blue-eyed, muscular ectomesomorphs so much alike to Aaron's eye, although Timofaev Bron was born in Omsk and Don Purcell in Ohio. Ten years ago those faces had held only simple dedication to the goal of getting to a supremely difficult place in one piece. The failures of their respective scout missions have brought them back to *Centaur* lined and dulled. But in the last twenty days since Lory's return something has awakened in their eyes; Aaron isn't too eager to know its name.

"Report, please, Lieutenant Foy," says Yellaston, his glance making it clear that Aaron is to be included. The official recorder is still on.

Francis Xavier Foy sucks air through his teeth importantly; this is his second big interrogation on their entire ten-year voyage.

"Sir, I must regretfully report that the protocol shows persistent, ah, anomalous responses. First, the subject shows a markedly elevated and labile emotionality—" He glances irritatedly at Aaron to whom this is no news.

"The level of affect is, ah, suggestive. More specifically, on the question of injury to Commander Kuh, Dr. Kaye—Dr. *Lory* Kaye, that is—the physiological reactions contraindicate her verbal responses, that is, they are not characteristic of her base-line truth-type—" He shuffles his printouts, not looking at Aaron.

"Lieutenant Foy, are you trying to tell us that in your professional judgment Dr. Kaye is lying about what happened to the Gamma scout crew?"

Frank Foy wriggles, reshuffling tapes. "Sir, I can only repeat that there are contraindications. Areas, of unclarity. In particular these three responses, sir, if you would care to compare these peaks I have marked?"

Yellaston looks at him thoughtfully, not taking the tapes.

"Sir, if we could reconsider the decision not to employ, ah, chemical supplementation," Foy says desperately. He means, scop and EDC. Aaron knows Yellaston won't do this; he supposes he is grateful.

Yellaston doesn't bother answering. "Leaving aside the question of injury to Commander Kuh, Frank, what about Dr. Kaye's responses on the general habitability of the planet?"

"Again, there are anomalies in Dr. Kaye's responses." Foy visibly disapproves of any suspicions being left aside.

"What type of anomalies?"

"Abnormal arousal, sir. Surges of, ah, emotionality. Taken together with terms like 'paradise,' 'ideal,' and so on in the verbal protocol, the indications are—"

"In your professional judgment, Lieutenant Foy, do

you conclude that Dr. Kaye is or is not lying when she says the planet is habitable?"

"Sir, the problem is variability, in a pinpoint sense. What you have suggests the classic pattern of a covert *area.*"

Yellaston ponders; behind him the two scout commanders watch impassively.

"Lieutenant Foy. If Dr. Kaye does in fact believe the planet to be eminently suitable for colonization, can you say that her emotion could be accounted for by extreme elation and excitement at the successful outcome of our long and difficult mission?"

Foy stares at him, mouth slightly open.

"Elation, extreme—I see what you mean, sir. I hadn't—yes, sir, I suppose that could be one interpretation."

"Then do I correctly summarize your findings at this stage by saying that while Dr. Kaye's account of the events concerning Commander Kuh remains unclear, you see no specific counter-indication of her statement that the planet is habitable?"

"Ah, yes, sir. Although—"

"Thank you, Lieutenant Foy. We will resume tomorrow."

The two scout commanders glance at each other. They are solidly united against Foy, Aaron sees. Like two combat captains waiting for an unruly pacifist to be disposed of so the contest can start. Aaron sympathizes, he can't make himself like Foy. But he didn't like that tone in Lory's voice, either.

"Man, the samples, the sensor records," Don Purcell says abruptly. "They don't lie. Even if they only got thirty hours on-planet, that place is perfect."

Tim Bron grins, nods at Aaron. Yellaston smiles remotely, his eyes reminding them of the official recorder. For the thousandth time Aaron is touched by the calm command presence of the man. Old Yellowstone. The solid whatever-it-is that has held them together, stuffed in this tin can all through the years. Where the hell did they find him? A New Zealander, educated at some extinct British school. Chief of the Jupiter mission, etcetera, etcetera. Last of the dinosaurs.

But now he notices an oddity: Yellaston, who has absolutely no nervous mannerisms, is massaging the knuckles of one hand. Is it indecision over Lory's answers? Or is it the spark that's sizzling behind the two scout commanders' eyes—the planet?

The planet . . .

A golden jackpot rushes uncontrollably up through some pipe in Aaron's midbrain. Is it really there at last? After all the gruelling years, after Don and then Tim came back reporting nothing but gas and rocks around the first two Centaurus suns—is it possible our last chance has won? If Lory is to be believed, Kuh's people are at this moment walking in Earth's new Eden that we need so desperately. While we hang here in darkness, two long years away. If Lory is to be believed—

Aaron realizes Captain Yellaston is speaking to him.

"—You judge her to be medically fit, Dr. Kaye?"

"Yes, sir. We've run the full program of tests designed for possible alien contact, plus the standard biomonitor spectrum. As of last night—I haven't checked the last six hours—and apart from weight loss and the ulcerative lesions in the duodenum which she suffered from when she got back to *Centaur,* Dr. Lory Kaye shows no significant change from her base-line norms when she departed two years ago."

"Those ulcers, Doctor; am I correct that you feel they can be fully accounted for by the strain of her solitary voyage back to this ship?"

"Yes, sir, I certainly do." Aaron has no reservations here. Almost a year alone, navigating for a moving point in space? My god, how did you do it, he thinks again. My little sister. She isn't human. And that alien thing on board, right behind her . . . For an instant Aaron can feel its location, down below the left wall. He glances at the recorder, suppressing the impulse to ask the others if they feel it too.

"Tomorrow is the final day of the twenty-one day quarantine period," Yellaston is saying. "An arbitrary interval, to be sure. You will continue the medical watch on Dr. Lory Kaye until the final debriefing session at oh-nine-hundred tomorrow." Aaron nods. "If there are still no adverse indications, the quarantine will terminate at noon. As soon as feasible thereafter we should proceed to examine the specimen now sealed in scoutship Gamma. Say the following day; will this give you sufficient time to coordinate your resources with the Xenobiology staff and be prepared to assist us, Dr. Kaye?"

"Yes, sir."

Yellaston voice-signs the log entry, clicks the recorder off.

"Are you going to wait to signal home until after we look at that specimen?" Don asks him.

"Certainly."

They go out then, four men moving carefully in cramped quarters. Roomier than they'd have on Earth now. Aaron sees Foy manage to get in Yellaston's way, feels a twinge of sympathy for the authority-cathected wretch. Anything to get Daddy's attention. He too has been moved by Yellaston's good-wise-father projection. Are his own responses more mature? The hell with it, he decides; after ten years self-analysis becomes ritual.

When he emerges into Isolation corridor Lory has vanished into her cubicle and Solange is nowhere in sight. He nods at Coby through the vitrex and punches the food-dispenser chute. His server arrives on a puff of kitchen-scented air. Protein loaf, with an unexpected garnish; the commissary staff seems to be in good form.

He munches, absently eyeing the three-di shot of Earth mounted above his desk in the office beyond the wall. That photo hangs all over the ship, a beautifully clear image from the early clean-air days. What are they eating there now, each other? But the thought has lost its impact after a decade away; like everyone else on *Centaur*, Aaron has no close ties left behind. Twenty billion humans swarming on that globe when they went; doubtless thirty by now, even with the famines. Waiting to explode to the stars now that the technology is—precariously—here. Waiting for the green light from *Centaur*. Not literally green, of course, Aaron thinks;

just one of the three simple codes they can send at this range. For ten long years they have been sending yellow—*Exploration continues*. And until twenty days ago they were facing the bleak red—*No planet found, returning to base*. But now, Lory's planet!

Aaron shakes his head, nibbling a slice of real egg, thinking of the green signal starting on its four-year trajectory back to Earth. *Planet found, launch emigration fleets, coordinates such-and-such*. Earth's teeming billions all pressing for the handful of places in those improbable transport cans.

Aaron frowns at himself; he rejects the "teeming billions" concept. Doggedly he thinks of them as people, no matter how many—individual human beings each with a face, a name, a unique personality, and a meaningful fate. He invokes now his personal ritual, his defense against mass-think, which is simply the recalling of people he has known. An invisible army streams through his mind as he chews. People . . . from each he has learned. What? Something, large or small. An existence . . . the face of Thomas Brown glances coldly from memory; Brown was the sad murderer who was his first psychosurgery patient a zillion years ago at Houston Enclave. Had he helped Brown? Probably not, but Aaron will be damned if he will forget the man. The living man, not a statistic. His thoughts veer to the reality of his present shipmates, the sixty chosen souls. Cream of Earth, he thinks, only half in sarcasm. He is proud of them. Their endurance, their resourcefulness, their effortful sanity. He thinks it is not impossible that Earth's sanest children are in this frail bubble of air and warmth twenty-six million million miles away.

He cycles his server, pulls himself together. He has eighteen hours of biomonitor tapes to check against the base-line medical norms of Tighe, Lory, and himself. And first he must talk to the two people who thought they saw Tighe. As he gets up, the image of Earth catches his eye again: their lonely, vulnerable jewel, hanging there in blackness. Suddenly last night's dream jumps back, he sees again the monster penis groping toward the stars with *Centaur* at its tip. Pulsing with pressure, barely able to wait for the trigger that will release the human deluge—

He swats his forehead; the hallucination snaps out. Angry with himself he plods back to the Observation cubby.

The image of Bruce Jang is waiting on the screen; his compatriot, the young Chinese-American engineer on a ship where everyone is a token something. Only not "young" any more, Aaron admonishes himself.

"They have me in the coop, Bruce. I'm told you saw Tighe. Where and when?"

Bruce considers. Two years ago Bruce had still looked like Supersquirrel, all fast reflexes, buck teeth, and mocking see-it-all eyes. Cal Tech's answer to the universe.

"He came by my quarters about oh-seven-hundred. I was cleaning up, the door was open, I saw him looking in at me. Sort of, you know, fon-nee." Bruce shrugs, a joyless parody of his old jive manner.

"Funny? You mean his expression? Or was there anything peculiar about him, I mean visually different?"

A complex pause.

"Now that you mention it, yes. His refraction index was a shade off."

Aaron puzzles, finally gets it. "Do you mean Tighe appeared somewhat blurred or translucent?"

"Yeah. Both," Bruce says tightly. "But it was him."

"Bruce, Tighe never left Isolation. We've checked his tapes."

Very complex pause; Aaron winces, remembering the shadow waiting to enshroud Bruce. The near-suicide had been horrible.

"I see," Bruce says too casually. "Where do I turn myself in?"

"You don't. Somebody else saw Tighe, too. I'm checking them out next."

"Somebody else?" The fast brain snaps, the shadow is gone. "Once is accident, twice is coincidence." Bruce grins, ghost of Supersquirrel. "Three times is enemy action."

"Check around for me, will you, Bruce? I'm stuck

here." Aaron doesn't believe in enemy action but he believes in helping Bruce Jang.

"Right. Not exactly my game of course, but—right."

He goes out. The Man Without a Country. Over the years Bruce had attached himself to the Chinese scout team and in particular to Mei-Lin, their ecologist. He had confidently expected to be one of the two nonnationals Commander Kuh would, by agreement, take on the planet-seeking mission. It had nearly been a mortal blow when Kuh, being more deeply Chinese, had chosen Lory and the Aussie mineralogist.

The second Tighe-seer is now coming on Aaron's screen: Åhlstrom, their tall, blonde, more-or-less human computer chief. Before Aaron can greet her she says resentfully, "It is not right you should let him out."

"Where did you see him, Chief Åhlstrom?"

"In my Number Five unit."

"Did you speak to him? Did he touch anything?"

"Nah. He went. But he was there. He should not be."

"Tell me, please, did he look different in any way?"

"Different, yah," the tall woman says scornfully. "He has half no head."

"I mean, outside of his injury," says Aaron carefully, recalling that Åhlstrom's humor had once struck him as hearty.

"Nah."

"Chief Åhlstrom, Lieutenant Tighe was never out of this Isolation ward. We've verified his heartrate and respiration record. He was here the entire time."

"You let him out."

"No, we did not. He was here."

"Nah."

Aaron argues, expecting Åhlstrom's customary punchline: "Okay, I am stubborn Swede. You show me." Her stubbornness is a *Centaur* legend; during acceleration she had saved the mission by refusing to believe her own computers' ranging data until the hull sensors were rechecked for crystallization. But now she suddenly stands up as if gazing into a cold wind and says bleakly, "I could wish to go home. I am tired of this machine."

This is so unusual that Aaron can find nothing useful to say before she strides out. He worries briefly; if Ahlstrom needs help, he is going to have a job reaching that closed crag of a mind. But he is all the same relieved; both the people who "saw" Tighe seem to have been under some personal stress.

Hallucinating Tighe, he thinks; that's logical. Tighe stands for disaster. Appropriate anxiety symbol, surprising more people haven't cathected on him. Again he feels pride in *Centaur's* people, so steady after ten years' deprivation of Earth, ten years of cramped living with death lying a skin of metal away. And now something more, that spark of alien life, sealed in *China Flower's* hold, tethered out there. Lory's alien. It is now hanging, he feels, directly under the rear of his chair.

"Two more people waiting to see you, boss," says Coby's voice on the intercom. This also is mildly unusual, *Centaur* is a healthy ship. The Peruvian oceanographer comes in, shamefacedly confessing to insomnia. He is religiously opposed to drugs, but Aaron persuades him to try an alpha regulator. Next is Kawabata, the hydroponics chief. He is bothered by leg spasms. Aaron prescribes quinine, and Kawabata pauses to chat enthusiastically about the state of the embryo cultures he has been testing.

"Ninety percent viability after ten year cryostasis," he grins. "We are ready for that planet. By the way, Doctor, is Lieutenant Tighe recovering so well? I see you are allowing him freedom."

Aaron is too startled to do more than mumble. The farm chief cuts him off with an encomium on chickens, an animal Aaron loathes, and departs.

Shaken, Aaron goes to look at Tighe. The sensor lights outside his door indicate all pickups functioning: pulse regular, EEG normal if a trifle flat. He watches the alpha-scope break into a weak REM, resume again. The printouts themselves are outside. Aaron opens the door.

Tighe is lying on his side, showing his poignant Nordic profile, deep in drugged sleep. He doesn't look over twenty: rose-petal flush on the high cheekbones, a

pale gold cowlick falling over his closed eyes. The pro-
totype Beautiful Boy who lives forever with his white
aviator's silk blowing in the wind of morning. As Aaron
watches, Tighe stirs, flings up an arm with the i.v. taped
to it, and shows his whole face, the long blond lashes
still on his cheek.

It is now visible that Tighe is a thirty-year-old boy
with an obscene dent where his left parietal arch
should be. Three years back, Tiger Tighe had been their
first—and so far, only—serious casualty. A stupid accident; he had returned safely from a difficult EVA and
nearly been beheaded by a loose oxy tank while unsuit-
ing in the freefall shaft.

As if sensing Aaron's presence Tighe smiles heart-
breakingly, his long lips still promising joy. The undamaged Tighe had been the focus of several homosexual
friendships, a development provided for in *Centaur's*
program. Like so much else that has brought us through
sane, Aaron reflects ruefully. He had never been one of
Tighe's lovers. Too conscious of his own graceless, utili-
tarian body. Safer for him, the impersonal receptivity of
Solange. Which was undoubtedly also in the program,
Aaron thinks. Everything but Lory.

Tighe's mouth is working, trying to say something in
his sleep.

"Hoo, huh." The speech circuits hunt across the
wastelands of his ruined lobe. "Huhhh . . . Huh-
home." His lashes lift, the sky-blue eyes find Aaron.

"It's all right, Tiger," Aaron lies, touches him com-
fortingly. Tighe makes saliva noises and fades back into
sleep, his elegant gymnast's body turning a slow ara-
besque in the low gee. Aaron checks the catheters and
goes.

The closed door opposite is Lory's. Aaron gives it a
brotherly thump and looks in, conscious of the ceiling
scanner. Lory is on the bunk reading. A nice, normal
scene.

"Tomorrow at oh-nine-hundred," he tells her. "The
wrap-up. You okay?"

"You should know." She grimaces cheerfully at the
biomonitor pickups.

Aaron squints at her, unable to imagine how he can voice some cosmic, lifelong suspicion with that scanner overhead. He goes out to talk to Coby.

"Is there any conceivable chance that Tiger could have got to where an intercom screen could have picked him up?"

"Absolute negative. See for yourself," Coby says, loading tape-spools into the Isolation pass-through. His eyes flick up at Aaron. "I didn't bugger them."

"Did I say that?" Aaron snaps. But he's guilty, they both know it; because it was Coby who was Frank Foy's other important case, five years back. Aaron had caught his fellow doctor making and dealing dream-drugs. Aaron sighs. A miserable business. There had been no question of "punishing" Coby, or anyone else on *Centaur* for that matter; no one could be spared. And Coby is their top pathologist. If and when they get back to Earth he will face—who knows what? Meanwhile he has simply gone on with his job; it was then he had started calling Aaron "boss."

Now Aaron sees a new animation flickering behind Coby's clever-ape face. Of course—the planet. Never to go back. Good, Aaron thinks. He likes Coby, he relishes the unquenchable primate ingenuity of the man.

Coby is telling him that the Drive chief Gomulka has come in with a broken knuckle, refusing to see Aaron. Coby pauses, waiting for Aaron to get the implication. Aaron gets it, unhappily; a physical fight, the first in years.

"Who did he hit?"

"One of the Russkies, if I had to guess."

Aaron nods wearily, pulling in the tapes he has to check. "Where's Solange?"

"Over with Xenobiology, checking out what you'll need to analyze that thing. Oh, by the way, boss—" Coby gestures at the service roster posted on their wall—"you missed your turn on the shit detail. Last night was Common Areas. I got Nan to swap you for a Kitchen shift next week, maybe you can talk Berryman into giving us some real coffee."

Aaron grunts and takes the tapes back to Interview

to start the comparator runs. It is a struggle to keep awake while the spools speed through the discrepancy analyzer, eliciting no reaction. His own and Lory's are all nominal, nominal, nominal, nominal—all variation within normative limits. Aaron goes out to the food dispenser, hoping that Solange will show. She doesn't. Reluctantly he returns to run Tighe's.

Here, finally, the discrepancy indicator stirs. After two hours of input the analyzer has summed a deviation bordering on significance; it hovers there as Aaron continues the run. Aaron is not surprised; it's the same set of deviations Tighe has shown all week, since his problematical contact with the alien. A slight, progressive flattening of vital function, most marked in the EEG. Always a little less theta. Assuming theta correlates with memory, Tighe is losing capacity to learn.

Aren't we all, Aaron thinks, wondering again what actually happened in Gamma corridor. The scoutship *China Flower* had been berthed there with the ports sealed, attended by a single guard. Boring duty, after two weeks of nothing. The guard had been down by the stern end having a cup of brew. When he turned around Tighe was lying on the deck up by the scout's cargo hatch and the port was open. Tighe must have come out of the access ramp right by the port; he had been EVA team-leader before his accident, it was a natural place for him to wander to. Had he been opening or closing the lock when he collapsed? Had he gone inside and looked at the alien, had the thing given him some sort of shock? Nobody can know.

Aaron tells himself that in all likelihood Tighe had simply suffered a spontaneous cerebral seizure as he approached the lock. He hopes so. Whatever happened, Yellaston ordered the scoutship to be undocked and detached from *Centaur* on a tether. And Tighe's level of vitality is on the downward trend, day after day. Unorthodox, unless there is unregistered midbrain deterioration. Aaron can think of nothing to do about it. Maybe better so.

Bone-weary now, he packs up and forces himself to

go attend to Tighe's necessities. Better say good night to Lory, too.

She is still curled on her bunk like a kid, deep in a book. *Centaur* has real books in addition to the standard microfiches; an amenity.

"Finding some good stuff?"

She looks up, brightly, fondly. The scanner will show that wholesome sisterly grin.

"Listen to this, Arn." She starts reading something convoluted; Aaron's ears adjust only in time to catch the last of it. ". . . *Grow upward, working out the beast, and let the ape and tiger die. . . .* It's very old, Arn. Tennyson." Her smile is private.

Aaron nods warily, acknowledging the earnest Victorian. He has had enough tiger and ape and he will not get drawn into another dialog with Lory, not with that scanner going.

"Don't stay up all night."

"Oh, this rests me," she tells him happily. "It's an escape into truth. I used to read and read on the way back."

Aaron flinches at the thought of that solitary trip. Dear Lory, little madwoman.

"Night."

"Good night, dear Arn."

He gets himself into his bunk, grumbling old curses at *Centaur's* selection board. Pedestrian clots, no intuition. Lory the non-sex-object, sure. Barring the fact that Lory's prepubescent body is capable of unhinging the occasional male with the notion that she contains some kind of latent sexual lightning, some secret supersensuality lurking like hot lava in the marrow of her narrow bones. In their years on Earth, Aaron had watched a series of such idiots breaking their balls in the attempt to penetrate to Lory's mythical marrow. Luckily none on *Centaur,* so far.

But that wasn't the main item the selection board missed. Aaron sighs, lying in the dark. He knows the secret lightning in Lory's bones. Not sex, would that it were. Her implacable innocence—what was the old phrase, *a fanatic heart.* A too-clear vision of good, a too-sure hatred of evil. No love lost, in between. Not much use for living people. Aaron sighs again, hearing the frightening condemnation in her unguarded voice. Has she changed? Probably not. Probably doesn't matter, he tells himself; how could it matter that chance has put Lory's head between us and whatever's on that planet? It's all a technical problem, air and water and bugs and so on . . .

Effortfully he pushes the thoughts away. I've been cooped up here twenty days with her and Tighe, he tells himself; I'm getting deprivation fantasies. As sleep claims him his last thought is of Captain Yellaston. The old man must be getting low on his supplies.

II

. . . Immensely tall, eternally noble, the woman paces through gray streaming clouds. In rituals of grief she moves, her heavy hair bound with dark jewels; she gestures to her head, her heart, a mourning queen pacing beside a leaden sea. Chained beasts move slowly at her heels, the tiger stepping with sad majesty, the ape mimicking her despair. She plucks the bindings from her hair in agony, it streams on the icy wind. She bends to loose the tiger, urging it to freedom. But the beast-form wavers and swells, thins out; the tiger floats to ghostly life among the stars. The ape is crouching at her feet; she lays her long fingers on its head. It has turned to stone. The woman begins a death chant, breaking her bracelets one by one beside the sea . . .

Aaron is awake now, his eyes streaming with grief. He hears his own throat gasping, *Uh—uhh-uhh*, a sound he hasn't made since—since his parents died, he remembers sharply. The pillow is soaked. What is it? What the hell is doing it? That was Lory's goddam ape and tiger, he thinks. Stop it! Quit.

He stumbles up, finds it's the middle of the night, not morning. As he douses his face he is acutely aware of a direction underfoot, an invisible line leading down through the hull to the sealed-up scouter, to the alien inside. Lory's alien in there.

All right. Face it.

He sits on his bunk in the dark. Do you believe in alien telepathic powers, Dr. Kaye? Is that vegetable in there broadcasting on a human wavelength, sending out despair?

Possible, I suppose, Doctor. Anything—almost anything—is *possible*.

But the tissue samples, the photos. They showed no differentiated structure, no neural organization. No brain. It's a sessile plant-thing. Like a cauliflower, like a big lichen; like a bunch of big grapes, she said. All it does is metabolize and put out a little bioluminescence. Discrete cellular potentials *cannot* generate anything complex enough to trigger human emotions. Or can they? No, he decides. We can't do it ourselves, for god's sake. And it's not anything physical like subsonics, not with the vacuum between. And besides, if it is doing this, Lory couldn't possibly have got back here sane. Nearly a year of living ten feet away from a thing sending out nightmares? Not even Lory. It has to be me. I'm projecting.

Okay; it's me.

He lies down again, reminding himself that it's time he ran another general checkup. He should expand the free-association session, too; other people may be getting stress phenomena. Those Tighe-sightings . . . Last time he caught two incipient depressions. And he'll do all that part himself, people won't take it from Coby, he thinks, and catches himself in the fatuity. The fact is that people talk a lot more to Coby than they do to him. Maybe I have some of Lory's holy-holies. He grins, drifting off.

. . . *Tighe drifts in through the walls, curled in a foetal clasp, his genital sac enormous. But it's a different Tighe. He's green, for one thing, Aaron sees. And vastly puffy, like a huge cauliflower or a cumulus cloud. Not frightening. Not anything, really; Aaron watches neutrally as cumulus-cloud-green Tighe swells, thins*

out, floats to ghostly life among the stars. One bulbous
baby hand waves slowly, Ta-ta . . .

With a jolt Aaron discovers it really is morning. He
lurches up, feeling vile. When he comes out Solange is
sitting at the desk beyond the vitrex; Aaron feels instantly better.

"Soli! Where the hell were you?"

"There are so many problems, Aaron." She frowns, a
severe flower. "When you come out you will see. I am
giving you no more supplies."

"Maybe I'm not coming out." Aaron draws his hot
cup.

"Oh?" The flower registers disbelief, dismay. "Captain Yellaston said three weeks, the period is over and
you are perfectly healthy."

"I don't feel so healthy, Soli."

"Don't you want to come out, Aaron?" Her dark
eyes twinkle, her bosom radiates the shapes of holding
and being held, she warms him through the vitrex.
Aaron tries to radiate back. They have been lovers five
years now, he loves her very much in his low-sex-drive
way.

"You know I do, Soli." He watches Coby come in
with Aaron's printouts. "How'm I doing, Bill? Any sign
of alien plague?"

Solange's face empathizes again: tender alarm. She's
like a play, Aaron thinks. If a brontosaurus stubbed its
toe, Soli would go *Oooh* in sympathy. Probably do the
same at the Crucifixion, but he doesn't hold that against
her. Only so much band-width for anybody; Soli is set
low.

"Don't pick up a thing on visual, boss, except you're
not sleeping too good."

"I know. Bad dreams. Too much excitement, buried
bogies stirring up. When I get out we're going to run
another general checkup."

"When the doc gets symptoms he checks everybody
else," Coby says cheerfully, the leer almost unnotice-
able. He's happy, all right. "By the way, Tiger's awake.
He just took a pee."

"Good. I'll see if I can bring him out to eat."

When Aaron goes in he finds Tighe trying to sit up. "Want to come out and eat, Tiger?" Aaron releases him from the tubes and electrodes, assists him outside to the dispenser. As Tighe sees Solange his hand whips up in his old, jaunty greeting. Eerie to see the well-practiced movements so swift and deft; for minutes the deficit is hidden. Quite normally he takes the server, begins to eat. But after a few mouthfuls a harsh noise erupts from his throat and the server falls, he stares at it tragically as Aaron retrieves it.

"Let me, Aaron, I have to come in." Solange is getting into her decontamination suit.

She brings in the new batch of tapes. Aaron goes down the hall to run them. The Interview room is normally their data processing unit. *Centaur's* builders really did a job, he muses while the spools spin nominal-nominal, as before. Adequate provision for quarantine, provision for every damn thing. Imagine it, a starship. I sit here in a ship among the stars. *Centaur,* the second one ever . . . *Pioneer* was the first, Aaron had been in third grade when *Pioneer* headed out for Barnard's star. He was in high school when the signal came back red: Nothing.

What circles Barnard's star, a rock? A gasball? He will never know, because *Pioneer* didn't make it back to structured-signal range. Aaron was an intern when they declared her lost. Her regular identity code had quit and there was a new faint radio source in her direction. What happened? No telling . . . She was a much smaller, slower ship. *Centaur's* builders had redesigned on the basis of the reports from *Pioneer* while she was still in talking distance.

Aaron pulls his attention back to the tapes, automatically suppressing the thought of what will happen if *Centaur* too finds nothing after all. They have all trained themselves not to think about that, about the fact that Earth is in no shape to mount another mission if *Centaur* fails. Even if they could, where next? Nine light-years to Sirius? Hopeless. The energy and resources to build *Centaur* almost weren't there ten years ago. Maybe by now they've cannibalized the emigration hulls, Aaron's submind mutters. Even if we've found a planet, maybe it's too late, maybe nobody is waiting for our signal.

He snaps his subconscious to order, confirms that the tapes show nothing, barring his own nightmare-generated peaks. Lory's resting rates are a little up too, that's within bounds. Tighe's another fraction down since yesterday. Failing; why?

It's time to pack up. Lory and Solange are waiting to come in and hook up for the final debriefing, as Yellaston courteously calls it. Aaron goes around into the Observation cubicle and prepares to observe.

Frank Foy bustles first onto his screen to run his response-standardizing questions. He's still at it when Yellaston and the two scout commanders come in. Aaron is hating the scene again; he makes himself admit that Don and Tim are wearing decently neutral expressions. Space training, they must know all about bodily humiliation.

Foy finishes. Captain Yellaston starts the sealed recorder and logs in the event-date.

"Dr. Kaye," Foy leads off, "referring to your voyage back to this ship. The cargo module in which you transported the alien life-form had a viewing system linked to the command module in which you lived. It was found welded closed. Did you weld it?"

"Yes. I did."

"Why did you weld it? Please answer concisely."

"The shutter wasn't light-tight. It would have allowed my daily light cycle to affect the alien: I thought this might harm it, it seems to be very photosensitive. This is the most important biological specimen we've ever had. I had to take every precaution. The module was equipped to give it a twenty-two hour circadian cycle with rheostatic graded changes, just like the planet—it has beautiful long evenings, you know."

Foy coughs reprovingly.

"You went to the length of welding it shut. Were you afraid of the alien?"

"No!"

"I repeat, were you afraid of the alien?"

"No. I was not—well, yes, I guess I was, a little, in a sense. You see I was going to be alone all that time. I was sure the life-form is harmless, but I thought it might, oh, grow toward the light, or even become motile. There's a common myxomycetes—a fungus that has a motile phase, *Lycogala epidendron,* called Coral Beads. I just didn't know. And I was afraid its luminescent activity might keep me awake. I have a little difficulty sleeping."

"Then you do believe the alien may be dangerous?"

"No! I know now it didn't do a thing, you can check the records."

"May I remind you to control your verbalization, Dr. Kaye. Referring again to the fact that the cover was welded; were you afraid to look at the alien?"

"Of course not. No."

Young Frank really is an oddy, Aaron thinks; more imagination than I figured.

"Dr. Kaye, you state that the welding instrument was left on the planet. Why?"

"Commander Kuh needed it."

"And the scoutship's normal tool complement is also missing. Why?"

"They needed everything. If something went wrong I couldn't make repairs; it was no use to me."

"Please, Dr. Kaye."

"Sorry."

"Were you afraid to have a means of unsealing the alien on board?"

"No!"

"I repeat. Dr. Kaye, were you afraid to keep with you a tool by which you could unseal the port to the alien?"

"No."

"I repeat. Were you afraid to have a means of unsealing the alien?"

"No. That's silly."

Foy makes checks on his tapes; Aaron's liver doesn't need tapes, it has already registered that hyped-up candor. Oh god—what is she lying about?

"Dr. Kaye, I repeat—" Foy starts doggedly, but Yellaston has lifted one hand. Foy puffs out his cheeks, switches tack.

"Dr. Kaye, will you explain again why you collected no computerized data after the first day of your stay on the planet?"

"We did collect data. A great deal of data. It went to the computer but it didn't get stored because the dump cycle had cut in. Nobody thought of checking it, I mean that's not a normal malfunction. The material we lost, it's sickening. Mei-Lin and Liu did a whole eco-geologic stream bed profile, all the biota, everything—"

She bites her lips like a kid, a flush rising around her freckles. After ten years in outer space Lory still has freckles.

"Did you dump that data, Dr. Kaye?"

"No!"

"Please, Dr. Kaye. Now, I want to refresh your memory of the voice recording allegedly made by Commander Kuh." He flips switches; a voice says thinly: "Very . . . well, Dr. Ka-yee. You . . . will go."

It's Kuh's voice all right; Aaron knows the audiograms match. But the human ear doesn't like it.

"Do you claim that Commander Kuh was in good health when he spoke those words?"

"Yes. He was tired, of course. We all were."

"Please restrict your answers, Dr. Kaye. I repeat. Was Commander Kuh in normal physical health other than fatigue when he made that recording?"

"Yes."

Aaron closed his eyes. Lory, what have you done?

"I repeat. Was Commander Kuh in normal physical and mental—"

"Oh, *all right!*" Lory is shaking her head desperately. "Stop it! Please, I didn't want to say this, sir." She gazes blindly at the screen behind which Yellaston must be, takes a breath. "It's really very minor. There was—there was a difference of opinion. On the second day."

Yellaston lifts a warning finger at Foy. The two scout commanders are statues.

"Two members of the crew felt it was safe to remove

their space suits," Lory swallows. "Commander Kuh—
did not agree. But they did so anyway. And they
didn't—they were reluctant to return to the scouter.
They wanted to camp outside." She stares up in appeal.
"You see, the planet is so pleasant and we'd been living
in that ship so long."

Foy scents a rat, pounces.

"You mean that Commander Kuh removed his suit
and became ill?"

"Oh no! There was a—an argument," Lory says
painfully. "He was, he sustained a bruise in the laryn-
geal area. That's why—" She slumps down in the chair,
almost crying.

Yellaston is up, brushing Foy away from the speaker.

"Very understandable, Doctor," he says calmly. "I
realize what a strain this report has been for you after
your heroic effort in returning to base alone. Now we
have, I think, a very full account—"

Foy is staring bewilderedly. He has started a rat all
right, but it is the wrong, wrong rat. Aaron understands
now. The supersensitive Chinese, the undesirability of
internal dissension on the official log. Implications, implications. There was a fracas among Kuh's crew and
somebody wiped *China Flower's* memory.

So that is Lory's secret. Aaron breathes out hard, euphoric with relief. So that's all it was!

Captain Yellaston, an old hand at implications, is
going on smoothly. "I take it, Doctor, that the situation
was quickly resolved by Commander Kuh's decision to
commence colonization, and his confidence that you
would convey his report to us for transmission to Earth,
as in fact you have done?"

"Yes, sir," says Lory gratefully. She is still trembling;
everyone knows that violence of any sort upsets Lory.
"You see, even if something serious happened to me,
the scoutship was on automatic after midpoint. It would
have come through. You picked it up."

She doesn't mention that she was unconscious from
ulcerative hemorrhage when *China Flower's* signal
came through the electronic hash from Centaurus's
suns; it had taken Don and Tim a day to grapple and

bring her in. Aaron looks at her with love. My little sister, the superwoman. Could I have done it? Don't ask.

He listens happily while Yellaston winds it up with a few harmless questions about the planet's moons and throws the screen open two-way to record a formal commendation for Lory. Foy is still blinking; the two scout commanders look like tickled tigers. Oh, that planet! They nod benevolently at Lory, glance at Yellaston as if willing him to fire the green signal out of the top of his head.

Yellaston is asking Aaron to confirm the medical clearance. Aaron confirms no discrepancies, and the quarantine is officially terminated. Solange starts unwiring Lory. As the command party goes out, Yellaston's eye flicks over Aaron with the expressionlessness he recognizes; the old man will expect him in his quarters that evening with the usual.

Aaron draws himself a hot drink, takes it into his cubicle to savor his relief. Lory really did a job there, he thinks. Whatever kind of dust-up the Chinese had, it must have shocked her sick. She used to get hives when I played hockey, he remembers. But she's really grown up, she didn't spill the bloody details all over the log. Don't mess up the mission. That idiot Foy . . . You did that nicely, little sister, Aaron tells the image at the back of his mind. You're not usually so considerate of our imperfect undertakings.

The image remains unmoving, smiling enigmatically. Not usually so considerate of official sensibilities? Aaron frowns.

Correction: Lory has *never* been considerate of man's imperfection. Lory has *never* been diplomatic. If I hadn't sat on her head Lory would be in an Adjustment Center with a burn in her cortex instead of on this ship. And she's been as prickly as a bastard with poor old Jan. Has a year alone in that scouter worked a miracle?

Aaron ponders queasily; he doesn't believe in miracles. Lory conscientiously lying to preserve the fragile unity of man? He shakes his head. Very unlikely. A point occurs unwelcomely; that story did save something. It saved her own credibility. Say the Chinese wrangle happened. Was Lory using it, letting Foy pry it out of her to account for those blips on the tape? To get herself—and something—through Francis Xavier Foy's PKG readouts? She had time to figure it, ample time—

Aaron shudders from neck to bladder and strides out of his cubicle to collide with Lory coming out of hers.

"Hi!" She has a plain little bag in her hand. Aaron realizes the scanners are still on overhead.

"Glad to be getting out?" he asks lamely.

"Oh, I didn't mind." She wrinkles her nose. "It was a rational precaution for the ship."

"You seem to have become more, ah, tolerant."

"Yes." She looks at him with what the scanner will show as sisterly humor. "Do you know when Captain Yellaston plans to examine the specimen I brought back?"

"No. Soon, I guess."

"Good." The smiley look in her eye infuriates him. "I really brought it back for you, Arn. I wanted us to look at it together. Remember how we used to share our treasures, that summer on the island?"

Aaron mumbles something, walks numbly back to his room. His eyes are squeezed like a man kicked in the guts. Lory, little devil—how could you? Her thirteen-year-old body shimmers in his mind, sends helpless heat into his penile arteries. He is imprinted forever, he fears; the rose-tipped nipples on her child's chest, the naked mons, the flushed-pearl labia. The incredible sweetness, lost forever. He had been fifteen, he had ended both their virginities on a spruce island in the Fort Ogilvy Officers' Recreational Reserve the year before their parents died. He groans, wondering if he has lost both their souls, too, though he doesn't believe in souls. Oh, Lory . . . is it really his own lost youth he aches for?

He groans again, his cortex knowing she is up to some damn thing while his medulla croons that he loves her only and forever, and she him. Damn the selection board who had dismissed such incidents as insignificant, even healthy!

"Coming out, boss?" Coby's head comes in. "I'm opening up, right? This place needs a shake-out."

Aaron shakes himself out and goes out to check over Coby's office log. Lots of catching up to do. Later on when he is more composed he will visit Lory and shake some truth out of her.

He walks through the now-open vitrex, finds freedom invigorating. The office log reveals three more insomnia complaints, that's four in all. Alice Berryman, the Canadian nutrition chief, is constipated; Jan Ing, his Xenobiology colleague, has the trots. Quartermaster Miriamne Stein had a migraine. Van Wal, the Belgian chemist, has back spasm again. The Nigerian photolab chief has sore eyes, his Russian assistant has cracked a toe-bone. And there's Gomulka's knuckle. No sign of whoever he hit, unless he broke Pavel's toe. Unlikely . . . For *Centaur,* it's a long list; understandable, with the excitement.

Solange bustles in carrying a mess of Isolation biomonitors. "We have much work to do on these, Aaron. Tighe will stay where he is, no? I have left his pickups on." She still pronounces it "peekups."

Warmed, Aaron watches her coiling input leads. Surprising, the forcefulness some small women show. Such a seductive little person. He knows he shouldn't find it mysterious and charming that she is so capable with any kind of faulty circuit.

"Tighe's not doing too well, Soli. Maybe you or Bill can lead him around a bit, stimulate him. But don't leave him alone at any time. Not even for a minute."

"I know, Aaron." Her face has been flashing through her tender repertory while her hands wham the sensor boxes around. "I know. People are saying he is out."

"Yeah . . . You aren't getting any, oh, anxiety symptoms yourself, are you? Bad dreams, maybe?"

"Only of you." She twinkles, closing a cabinet emphatically, and comes over to lay her hand on the faulty circuits in Aaron's head. His arms go gratefully around her hips.

"Oh, Soli, I missed you."

"Ah, poor Aaron. But now we have the big meeting downstairs. Fifteen hundred, that is twenty minutes. And you must help me with Tighe."

"Right." Reluctantly he lets sweet comfort go.

By fifteen hundred he is in a state of tentative stability, going down-ramp to the main Commons Ring where gravity is Earth-normal. Commons is *Centaur's* chief amenity, as her designers put it. It really is an amenity, too, Aaron thinks as he comes around a tubbed sweet-olive tree and looks out into the huge toroid space stretching all the way round the hull, fragrant with greenery from the Farm. Kawabata's people must have moved in a fresh lot.

The unaccustomed sounds of voices and music intimidate him slightly; he peers into the varied lights and shadows, finding people everywhere. He can see only a chord of the great ring, with its rising perspective at each end showing only leaning legs and feet beyond the farthest banks of plants. He hasn't seen so many people all here at once since Freefall Day, their annual holiday when *Centaur's* roll is stopped and the floor viewports opened. And even the last few viewing days people tended to slip in and look alone. Now they are all here together, talking animatedly. Moving around some sort of display. Aaron follows Miriamne Stein and finds himself looking at a bank of magnificent back-lighted photos.

Lory's planet.

He has been shown a few small frames from *China Flower's* cameras, but these blow-ups are overpowering. The planet seen from orbit—it looks like a flower-painted textile. Its terrain seems old, eroded to gentleness. The mountains or hills are capped with enormous gaudy rosettes, multi-ringed labyrinths ruffled in lemon-yellow, coral, emerald, gold, turquoise, bile-green, orange, lavender, scarlet—more colors than he can name. The alien vegetables or whatever. Beautiful! Aaron gapes, oblivious of shoulders touching him. Those "plants" must cover miles!

The next shots are from atmosphere, they show horizon and sky. The sky of Lory's planet is violet-blue, spangled with pearl-edged cirrus wisps. Another view shows alto-stratus over a clear silver-green expanse of sea or lake, reflecting cobalt veins—an enchanting effect. Everything exhales mildness; there is a view of an immense smooth white beach lapped by quiet water. Farther on, a misty mountain of flowers.

"Isn't it wonderful?" Alice Berryman murmurs in his general direction. She's flushed, breathing strongly; the medical fraction of Aaron's mind surmises that her constipation problem has passed.

They move on together, following the display which goes on and on across the Common's normal hobby bays and alcoves. Aaron cannot get his fill of looking at the great vegetable forms, their fantastic color and variety. It is hard to grasp their size; here and there Photolab has drawn in scales and arrows pointing out what appear to be fruits or huge seed-clusters. No wonder Akin's crew has sore eyes and stubbed toes, Aaron thinks; a tremendous job. He goes around an aviary cage and finds a spectacular array of night-shots showing the "plants'" bioluminescence. Weird auroral colors, apparently flickering or changing continuously. What the nights must be like! Aaron peers at the dark sky, identifies the two small moons of Lory's planet. He really must stop calling it Lory's planet, he tells himself. It's Kuh's now if it's anybody's. Doubtless it will be given some dismal official name.

The mynah bird squawks, drawing his attention to another panel in the chess alcove: close-ups of the detached fruit-clusters or whatever they are, with infrared and high-frequency collations. It was one of these detached clusters that Lory brought back, along with samples of soil and water and so on. Aaron studies the display; the "fruits" are slightly warm and a trifle above background radiation level. They luminesce, too. Not dormant. A logical choice, Aaron decides, momentarily aware that the thing is out there on a line with his shoulder. Is it menacing? Are you giving me bad dreams, vegetable? He stares probingly at the pictures. They don't look menacing.

Beyond the aquariums he comes upon the ground pictures taken before the computer was dumped. The official first-landing photo, almost life-size, showing everybody in suits and helmets beside *China Flower's* port. Behind them is that enormous flat beach and a far-off sea. Faces are almost invisible; Aaron makes out Lory in her blue suit. Beside her is the Australian girl, her gloved hand very close to that of Kuh's navigator, whose name is also Kuh; "little" Kuh is identifiable by his two-meter height. In front of the group is a flagstaff flying the United Nations flag. Ridiculous. Aaron feels his throat tighten. Ludicrous, wondrous. And the flag, he sees, is blowing. The planet has winds. Moving air, imagine!

He has been too fascinated to read the texts by each display, but now the word "wind" catches his attention. "Ten to forty knots," he reads. "Continuous during the period. We speculate that the dominant life-forms, being sessile, obtain at least some nourishment from the air constantly moving through their fringed 'foliage.' (See atmospheric analyses.) A number of types of airborne cells resembling gametes or pollen have been examined. Although the dominant plantlike forms apparently reproduce by broadcast methods, they may represent the culmination of a long evolutionary history. Over two hundred less-differentiated forms ranging in size from meters to a single cell have been tentatively identified. No self-motile life of any kind has been found."

Looking more closely at the picture, Aaron sees that the foreground is covered with a tapestry of lichenlike small growths and soft-looking tufts. The smaller forms. He moves on through to a series of photos showing the crew deploying vehicles out of *China Flower's* cargo port, and bumps into a ring of people around the end of the display.

"Look at that," somebody sighs. "Would you look at that." The group makes way and Aaron sees what it is. The last photo, showing three suited figures—with their helmets off.

Aaron's eyes open wide, he feels his guts stir. There

is Mei-Lin, her short hair blowing in the wind. Liu En-Do, his bare head turned away to look at a range of hills encrusted with the great flower-castles. And "little" Kuh, smiling broadly at the camera. Immediately behind them is a ridge which seems to be covered with vermilion lace-fronds bending to the breeze.

Air, free air! Aaron can almost feel that sweet wind, he longs to hurl himself into the viewer, to stride out across the meadows, up to the hills. A paradise. Was it just after this that the crew ripped off their foul space suits and refused to go back to the ship?

Who could blame them, Aaron thinks. Not he. God, they look happy! It's hard to remember when we lived, really lived. A corner of his mind remembers Bruce Jang, hopes he will not linger too long by that picture.

The crowd has carried him half around the toroid now; he is entering a wide section full of individual console seats that is normally the library. With the privacy partitions down it is used for their rare general assemblies. The rostrum is at the middle, where the speaker's whole figure will be most visible. It's empty. Beyond it is a screen projecting the star-field ahead; year by year Aaron and his shipmates have watched the suns of Centaurus growing on that screen, separating to doubles and double-doubles. Now it shows only a single sun. The great blazing component of Alpha around which Lory's planet circles.

Several people are using the scanners while they wait. Aaron sits down beside a feminine back he recognizes as Lieutenant Pauli, Tim Bron's navigator. Her head is buried in the scanner hood. The title-panel on the console reads: GAMMA CENTAURUS MISSION. V, VERBAL REPORT BY DR. LORY KAYE, EXCERPTS FROM. That would be Lory's original narrative session, Aaron decides. Nothing about the "argument" there.

Pauli clicks off and folds down the scanner hood. When Aaron catches her eye she smiles dreamily, looking through him. Ahlstrom is sitting down just beyond; unbelievably, she's smiling too. Aaron looks around sharply at the rows of faces, thinking I've been shut away three weeks, I haven't realized what the planet is doing to them. Them? He finds his own risor muscle is tight.

Captain Yellaston is moving to the speaker's stand, being stopped by questions, Aaron hasn't heard so much chatter in years. The hall seems to be growing hot with so many bodies bouncing around. He isn't used to crowds any more, none of them are. And this is only sixty people. Dear god—*what if we have to go back to Earth*? The thought is horrible. He remembers their first year when there was another viewscreen showing the view astern: yellow Sol, shrinking, dwindling. That had been a rotten idea, soon abolished. What if the planet is somehow no good, is toxic or whatever—what if they have to turn around and spend ten years watching Sol expand again? Unbearable. It would finish him. Finish them all. Others must be thinking this too, he realizes. Doctor, you could have a problem. A big, big problem. But that planet *has* to be all right. It looks all right, it looks beautiful.

The hall is falling silent, ready for Yellaston. Aaron catches sight of Soli on the far side, Coby is by her with Tighe between them. And there's Lory by the other wall, sitting with Don and Tim. She's holding herself in a tight huddle, like a rape victim in court; probably agonized by her tapes being on the scanners. Aaron curses himself routinely for his sensitivity to her, realizes he has missed Yellaston's opening words.

". . . the hope which we may now entertain." Yellaston's voice is reticent but warm; it is also a rare sound on *Centaur*—the captain is no speechmaker. "I have a thought to share with you. Doubtless it has occurred to others, too. One of my occupations in the abundant leisure of our recent years—" pause for the ritual smiles—"has been the reading of the history of human exploration and migrations on our own planet. Most of the story is unrecorded, of course. But in the history of new colonies one fact appears again and again. That is that people have suffered appalling casualties when they attempted to move to a new habitation in even the more favorable areas of our own home world.

"For example, the attempts by Europeans to settle on the Northeast coast of America. The early Scandinavian colonies may have lasted a few generations before they vanished. The first English colony in fertile, temperate Virginia met disaster and the survivors were recalled. The Plymouth colony succeeded in the end, but only because they were continuously resupplied from Europe and helped by the original Indian inhabitants. The catastrophe that struck them interested me greatly.

"They came from northern Europe, from above fifty degrees north. Winters there are mild because the coast is warmed by the Gulf Stream, but this ocean current was not understood at that time. They sailed south by west, to what should have been a warmer land. Massachusetts was then covered by wild forests, like a park if we can imagine such a thing, and it was indeed warm summer when they landed. But when winter came it brought a fierce cold like nothing they had ever experienced, because that coast has no warming sea-current. A simple problem to us. But their technical knowledge had not foreseen it and their resources could not meet it. The effect of the bitter cold was compounded by disease and malnutrition. They suffered a fearful toll of lives. Consider: There were seventeen married women in that colony; of these, fifteen died the first winter."

Yellaston pauses, looking over their heads.

"Similar misfortunes befell numberless other colonies from unforeseen conditions of heat or drought or disease or predators. I am thinking also of the European settlers in my own New Zealand and in Australia and of the peoples who colonized the islands of the Pacific. The archeological records of Earth are filled with instance after instance of peoples who arrived in an area and seemingly vanished away. What impresses me here is that these disasters occurred in places that we now regard as eminently favorable to human life. The people were moving to an only slightly different terrain of our familiar Earth, the Earth on which we have evolved. They were under our familiar sun, in our atmosphere and gravity and other geophysical conditions. They met only very small differences. And yet these small differences killed them."

He was looking directly at them now, his fine light greenish eyes moving unhurriedly from face to face.

"I believe we should remind ourselves of this history as we look at the splendid photographs of this new planet which Commander Kuh has sent back to us. It is not another corner of Earth nor an airless desert like Mars. It is the first totally alien living world that man has touched. We may have no more concept of its true nature and conditions than the British migrants had of an American winter.

"Commander Kuh and his people have bravely volunteered themselves to test its viability. We see them in these photographs apparently at ease and unharmed. But I would remind you that a year has passed since these pictures were made, a year during which they have had only the meagre resources of their camp. We hope and trust that they are alive and well today. But we must remember that unforeseeable hazards may have assailed them. They may be wounded, ill, in dire straits. I believe it is appropriate to hold this in mind. We here are safe and well, able to proceed with caution to the next step. They may not be."

Very nice, Aaron thinks. He has been watching faces, seeing here and there a lip quirked at the captain's little homily, but mostly expressions like his own. Moved and sobered. He's our pacemaker, as usual. And he's taken the edge off our envy of the *China* crew. Dire straits—wonderful old phrase. Are they really in dire straits, maybe? Yellaston is concluding a congratulatory remark for Lory. With a start Aaron recalls his own suspicion of her, his conviction that she is hiding something. And ten minutes ago I was ready to rush out onto that planet, he chides himself. I'm losing balance, I have to stop these mood swings. A thought has been percolating in him, something about Kuh. It surfaces. Yes. Bruised larynxes croak or wheeze. But Kuh's weak voice had been clear. Should check on that.

People are moving away. Aaron moves with them,

sees Lory over by the ramp, surrounded by a group. She's come out of her huddle, she's answering their questions. No use trying to talk to her now. He wanders back through the displays. They still look tempting, but Yellaston has broken the spell, at least for him. Are those happy people now lying dead on the bright ground, perhaps devoured, only skeletons left? Aaron jumps; a voice is speaking in his ear.

"Dr. Kaye?"

It's Frank Foy, of all people.

"Doctor, I wanted to say—I hope you understand? My role, the distressing aspects. One sometimes has to perform duties that are most repugnant, as a medical man you too must have had similar—"

"No problem." Aaron collects himself. Why is Frank so embarrassing? "It was your job."

Foy looks at him emotionally. "I'm so glad you feel that way. Your sister—I mean, Dr. Lory Kaye—such an admirable person. It seems incredible a woman could make that trip all alone."

"Yeah . . . By the way, speaking of incredible, Frank, I know Lory's voice pretty well. I believe I was able to spot the points that were bothering you, in fact I'm inclined to share your—"

"Oh, not at all, Aaron," Foy cuts him off. "You need say no more, I'm entirely satisfied. *Entirely*. Her explanation clears up every point." He ticks them off on his fingers. "The fate of the recording system, the absence of the welder and other tools, Commander Kuh's words, the question of injury—he *was* injured—the emotion about living on the planet. Dr. Kaye's revelation of the, ah, conflict dovetails perfectly."

Aaron has to admit that it does. Frank goes in for chess problems, he remembers; a weakness for elegant solutions.

"What about welding that alien in and being afraid to look at it? Between us, that thing gives me willies, too."

"Yes," Foy says soberly. "Yes, I fear I was giving in to my natural, well, is *xenophobia* the word? But we mustn't let it blind us. Undoubtedly Commander Kuh's people stripped that ship, Aaron. A dreadful experience for your sister, I felt no need to make her relive all that must have gone on. Among all those Chinese, poor girl."

When xenophobias collide . . . Aaron sees Foy isn't going to be much help, but he tries again.

"The business of the planet being ideal, a paradise and so on, that bothered me, too."

"Oh, I feel that Captain Yellaston put his finger on the answer there, Aaron. The excitement, the elation. I hadn't appreciated it. Now that I've seen these, I confess I feel it myself."

"Yeah." Aaron sighs. In addition to the elegant solution, Frank has received the Word. Captain Yellaston (who art in Heaven) has explained.

"Aaron, I confess I *hate* these things!" Foy says unexpectedly.

Aaron mumbles, thinking, possible, maybe he does. On the surface, anyway. With a peculiar smiling-through-tears look Foy goes on, "Your sister is such a wonderful person. Her strength is as the strength of ten, because her heart is pure."

"Yeah, well . . ." Suddenly the evening chow-call chimes out, saving him. Aaron bolts into the nearest passageway. Oh, no. Not Frank Foy. No ball-breaking here, though. Abelard and Heloise, so pure. A perfect match, really . . . What would Frank say if he told him about Lory and himself? Hey, Frank, when we were kids I humped my little sister all over the Sixth Army District, she screwed like a mink in those days. On second thought, forget it, Aaron tells himself. He knows how Frank would react. "Oh." Long grave pause. "I'm terribly sorry, Aaron. For you." Maybe even in priestly tones, "Would it help you to talk about it?" Etsanctimoniouscetera. A tough case, will the real Frank Foy ever stand up? No. Lucky it doesn't interfere with his being a damn good mathematician. Maybe it helps, for all I know. Humans! . . . A good food-smell is in his nose, lifting his mood. Chemoreceptors have pathways to the primitive brain. Ahead are voices, music, lights.

Maybe Foy's right, Aaron muses. How about that?

Lory's story does dovetail. Am I getting weird? Sex-fantasies about Sis, I haven't had that trouble for years. It's being locked up with her, Tighe, that alien—a big armful of Soli, that's what I need. Solace, Soul-ass . . . Resolutely ignoring a sensation that the alien is now straight overhead outside the hull, Aaron fills a server and takes it over to a seat by Coby and Jan Ing, the Xenobiology chief with whom he will be working tomorrow. He's Lory's boss; Lory herself isn't here.

"Quite a crowd tonight."

"Yeah." In recent years more and more of *Centaur's* people have been eating alone at odd hours, taking their food to their rooms. Now there's a hubbub here. Aaron sees the Peruvian oceanographer has a chart propped by his server, he's talking to a circle of people with his mouth full, pointing. Miriamne Stein and her two girl friends—*women* friends, Aaron corrects himself—who usually eat together are sitting with Bruce Jang and two men from Don's crew. EVA Chief George Brokeshoulder has shaved a black black war-crest on his copper scalp, he hasn't bothered to do that in years. Ahlstrom is over there with Akin the Photo chief, for heaven's sake. The whole tranquillized ship is coming to life, tiger-eyes opening, ape-brains reaching. Even the neat sign which for so long has read, THE CENTRAL PROBLEM OF OUR LIVES IS GARBAGE. PLEASE CLEAN YOUR SERVERS has been changed: someone has taped over GARBAGE and lettered BEAUTY.

"Notice the treat we're getting, boss," says Coby munching. "How did Alice get Kawabata to let loose some chicken? Oh, oh—look."

The room falls silent as Alice Berryman holds up dessert—a plate of real, whole peaches.

"One half for each person," she says severely. She is wearing a live flower over her ear.

"People are becoming excited," the XB chief observes. "How will it sustain itself for nearly two years?"

"*If* we go to that planet," Aaron mutters.

"I could make an amoral suggestion," Coby grins. "Tranks in the water supply."

Nobody laughs. "We've made out so far without,

uh, chemical supplementation, as Frank would say," says Aaron. "I think we'll hold out."

"Oh, I know, I know. But don't say I didn't warn you it may come to that."

"About tomorrow," Jan Ing says. "The first thing we will get will be the biomonitor records from the personnel section of the scoutship, right? Before we proceed to open the cargo space?"

"That's the way I hear it."

"Immediately after opening the alien's module I plan to secure biopsy sections. Very minimal, of course. Dr. Kaye says she doesn't believe that will harm the alien. We're working on extension probes that can be manipulated from outside the hatch."

"The longer the better," Aaron says, imagining tentacles.

"Assuming the alien life-form is still alive . . ." The XB chief taps out a silent theme, probably from Sibelius. "We'll know when we get our hands on the record."

"It should be." Aaron has been feeling the thing lying out beyond the buffet wall. "Tell me, Jan, do you ever have an impression that the thing is, well, *present?*"

"Oh, we're all conscious of that." Ing laughs. "Biggest event in scientific history, isn't that so? If only it is alive."

"You getting bad vibrations, boss? The dreams?" Coby inquires.

"Yeah." But Aaron can't go on, not with Coby's expression. "Yeah, I am. A xenophobe at heart."

They go into a discussion of the tissue-analyzing program and the type of bioscanners that will be placed inside the alien's module.

"What if that thing comes charging out into the corridor?" Coby interjects. "What if it's had kittens or split into a million little wigglers?"

"Well, we have the standard decontaminant aerosols," Jan frowns. "Captain Yellaston has emphasized the precautionary aspect. He will, I believe, be personally standing by the emergency vent control which could very quickly depressurize the corridor in case of real emergency. This means we will be wearing suits. Awkward working."

"Good." Aaron bites the delicious peach, delighted to hear that old Yellaston's hand will be on the button. "Jan, I want a clear understanding that no part of that thing is taken into the ship. Beyond the corridor, I mean."

"Oh, I entirely agree. We'll have a complete satellite system there. Including mice. It will be crowded." He swabs his server with cellulose granules from the dispenser, frowning harder. "It would be unthinkable to harm the specimen."

"Yeah." Lory has still not come in, Aaron sees. Probably eating in her room after that mob scene. He joins the recycle line, noticing that the usual glumness of the routine seems to have evaporated. Even Coby omits his scatological joke. What are Kuh's people eating now, Aaron wonders, telepathic vegetable steaks?

Lory is quartered—naturally—in the all-female dorm on the opposite side of the ship. Aaron hikes up a spiral cross-ship ramp, as usual not quite enjoying the sharp onset of weightlessness as he comes to *Centaur's* core. Her central core is a wide freefall service shaft from bow to stern, much patronized by the more athletic members of the crew. Aaron kicks awkwardly across it, savoring the rich air. It comes from a green-and-blue radiance far away at the stern end—the Hydroponics Farm and the Hull Pool, their other chief amenity. He shudders slightly, recalling the horrible months when the air even here was foul and the passageways dark. Five years ago an antibiotic from somebody's intestinal tract had mutated instead of being broken down by passage through the reactor coolant system. When it reached the plant beds it behaved as a chlorophyll-binding quasi-virus and Kawabata had had to destroy 75 percent of the oxygenating beds. A terrible time, waiting with all oxygen-consuming devices shut down for the new seedlings to grow and prove clean. Brr. . . . He starts "down" the exit ramp to Lory's dorm, past the cargo stores and service areas. People aren't allowed to live in less than three-quarters gee. Corridors branch out every few meters leading to other dorms and living units. *Centaur* is a warren of corridors, that's part of the program, too.

He comes to the tiny foyer or commons room outside the dorm proper and sees red hair beyond a bank of ferns: Lory—chewing on her supper, as he'd guessed. What he hadn't expected is the large form of Don Purcell, hunched opposite her deep in conversation.

Well, well! Mildly astounded, Aaron right flanks into another passage and takes himself off toward his office, blessing *Centaur's* design. The people of *Pioneer* had suffered severely from the stress of too much social contact in every waking moment; the answer found for *Centaur* was not larger spaces but an abundance of alternative routes that allow her people to enjoy privacy in their comings and goings about the ship, as they would in a village. Two persons in a two-meter corridor must confront each other but in two one-meter corridors each is alone and free to be his private self. It has worked well, Aaron thinks; he has noticed that over the years people have developed private "trails" through the ship. Kawabata, for instance, makes his long way from Farm to Messhall by a weird route through the cold sensor blister. He himself has a few. He grins, aware that his mind is demonstrating his total lack of irritation at finding Lory with another man.

In the clinic office Bruce Jang is chatting up Solange. When Aaron comes in Bruce holds up five spread fingers meaningfully. Aaron blinks, finally remembers.

"Five more people think they've seen Tighe?"

"Five and a half. I'm the half. I only heard him this time."

"You heard Tighe's voice? What did he say?"

"He said good-bye. That's all right with me, you know?" Bruce shows his teeth.

"Bruce, does your five include Ahlstrom or Kawabata?"

"Kawabata, yes. Ahlstrom, no. Six then."

Solange is registering discovery, puzzlement. "Do these people understand they have not really seen him?"

"Kidua and Morelli, definitely no. Legerski is suspicious, he said Tighe looked weird. Kawabata—who knows? The oriental physiognomy, very opaque." Supersquirrel lives.

"I think it is good I brought him to the meeting," Solange said. "I had the hunch, so people will see he is around and not worry."

"Yeah, good." Aaron takes a breath. "I've been having nightmares lately, if it's of any interest. The last one featured Tighe. He said good-bye to me, too."

Bruce's eyes snap. "Oh? You're in Beta section. That's bad."

"Bad?"

"My five sightings had a common factor before you blew it. Everyone was in Gamma section, fairly near the hull, too. That was nice."

"Nice." Aaron knows at once what Bruce means: *China Flower's* official name is *Gamma,* and the Gamma section is above her berth. But of course she isn't docked, now.

"Bruce, does that tether extend straight out? I'm no engineer. I mean, we're rotating; is she trailing?"

"Not much. A shallow tractrix. She already had our rotation when they ran her out."

"Then that alien is right under all the people who hallucinated Tighe."

"Yeah. All but you. We're in Beta here. And of course Ahlstrom is pretty far forward."

"But Tighe himself is here," says Solange. "In Beta with you."

"Yeah, but look," Aaron leans back. "Aren't we getting into witch-doctoring? There are other common factors. First, we've all been under stress for a long time and we're in a damn spooky place. Then along come two big jolts—the news about the planet and a genuine alien from outer space no one can look at. You've seen the ship, Bruce, people are lighted up like Christmas. Hope is a terrible thing, it brings fear that the hope won't be realized. Suppress the fear and it surfaces as symbol—and poor Tiger is our official disaster symbol, isn't he? Talk about common factors, it's a wonder we aren't all seeing green space-boogies."

Aaron is pleased to find he believes his own agreement; it sounds very convincing. "Moreover, Tighe is linked with the alien now."

"If you say so, Doc," says Bruce lightly.

"Well, I do say so. I say there's sufficient cause to account for the phenomena. Occam's razor, the best explanation is that requiring fewer unsupported postulates, or whatever."

Bruce chuckles. "You're citing the law of parsimony, actually." He jumps up, turns to examine a telescoping metal rod on Solange's desk. "Don't forget, Aaron, old William ended up proving god loves us. I shall continue to count."

"Do that," Aaron grins.

Bruce comes close, says softly to Aaron alone, "What would you say if I told you I also saw . . . Mei-Lin?"

Aaron looks up wordlessly. Bruce lays the rod diagonally across Aaron's console. "I thought so," he says dryly and goes out.

Solange comes over to take the rod, her face automatically tuned to the pity on his. Bruce hallucinating Mei-Lin? That fits, too. It doesn't upset Aaron's theory. "What's this for, Soli?"

"The extension for the section cutter," she tells him, striking a fencing pose. "It needs many wires, it will be a mess."

"Oh Soli—" Aaron finally gets his arms around her, where they begin to feel alive at last. "Smart and beautiful, beautiful and smart. You're such a healthy person. What would I do without you?" He buries his unhealthy nose in her fragrant flesh.

"You would do your house calls," she tells him tenderly, her hips delicious in his hands.

"Oh god. Do I have to, now?"

"Yes, Aaron. Now. Think how it will be nice, afterward."

Ruefully Aaron extricates himself, confirming the board's estimate of his drives. Getting out his kit he recalls another duty and stuffs two liter flasks into the kit while Solange checks her file.

"Bustamente number one," she tells him. "I think he is very tense."

"I wish to god we could get him in here for an EKG."

"He will not come. You must do your best." She ticks off two more people Aaron would have visited during his weeks in quarantine. "And your sister, h'mm?"

"Yeah." Closing the kit, he wonders for the thousandth time if Solange knows about the flasks inside. And Coby? Christ, Coby has to know, he'd have been checking that distillation apparatus from Day One. Probably saving it for some blackmail scheme, who knows, Aaron thinks. Could I ever explain that I'm not doing what I damned him for? Or am I?

"Make the records nicely, please, Aaron."

"I will, Soli, I will. For you."

"Ha ha."

He wants poignantly to turn back, forces himself to trot up a ramp at random and discovers he is heading again toward Lory's dorm. Don must be long gone now, but still he reconnoiters the lounge area before going in. Lory's head—and good god, Don is still there! Aaron retreats, but not before he has seen that the shoulders actually belong to Timofaev Bron.

Feeling almost ludicrously dismayed, like a character in a bedroom farce, Aaron strides through the mixed-dorm commons, vaguely aware of the number of couples among the shadows. What the hell is Lory becoming, Miss Centaur? They have no right to bother Lory this way, he fumes, not with that ulcer still unhealed. Don't they know she needs rest? *I am the doctor* . . . The inner voice comments that more than Lory's ulcers are unhealed; he disregards it. If Tim is not out of there in thirty minutes he will break it up, and—what?

Sheepishly, he admits his intention to, well, question her, although he cannot for the moment recall the urgency of what he had to ask. Well, confession is good for ulcers, too.

The next turn-off leads to the quarters of his first

patient, a member of Tim Bron's crew who came back to *Centaur* in full depressive retreat. Aaron has worked hard over him, prides himself on having involved the man in a set of correspondence chess games which he plays in solitary, never leaving his room. Now he finds the privacy-lock open, the room empty. Has Igor gone to Commons? His chess book is gone. Another point for the planet, Aaron decides, and goes cheerfully on to André Bachi's room.

Bachi is out of bed, his slender Latin face looking almost like its old self despite the ugly heaviness of glomerule dysfunction.

"To think I will live to see it," he tells Aaron. "Look, I have here the actual water, Jan sent it to me. Virgin water, Aaron. The water of a world, never passed through our bodies. Maybe it will cure me."

"Why not?" The man's intensity is heartbreaking; can he live two years, assuming they do go to Lory's world? Maybe . . . Bachi is the board's only failure so far. Merhan-Briggs syndrome, exceedingly rare, Coby's brilliant diagnosis.

"With this I can die happy, Aaron," Bachi says. "My god, for an organic chemist to experience this!"

"Is there life in it?" Aaron gestures at Bachi's scanning scope.

"Oh yes. Fantastic. So like, so unlike. Ten lifetimes' work. I have only two mounts made yet; I am slow."

"I'll leave you to it." Aaron puts Bachi's urine and saliva vials in his kit.

When he comes out he will not turn back toward Lory; instead he takes a midship passage toward the bridge. *Centaur's* bridge is in her big, shielded nose-module, which is theoretically capable of sustaining them all in an emergency. Theoretically; Aaron does not believe that most of his fellow crewmen could bear to pack themselves into it now, merely to survive. Up here is most of their important hardware, Ahlstrom's computers, astrogation gear, backup generators, and the gyros and laser system, which are their only link with Earth. Yellaston, Don, and Tim have quarters just aft of the bridge command room. Aaron turns off before Computers at a complex of panels giving access to *Centaur's* circuitry and stops under the door-eye of *Centaur's* Communications chief. There is no visible call-plate.

Nothing happens—and then the wall beside his knee utters a grating cough. Aaron jumps.

"Enter, Doc, enter," says Bustamente's bass voice.

. The door slides open. Aaron goes warily into a maze of low music and shifting light-forms in which six or seven big black men in various perspectives are watching him.

"I'm working on something in your field, Doc. Comparing startle stimuli. Nonlinear, low decibels give a bigger jump."

"Interesting." Aaron advances gingerly through unreal dimensions; visiting Ray Bustamente is always an experience. "Which one is you?"

"Over here." Aaron strikes some kind of mirrored surface and makes his way around it to comparative normality. Bustamente is on his lounger in a pose of slightly spurious relaxation.

"Roll up that sleeve, Ray. We have to do this, you know that."

Bustamente complies, grumbling. Aaron winds on the cuff, admiring the immense biceps. No fat on the triceps either; maybe the big man really does pay some heed to his advice. Aaron watches his digital read-out swing, relishing his feelings for Ray, what he thinks of as Ray's secret. The man is another rarity, a natural-born king. The real living original of which Yellaston is only the abstraction. Not a team-leader like Don or Tim. The archaic model, the Boss, Jefe, Honcho, whatever—the alpha human male who outfights you, outdrinks you, outroars you, outsmarts you, kills your enemies, begets his bastards on your woman, cares for you as his property, tells you what to do—and you do it. The primordial Big Man who organized the race and for whom the race has so little more use. Ten years ago it hadn't been visible; ten years ago there was a tall, quiet young Afro-American naval electronics officer with impeccable degrees and the ability to tune a Mannheim circuit in boxing gloves. That was before the shoulders thickened and the brow-ridges grew heavy over the watchful eyes.

"I really wish you'd come by the clinic, Ray," Aaron tells him, unwinding the cuff. "This thing isn't a precision instrument."

"What the hell can you do if you don't like my sound? Give me a stupid-pill?"

"Maybe."

"I'm making that planet, you know, Doc. Dead or alive."

"You will." Aaron puts his instruments away, admiring Bustamente's solution to his problem. What does a king do, born into a termite world, barred even from the thrones of termites? Ray had seen the scene, spotted his one crazy chance. And his decision has brought him twenty trillion miles from the termite heap, headed for a virgin planet. A planet with room, maybe, for kings.

A girl-shape is wavering among the mirrors, suddenly materializes into Melanie, the little white-mouse air-plant tech. She has an odd utensil in her hand. Aaron identifies it as a food-cooking device.

"We're working on a few primitive arts," Bustamente grins. "What's it going to be tonight, Mela?"

"A tuber," she says seriously, pushing back her ash-pale hair. "It's sweet but not much protein, it would have to be combined with fish or meat. You'll get fat." She nods impersonally at Aaron, goes back behind the screens.

"She's mine, you know." Bustamente stretches, one eye on Aaron. "Is that air as good as it looks? Ask your sister if it *smells* good, will you?"

"I'll ask her when I drop by tonight."

"Lot of dropping by recently." Bustamente suddenly flicks a switch and a screen Aaron hadn't noticed comes to life. It's an overhead shot of the communications office. The gyro chamber beyond is empty. Bustamente grunts, rolls his switch; the view flips to the bridge corridor, flip-flip-flips to others he can't identify. No people in sight. Aaron goggles; the extent of Bustamente's electronic surveillance network is one of *Centaur's* standing myths. Not so mythical, it seems; Ray really has been weaving in *Centaur's* walls. Oddly, Aaron doesn't resent it.

"Tim dropped by the shop today. Just looking to talk, he said." Bustamente flips back to the gyro chamber, zooms in on the locked laser-console. There is a definitely menacing flavor to the show; Aaron recalls with pleasure the time Frank Foy tried to set a scanner on Coby without clearing with the Commo chief.

As if reading his thought, Bustamente chuckles. "To quote the words of an ancient heavyweight boxing champion, George Foreman, *'Many a million has fall and stumble when he meet Big George in that ol' black jungle. . . .'* Plans to make, you know, Aaron? Melanie, that's one. She's tougher than she looks but she's kind of puny. Need some muscle. That big old Daniela, she's my number two. Marine biology, she knows fish."

He flicks another image on the screen. Aaron gets a flash of a strong female back, apparently in the Commons game-bay.

"You're selecting your, your prospective family?" Aaron is charmed by the big man's grab at the guts of life. A king, all right.

"I don't plan to hang in too close, you know, Doc." His eye is on Aaron. "Should have medical capability. You'll be sticking with the others, right? So I figure number three is Solange."

"Soli?" Aaron stares, forces himself to hold his own grin. "But have you, I mean what does she—Ray, we're nearly two years away, we may not even—"

"Don't worry about that, Doc. Just thought I'd warn you. You can use the time to teach Soli what to do when the babies come."

"Babies." Aaron reels mentally; the word hasn't been heard on *Centaur* for years.

"Maybe time you did a little planning yourself. Never too soon, you know."

"Good thought, Ray." Aaron makes his way out through the light-show jungle, hoping his smile expresses professional cheer rather than the sickly grin of one whose mate has just been appropriated by The Man. Soli! Oh, Soli, my only joy . . . but there's years yet, nearly two years, he tells himself. Surely he can think of something. Or can he?

A ridiculous vision of himself fighting Bustamente in a field of giant cauliflowers floats through his mind. But the woman they're fighting for isn't Solange, Aaron realizes. It's Lory.

Shaking his head at his subconscious, Aaron goes on up to the command corridor, taps the viewplate at Captain Yellaston's door. He feels a renewed appreciation for the more abstract forms of leadership.

"Come in, Aaron." Yellaston is at his console, filing his nails. His eyes don't flicker; Aaron has never been able to catch him checking on his loaded kit. The old bastard knows.

"That speech was a good idea, sir," Aaron says formally.

"For the time being." Yellaston smiles—a surprisingly warm, almost maternal smile on the worn Caucasian face. He puts the file away. "There's a point or two we should discuss, Aaron, if you're not too pressed."

Aaron sits, noting that Yellaston's faint maxillary tic has surfaced again. The only indicator he has ever given of the solitary self-combat locked in there; Yellaston has an inhuman ability to function despite what must be extensive CNS toxicity. Aaron will never forget the day *Centaur* officially passed beyond Pluto's orbit; that night Yellaston had summoned him and announced without preamble, "Doctor, I am accustomed to taking an average of six ounces of alcohol nightly. I have done so all my life. For this trip I shall reduce it to four. You will provide them." Staggered, Aaron had asked him how he had come through the selection year? "Without." Yellaston's face had sagged then, his eyes had frightened Aaron. "If you care for the mission, Doctor, you will do as I say." Against every tenet of his training, Aaron had. Why? He has wondered that many times. He knows all the conventional names for the demons the old man must poison nightly. Hidden ragings and cravings and panics, all to be exorcised thusly. His business is those names—but the fact is that Aaron suspects the true name of Yellaston's demon is something different. Something inherent in life itself, time or evil maybe, for which he has no cure. He sees Yellaston as a complicated fortress surviving by strange rituals. Perhaps the demon is dead now, the fort empty. But he has never dared to risk inquiring.

"Your sister is a very brave girl." Yellaston's voice is extra warm.

"Yes, incredible."

"I want to be sure you know that I appreciate the full extent of Dr. Kaye's heroism. The record will so show. I am recommending her for the Legion of Space."

"Thank you, sir." Glumly Aaron acknowledges Yellaston's membership in the Love-Lory Club. Suddenly he wonders, Is this the start of one of Yellaston's breaks? It has only happened a few times, the giving-way of the iron man's defenses, but it has caused Aaron much grief. The first was when they were about two years out, Yellaston began chatting with young Alice Berryman. The chats became increasingly intense. Alice was star-eyed. So far nothing wrong, only puzzling. Alice told Miriamne that he spoke of strange strategic and philosophical principles that she found hard to grasp. The culmination came when Aaron found her weeping before breakfast and hauled her to his office to let the story out. He had been dismayed. Not sex—worse. A night of incoherent, unstoppable talk, ending in maudlin childhood. "How can he be so, so *silly*—?" All stars gone, traumatic disgust. Daddy is dead. Aaron had tried to explain to her the working of a very senior, idiosyncratic old primate; hopeless. He had given up and shamelessly narco-twisted her memory, made her believe it was she who had been drunk. For the good of the mission . . . After that he had kept watch. There were three more, periodicity about two years. The poor bastard, Aaron thinks; childhood must have been the last time he was free. Before the battle began. So far Yellaston has never used him for release. Perhaps he values his bootlegger; more likely, Aaron has decided, he is simply too old. Is that about to change?

"Her courage and her accomplishment will be an inspiration."

Aaron nods again, warily.

"I wanted to be sure you understand I have full confidence in your sister's report."

She snowed him, Aaron thinks dismally. Oh Lory. Then he catches the tension in the pause and looks up. Is this leading somewhere?

"There is too much at stake here, Aaron."

"That's right, sir," says Aaron with infinite relief. "That's what I feel, too."

"Without in any way subtracting from your sister's achievement, it is simply too much to risk on anyone's unsupported word. Anyone's. We have no objective data on the fate of the Gamma crew. Therefore I shall continue to send code yellow, not code green, until we arrive at the planet and confirm."

"Thank god," says Aaron the atheist.

Yellaston looks at him curiously. It's the moment for Aaron to speak about the Tighe-sightings, the dreams, to confess his fears of Lory and alien telepathic vegetables. But there's no need now, Yellaston wasn't snowed, it was just his weird courtesy.

"I mean I do agree . . . Does this mean we're going to the planet, that is, you've decided before we check out that specimen?"

"Yes. Regardless of what we find, there is no alternative. Which brings up this point." Yellaston pauses. "My decision with respect to the signal may not be entirely popular. Although two years is a very short time."

"Two years is an eternity, sir." Aaron thinks of the flushed faces, the voices; he thinks of Bustamente.

"I realize it may seem so to some. I wish it could be shortened. *Centaur* does not have the acceleration of the scouters. More pertinently, Aaron, some crew members may also feel that we owe it to the home world to let them know as soon as possible. The situation there must be increasingly acute."

They are both silent for a moment, in deference to the acuteness of Earth's "situation."

"If *Centaur* were to have an accident before we verify the planet, this could deprive Earth of knowledge of the planet's existence, perhaps forever. The fear of such a catastrophe will weigh heavily with some. On the other hand, we have had no major malfunctions and no reason to think we shall. We are proceeding as planned. The most abysmal error we could make would be to send the green code now and then discover, after the ships have been irreversibly launched, that the planet is uninhabitable. Those ships cannot turn back."

Aaron perceives that Yellaston is using him to try out pieces of his formal announcement; a bootlegger has many uses. But why not his logical advisors, his execs, Don and Tim? Oh, oh. Aaron begins to suspect who "some" people may include.

"We would doom all the people in the pipeline. Worse, we would end forever any hope of a new emigration effort. Our hastiness would be criminal. Earth has trusted us. We must not risk betraying her."

"Amen."

Yellaston broods a moment, suddenly gets up and goes over to his cabinet wall. Aaron hears a gurgle. The old man must have saved his last one until relief arrived.

"God damn it." Yellaston suddenly sets a flask down hard. "We never should have had women on this mission."

Aaron grins involuntarily, thinking, there speaks the dead dick. Thinking also of Soli, of Ahlstrom, of all the female competences on *Centaur,* of the debates on female command that had yielded finally to the policy of minimal innovation on a mission where so much else would be new. But he knows exactly what Yellaston means.

Yellaston turns around, letting Aaron see his glass; an unusual intimacy. "Going to be a bitch, Doctor. These two will be the toughest we've had to face. Two years. The fact that we're going to the planet ourselves will suffice for most, I think." He massages his knuckles again. "It might not be a bad idea for you to keep your eyes and ears rather carefully open, Aaron, during the time ahead."

Implications, implications. Doctors, like bootleggers, have their uses, too.

"I believe I see what you mean, sir."

Yellaston nods. "On a continuing basis," he says authoritatively. He and Aaron exchange regards in which is implicit their mutual view of the relevance of Francis Xavier Foy.

"I'll do my best," Aaron promises; he has recalled his general checkup plan, maybe he can use that projective-recall session to spot trouble.

"Good. Now, tomorrow we examine that specimen. I'd like to hear your plans." Yellaston comes back, glassless, to his console and Aaron gives him a rundown on his arrangements with the Xenobiology chief.

"All the initial work will take place in *situ*, right?" Aaron concludes, conscious that the alien's *situ* is now directly to his left. "Nothing goes into the ship?"

"Right."

"I'd like to have authority to enforce that. And guards on the corridor entrances, too."

"The authority is yours, Doctor. You'll have the guards."

"That's fine." Aaron rubs his neck. "There've been a couple of, oh, call them psychological reactions to the alien I'm looking into. Nothing serious, I think. For instance, have you experienced an impression of localization, about the alien, I mean? A sense of where the thing is, physically?"

Yellaston chuckles. "Why yes, as a matter of fact I do. Right north, over there." He points high toward Aaron's right. "Is that significant, Doctor?"

Aaron grins in relief. "Yeah, it is to me. It signifies that my personal orientation still isn't any good after ten years." He picks up his kit, moves over to Yellaston's cabinets. "I thought the thing was down under your bunk." Unobtrusively he substitutes the full flasks, noting that that drink had been indeed the old man's last.

"Give your sister my personal regards, Aaron. And don't forget."

"I'll remember, Captain."

Obscurely moved, Aaron goes out. He knows he must do some serious thinking; if Don or Tim decide to kick up, what the hell can Dr. Aaron Kaye do about it?

But he is euphoric. The old man isn't buying Lory's story blind, he isn't going to rush it. Daddy will save us from the giant cauliflowers. I better get some exercise, he thinks, and trots down-ramp to one of the long outer corridors on the hull. There are six of these bow-stern blisters; they form the berths that hold the three big scoutships. Gravity is strong down here, slightly above Earth-normal, and people use the long tubes for games and exercise—another good program-element, Aaron thinks approvingly. He comes out into Corridor Beta, named for Don Purcell's scouter. *Beta* has long been known as the *Beast,* as in Beast-of-Fascist-Imperialism, a joke of *Centaur's* early years when Tim's *Alpha* was likewise christened the *Atheist Bastard.* Kuh's *Gamma* became only *China Flower*—the flower which is now hanging on her stem with her cryptic freight.

This corridor is identical to Gamma where the alien will be examined tomorrow. Aaron strides along effortfully savoring the gee-loading, counting access portals which will need guards. There are fourteen, more than he had thought. Ramps lead down here from all over the ship—the scouters were designed as lifeboats, too. The corridor is so long the far end is hazy. He fancies he can feel a chill on his soles. Imagine, he is in a starship! A fly walking the wall of a rotating can in cosmic space: *There are suns beneath my feet.*

He remembers the scenes of ceremony that had taken place in these corridors three years back, when the scoutships were launched to reconnoiter the suns of Centaurus. And the sad returns four months ago when first Don and then Tim had come back bearing news of nothing but methane and rock. Will the *Beast* and the *Bastard* soon be ferrying us down to Lory's planet?—I mean in two years, and it's Kuh's planet, Aaron corrects himself, so preoccupied that he bumps blindly into the rear of Don Purcell, backing out of Beta's command lock.

"Getting ready to land us, Don?"

Don only grins, the all-purpose calm grin that Aaron believes he would wear if he were going down in flames. Tough to get behind a grin like that if Don really was, well, disaffected. He doesn't look mutinous, Aaron thinks. Hard to imagine him leading an assault on Ray's gyros. He looks like an order man, a good jock. Like Tim. Kuh was the same breed, too, transistorized. The genotype that got us here, the heavy-duty transport of the race.

Aaron ducks into the ramp that leads to Lory's quarters, imagining Don and the scoutships and them all superimposed on that planet, that mellow flowery world. Pouring out to make a new Earth. Will they find Kuh's colony, or silent bones? But the freedom, the building . . . and then, then will come the fleet from Earth. Fifteen years, that's what we'll have, Aaron thinks, assuming we send the green signal when we land. Fifteen years. And then the emigration ships will start coming in, the—what was it Yellaston called it—the pipeline. Typical anal imagery. The pipeline spewing Earth's crap across the light-years. Technicians first, of course, basic machinery, agriculture. Pioneer-type colonists. And then pretty soon people-type people, administrators, families, politicians—whole industries and nations all whirling down that pipeline onto the virgin world. Covering it, spreading out. What of Bustamente, then? What of himself and Lory?

He is by Lory's door now, the lounge is empty at last.

When she opens it Aaron is pleased to see she's doing nothing more enigmatic than brushing her hair; the same old hygienic black bristles pulling through the coppery curls which are now just frosted gray, nice effect, really. She beckons him in, brushing steadily; counting, he guesses.

"Captain sends you his personal regards." As he sits it occurs to him that Foy may have bugged her room. No visuals, though. Not Foy.

"Thank you, Arn . . . seventy . . . Your personal regards, too?"

"Mine too. You must be tired, I notice you had company. Tried to look in earlier."

"Seventy-five . . . Everybody wants to hear about it, it means so much to them."

"Yeah. By the way, I admired your tactfulness about

our battling Chinese. I didn't know you had it in you, Sis."

She brushes harder. "I didn't want to *spoil* it. They—they stopped all that, anyway. There." She lays the brush down, smiles. "It's such a peaceful place, Arn. I think we could really live a new way there. Without violence and hatred and greed. Oh, I know how you—but that's the feeling it gave me, anyway."

The light tone doesn't fool him. Lory, lost child of paradise striving ever to return. That look in her eye, you could cast her as the young Jeanne, reminding the Dauphin of the Holy Cause. Aaron has always had a guilty sympathy for the Dauphin.

"There'll always be some bad stuff as long as you have people, Lor. People aren't all that rotten. Look at us here."

"Here? You look, Arn. Sixty hand-picked indoctrinated specimens. Are we really good? Are we even gentle with each other? I can feel the—the savagery underneath, just waiting to break loose. Why, there was a *fight* yesterday. Here."

How does she hear these things?

"It's a hell of a strain, Lor. We're human beings."

"Human beings must change."

"Goddamnit, we don't have to change. Basically, I mean," he adds guiltily. Why does she do this to him? She makes me defend what I hate, too. She's right, really, but, but—"You might try caring a little for people as they are—it's been recommended," he says angrily and hates the unctuousness in his voice.

She sighs, straightens the few oddments on her stand. Her room looks like a cell. "Why do we use the word human for the animal part of us, Arn? Aggression—that's human. Cruelty, hatred, greed—that's human. That's just what *isn't* human, Arn. It's so sad. To be truly human we must leave all that behind. Why can't we try?"

"We do, Lor. We do."

"You'd make this new world into another hell like Earth."

He can only sigh, acknowledging her words, remembering too the horrible time after their parents died, when Lory was sixteen . . . Their father had been Lieutenant-General Kaye, they had grown up sheltered, achievement-oriented in the Army enclaves' excellent schools. Lory had been into her biology program when the accident orphaned them. Suddenly she had looked up and seen the world outside—and the next thing Aaron knew he was hauling her out of a Cleveland detention center in the middle of the night. The ghetto command post had recognized her Army ID plate.

"Oh, Arn," she had wept to him in the copter going home. "It isn't right! it isn't *right*." Her face was blotched and raw where the gas had caught her, he couldn't bear to look.

"Lor, this is too big for you. I know it isn't right. But this is not like setting up a dog shelter on Ogilvy Island. Don't you understand you can get your brains cut?"

"That's what I mean, they're doing obscene things to people. It isn't *right*."

"You can't fix it," he'd snapped at her in pain. "Politics is the art of the possible. This isn't possible, you'll only get killed."

"How do we know what's possible unless we try?"

Oh god, that next year. Their father's name had helped some, luck had helped more. In the end what probably saved her was her own implacable innocence. He had finally tracked her down in the back shed of a mortuary in the old barrio section of Dallas; emaciated, trembling, barely able to speak.

"Arn, oh—they—" she whimpered while he wiped vomit off her chin, "Dave refused to help Vicky, he—he wants him to get caught . . . So he can be leader . . . He won't let us help him."

"I think that happens, Lor." He held her thin shoulders, trying to stop the shaking. "That does happen, people are human."

"No!" She jerked away fiercely. "It's terrible. It's terrible. They—*we* were fighting among ourselves, Arn. Fighting over *power*. Dave even wants his woman, I think—they hit each other. She, she was just property."

She heaved up the rest of the soup he'd brought her.

"When I said that they threw me out."

Aaron held her helplessly, thinking, her new friends can't live up to her any more than I can. Thank god.

"Arn," she whispered. "Vicky . . . *he took some money*. I know . . ."

"Lor, come on home now. I fixed it, you can still take your exams if you come back now."

". . . All right."

Aaron shakes his head, sitting in *Centaur* twenty trillion miles from Dallas, looking at that same fierce vision on the face of his little sister now going gray. His little sister whom chance has made their sole link with that planet, that thing out there.

"All right, Lor." He gets up, turns her around to face him. "I know you. What the hell happened on that planet? What are you covering?"

"Why, nothing, Arn. Except what I told you. What's the *matter* with you?"

Is it too innocent? He distrusts everything, cannot tell.

"Please let go of me."

Conscious of Foy's problematical ears he lets go, steps back. This would sound crazy.

"Do you realize this isn't games, Lor? Our lives are depending on it. Real people's lives, much as you hate humanity. You better not be playing."

"I don't hate humanity, I just hate some of the things people do. I wouldn't *hurt* people, Arn."

"You'd liquidate ninety percent of the race to achieve your utopia."

"What a terrible thing to say!"

Her face is all soul, he aches for her. But Torquemada was trying to help people, too.

"Lor, give me your word that Kuh and his people are absolutely okay. Your faithful word."

"They *are*, Arn. I give you my word. They're beautiful."

"The hell with beauty. Are they physically okay?"

"Of course they are."

Her eyes still have that look, but he can't think of anything else to try. Praise be for Yellaston's caution.

She reaches out for him, thin electric hand burning his. "You'll see, Arn. Isn't it wonderful, we'll be together? That's what kept me going, all the way back. I'll be there tomorrow when we look at it."

"Oh, no!"

"Jan Ing wants me. You said I'm medically fit. I'm his chief botanist, remember?" She smiles mischievously.

"I don't think you should, Lor. Your ulcers."

"Waiting around would be much worse for them." She sobers, grips his arm. "Captain Yellaston—he's going to send the green, isn't he?"

"Ask him yourself. I'm only the doctor."

"How sad. Oh well, he'll see. You'll all see." She pats his arm, turns away.

"*What*'ll we see?"

"How harmless it is, of course . . . Listen, Arn. This is from some ancient work, the martyr Robert Kennedy quoted it before he was killed. 'To tame the savage heart of man, to make gentle the life of this world' . . . Isn't that fine?"

"Yeah, that's fine, Lor."

He goes away less than comforted, thinking, the life of this world is not gentle, Lory. It wasn't gentleness that got you out here. It was the drives of ungentle, desperate, glory-hunting human apes. The fallible humanity you somehow can't see . . .

He finds he has taken a path through the main Commons. Under the displays the nightly bridge and poker games are in session as usual, but neither Don nor Tim are visible. As he goes out of earshot he hears the Israeli physicist ante what sounds like an island. An island? He climbs up toward the clinic, hoping he heard wrong.

Solange is waiting for him with the medical log. He recites Ray and Bachi's data with his head leaning against her warm front, remembering he has another problem. Forget it, he tells himself, I have two years to worry about Bustamente.

"Soli, tomorrow I want to rig up an array of decontaminant canisters over the examination area. With the release at my station. Say a good strong phytocide plus a fungicide with a mercury base. What should I get from Stores?"

"Decon Seven is the strongest, Aaron. But it cannot be mixed, we will have to place many tanks." Her face is mirroring pity for the hypothetically killed plants, concern for the crew.

"Okay, so we'll place many tanks. Everything the suits will take. I don't trust that thing."

Soli comes into his arms, holds him with her strong small hands. Peace, comfort. *To make gentle the life of mankind.* His body has missed her painfully, demonstrates it with a superior erection. Soli giggles. Fondly he caresses her, feeling like himself for the first time in weeks. Do I see you as property, Soli? Surely not . . . The thought of Bustamente's huge body covering her floats through his mind; his erection increases markedly. Maybe the big black brother will have to revise his planning, Aaron thinks genially, hobbling with her to his comfortable, comforting bunk. Two years is a long time . . .

Drifting asleep with Soli's warm buttocks in his lap Aaron has a neutral, almost comic hypnagogic vision: Tighe's face big as the wall, garlanded with fruits and flowers like an Italian bambino plaque. The pink and green flowers tinkle, chime elfland horns. *Tan tara!* Centripetal melodies. *Tan tara! Tara! TARA!*

—and fairy horns turn into his medical alarm signal, with Soli shaking him awake. The call is from the bridge.

He leaps out of bed, yanking shorts on, hits the doorway with one shoulder and runs "up" to the freefall shaft. His kit is somehow in his hand. He has no idea what time it is. The thought that Yellaston has had a heart attack is scaring him to death. Oh god, what will they do without Yellaston?

He kicks free, sails and grabs clumsily like a three-legged ape, clutching the kit, is so busy figuring alternative treatment spectrums that he almost misses the voices coming from the Commo corridor. He gets himself into the access, finds his feet and scurries "down" still so preoccupied that he does not at first identify the dark columns occupying the Communication step. They are Bustamente's legs.

Aaron pushes in past him and confronts a dreadful sight. Commander Timofaev Bron is sagging from Bustamente's grasp, bleeding briskly from his left eye.

"All right, all right," Tim mutters. Bustamente shakes him.

"What the hell was that power drain?" Don Purcell comes in behind Aaron.

"This booger was sending," Bustamente growls. "Shit-eater, I was too slow. He was sending *on my beam.*" He shakes the Russian again.

"All right," Tim repeats unemotionally. "It is done."

The blood is coming from a supra-orbital split. Aaron disengages Tim from Bustamente, sits him down with his head back to clamp the wound. As he opens his kit a figure comes slowly through the side door from Astrogation: Captain Yellaston.

"Sir—" Aaron is still confusedly thinking of that coronary. Then Yellaston's peculiar rigidity gets through to him. Oh Jesus, no. The man is not sick but smashed to the gills.

Bustamente is yanking open the gyro housing. The room fills with a huge humming tone.

"I did not harm the beam," Tim says under Aaron's hands. "Certain equipment was installed when we built it; you did not look carefully enough."

"Son of a bitch," says Don Purcell.

"What do you mean, equipment?" Bustamente's voice rises, harmonic with the precessing gyros. "What have you done, flyboy?"

"I was not sent here to wait. The planet is there."

Aaron sees Captain Yellaston's lips moving effortfully, achieving a strange pursed look. "You indicated . . ." he says eerily, "You indicated . . . that is, you have preempted the green . . ."

The others stare at him, look away one by one. Aaron is stabbed with unbearable pity, he is suspecting that what has happened is so terrible it isn't real yet.

"Son of a bitch," Don Purcell repeats neutrally.

The green signal has been sent, Aaron realizes. To

the Russians, anyway, but everybody will find out, everybody will start. It's all over, he's committed us whether that planet's any good or not. Oh god, Yellaston—he saw this coming, if he'd been younger, if he'd moved faster—if half his brains hadn't been scrambled in alcohol. I brought it to him.

Automatically his hands have completed their work. The Russian gets up. Don Purcell has left, Bustamente is probing the gyro-chamber with a resonator, not looking at Tim. Yellaston is still rigid in the shadows.

"It was in the hull shielding," Tim says to Bustamente. "The contact is under the toggles. Don't worry, it was one-time."

Aaron follows him out, unable to believe in any of this. Lieutenant Pauli is waiting outside; she must be in it, too.

"Tim, how could you be so goddam sure? You may have killed everybody."

The cosmonaut looks down at him calmly, one-eyed. "The records don't lie. They are enough, we will find nothing else. That old man would have waited forever." He chuckles, a dream-planet in his eye.

Aaron goes back in, leads Yellaston to his quarters. The captain's arm is trembling faintly. Aaron is trembling too with pity and disgust. That old man, Tim had called him. That old man . . . Suddenly he realizes the full dimensions of this night's disaster.

Two years. The hell with the planet, maybe they won't even get there. Two years in this metal can with a captain who has failed, an old man mocked at in his drunkenness? No one to hold us together, as Yellaston had done during those unbearable weeks when the oxygen ran low, when panic had hung over all their heads. He had been so good then, so right. Now he's let Tim take it all away from him, he's lost it. We aren't together any more, not after this. It'll get worse. *Two years . . .*

"In the . . . fan," Yellaston whispers with tragic dignity, letting Aaron put him onto his bed. "In . . . the fan . . . my fault."

"In the morning," Aaron tells him gently, dreading the thought. "Maybe Ray can figure some way."

" . . . "

Aaron heads hopelessly for his bunk. He knows he won't sleep. *Two years . . .*

III

Silence . . . Bright, clinical emptiness, no clouds, no weeping. Horizon, infinity. Somewhere words rise, speaking silence: I AM THE SPOUSE. Cancel sound. Aaron, invisible and microbe-sized, sees on the floor of infinity a very beautifully veined silver membrane which he now recognizes as an adolescent's prepuce, the disjecta of his first operation . . .

Almost awake now, in foetal position; something terrible ahead if he wakes up. He tries to burrow back into dream but a hand is preventing him, jostling him back to consciousness.

He opens his eyes and sees Coby handing him a hot cup; a very bad sign.

"You know about Tim." Aaron nods, sipping clumsily.

"You haven't heard about Don Purcell, though. I didn't wake you. No medical aspects."

"What about Don Purcell? What happened?"

"Brace yourself, boss."

"For Christ's sake, don't piss around, Bill."

"Well, about oh-three-hundred we had this hull tremor. Blipped all Tighe's tapes. I called around, big flap, finally got the story. Seems Don fired his whole scouter off on automatic. It's loaded with a complete set of tapes, records, everything he could get his hands on. The planet, see? They say it can punch a signal through to Earth when it gets up speed."

"But Don, is Don in it?"

"Nobody's in it. It's set on autopilot. The *Beast* had some special goodies, too, our people must have a new ear up someplace. Mars, I heard."

"Jesus Christ . . ." So fast, it's happening, Aaron

thinks. Where does Coby get his information, anything bad he knows it all. Then he sees the faint appeal under Coby's grin; this is what he can do, his wretched offering.

"Thanks, Bill." Aaron gets up effortfully . . . First Tim and now Don—war games on *Centaur*. It's all wrecked, all gone.

"Things are moving too fast for the old man." Coby leans back familiarly on Aaron's bunk. "Good thing, too. We have to get a more realistic political organization. This great leader stuff, he's finished. Oh, we can keep him on as a figurehead . . . Don and Tim are out, too, for now anyway. First thing to start with, we elect a working committee."

"You're crazy, Bill. You can't run a ship with a committee. We'll kill ourselves if we start politics."

"Want to bet?" Coby grins. "Going to see some changes, boss."

Aaron sluices water over his head to shut off the voice. Elections, two years from nowhere? That'll mean the Russian faction, the U.S. faction, the Third and Fourth Worlders; scientists versus humanists versus techs versus ecologists versus theists versus Smithites— all the factions of Earth in one fragile ship. What shape will we be in when we reach the planet, if we live that long? And any colony we start—Oh, damn Yellaston, damn me—

"General meeting at eleven hundred," Coby is saying. "And by the way, Tighe really did go wandering for about twenty minutes last night. My fault, I admit it, I forgot the isolation seal was off. No harm done. I got him right back in."

"Where was he?"

"Same place. By the port where *China* was."

"Take him with you to the meeting," Aaron says impulsively, punishing them all.

He goes out to get some breakfast, trying to shake out of the leaden feeling of oversleep, of doom impending. He dreads the meeting, dreads it. Poor old Yellaston trying futilely to cover his lapse, trying to save public face. A figurehead. He can't take that, he'll go into depression. Aaron makes himself set up Tighe's tapes to occupy his thoughts.

Tighe's tapes are worse than before, composite score down another five points, Aaron sees, even before the twenty-minute gap. His CNS functions are coming out of synch, too, an effect he hasn't seen in an ambulant patient, especially one as coordinated as Tighe. Curious . . . Have to study it, Aaron thinks apathetically. All our curves are coming out of synch, we're breaking up. Yellaston was our pacemaker. Can we make it without him? . . . Am I as dependent as Foy?

It is time for the meeting. He plods down to the Commons, sick with pity and dread; he is so reluctant to listen that he does not at first notice the miracle: There is nothing to pity. The Yellaston before his eyes is firm-voiced, erect, radiating leaderly charisma; is announcing, in fact that *Centaur's* official green code for the Alpha sun was beamed to Earth at oh-five-hundred this morning.

What?

"As some of you are aware," Yellaston says pleasantly, "our two scout commanders have also taken independent initiative to the same effect in messaging their respective Terrestrial governments. I want to emphasize that their actions were pursuant to specific orders from their superiors prior to embarkation. We all regret, we here who are joined in this mission have always regretted—that the United Nations of Earth who sponsored our mission were not more perfectly united when we left. We may hope they are so now. But this is a past matter of no concern to us, arising from tensions on a world none of us may ever visit again. I want to say now that both Tim Bron and Don Purcell—" Yellaston makes a just-perceptible fatherly nod toward the two commanders, who are sitting quite normally on his left, despite Tim's taped eye "—faithfully carried out orders, however obsolete, just as I or any of us would have felt obligated to do in their places, had we been so burdened. Their duties have now been discharged. Their independent signals, if they arrive, will serve as confirmation to our official transmission to Earth as a whole.

"Now we must consider our immediate tasks."

Jesus god, Aaron thinks, the old bastard. The old fox, he's got it all back, he took the initiative right out from under them while I thought he was dead out. Fantastic. But how the hell? Running those lasers up is a job. Aaron looks around, catches a hooded gleam from Bustamente. Ol' Black George was cooking in his electronic jungle, he and Yellaston. Aaron grins to himself. He is happy, so happy that he ignores the inner murmur: *At a price.*

"The biologic examination of the planetary life-form returned to us by Commander Kuh will start at about sixteen hundred this afternoon. It will be conducted in Corridor Gamma One under decontaminant seal, but the entire operation will be displayed on your viewers." Yellaston smiles. "You will probably see it better than I will. Next, and concurrently, the Drive section will prepare to initiate change of course toward the Alpha planet. Each of you will secure your areas for acceleration and course-change as speedily as possible. The vector loadings will be posted tomorrow. Advise Don and Tim of any problems in their respective sections. First Engineer Singh will deal with Gamma section in the absence of Commander Kuh. And finally, we must commence the work of adapting and refining our general colonization plan to the planetary data now at hand. Our first objective is a planetary atlas incorporating every indicator that your specialties can extract from the *Gamma* tapes. On this we can build our plans. I remind you that this is a task requiring imagination and careful thought of every contingency and parameter. Gentlemen, ladies: The die is cast. We have only two years to prepare for the greatest adventure our race has known."

Aaron starts to smile at the archaism, finds he has a fullness in the throat. The hush around him holds for a minute; Yellaston nods to Don and Tim and they get up and exit with him. Perfect, Aaron thinks. We'll make it, we're okay. Screw Coby. Daddy lives. Everyone is jabbering now, Aaron makes his way through them past the great flowering wonder of Lory's—of the Alpha planet. Our future home. Yellaston will get us there, he's pulled it out.

But at a price, the gloomy corner of his forebrain repeats. The big green light is on its way to Earth. Not only we but all the people of Earth are committed, committed to that world. That planet *has* to be all right now.

He goes to assemble his equipment, irrationally resolved to double his emergency decontaminant array.

log 124 586 *sd* 4100 *x* 1200 *notice to all personnel corridor gamma one will be under space hazard seal starting 1545 this day for the purpose of bioanalysis of alien life specimen/ /attendance will be limited to: [1] centaur command cadre alpha [2] designated xenobiosurvey/medical personnel [3] eva team charlie [4] safety/survival staff assigned to corridor access locks/ /the foregoing personnel will be suited at all times until the unsealing of the corridor/ /because of the unknown risk-factor in this operation additional guards will also be stationed on the inboard side of all access ports: see special-duty roster attached/ /unauthorized personnel will not, repeat not, enter gamma one starting as of now/ /video cover of the entire operation from the closest feasible points will be available on all screens on ship channel one, starting approximately 1515 hours*

yellaston, cmdg

In Corridor Gamma One, the major risk-factor is wires. Aaron leans on a bulkhead amid his tangle of equipment, holding his bulky suit and watching Jan Ing wrangle with Electronics. The Xenobiology chief wants a complete computer capability in the corridor; there is no way of passing the cable through the lock seals. The EVA team is appealed to but they refuse to give up any of their service terminals. Finally the issue is resolved by sacrificing an access-lock indicator panel. Engineer Gomulka, who will double as a guard, starts cutting it out to bring the computer leads in.

Wires are snaking all over the deck. XB has brought in half their laboratory, and he can see at least eight other waldo-type devices in addition to the biomonitor extension equipment. On top of it all the camera crew is setting up. One camera is opposite the small hatch that will open into *China Flower's* personnel section, two by the big cargo hatch behind which the alien thing will be, plus a couple of overhead views. They are also mounting some ceiling slave screens for the corridor, Aaron is glad to find. He is too far back to see the hatches. The Safety team is trying to get the cables cleared into bundles along the wall, but the mess is bound to get worse when the suit umbilicals come into use. Mercifully, general suiting-up will not take place until the EVA team has winched *China Flower* up to her berth.

Aaron's station is the farthest one away at the stern end of the corridor. In front of him is an open space with the EVA floor lock, and then starts the long Xeno-biology clutter. Beyond XB is the big cargo hatch and then the small hatch, and finally in the distance is the corridor command station. Command Cadre Alpha means Yellaston and Tim Bron. Aaron can just make out Tim's eye-patch, he's talking with Don Purcell who will go back to man *Centaur's* bridge. In case of trouble . . . Aaron peers at his racks of decontaminant aerosols mounted opposite the hatches. They have wires, too, running to a switch beside his hand. He had trouble with XB about those cans; Jan Ing would rather be eaten alive than risk damaging their precious specimen of alien life.

A hand falls on his shoulder—Captain Yellaston, coming in the long way round, his observant face giving no hint of what must be the chemical conditions in his bloodstream.

"The die is cast," Aaron observes.

Yellaston nods. "A gamble," he says quietly. "The mission . . . I may have done a fearful thing, Aaron. They were bound to come, on the strength of the other two."

"The only thing you could have done, sir."

"No." Aaron looks up. Yellaston isn't talking to him; his eyes are on some cold cosmic scoreboard. "No. I should have sent code yellow and announced I had sent the green. Ray would have kept silent. That would have held back the U.N. ships at least. It was the correct move. I failed to think it through in time."

He moves on down the corridor, leaving Aaron stunned. Sent the yellow and lied to us for two years? *Captain Yellaston*? But yes, Aaron sees slowly, that would have saved something, in case the planet is no good. It would have been better. What he did was good but it wasn't the best. Because he was drunk . . . My fault. My stupid susceptibilities, my—

People are jostling past him, it's the EVA team, suited and ready to go out. Chief George Brokeshoulder's suit is a work of art, painted with blazing Amerind symbols. The last man by punches Aaron's arm—Bruce Jang, giving him a mean wink through his gold-washed faceplate. Aaron watches them file down into the EVA blister lock, remembering the same thing three weeks ago when they had gone out to bring in *China Flower* with Lory unconscious inside. This time all they have to do is reel up the tether. Risky enough. The rotational mechanics could send a man into space, Aaron thinks; he is always awed by skills he doesn't have.

A videoscreen comes to life, showing spinning stars. A space suit occults them; when it passes, three small yellow lights are moving toward a blackness—the helmet lights of the team going down to *China Flower* far below. Aaron's gut jumps; an *alien* is out there, he is about to meet an *alien*. He blinks, begins to sort and assemble the extensor mounts on which his sensors will be intruded into the scouter's cargo hold. As he does so, he notices faces peering at him through the vitrex of the nearest access lock. He waves. The faces, perceiving that the scenario has not yet started, go away. It will be, Aaron realizes, a long afternoon.

By the time he and Ing have lined up their equipment all nonoperational people except the suit team have left the corridor. The hull has been groaning softly; *China Flower* is rising to them on her winch. Suddenly the wall beside him clanks, grinds reverberatingly—the port probes engage, the grinding stops. Aaron shivers involuntarily: the alien is here.

As the EVA lock cycle begins flashing, Tim Bron's voice says on the audio, "All hands will now suit up."

The EVA team is coming back inside. The suit men work down the corridor, checking and paying out the umbilicals as neatly as they can. It's going to be cramped working. The suit team reach him last. As he seals in he sees more faces at the side lock. The videoscreens are all on now, giving a much better view, but still the faces remain. Aaron chuckles to himself; the old ape impulse to see with the living eye.

"All nonoperational personnel will now clear the area."

The EVA team is lined up along the wall opposite *China Flower's* personnel hatch. The plan is to open this first in order to retrieve the scoutship's automatic records of the alien's life-processes. Is it still alive in there? Aaron has no mystic intuitions now, only a great and growing tension in his gut. He makes himself breathe normally.

"Guards, secure the area."

The last corridor entrances are dogged tight. Aaron sees a face-plate turned toward him three stations up the XB line. The face belongs to Lory. He flinches slightly; he had forgotten she would be here. He lifts his gloved hand, wishing he was between her and that cargo port.

The area is secure, the guards stationed. George Brokeshoulder and two other EVA men move up to open the lock coupled to *China Flower's* personnel port. Aaron watches the close-up on the overhead screen. Metal clinks, the lock hatch slides sideways. The EVA men go in carrying vapor analyzers, the hatch rolls shut. Another wait. Aaron sees the XB people tuning their suit radios, realizes the EVA men are reporting. He gets the channel: "Nominal. . . . Atmosphere nominal (crackle, crackle) . . ." The hatch is sliding back again, the men come out accompanied by a barely perceptible fogginess. Lory looks back at him again; he understands. This is the air she had breathed for nearly a year.

The ship's tapes are being handed out. The alien is, it appears, alive.

"Metabolic trace regular to preliminary inspection, envelope unchanged," Jan Ing's voice comes on the audio. "Intermittent bioluminescence, two to eighty candlepower." Eighty candlepower, that's *bright*. So Lory hadn't lied about that, anyway. "A strong peak coinciding with the original docking with *Centaur* . . . a second peak occurred, yes, about the time the scoutship was removed from its berth."

That would be about when Tighe did—or didn't—open the container, Aaron thinks. Or maybe it was stimulated by moving the ship.

"One of the fans which circulate its atmosphere is not operating," the XB chief goes on, "but the remaining fans seem to have provided sufficient movement for adequate gas exchange. Its surface atmosphere requires continuous renewal, since it is adapted to constant planetary wind. It also exhibits pulselike internal pressure changes—"

Aaron's mind is momentarily distracted by the vision of himself stepping out into planetary wind, a stream of wild unrecycled air. That creature in there dwells on wind. A podlike mass about four meters long, Lory had described it. Like a big bag of fruit. Squatting in there for a year, metabolizing, pulsing, luminescing—what else has it been doing? The functions of life: assimilation, excitation, reproduction. Has it been reproducing? Is the hold full of Coby's tiny monsters waiting to pounce out? Or ooze out, swallowing us all? Aaron notices he has drifted away from his decontaminant switches; he moves back.

"The mass is constant, activity vectors stable," Jan concludes.

So it hasn't been multiplying. Just squatting there. Thinking, maybe? Aaron wonders if those biolumines-cence peaks would correlate with any phenomena on *Centaur*. What phenomena? Tighe sightings, maybe, or nightmares? Don't be an idiot, he tells himself; the imp in his ear replies that those New England colonists didn't correlate ocean currents and winter temperatures, either . . . Absently he has been following the EVA team's debate on whether to cut open the viewport to the alien that Lory welded shut. It is decided not to try this but to proceed directly to the main cargo lock.

The team comes out and the men assigned to the extension probes pick up their equipment, cables writhing in a slow snake dance. Bruce and the EVA chief undog the heavy cargo hatch. This is the port through which the scoutship's groundside equipment, their vehicles and flier and generator were loaded in. The hatch rolls silently aside, the two men go into the lock. Aaron can see them on the videoscreen, unsealing the scouter's port. It opens; no vapor comes out because the hold is unpressurized. Beyond the suited figures Aaron can see the shiny side of the cargo-module in which the alien is confined. The sensor men advance, angling their probes into the lock like long-necked beasts. Aaron glances up at another screen which shows the corridor as a whole and experiences an odd, oceanic awareness.

Here we are, he thinks, tiny blobs of life millions and millions of miles from the speck that spawned us, hanging out here in the dark wastes, preparing with such complex pains to encounter a different mode of life. All of us, peculiar, wretchedly imperfect—somehow we have done this thing. Incredible, really, the ludicrous tangle of equipment, the awkward suited men, the precautions, the labor, the solemnity—Jan, Bruce, Yellaston, Tim Bron, Bustamente, Alice Berryman, Coby, Kawabata, my saintly sister, poor Frank Foy, stupid Aaron Kaye—a stream of faces pours through his mind, hostile or smiling, suffering each in his separate flawed reality: all of us. Somehow we have brought ourselves to this amazement. Perhaps we really are saving our race, he thinks, perhaps there really is a new earth and heaven ahead . . .

The moment passes; he watches the backs of the men inside *China,* still struggling with the module port. The sensor men have closed in, blocked the view. Aaron glances up at the bow end of the corridor where Yellaston and Tim Bron stand. Yellaston's arm is extended stiffly to the top of his console. That must be the evacuation control; if he pulls it the air ducts will open, the corridor will depressurize in a couple of minutes. So will the alien's module if it's open. Good; Aaron feels reassured. He checks his own canister-release switch, finds he has again strayed forward and moves back.

Confused exclamations, grunts are coming over the suit channel; apparently there is a difficulty with the module port. One of the sensor men drops his probe, moves in. Another follows. What's the trouble?

The screen shows nothing but suit backs, the whole EVA team is in there—Oh! Sudden light, cracks of radiance between the men silhouetting them blue against a weird pink light—Is it fire? Aaron's heart jumps, he clambers onto a stanchion to see over heads. Not fire, there's no smoke. Oh, of course, he realizes—that light is the alien's own luminescence! They have opened the module.

But why are they all in there, why aren't they falling back to push the sensors in? Wide rosy light flashes, hidden by bodies. They must have opened the whole damn port instead of just cracking it. Is that thing trying to come out?

"Close it, get out!" Aaron calls into his suit mike. But the channel is a bedlam of static. Everybody is crowding forward toward that hatch, too. That's dangerous. "Captain!" Aaron shouts futilely. He can see Yellaston's hand still on the panel, but Tim Bron seems to be holding onto his arm. The EVA men are all inside *China Flower,* inside the module even, it's impossible to tell. A pink flare lights up the corridor, winks out again.

"Move back! Get back to your stations!" Yellaston's voice cuts in on the command channel override and the intercom babble goes dead. Aaron is suddenly aware of pressure around him, discovers that he is all the way up at the XB stations, being crowded by someone behind. It's Akin's face inside the safety guard visor. They disengage clumsily, move back.

"Go back to your stations! EVA team, report."

Aaron is finding movement oddly effortful. He wants very much to open his stifling helmet.

"George, can you hear me? Get your men out."

The screen is showing confused movement, more colored flashes. Is somebody hurt? There's a figure, coming slowly out of the hatch.

"What's going on in there, George? Why is your helmet open?"

Aaron stares incredulously as the EVA chief emerges into the corridor—his faceplate is open, tipped back showing his bronze, axe-shaped face. What the hell is happening? Did the alien grab them? George's arm goes up, he is making the okay signal; the suit-to-suit channel is still out. The others are coming out behind him, the strange light shining on their backs, making a great peach-colored glow in the corridor. Their visors are open, too. But they seem to be all right, whatever happened in there.

The screen is showing the module port; all Aaron can make out is a big rectangle of warm-colored light. It seems to be softly bubbling or shifting, like a light show—globes of rose, yellow, lilac—it's beautiful, really. Hypnotic. They should close it, he thinks, hearing Yellaston ordering the men to seal their helmets. With an effort Aaron looks away, sees Yellaston still by his station, his arm rigid. Tim Bron seems to have moved away. It's all right, nothing has happened. It's all right.

"Get those suits closed before I depressurize!"

The EVA chief is slowly pulling his face-plate down, so are the others. Their movements seem vague, unfocussed. One of them stumbles over the biopsy equipment. Why doesn't he pick it up? Something *is* wrong with them. Aaron frowns. His brain feels gassy. Why aren't they carrying out the program, doing something about the bioluminescence? It's probably all right, though, Yellaston is there. He's watching.

At this moment he is jostled hard. He blinks, recovers balance, looks around. Jesus—he's in the wrong place—everybody is in the wrong place. The whole corridor is jamming forward of where it's supposed to be, staring at that marvelous glow. The guards—they're not by the ports! Something is not all right at all, Aaron realizes. It's that light, it's doing something to us! *Close the port*, he wills, trying to get back to his station. It's like moving in water. The emergency switch—he has to reach it, how did he ever get so far away? And the ports, he sees, the vitrex is crowded with faces, people are in the access ramps staring into the corridor. They've come from all over the ship. What's wrong? What's happening to us?

Cold fear bursts up in his gut. He catches the EVA lock and clings to it fighting an invisible slow tide. Part of him wants to push his helmet off and run forward to the radiance coming from that port. People ahead of him are opening their visors—he can see Jan Ing's sharp Danish nose.

"Stand away from that port!" Yellaston shouts. At that Jan Ing darts forward, pushing people aside. "Stop," Aaron yells into his useless mike, finds himself opening his own visor, moving after Jan. Voices, sounds fill his ears. He grabs another stanchion, pulls himself up to look for Yellaston. The captain is still there; he seems to be struggling slowly with Tim Bron. The light is gone now, hidden by a press of bodies around the port. That thing in there is doing this, Aaron tells himself; he is terrified in a curious unreal way, his head is singing thickly. He is also angry with those people down there—they are going in, blocking it. Lost! But is it they who are lost or the wonderful light?

Someone bumps breast-to-breast with him, pulling at his arm. He looks down into Lory's blazing face. Her helmet is gone.

"Come on, Arn! We'll go together."

Primal distrust sends an icicle into his mind; he grabs her suit, anchors himself to a console with his other arm. Lory! She's in league with that thing, he knows it, this is her crazy plot. He has to stop it. Kill it! Where is his emergency release? It's too far, too far—

"Captain!" he shouts with all his strength, fighting Lory, thinking, two minutes, we can get out. "Depressurize! Dump the air!"

"No, Arn! It's beautiful—don't be afraid!"

"Dump the air, kill it!" he yells again, but his voice can't override the confusion. Lory is yanking on his arm, her exultant face fills him with sharp fright. "What is it?" He shakes her by the belt. "What are you trying to do?"

"It's time, Arn! It's *time,* come on—there're so many people—"

He tries to get a better grip on her, hearing metal clang behind him and realizes too late he has let go his hold on the console. But her words are now making a kind of sense to him—there *are* too many people, it is important, quite important to get there before something is all used up. Why is he letting them hide that light? Lory has his hand now, drawing him toward the press of people ahead.

"You'll see, it will all be gone, the pain . . . Arn dear, we'll be together."

The beauty of it floods Aaron's soul, washes all fear away. Just beyond those bodies is the goal of man's desiring, the fountain—the Grail itself maybe, the living radiance! He sees an opening by the wall, pulls Lory through—and is suddenly squeezed by more bodies from the side, a wall of people flooding out of the access port. Aaron fights to hold his ground, hold Lory, only dimly aware that he is struggling against familiar faces—Ahlstrom is beside him, smiling orgasmically, he pushes past Kawabata, ducks under somebody's arm. As he does, a force slams their backs—he is clouted into something entangling and falls down under an XB analyzer still clutching Lory's wrist.

"Arn, Arn, come on!"

Legs are going by him. It was Bustamente who hit him, forging past followed by a forest of legs. They have all come here to claim the shining glory in the port! Wildly enraged, Aaron struggles up, falls again with his own leg deep in a web of cables.

"Arn, get up!" She jerks at him fiercely. But he is suddenly calmer, although he does not cease to wrench at his trapped leg. There is a small intercom screen by his head, he can see two tiny struggling figures—

Yellaston and Tim Bron, their helmets gone. Dream-like, tiny . . . Tim breaks away. Yellaston nods once, and fells Tim from behind with a blow of both locked fists. Then he slowly steps over the fallen man and goes off screen. Pink light flares out.

They have all gone in there, Aaron realizes, heart-broken. It has called us and we have come—*I must go.* But he frowns, blinks; a part of him has doubts about the pull, the sweet longing. It feels fainter down here. Maybe that pile of stuff is shielding me, he thinks confusedly. Lory is yanking at the cables around his legs. He pulls her in to him.

"Lor, what's happening to them? What happened to—" he cannot recall the Chinese commander's name "—what happened to your, your crew?"

"Changed," she is panting. Her face is incredibly beautiful. "Merged, healed. Made whole. Oh, you'll see, hurry—Can't you *feel* it, Arn?"

"But—" He can feel it all right, the pull, the promising urgency, but he feels something else too—the ghost of Dr. Aaron Kaye is screaming faintly in his head, threatening him. Lory is trying to lift him bodily. He resists, fearing to be drawn from his shielded nook. The corridor around them is empty now but he can hear people in the distance, a thick babbling down by that hatch. No screams, nothing like panic. Disregarding Lory, he cranes to get a look at the big ceiling screen. They are all there, milling rather aimlessly, he has never seen so many people pressed so close. This is a medical emergency, he thinks. I am the doctor. He has a vision of Dr. Aaron Kaye getting to the levers that will seal that cargo hatch, standing firm against the crowd, saving them from whatever is in that hold. But he cannot; Dr. Aaron Kaye is only a thin froth of fear on a helpless, lunging desire to go there himself, to fling himself into that beautiful warm light. He is going to be very ashamed, he thinks vaguely, tied here like Ulysses against the siren call, huddling under an analyzer bench while the others—What? He studies the screen again, he can see no apparent trouble, no one has fallen. The

EVA men came out all right, he tells himself. What I have to do is get out of here.

Lory laughs, pulling at his legs; she has freed him, he sees. He is sliding. Effortfully he reaches into his suit, finds the panic syringe.

"Arn dear—" Her slender neck muscles are exposed; he grabs her hair, seats the spray. She wails and struggles maniacally but he holds on, waiting for the shot to work. His head feels clearer. The aching pull is less; maybe all those people are blocking it somehow. The thought hurts him. He tries to disregard it, thinking, if I can get across the corridor, into that access ramp, I can seal it behind me. Maybe.

Suddenly there is movement to his left—a pair of legs, slowly stepping by his refuge. Pale gold legs he recognizes.

"Soli! Soli, stop!"

The legs pause, a small hand settles on the overturned stand beyond him. Just within reach—he can spring and grab her, letting go of Lory—to reach her he must let Lory go. He lunges, feels Lory pull away and clutches her again. He falls short. The hand is gone.

"Soli! Soli! Come back!" Her footsteps move on down the corridor. Dr. Aaron Kaye will be ashamed, ashamed; he knows it. "The EVA men were okay," he mutters. Lory is weakening now, her eyes vague. "No, Arn," she sighs, sighs deeply again. Aaron rolls her, gets a firm grip on her suit-belt and crawls out into the corridor.

As his head clears the shelter, the sweet pull grabs him again. There—down there is the goal! "I'm a doctor," he groans, willing his limbs. A thick cable is under his hand. From miles away he recognizes it—the XB computer lead, running toward the inboard lock. If he can follow that across the corridor he will be at the ramp.

He clasps it, starts to shuffle on his knees, dragging Lory. The thing down there is pulling at the atoms of his soul, his head is filled with urgent radiance calling to him to drop the foolish cable and run to join his mates. "I'm a *doctor,*" he mumbles; it requires all his strength to slide his gloved hand along his lifeline, he is turning away from bliss beyond his dreams. Only meters to go. It is impossible. Why is he refusing, going the wrong way? He will turn. But something has changed . . . He is at the lock, he sees; he must let go the cable and drag Lory over the sill.

Sobbing, he does so; it is almost more than he can bear to nudge the heavy port with his heel and send it swinging closed behind them.

As it closes the longing lessens perceptibly. Metal, he thinks vacantly, it has blocked it a little, maybe it is some kind of EM field. He looks up. A figure is standing by the lock.

"Tiger! What are you doing here?" Aaron pulls himself upright with Lory huddled by his feet. Tighe looks at them uncertainly, says nothing.

"What's in that boat, Tiger? The alien, did you see it? What is it?"

Tighe's face wavers, crumples. "Mu . . . muh," his mouth jerks. "Mother."

No help here. Just in time, Aaron notices his own hands opening the port-lever. He takes Lory under the arms and drags her farther away up the ramp to the emergency intercom panel. Her eyes are still open, her hands are fumbling weakly at her suit-fastenings.

Aaron breaks out the caller. It's an all-ship channel.

"Don! Commander Purcell, can you hear me? This is Dr. Kaye, I'm in ramp six, there's been trouble down here."

No answer. Aaron calls again, calls Coby, calls the Commo and Safety CQs, calls everybody he can think of, calls himself hoarse. No answer. Has everybody on *Centaur* gone into corridor Gamma One, is the whole damned ship out there with that—

Except Tighe. Aaron frowns at the damaged man. He was in here, he didn't join the stampede.

"Tiger, did you go out there?"

Tighe mouths, emits what could be a negative. He seems uninterested in the port. What does it take to stay sane near that thing, Aaron wonders, cortical suppressants? Or did one contact immunize him? Can we prepare drugs, can I lobotomize myself and still function? He notices he has drifted closer to the port, that Lory is crawling toward it, half out of her suit. He pulls her out of it, gets them both back up the ramp.

When he looks up there is a shadow on the port view-panel.

For a terrified instant Aaron is sure it is the alien coming for him. Then he sees a human hand, slowly tapping. Somebody trying to get in—but he dare not go down there.

"Tiger! Open the port, let the man in." He gestures wildly at Tighe. "The port, look! You remember, hit the latch, Tiger. Open up!"

Tighe hesitates, turns in place. Then an old reflex fires; he sidesteps and slaps double-handed at the latch with perfect coordination—and as quickly sags again. The port swings open. Captain Yellaston stands there. Deliberately he steps through.

"Captain, captain, are you all right?" Aaron starts to run forward, checks himself. "Tiger, close the port."

Yellaston is walking stiffly toward him, looking straight ahead. Face a little pale, Aaron thinks, no injuries visible. He's all right, whatever happened. It's all right.

"Captain, I—" But there are more figures at the port, Aaron sees, Tim Bron and Coby, coming in past Tighe. Others beyond. Aaron has never been so glad to see his assistant, he yells something at him and turns to catch up with Yellaston.

"Captain—" He wants to talk about sealing off the corridor, about examining them all. But Yellaston does not look around.

"The red," Yellaston says in a faint remote voice. "The red . . . is the correct . . . signal." He walks on, toward the bridge.

Some sort of shock, Aaron thinks, and sees movement by the wall ahead—it is Lory, up and staggering away from him. But she isn't going toward the corridor, she's going up a ramp into the ship. The clinic is where she belongs. Aaron starts after her, confident that the drug will slow her down. But his suit is awkward, he has not counted on that feral vitality. She stays ahead of him, she gains speed up the twisting tube as the gees let go. He pounds up after her, past the dormitory levels, past Stores; he is half-sailing now. Lory dives into the central freefall shaft—but not going straight, he sees her twist left, toward the bridge.

Cursing, Aaron follows her in. His feet miss the guides, he ricochets, has trouble regaining speed. Lory is a receding minnow-shape ahead of him, going like a streak. She shoots through the command-section sphincter, checks. Damn, she's closing it against him.

By the time he gets it open and goes through, the core shaft is empty. Aaron kicks on into the Astrogation dome. Nobody there. He climbs out of the freefall area and starts back around the computer corridor. Nobody here either. Ahlstrom's gleaming pets are untended. This has never happened before. It's like a ghost ship. Station after station is empty. The physics display-screen is running a calculation, unobserved.

A sound breaks the silence, coming from the next ring aft. Oh god, Bustamente's Commo room! Aaron can't find the inside door, he doubles back out into the corridor, races clumsily sternwards, terror in his guts as the sound rises to a scream.

The Commo room is open. Aaron plunges in, checks in horror. Lory is standing in the sacred gyro chamber. The scream is coming from the open gyro housings. Her arm jerks out, sending a stream of objects—headsets, jacks, wrenches—into the flying wheels.

"Stop!" He lunges for her, but the sound has risen to a terrible yammering. A death cry—the great pure beings who have spun there faultlessly for a decade holding their lifeline to Earth are in mortal agony. They clash, collide horribly. A cam shoots past him, buries itself in the wall. She has killed them, his mad sister.

Gripping her he stands there stunned, scarcely able to take in other damage. The housing of the main laser crystals is wrecked; they have been hit with something. That hardly matters now, Aaron thinks numbly. Without the gyros to aim them the beam is only an idiot's finger flailing across the stars.

"We, we'll go together, Arn," Lory hangs on him, weak now. "They can't—stop us any more."

Aaron's substrate takes over; he utters a howl and starts to shake her by the neck, squeezing, crushing—but is startled into stasis by a voice behind him, saying "Bustamente."

He wheels. It is Captain Yellaston.

"I will send . . . the red signal . . . now."

"You can't!" Aaron yells in rage. "You can't, it's broken! *She* broke it!" Preadolescent fury floods him, ebbs as he sees that remote, uncomprehending face.

"You will send . . . the red signal." The man is in shock, all right.

"Sir, we can't—we can't send anything right now." Aaron releases Lory, takes Yellaston's arm. Yellaston frowns down at him, purses his lips. A two-liter night. He lets himself be turned away, headed toward his quarters. Aaron is irrationally grateful: As long as Yellaston hasn't seen the enormity it isn't real. He pulls back the captain's glove, checks the pulse as they go. About sixty; slow but not arrhythmic.

"The technical capacity . . ." Yellaston mutters, going into his room. "If you have the efficiency . . . you'll wake up in the morning . . ."

"Please lie down awhile, Captain." Aaron closes the door, sees Lory wandering behind him. He takes her arm and starts back toward his office, resisting the faint urge to turn toward Gamma One. If he can only get to his office he can begin to function, decide what to do. What has hit *Centaur's* people, what did that alien do? A static discharge, maybe, like an electric eel? Better try his standard adrenergic stim-shot, if the heartrates are okay. That overwhelming attractant—he can feel it now, even here in Beta corridor on the far side of the ship. Like a pheromone, Aaron decides. That thing is a sessile life-form, maybe it attracts food, maybe it gets itself fertilized that way. Just happens that it works on man. A field, maybe, like gravity. Or some fantastically attenuated particle. The suits didn't stop it completely. I should seal it off, that's the first thing, he tells himself, leading Lory, docile now. They are passing Don's scoutship berth. But the *Beast* isn't here, it's god knows how many thousand miles away now, blatting out its message.

Someone is here—Don Purcell is standing by an access ramp, staring at the deck. Aaron drags Lory faster.

"Don! Commander, are you okay?"

Don's head turns to him; the grin is there, the eyes have smile-wrinkles. But Aaron sees his pupils are unequally dilated, like a poleaxed steer. How severe was that shock? He takes the unresisting wrist.

"Can you recognize me, Don? It's Aaron. It's Doc. You've had a physical shock, you shouldn't be wandering around." Pulse slow, like Yellaston's; no irregularity Aaron can catch. "I want you to come with me to the clinic."

The strong body doesn't move. Aaron pulls at him, realizes he can't budge him alone. He needs his syringe-kit, too.

"That's a medical order, Don. Report for treatment."

The smile slowly focusses on him, puzzled.

"The power," Don says in the voice he uses at chapel. "The hand of the Almighty on the deep . . ."

"See, Arn?" Lory reaches out toward Don, pats him. "He's changed. He's gentle." She smiles tremulously.

Aaron leads her on, wondering how seriously people have been hit. *Centaur* can sustain itself for days, that part's all right. He will not think of the more fearful hurt, the murdered gyros; Bustamente—Bustamente can do something, somehow. But how long are people going to remain in shock? How many of them got hit by that thing, who is functioning besides himself? Could it be permanent damage? Impossible, he tells himself firmly; a shock that severe would have finished poor Tighe. Impossible.

As he turns off to the clinic Lory suddenly pulls back. "No, Arn, this way!"

"We're going to the office, Lor. I have work to do."

"Oh no, Arn. Don't you *understand*? We're going now, together." Her voice is plaintive, with a loose, slurred quality. Aaron's training wakes up. Chemical supplementation, as Foy said—this is the time to get some answers from the subject.

"Sis, talk to me a minute, then we'll go. What happened to them, what happened to Mei-Lin and the others on the planet?"

"Mei-Lin?" she frowns.

"Yes, what did you see them do? You can tell me now, Lor. Did you see them out there?"

"Oh, yes . . ." She gives a vague little laugh. "I saw them. They left me in the ship, Arn. They, they didn't want me." Her lips quiver.

"What did they do, Lor?"

"Oh, they walked. Little Kuh had the video, I could see where they went. Up the hills, toward the, toward the beauty . . . It was hours, hours and hours. And then Mei-Lin and Liu went on ahead, I could see them running—Oh, Arn, I wanted to run too, you can't imagine how they look—"

"What happened then, Lor?"

"They took off their helmets and then the camera fell down, I guess the others were all running too. I could see their feet—it was like a mountain of jewels in the sun—" Tears are running down her face, she rubs her fist at them like a child.

"What did you see then? What did the jewel-thing do to them?"

"It didn't do anything." She smiles, sniffing. "They just touched it, you know, with their minds. You'll *see,* Arn. Please—let's go now."

"In a minute, Lor. Tell me, did they fight?"

"Oh, no!" Her eyes widen at him. "No! Oh, I made that up to protect it. No hurting any more, never. They came back so gentle, so happy. They were all changed, they shed all that. It's waiting for us, Arn, see? It wants to deliver us. We'll be truly human at last." She sighs. "Oh, I wanted so much to go, too, it was terrible. I had to tie myself, even in the suit. I *had* to bring it back to you. And I did, didn't I?"

"You got that thing in the scouter all by yourself, Lor?"

She nods, dream-eyed. "I found a little one, I poked

it with the front-end loader." The contrast between her words and her face is weird.

"What were Kuh and his men doing all this time? Didn't they try to stop you?"

"Oh no, they watched. They were around. Please Arn, come *on*."

"How long did it take you!"

"Oh, days, Arn, it was so hard. I could only do a little at a time."

"You mean they didn't recover for days? What about that tape, Lor; you faked it, didn't you?"

"I, I edited it a little. He wasn't . . . interested." Her eyes shift evasively. Control returning. "Arn, don't be *afraid*. The bad things are over now. Can't you feel it, the goodness?"

He can—it's there, pulling at him faint and bliss-laden. He shudders awake, discovers he has let her lead him nearly to the core, toward Gamma One. Angrily he makes himself grab the handrail and start hauling her back toward the clinic. It is like moving through glue, his body doesn't want to.

"No, Arn, no!" She pulls back, sobbing. "You *have* to, I worked so hard—"

He concentrates grimly on his feet. The clinic door is ahead now, to his infinite relief he can see Coby inside at the desk.

"You aren't coming!" Lory wails and jerks violently out of his grasp. "You—Oh—"

He jumps for her, but she is running away again, running like a goddamned deer. Aaron checks himself. He cannot chase after her now, he has evaded his duty too long as it is. Days, she said. This is appalling. And they were walking around. Brain damage . . . Don't think of it.

He goes into the office. Coby is looking at him.

"My sister is in psychotic fugue," Aaron tells him. "She damaged our communication equipment. Sedation ineffective—" He perceives he is acting irrationally, he should tackle the major medical situation first.

"How many people got shocked by that thing, Bill?"

Coby's noncommittal gaze does not change. Finally

he says dully, "Shock. Oh, yes. Shock." His lip twists in a ghostly sneer.

Oh, god no . . . Coby was in that corridor, too.

"Jesus, Bill, did it get you? I'm going to give you a shot of AD-twelve. Unless you have other ideas?"

Coby's eyes are following him. Maybe he isn't as severely affected, Aaron thinks.

"Post coitum tristum." Coby's voice is very low. "I am tristum."

"What did it do to you, Bill, can you tell me?"

The silent, sad stare continues. Just as Aaron opens the hypo-kit Coby says clearly, "I know a ripe corpus luteum when I see one." He gives a faint, nasty chuckle.

"What?" Obscene visions leap to life in Aaron's head as he bares Coby's elbow and sends the epidermal jet into the vein. "Did you, you didn't have some sort of intercourse with that thing, Bill?"

"In-ter-course?" Coby echoes in a whisper. "No . . . not us, anyway. If somebody had . . . in-ter-course it was god, maybe . . . Or a planet . . . Not us . . . It had *us*."

His pulse is slow, skin cold. "What do you mean, Bill?"

Coby's face quivers, he stares up into Aaron's eyes, fighting to hang on to consciousness. "Say we were carrying it . . . carrying a load of jizzum in our heads, I guess . . . And the jizzum meets . . . the queen couzy, the queen couzy of all time . . . and it jumps . . . jumps across. It makes some kind of holy . . . zygote, out there . . . see? Only we're left . . . empty . . . What happens to a sperm's tail . . . afterwards?"

"Take it easy, Bill." Aaron will not listen, oh no, not to delirium. His best diagnostician raving.

Coby emits another ghastly snicker. "Good old Aaron," he whispers. "You didn't . . ." His eyes go blank.

"Bill, try to pull yourself together. Stay right there. People are in shock, they're wandering around disoriented. I have work to do, can you hear me? Stay here, I'll be back."

Visions of himself hustling through the ship, reviving people—more important, sealing off that corridor, too. He loads a kit of stim-hypos, adds cardiotropics, detoxicants. An hour too late, Dr. Aaron Kaye is on the job. He draws hot brew for them both. Coby doesn't look.

"Drink up, Bill. I'll be back."

He sets off to Stores, steering against the pull from Gamma One. It is weak here. He can make it quite easily. Is it in refractory phase, maybe? Shot its bolt. How long to recovery? Better attend to that first, can't let it get them all over again.

Miriamne Stein is at her desk, her face absolutely quiet.

"It's Doc, Miri. You've had a shock, this will help you." He hopes, administering it to her passive arm. Her empty eyes slowly turn. "I'm checking out some EVA rope, see? I'll leave you a receipt right here, Miri, look. You stay there until you feel better."

Outside, he lets himself start across the ship, going with the pull. Joy opens in him, it is like a delicious sliding, like letting go sexually in his head . . . Am I acting rationally? He probes himself, scared. Yes—he can make himself turn, make himself go forward toward the first bow-ramp. His plan is to close all the ports the crowd left open on their way into the corridor. Fourteen. After that—after that he can, he knows, vent the air from the inboard side. Depressurizing will kill it, of course. The sensible thing to do. No, surely that isn't necessary? He will think about it later, something is hurting him right now.

At the bow-ramp his head still feels okay, the thing's . . . lure is weak. The port is open; Don probably came this way. Cautiously, Aaron risks going down to it without tying his rope. All right; he has it swinging shut. As it closes he peeks out down the corridor. A mess, no people he can see—but the rosy living radiance—his heart misses, jumps—and the port closes almost on his nose.

A near thing. He must take no chances on the next one—it will be nearer to that marvelous light, will be in fact behind the command console where Yellaston was.

Aaron finds his feet hurrying, stops himself at the last turn in the ramp and ties one end of the tether to a wall-hold. The other end he knots around his waist. Multiple knottings, must not be able to untie these in a hurry.

It's well he did so, he finds; he is already stepping into the corridor itself, stumbling on helmets, gloves, cables. The great flare of warm light is about twenty meters ahead. He must go back, go back and close the port. He stops himself at the command console and looks up at the videoscreen, still focussed on *China Flower*'s fiery heart. It *is* like jewels in there, he sees, awestruck—great softly glowing globes, dazzling, changing color as he looks . . . some are dark, like a heap of fiery embers burning out. *Dying?* Grief wells up in him, he puts his hand up to hide it, looks away. There are his useless, evil canisters . . . and the corridor a shambles. Aftermath of a stampede . . . What was Coby muttering about, sperm. They went through here, tails thrashing—

"Arn—you came!"

From nowhere Lory is hugging his arm.

"Oh, Arn dear, I waited—"

"Get out of here, Lor!" But she is working at his waist, trying to untie knots. Her face is ecstatic—a load of jizzum in the head, all right. "Go away, Lor. I'm going to depressurize."

"We'll be *together*, don't be afraid."

Angrily he pushes her behind him. "I'm going to vent the air, can't you hear me? The air is going out!"

He tries to head her back toward the ramp, but she twists away from him, gasping, "Oh, Arn, please Arn, I can't—" And she is running to the light, to *China*'s hatch.

"Come back here!" He runs at her, is brought up by the rope. She wavers just beyond him outlined in pale fire, turning, turning, her fists at her mouth, sobbing, "I—I'm going—alone—"

"No! Lor, wait!"

His own hands are ripping at the knots but she is going, slipping away from him across the tangled floor.

"No, no—" The warm light enwraps her, she has turned, is walking into it, is gone—

A harsh warble breaks into his ears, waking him. He staggers back, finally makes out that the flashings on the console are launch warnings. Somebody is in *China Flower,* taking off!

"Who's in there? Stop!" He flips channels at random. "You in the ship, answer me!"

"Good-bye . . . boy." Bustamente's voice echoes from the speakers.

"Ray, are you in there? This is Aaron, Ray, come out, you don't know what you're doing—"

"I know to . . . set course. Keep your shit . . . world." The deep voice is flat, mechanical.

"Come out here! Ray, we need you. Please listen, Ray—the gyros are broken. The *gyros.*"

". . . Tough."

A heavy metal purring shivers the walls.

"Ray, wait!" Aaron screams. "My sister is in there, she'll be killed—your hatch is open! I'll be killed too, please, Ray, let her come out. I'll close it. Lory! Lory, get out!"

His eyes are seeking desperately for the hatch control, his hands tear at the knots.

"She can come, too." A deathlike chuckle—another lighter voice briefly there, too. Ray's women—is Soli in there? The knots are giving.

"I'm going to . . . that planet . . . boy."

"Ray, you'll wake up a million miles in space, for Christ's sake wait!" He jerks, pulls loose—he has to get there, get Lory out—he has to save that living beauty, that promise—

Other lights are flashing, there is a shudder in the walls. *The ship, Lory,* his brain cries faintly. He pulls the rope free and sees her shadow, her body wavering out blue against the radiance waiting there, waiting for him. With his last sanity he strikes the hatch lever, shoves it home.

The big hatch starts to slide shut across the radiant port.

"No, wait! No!" Aaron starts to run to it, his hand

still grasping the rope, he is running toward all he has ever longed for—but the walls clang, scrape thunderously, and a wind buffets him sideways. He grips the rope in reflex, sees Lory stagger and start to slide in the howling air, everything is sliding toward the closing hatch. *China Flower* is going, falling away—taking it from him. They will all be blown out after her—but as Lory nears it the hatch slides home, the last ray vanishes.

The wind stops, the corridor is totally silent.

He stands there, a foolish man holding a rope, knowing that all sweetness is fading. Life itself is falling out to the dark beneath him, going away forever. Come back, he whispers, aching. Oh, come back.

Lory stirs. He lets fall the idiotic rope, goes to her bowed under a loss beyond bearing. What have I saved, what have I lost? Going away, fainter, fainter yet.

She looks up. Her face is clear, empty. Very young. All gone now, the load in her head . . . A feeling of dumb weight comes over him. It is *Centaur,* the whole wonderful ship he had been so proud of, hanging over him mute and flaccid in the dark. The life-spark gone away. Voiceless, unfindable in the icy wastes . . . His gut knows it is forever now, nothing will ever be all right again.

Gently he helps Lory up and starts walking with her to noplace, she trustful to his hand; little sister as she had been long ago. As they move away from the corridor his eyes notice a body lying by the wall. It is Tighe.

IV

. . . Dr. Aaron Kaye recording. The ghosts, the new things I mean, they're starting to go. I see them quite well now awake. Yesterday—wait, was it yesterday? Yes, because Tim has only been here one night, I brought him in yesterday. His, his body, I mean. It was his ghost I saw—Christ, I keep calling them that—the *things,* the new things, I mean. The ghost is in Tim's bed. But I saw his go, it was still out in Beta corridor.

Did I say they're fairly stationary? I forget what I said. Maybe I should go over it, I have the time. They're more or less transparent, of course, even at the end. They float. I think they're partly out of the ship. It's hard to tell their size, like a projection or afterimage. They seem big, say six or eight meters in diameter, but once or twice I've thought they may be very small. They're alive, you can tell that. They don't respond or communicate. They're not . . . rational. Not at all. They change, too, they take on colors or something from your mind. Did I say that? I'm not sure they're really visible at all, maybe the mind senses them and constructs an appearance. But recognizable. You can see . . . traces. I can identify most of them. Tim's was by ramp seven. It was partly Tim and partly something else, very alien. It seemed to swell up and float away out through the hull, as if it was getting closer and farther at the same time. The first one to go, so far as I know. Except Tighe's, I dreamed that. They do *not* dissipate. It throbbed—no, that isn't quite right. It swelled and floated. Away.

They're not ghosts, I should repeat that.

What I think they are—my subjective impression, I mean, a possible explanatory hypothesis—Oh, hell, I don't have to talk that way any more. What I think they are is some kind of energy-thing, some—

What I think they are is blastomeres.

Holy zygotes, Coby said. I don't think they're holy. They're just there, growing. Definitely not spirits or ghosts or higher essences, they're not the *person* at all. They're a, a combined product. They develop. They stay at the site awhile and then . . . move on out.

Maybe I should record the order they go in, maybe it will correlate with the person's condition. That would be of scientific interest. The whole thing is of deep scientific interest, of course. Who will it be of scientific interest to? That's a good question. Maybe somebody will stumble on this ship in about a thousand years. Hello, friend. Are you human? If you are you won't be long. Kindly listen to Dr. Aaron Kaye before you—Oh, god, wait—

This is Dr. Aaron Kaye recording a message of deep scientific interest. Where was I? It doesn't matter. Tim—I mean Commander Timofaev Bron died today. I mean Tim himself. That's the first actual death except Tighe. Oh, and Bachi—I reported him, didn't I? Yes. The others are still functioning more or less. In a vegetable way. They feed themselves now and then. Since the meals stopped I carry rations around. We go over the ship every day or so. I'm pretty sure no one else has died. Some of them are still playing cards in Commons, they even say a word or two sometimes. Some cards have fallen down, the ten of spades has been by Don's foot for days. I made them drink water yesterday. I'm afraid they're badly dehydrated . . . Kawabata's the worst off, I think, he's sleeping in a soil bed. Earth to earth . . . He'll probably go soon. I have to learn to run all that, I suppose. If I go on.

. . . I know now I'll never be able to fix that laser. Christ, I spent a week in Ray's spookhouse. Funny thing, they gave us a big nondirectional Mayday transmitter. That means, "Come here and rescue us." But how can I send, "Stay the hell away?" Flaw in the program. That's all too short-range, anyway . . . I could blow up the ship, I guess I could work that out. What good would it do? It wouldn't stop them coming. They'd figure we had an accident. Too bad, hazards of space. Baby, you'll find out . . .

. . . Wonder where Ray is now, how long he lasted? His, his thing is here, of course. In Gamma One. The women too. I found Soli's, it's, no, I think we won't talk about that. They were with him, their bodies, I mean. *Them* . . . He was so strong, he did something, he acted, afterward. No use of course. The dead saving the dead. Help me make it through the night—quit that.

. . . Functioning, we were discussing functioning. The most intact is Yellaston. I mean, he isn't intact at all but we talk a little, sort of, when I go up there. Maybe a lifetime practice in carrying on with half of his cortex shot. I think he understands. It's not a highly technical concept, after all. He knows he's dying. He saw it as death, the whole thing. Intuition in his locked-up guts, the fear—Sex equals death. How right you are, old man. Funny, I used to treat patients for thinking that. Therapy—Of course it was a different, let's say order of sex. He's quit drinking. The thing he was holding in, the load, it's gone . . . I think of what's left as him, damn it, it *is* him, the human part. I've seen his, his product, it's by the bow-port. It's very strange. I wonder, has he seen it? Does a spent sperm recognize the blastomere? I think he must have. I found him crying, once. Maybe it was joy, I don't think so . . .

. . . Hello, friend. This is Dr. Aaron Kaye, your friendly scientific reporter. Dr. Aaron Kaye is also getting the tiniest bit ethanolized, maybe you'll forgive it. It has occurred to me as a matter of scientific justice that Coby deserves credit for the, the formulation of the hypothesis. Superb diagnostician, Coby, to the end. That's Dr. William F. Coby, late of Johns Hopkins/M.I.T Originator of Coby's final solution—hypothesis, I mean. Remember his name, friend. While you can. I tried to get him to record this but he doesn't talk any more. I think he's right; I know he's right. He still functions, though, in a dying way. Goes to the narcotics locker quite openly. I let him. Maybe he's trying something. Why is he so intact? Didn't he have much of whatever it is they lost, not much jizzum there? No—that's not fair. Not even true . . . Funny thing, I find myself liking him now, really liking him. Dangerous stuff all gone, I guess. Comment on me. Call me Lory—no, we aren't going to talk about Lory, either. We were talking about, I was talking about Coby. His hypothesis. Listen, friend. You on your way with a load in your head.

Coby's right, I know he's right. We're gametes.

Nothing but gametes. The dimorphic set—call it sperm. Two types, little boy sperms, little girl sperms—half of the germ-plasm of . . . something. Not complete beings at all. Half of the gametes of some . . . creatures, some race. Maybe they live in space, I think so. The, their zygotes do. Maybe they aren't even intelligent. Say they use planets to breed on, like amphibians going to the water. And they sowed their primordial seed-stuff around here, their milt and roe among the stars. On suitable planets. And the stuff germinated. And after the usual interval—say three billion years, that's what it took us, didn't it?—the milt, the sperm evolved to *motility*, see? And we made it to the stars. To the roe-planet. To fertilize them. And that's all we are, the whole damn thing—the evolving, the achieving and fighting and hoping—all the pain and effort, just to get us there with the loads of jizzum in our heads. Nothing but sperms' tails. Human beings—does a sperm think it's somebody, too? Those beautiful egg-things, the creatures on that planet, evolving in their own way for millions of years . . . maybe they think and dream, too, maybe they think they're people. All the whole thing, just to make something else, all for nothing—

. . . Excuse me. This is Dr. Aaron Kaye, recording two more deaths. They are Dr. James Kawabata and Quartermaster Miriamne Stein. I found her when I was taking Kawabata's body to cold Stores. They'll all be there, you'll find them, friend. Fifty-five icicles and one dust pile . . . maybe. Cause of death—have I been reporting cause of death? Cause of death, acute—Oh, hell, what does a sperm's tail die of? Acute loss of ability to live any more. Acute post-functional irrelevance . . . Symptoms; maybe you'd like to know the symptoms. You should be interested. The symptoms start after brief contact with a certain life-form from the Alpha planet—did I mention that there does seem to have been momentary physical contact, apparently through the forehead? The gross symptoms are disorientation, apathy, some aphasia, ataxia, anorexia. All responses depressed; aprosexia, speech echolalic. Reflexes weakly present, no typical catatonia. Cardiac functions subnormal, nonacute. Clinically—I've been able to test six of them—clinically the EEG shows generalized flattening, asynchrony. Early theta and alpha deficits. It is unlike, repeat totally unlike, post-ECS syndrome. Symptoms cannot be interpreted as due to a physical shock, electric or otherwise. Adrenergic systems most affected, cholinergic relatively less so. Adrenal insufficiency is not, repeat not, confirmed by hormonal bioassay. Oh hell—they've been drained, that's what it is. Drained of something . . . something vital. Prognosis . . . yes.

The prognosis is death.

This is of great scientific interest, friend. But you won't believe it, of course. You're on your way there, aren't you? Nothing will stop you, you have reasons. All kinds of reasons—saving the race, building a new world, national honor, personal glory, scientific truth, dreams, hopes, plans—does every little sperm have its reasons, thrashing up the pipe?

It calls, you see. The roe calls us across the light-years, don't ask me how. It's even calling Dr. Aaron Kaye, the sperm who said no—Oh, Christ, I can feel it, the sweet pull. *Why did I let it go?* . . . Excuse me. Dr. Aaron Kaye is having another drink now. Quite a few, actually. Yellaston was right, it helps . . . The infinite variety of us, all for nothing. Where was I? . . . We make our rounds, I check them all. They don't move much any more. I look at the new things, too . . . Lory comes with me, she helps me carry things. Like she used to, little sister—we're particularly not going to talk about Lory. The things, the zygotes—three more of them went away today, Kawabata's and the two Danes. Don's is still in Commons, I think it's going soon. Do they leave when the, the *person* dies? I think that's just coincidence. We're totally . . . *irrelevant,* afterward. The zygote remains near the site of impregnation for a variable period before moving on to implant. Where do they implant, in space, maybe? Where do they get born?—Oh, god, what are they like, the creatures that generated us, that we die to form? Can a gamete look at a king? Are they brutes or angels? Ah, Christ, it isn't fair, *it isn't fair!*

 . . . Sorry, friend. I'm all right now. Don Purcell collapsed today, I left him in Commons. I visit my patients daily. Most of them are still sitting. Sitting at their stations, in their graves. We do what we can, Lory and I. *Making gentle the life of this world* . . . It may be of great scientific interest that they all saw it different, the egg-things I mean. Don said it was god, Coby saw ova. Åhlstrom was whispering about the tree Yggdrasil. Bruce Jang saw Mei-Lin there. Yellaston saw death. Tighe saw Mother, I think. All Dr. Aaron Kaye saw was colored lights. Why didn't I go, too? Who knows. Statistical phenomenon. Defective tail. My foot got caught . . . Lory saw utopia, heaven on earth, I guess. We will not talk about Lory . . . She goes 'round with me, looking at the dying sperms, our friends. All the things in their rooms, the personal life, all this ship we were so proud of. *Mono no aware,* that's the pathos of things, Kawabata told me. The wristwatch after the wearer has died, the eyeglasses . . . the pathos of all our things now.

. . . Yes, Dr. Aaron Kaye is getting fairly well pissed, friend. Dr. Aaron Kaye, you see, is avoiding contemplating what he'll do, afterward . . . after they are all gone. Coby broke his leg today. I found him, I think he was pleased when I put him to bed. He didn't seem to be in much pain. His, the thing he made, it went away quite a while ago, I guess I haven't been recording too well. A lot of them have gone. Not Yellaston's last time I looked. He's up in Astrogation, I mean Yellaston himself. Gazing out the dome. I know he wants to end there. Ah Christ, the poor old tiger, the poor ape, everything Lory hated—all gone now. Who cares about a sperm's personality? Answer: Another sperm . . . Dr. Kaye grows maudlin. Dr. Kaye weeps, in fact. Remember that, friend. It has scientific interest. What will Dr. Kaye do, afterward? It will be quiet around here on the good ship *Centaur,* which will probably last forever, unless it falls into a star . . . Will Dr. Kaye live out the rest of his life here, twenty-six trillion miles from his home testis? Reading, listening to music, tending his garden, writing notes of great scientific interest? Fifty-five frozen bodies and one skeleton. Keep your eye on the skeleton, friend . . . or check on that last scoutship, *Alpha.* Will Dr. Kaye one day take off in little old *Alpha,* trying to head for somewhere? Where? You guess . . . Tail-end Charlie, last man in

the oviduct. Over the viaduct, via the oviduct. Excuse me.
. . . Not the last. Not at all, let's not forget all those
fleets of ships, they'll start from Earth when the green
signal gets there. And they'll keep on coming for a
while anyway . . . The green got sent, didn't it, no
matter how we tried? The goal of man's desiring. No
way to stop it. No hope at all, really.

But of course it's only a handful, the ones that will
ever make it to the planet, compared to the total population of Earth. About the proportion of one ejaculandum
to total sperm production, wouldn't you say? Should
compute sometime, great scientific interest there. So most
of the egg-creatures will die unfertilized, too. Nature's
notorious wastefulness. Fifty million eggs, a billion sperm
—one salmon . . .

. . . What happens to the people who don't go, the
ones who stay on Earth, all the rest of the race? Let us
speculate, Dr. Kaye. What happens to unused sperm?
Stuck in testes, die of overheating. Reabsorbed. Remind
you of anything? Calcutta, say. Rio de Janeiro, Los An-
geles . . . Previews. Born too soon or too late—too
bad. Rot away unused. Function fulfilled, organs atro-
phy . . . End of it all, just rot away. *Not even knowing*—thinking they were people, thinking they had a
chance . . .

Dr. Kaye is getting rather conclusively intoxicated,
friend. Dr. Kaye is also getting tired of talking to you.
What good will it do you on your way up the pipe? Can
you stop, man? Can you? Ha ha. As—someone used to
say . . . God damn it, why can't you try? Can't you
stop, can't you stay human even if we're—Oh Lord, can
a half of something, can a gamete build a culture? I
don't think so . . . You poor doomed bastard with a
load in your head, you'll get there or die trying—

Excuse me. Lory stumbled a lot today . . . Little
sister, you were a good sperm, you swam hard. You
made the connection. She wasn't crazy, you know.
Ever, really. She knew something was wrong with us . . .
Healed, made whole? All those months . . . a wall
away from heaven, the golden breasts of god. The end
of pain, the queen couzy . . . fighting it all the way . . .

Oh, Lory, stay with me, don't die—*Christ, the pull, the terrible sweet pull—*

. . . This is Dr. Aaron Kaye signing off. Maybe my condition is of deep scientific interest . . . I don't dream any more.

Houston, Houston, Do You Read?

Lorimer gazes around the big crowded cabin, trying to listen to the voices, trying also to ignore the twitch in his insides that means he is about to remember something bad. No help; he lives it again, that long-ago moment. Himself running blindly—or was he pushed?—into the strange toilet at Evanston Junior High. His fly open, his dick in his hand, he can still see the grey zipper edge of his jeans around his pale exposed pecker. The hush. The sickening wrongness of shapes, faces turning. The first blaring giggle. *Girls*. He was in the *girls' can*.

He flinches now wryly, so many years later, not looking at the women's faces. The cabin curves around over his head, surrounding him with their alien things: the beading rack, the twins' loom, Andy's leather work, the damned kudzu vine wriggling everywhere, the chickens. So cosy. . . . Trapped, he is. Irretrievably trapped for life in everything he does not enjoy. Structurelessness. Personal trivia, unmeaning intimacies. The claims he can somehow never meet. Ginny: *You never talk to me* . . . Ginny, love, he thinks involuntarily. The hurt doesn't come.

Bud Geirr's loud chuckle breaks in on him. Bud is joking with some of them, out of sight around a bulkhead. Dave is visible, though. Major Norman Davis on the far side of the cabin, his bearded profile bent toward a small dark woman Lorimer can't quite focus on. But Dave's head seems oddly tiny and sharp, in fact the whole cabin looks unreal. A cackle bursts out from the "ceiling"—the bantam hen in her basket.

At this moment Lorimer becomes sure he has been drugged.

Curiously, the idea does not anger him. He leans or rather tips back, perching cross-legged in the zero gee, letting his gaze go to the face of the woman he has been talking with. Connie. Constantia Morelos. A tall moon-faced woman in capacious green pajamas. He has never really cared for talking to women. Ironic.

"I suppose," he says aloud, "it's possible that in some sense we are not here."

That doesn't sound too clear, but she nods interestedly. *She's watching my reactions,* Lorimer tells himself. *Women are natural poisoners.* Has he said that aloud too? Her expression doesn't change. His vision is taking on a pleasing local clarity. Connie's skin strikes him as quite fine, healthy-looking. Olive tan even after two years in space. She was a farmer, he recalls. Big pores, but without the caked look he associates with women her age.

"You probably never wore make-up," he says. She looks puzzled. "Face paint, powder. None of you have."

"Oh!" Her smile shows a chipped front tooth. "Oh yes, I think Andy has."

"Andy?"

"For plays. Historical plays, Andy's good at that."

"Of course. Historical plays."

Lorimer's brain seems to be expanding, letting in light. He is understanding actively now, the myriad bits and pieces linking into patterns. Deadly patterns, he perceives; but the drug is shielding him in some way. Like an amphetamine high without the pressure. Maybe it's something they use socially? No, they're watching, too.

"Space bunnies, I still don't dig it," Bud Geirr laughs infectiously. He has a friendly buoyant voice people like; Lorimer still likes it after two years.

"You chicks have kids back home, what do your

folks think about you flying around out here with old Andy, h'mm?" Bud floats into view, his arm draped around a twin's shoulders. The one called Judy Paris, Lorimer decides; the twins are hard to tell. She drifts passively at an angle to Bud's big body: a jut-breasted plain girl in flowing yellow pajamas, her black hair raying out. Andy's red head swims up to them. He is holding a big green spaceball, looking about sixteen.

"Old Andy." Bud shakes his head, his grin flashing under his thick dark mustache. "When I was your age folks didn't let their women fly around with me."

Connie's lips quirk faintly. In Lorimer's head the pieces slide toward pattern. I know, he thinks. Do you know I know? His head is vast and crystalline, very nice really. Easier to think. Women. . . . No compact generalisation forms in his mind, only a few speaking faces on a matrix of pervasive irrelevance. Human, of course. Biological necessity. Only so, so . . . diffuse? Pointless? . . . His sister Amy, *soprano con tremulo: Of course women could contribute as much as men if you'd treat us as equals. You'll see!* And then marrying that idiot the second time. Well, now he can see.

"Kudzu vines," he says aloud. Connie smiles. How they all smile.

"How 'boot that?" Bud says happily, "Ever think we'd see chicks in zero gee, hey, Dave? Artits-stico. Woo-ee!" Across the cabin Dave's bearded head turns to him, not smiling.

"And ol' Andy's had it all to his self. Stunt your growth, lad." He punches Andy genially on the arm, Andy catches himself on the bulkhead. Bud can't be drunk, Lorimer thinks; not on that fruit cider. But he doesn't usually sound so much like a stage Texan either. A drug.

"Hey, no offense," Bud is saying earnestly to the boy, "I mean that. You have to forgive one underprilly, underprivileged brother. These chicks are good people. Know what?" he tells the girl, "You could look stu-pen-dous if you fix yourself up a speck. Hey, I can show you, old Buddy's a expert. I hope you don't mind my saying that. As a matter of fact you look real stupendous to me right now."

He hugs her shoulders, flings out his arm and hugs Andy too. They float upwards in his grasp, Judy grinning excitedly, almost pretty.

"Let's get some more of that good stuff." Bud propels them both toward the serving rack which is decorated for the occasion with sprays of greens and small real daisies.

"Happy New Year! Hey, Happy New Year, y'all!"

Faces turn, more smiles. Genuine smiles, Lorimer thinks, maybe they really like their new years. He feels he has infinite time to examine every event, the implications evolving in crystal facets. I'm an echo chamber. Enjoyable, to be the observer. But others are observing too. They've started something here. Do they realise? So vulnerable, three of us, five of them in this fragile ship. They don't know. A dread unconnected to action lurks behind his mind.

"By god we made it," Bud laughs. "You space chickies, I have to give it to you. I commend you, by god I say it. We wouldn't be here, wherever we are. Know what, I jus' might decide to stay in the service after all. Think they have room for old Bud in your space program, sweetie?"

"Knock that off, Bud," Dave says quietly from the far wall. "I don't want to hear us use the name of the Creator like that." The full chestnut beard gives him a patriarchal gravity. Dave is forty-six, a decade older than Bud and Lorimer. Veteran of six successful missions.

"Oh my apologies, Major Dave old buddy." Bud chuckles intimately to the girl. "Our commanding ossifer. Stupendous guy. Hey, Doc!" he calls, "How's your attitude? You making out dinko?"

"Cheers," Lorimer hears his voice reply, the complex stratum of his feelings about Bud rising like a kraken in the moonlight of his mind. The submerged silent thing he has about them all, all the Buds and Daves and big, indomitable, cheerful, able, disciplined, slow-minded mesomorphs he has cast his life with. Meso-ectos, he corrected himself; astronauts aren't muscleheads. They like him, he has been careful about that. Liked him well enough to get him on *Sunbird,* to make him the official scientist on the first circumsolar mission. That little Doc Lorimer, he's cool, he's on the team. No shit from Lorimer, not like those other scientific assholes. He does the bit well with his small neat build and his dead-pan remarks. And the years of turning out for the bowling, the volleyball, the tennis, the skeet, the skiing that broke his ankle, the touch football that broke his collarbone. Watch that Doc, he's a sneaky one. And the big men banging him on the back, accepting him. Their token scientist . . . The trouble is, he isn't any kind of scientist any more. Living off his postdoctoral plasma work, a lucky hit. He hasn't really been into the math for years, he isn't up to it now. Too many other interests, too much time spent explaining elementary stuff. I'm a half-jock, he thinks. A foot taller and a hundred pounds heavier and I'd be just like them. One of them. An alpha. They probably sense it underneath, the beta bile. Had the jokes worn a shade thin in *Sunbird,* all that year going out? A year of Bud and Dave playing gin. That damn exercycle, gearing it up too tough for me. They didn't mean it, though. We were a team.

The memory of gaping jeans flicks at him, the painful end part—the grinning faces waiting for him when he stumbled out. The howls, the dribble down his leg. Being cool, pretending to laugh too. You shit-heads, I'll show you. I am not a girl.

Bud's voice rings out, chanting "And a hap-pee New Year to you-all down there!" Parody of the oily NASA tone. "Hey, why don't we shoot 'em a signal? Greetings to all you Earthlings, I mean, all you little Lunies. Happy New Year in the good year whatsis." He snuffles comically. "There is a Santy Claus, Houston, ye-ew nevah saw nothin' like this! Houston, wherever you are," he sings out. "Hey, Houston! Do you read?"

In the silence Lorimer sees Dave's face set into Major Norman Davis, commanding.

And without warning he is suddenly back there, back a year ago in the cramped, shook-up command module of *Sunbird,* coming out from behind the sun. It's the drug doing this, he thinks as memory closes around him, it's so real. Stop. He tries to hang onto reality, to the sense of trouble building underneath.

—But he can't, he is *there,* hovering behind Dave and Bud in the triple couches, as usual avoiding his official station in the middle, seeing beside them their reflections against blackness in the useless port window. The outer layer has been annealed, he can just make out a bright smear that has to be Spica floating through the image of Dave's head, making the bandage look like a kid's crown.

"Houston, Houston, *Sunbird,*" Dave repeats; *"Sunbird* calling Houston. Houston, do you read? Come in, Houston."

The minutes start by. They are giving it seven out, seven back; seventy-eight million miles, ample margin.

"The high gain's shot, that's what it is," Bud says cheerfully. He says it almost every day.

"No way." Dave's voice is patient, also as usual. "It checks out. Still too much crap from the sun, isn't that right, Doc?"

"The residual radiation from the flare is just about in line with us," Lorimer says. "They could have a hard time sorting us out." For the thousandth time he registers his own faint, ridiculous gratification at being consulted.

"Shit, we're outside Mercury." Bud shakes his head. "How we gonna find out who won the Series?"

He often says that too. A ritual, out here in eternal night. Lorimer watches the sparkle of Spica drift by the reflection of Bud's curly face-bush. His own whiskers are scant and scraggly, like a blond Fu Manchu. In the aft corner of the window is a striped glare that must be the remains of their port energy accumulators, fried off in the solar explosion that hit them a month ago and fused the outer layers of their windows. That was when Dave cut his head open on the sexlogic panel. Lorimer had been banged in among the gravity wave experiment, he still doesn't trust the readings. Luckily the particle stream has missed one piece of the front window;

they still have about twenty degrees of clear vision straight ahead. The brilliant web of the Pleiades shows there, running off into a blur of light.

Twelve minutes . . . thirteen. The speaker sighs and clicks emptily. Fourteen. Nothing.

"*Sunbird* to Houston, *Sunbird* to Houston. Come in, Houston. *Sunbird* out." Dave puts the mike back in its holder. "Give it another twenty-four."

They wait ritually. Tomorrow Packard will reply. Maybe.

"Be good to see old Earth again," Bud remarks.

"We're not using any more fuel on attitude," Dave reminds him. "I trust Doc's figures."

It's not my figures, it's the elementary facts of celestial mechanics, Lorimer thinks; in October there's only one place for Earth to be. He never says it. Not to a man who can fly two-body solutions by intuition once he knows where the bodies are. Bud is a good pilot and a better engineer; Dave is the best there is. He takes no pride in it. "The Lord helps us, Doc, if we let Him."

"Going to be a bitch docking if the radar's screwed up," Bud says idly. They all think about that for the hundredth time. It will be a bitch. Dave will do it. That was why he is hoarding fuel.

The minutes tick off.

"That's it," Dave says—and a voice fills the cabin, shockingly.

"Judy?" It is high and clear. A girl's voice.

"Judy, I'm so glad we got you. What are you doing on this band?"

Bud blows out his breath; there is a frozen instant before Dave snatches up the mike.

"*Sunbird*, we read you. This is Mission *Sunbird* calling Houston, ah, *Sunbird One* calling Houston Ground Control. Identify, who are you? Can you relay our signal? Over."

"Some skip," Bud says. "Some incredible ham."

"Are you in trouble, Judy?" the girl's voice asks. "I can't hear, you sound terrible. Wait a minute."

"This is United States Space Mission *Sunbird One*," Dave repeats. "Mission *Sunbird* calling Houston Space

Center. You are dee-exxing our channel. Identify, repeat identify yourself and say if you can relay to Houston. Over."

"Dinko, Judy, try it again," the girl says.

Lorimer abruptly pushes himself up to the Lurp, the Long-Range Particle Density Cumulator experiment, and activates its shaft motor. The shaft whines, jars; lucky it was retracted during the flare, lucky it hasn't fused shut. He sets the probe pulse on max and begins a rough manual scan.

"You are intercepting official traffic from the United States space mission to Houston Control," Dave is saying forcefully. "If you cannot relay to Houston get off the air, you are committing a federal offence. Say again, can you relay our signal to Houston Space Center? Over."

"You still sound terrible," the girl says. "What's Houston? Who's talking, anyway? You know we don't have much time." Her voice is sweet but very nasal.

"Jesus, that's close," Bud says. "That is close."

"Hold it." Dave twists around to Lorimer's improvised radarscope.

"There." Lorimer points out a tiny stable peak at the extreme edge of the read-out slot, in the transcoronal scatter. Bud cranes too.

"A bogey!"

"Somebody else out here."

"Hello, hello? We have you now," the girl says. "Why are you so far out? Are you dinko, did you catch the flare?"

"Hold it," warns Dave. "What's the status, Doc?"

"Over three hundred thousand kilometers, guesstimated. Possibly headed away from us, going around the sun. Could be cosmonauts, a Soviet mission?"

"Out to beat us. They missed."

"With a *girl?*" Bud objects.

"They've done that. You taping this, Bud?"

"Roger-r-r." He grins. "That sure didn't sound like a Russky chick. Who the hell's Judy?"

Dave thinks for a second, clicks on the mike. "This is Major Norman Davis commanding United States spacecraft *Sunbird One.* We have you on scope. Request you identify yourself. Repeat, who are you? Over."

"Judy, stop joking," the voice complains. "We'll lose you in a minute, don't you realise we worried about you?"

"Sunbird to unidentified craft. This is not Judy. I say again, this is not Judy. Who are you? Over."

"What—" the girl says, and is cut off by someone saying, "Wait a minute, Ann." The speaker squeals. Then a different woman says, "This is Lorna Bethune in *Escondita.* What is going on here?"

"This is Major Davis commanding United States Mission *Sunbird* on course for Earth. We do not recognise any spacecraft *Escondita.* Will you identify yourself? Over."

"I just did." She sounds older with the same nasal drawl. "There is no spaceship *Sunbird* and you're not on course for Earth. If this is an andy joke it isn't any good."

"This is no joke, madam!" Dave explodes. "This is the American circumsolar mission and we are American astronauts. We do not appreciate your interference. Out."

The woman starts to speak and is drowned in a jibber of static. Two voices come through briefly. Lorimer thinks he hears the words *"Sunbird* program" and something else. Bud works the squelcher; the interference subsides to a drone.

"Ah, Major Davis?" The voice is fainter. "Did I hear you say you are on course for Earth?"

Dave frowns at the speaker and then says curtly, "Affirmative."

"Well, we don't understand your orbit. You must have very unusual flight characteristics, our readings show you won't node with anything on your present course. We'll lose the signal in a minute or two. Ah, would you tell us where you see Earth now? Never mind the coordinates, just tell us the constellation."

Dave hesitates and then holds up the mike. "Doc."

"Earth's apparent position is in Pisces," Lorimer says

to the voice. "Approximately three degrees from P. Gamma."

"It is not," the woman says. "Can't you see it's in Virgo? Can't you see out at all?"

Lorimer's eyes go to the bright smear in the port window. "We sustained some damage—"

"Hold it," snaps Dave.

"—to one window during a disturbance we ran into at perihelion. Naturally we know the relative direction of Earth on this date, October nineteen."

"October? It's March, March fifteen. You must—" Her voice is lost in a shriek.

"E-M front," Bud says, tuning. They are all leaning at the speaker from different angles, Lorimer is head-down. Space-noise wails and crashes like surf, the strange ship is too close to the coronal horizon. "—Behind you," they hear. More howls. "Band, try . . . ship . . . if you can, your signal—" Nothing more comes through.

Lorimer pushes back, staring at the spark in the window. It has to be Spica. But is it elongated, as if a second point-source is beside it? Impossible. An excitement is trying to flare out inside him, the women's voices resonate in his head.

"Playback," Dave says. "Houston will really like to hear this."

They listen again to the girl calling Judy, the woman saying she is Lorna Bethune. Bud holds up a finger. "Man's voice in there." Lorimer listens hard for the words he thought he heard. The tape ends.

"Wait til Packard gets this one." Dave rubs his arms. "Remember what they pulled on Howie? Claiming they rescued him."

"Seems like they want us on their frequency." Bud grins. "They must think we're fa-a-ar gone. Hey, looks like this other capsule's going to show up, getting crowded out here."

"If it shows up," Dave says. "Leave it on voice alert, Bud. The batteries will do that."

Lorimer watches the spark of Spica, or Spica-plus-something, wondering if he will ever understand. The casual acceptance of some trick or ploy out here in this incredible loneliness. Well, if these strangers are from the same mold, maybe that is it. Aloud he says, *"Escondita* is an odd name for a Soviet mission. I believe it means 'hidden' in Spanish."

"Yeah," says Bud. "Hey, I know what that accent is, it's Australian. We had some Aussie bunnies at Hickam. Or-stryle-ya, woo-ee! You s'pose Woomara is sending up some kind of com-bined do?"

Dave shakes his head. "They have no capability whatsoever."

"We ran into some fairly strange phenomena back there, Dave," Lorimer says thoughtfully. "I'm beginning to wish we could take a visual check."

"Did you goof, Doc?"

"No. Earth is where I said, if it's October. Virgo is where it would appear in March."

"Then that's it," Dave grins, pushing out of the couch. "You been asleep five months, Rip van Winkle? Time for a hand before we do the roadwork."

"What I'd like to know is what that chick looks like," says Bud, closing down the transceiver. "Can I help you into your space-suit, Miss? Hey, Miss, pull that in, psst-psst-psst! You going to listen, Doc?"

"Right." Lorimer is getting out his charts. The others go aft through the tunnel to the small day-room, making no further comment on the presence of the strange ship or ships out here. Lorimer himself is more shaken than he likes; it was that damn phrase.

The tedious exercise period comes and goes. Lunchtime: They give the containers a minimum warm to conserve the batteries. Chicken *à la* again; Bud puts ketchup on his and breaks their usual silence with a funny anecdote about an Australian girl, laboriously censoring himself to conform to *Sunbird's* unwritten code on talk. After lunch Dave goes forward to the command module. Bud and Lorimer continue their current task of checking out the suits and packs for a damage-assessment EVA to take place as soon as the radiation count drops.

They are just clearing away when Dave calls them.

Lorimer comes through the tunnel to hear a girl's voice blare, "—dinko trip. What did Lorna say? *Gloria* over!"

He starts up the Lurp and begins scanning. No results this time. "They're either in line behind us or in the sunward quadrant," he reports finally. "I can't isolate them."

Presently the speaker holds another thin thread of sound.

"That could be their ground control," says Dave. "How's the horizon, Doc?"

"Five hours; Northwest Siberia, Japan, Australia."

"I told you the high gain is fucked up." Bud gingerly feeds power to his antenna motor. "Easy, eas-ee. The frame is twisted, that's what it is."

"Don't snap it," Dave says, knowing Bud will not.

The squeaking fades, pulses back. "Hey, we can really use this," Bud says. "We can calibrate on them."

A hard soprano says suddenly "—should be outside your orbit. Try around Beta Aries."

"Another chick. We have a fix," Bud says happily. "We have a fix now. I do believe our troubles are over. That monkey was torqued one hundred forty-nine degrees. Woo-ee!"

The first girl comes back. "We see them, Margo! But they're so small, how can they live in there? Maybe they're tiny aliens! Over."

"That's Judy," Bud chuckles. "Dave, this is screwy, it's all in English. It has to be some U.N. thingie."

Dave massages his elbows, flexes his fists; thinking. They wait. Lorimer considers a hundred and forty-nine degrees from Gamma Piscium.

In thirteen minutes the voice from Earth says, "Judy, call the others, will you? We're going to play you the conversation, we think you should all hear. Two minutes. Oh, while we're waiting, Zebra wants to tell Connie the baby is fine. And we have a new cow."

"Code," says Dave.

The recording comes on. The three men listen once more to Dave calling Houston in a rattle of solar noise. The transmission clears up rapidly and cuts off with the

woman saying that another ship, the *Gloria,* is behind
them, closer to the sun.

"We looked up history," the Earth voice resumes.
"There was a Major Norman Davis on the first *Sunbird*
flight. Major was a military title. Did you hear them say
'Doc'? There was a scientific doctor on board, Doctor
Orren Lorimer. The third member was Captain—that's
another title—Bernhard Geirr. Just the three of them,
all males of course. We think they had an early reaction
engine and not too much fuel. The point is, the first
Sunbird mission was lost in space. They never came out
from behind the sun. That was about when the big
flares started. Jan thinks they must have been close to
one, you heard them say they were damaged."

Dave grunts. Lorimer is fighting excitement like a
brush discharge sparking in his gut.

"Either they are who they say they are or they're
ghosts; or they're aliens pretending to be people. Jan
says maybe the disruption in those super-flares could
collapse the local time dimension. Pluggo. What did you
observe there, I mean the highlights?"

Time dimension . . . never came back . . . Lorimer's mind narrows onto the reality of the two unmoving bearded heads before him, refuses to admit the
words he thought he heard: *Before the year two thousand.* The language, he thinks. The language would
have to have changed. He feels better.

A deep baritone voice says, "Margo?" In *Sunbird*
eyes come alert.

"—like the big one fifty years ago." The man has the
accent too. "We were really lucky being right there
when it popped. The most interesting part is that we
confirmed the gravity turbulence. Periodic but not
waves. It's violent, we got pushed around some. Space is
under monster stess in those things. We think France's
theory that our system is passing through a micro-black-
hole cluster looks right. So long as one doesn't plonk
us."

"France?" Bud mutters. Dave looks at him specula-
tively.

"It's hard to imagine anything being kicked out in

time. But they're here, whatever they are, they're over eight hundred kays outside us scooting out toward Aldebaran. As Lorna said, if they're trying to reach Earth they're in trouble unless they have a lot of spare gees. Should we try to talk to them? Over. Oh, great about the cow. Over again."

"Black holes," Bud whistles softly. "That's one for you, Doc. Was we in a black hole?"

"Not in one or we wouldn't be here." If we are here, Lorimer adds to himself. A micro-black-hole cluster ... what happens when fragments of totally collapsed matter approach each other, or collide, say in the photosphere of a star? Time disruption? Stop it. Aloud he says, "They could be telling us something, Dave."

Dave says nothing. The minutes pass.

Finally the Earth voice comes back, saying that it will try to contact the strangers on their original frequency. Bud glances at Dave, tunes the selector.

"Calling *Sunbird One?*" the girl says slowly through her nose. "This is Luna Central calling Major Norman Davis of *Sunbird One*. We have picked up your conversation with our ship *Escondita*. We are very puzzled as to who you are and how you got here. If you really are *Sunbird One* we think you must have been jumped forward in time when you passed the solar flare." She pronounces it Cockney-style, "toime."

"Our ship *Gloria* is near you, they see you on their radar. We think you may have a serious course problem because you told Lorna you were headed for Earth and you think it is now October with Earth in Pisces. It is not October, it is March fifteen. I repeat, the Earth date—" she says "dyte" "—is March fifteen, time twenty hundred hours. You should be able to see Earth very close to Spica in Virgo. You said your window is damaged. Can't you go out and look? We think you have to make a big course correction. Do you have enough fuel? Do you have a computer? Do you have enough air and water and food? Can we help you? We're listening on this frequency. Luna to *Sunbird One*, come in."

On *Sunbird* nobody stirs. Lorimer struggles against

internal eruptions. *Never came back. Jumped forward in time.* The cyst of memories he has schooled himself to suppress bulges up in the lengthening silence. "Aren't you going to answer?"

"Don't be stupid," Dave says.

"Dave. A hundred and forty-nine degrees is the difference between Gamma Piscium and Spica. That transmission is coming from where they say Earth is."

"You goofed."

"I did not goof. It has to be March."

Dave blinks as if a fly is bothering him.

In fifteen minutes the Luna voice runs through the whole thing again, ending "Please, come in."

"Not a tape." Bud unwraps a stick of gum, adding the plastic to the neat wad back of the gyro leads. Lorimer's skin crawls, watching the ambiguous dazzle of Spica. Spica-plus-Earth? Unbelief grips him, rocks him with a complex pang compounded of faces, voices, the sizzle of bacon frying, the creak of his father's wheelchair, chalk on a sunlit blackboard, Ginny's bare legs on the flowered couch, Jenny and Penny running dangerously close to the lawnmower. The girls will be taller now, Jenny is already as tall as her mother. His father is living with Amy in Denver, determined to last till his son gets home. *When I get home.* This has to be insanity, Dave's right; it's a trick, some crazy trick. The language.

Fifteen minutes more; the flat, earnest female voice comes back and repeats it all, putting in more stresses. Dave wears a remote frown, like a man listening to a lousy sports program. Lorimer has the notion he might switch off and propose a hand of gin; wills him to do so. The voice says it will now change frequencies.

Bud tunes back, chewing calmly. This time the voice stumbles on a couple of phrases. It sounds tired.

Another wait; an hour, now. Lorimer's mind holds only the bright point of Spica digging at him. Bud hums a bar of *Yellow Ribbons,* falls silent again.

"Dave," Lorimer says finally, "our antenna is pointed straight at Spica. I don't care if you think I goofed, if Earth is over there we have to change course soon. Look, you can see it could be a double light source. We have to check this out."

Dave says nothing. Bud says nothing but his eyes rove to the port window, back to his instrument panel, to the window again. In the corner of the panel is a polaroid snap of his wife. Patty: a tall, giggling, rump-switching red-head; Lorimer has occasional fantasies about her. Little-girl voice, though. And so tall. . . . Some short men chase tall women; it strikes Lorimer as undignified. Ginny is an inch shorted than he. Their girls will be taller. And Ginny insisted on starting a pregnancy before he left, even though he'll be out of commo. Maybe, maybe a boy, a son—*stop it*. Think about anything. Bud. . . . Does Bud love Patty? Who knows? He loves Ginny. At seventy million miles. . . .

"Judy?" Luna Central or whoever it is says. "They don't answer. You want to try? But listen, we've been thinking. If these people really are from the past this must be very traumatic for them. They could be just realising they'll never see their world again. Myda says these males had children and women they stayed with, they'll miss them terribly. This is exciting for us but it may seem awful to them. They could be too shocked to answer. They could be frightened, maybe they think we're aliens or hallucinations even. See?"

Five seconds later the nearby girl says, "Da, Margo, we were into that too. Dinko. Ah, *Sunbird?* Major Davis of *Sunbird,* are you there? This is Judy Paris in the ship *Gloria,* we're only about a million kay from you, we see you on our screen." She sounds young and excited. "Luna Central has been trying to reach you, we think you're in trouble and we want to help. Please don't be frightened, we're people just like you. We think you're way off course if you want to reach Earth. Are you in trouble? Can we help? If your radio is out can you make any sort of signal? Do you know Old Morse? You'll be off our screen soon, we're truly worried about you. Please reply somehow if you possibly can, *Sunbird,* come in!"

Dave sits impassive. Bud glances at him, at the port window, gazes stolidly at the speaker, his face blank.

Lorimer has exhausted surprise, he wants only to reply to the voices. He can manage a rough signal by heterodyning the probe beam. But what then, with them both against him?

The girl's voice tries again determinedly. Finally she says, "Margo, they won't peep. Maybe they're dead? I think they're aliens."

Are we not?, Lorimer thinks. The Luna station comes back with a different, older voice.

"Judy, Myda here, I've had another thought. These people had a very rigid authority code. You remember your history, they peck-ordered everything. You notice Major Davis repeated about being commanding. That's called dominance-submission structure, one of them gave orders and the others did whatever they were told, we don't know quite why. Perhaps they were frightened. The point is that if the dominant one is in shock or panicked maybe the others can't reply unless this Davis lets them."

Jesus Christ, Lorimer thinks. Jesus H. Christ in colors. It is his father's expression for the inexpressible. Dave and Bud sit unstirring.

"How weird," the Judy voice says. "But don't they know they're on a bad course? I mean, could the dominant one make the others fly right out of the system? Truly?"

It's happened, Lorimer thinks; it has happened. I have to stop this. I have to act now, before they lose us. Desperate visions of himself defying Dave and Bud loom before him. Try persuasion first.

Just as he opens his mouth he sees Bud stir slightly, and with immeasurable gratitude hears him say, "Dave-o, what say we take an eyeball look? One little old burp won't hurt us."

Dave's head turns a degree or two.

"Or should I go out and see, like the chick said?" Bud's voice is mild.

After a long minute Dave says neutrally, "All right. . . . Attitude change." His arm moves up as though heavy; he starts methodically setting in the values for the vector that will bring Spica in line with their functional window.

Now why couldn't I have done that, Lorimer asks himself for the thousandth time, following the familiar check sequence. Don't answer. . . . And for the thousandth time he is obscurely moved by the rightness of them. The authentic ones, the alphas. Their bond. The awe he had felt first for the absurd jocks of his school ball team.

"That's go, Dave, assuming nothing got creamed."

Dave throws the ignition safety, puts the computer on real time. The hull shudders. Everything in the cabin drifts sidewise while the bright point of Spica swims the other way, appears on the front window as the retros cut in. When the star creeps out onto clear glass Lorimer can clearly see its companion. The double light steadies there; a beautiful job. He hands Bud the telescope.

"The one on the left."

Bud looks. "There she is, all right. Hey, Dave, look at that!"

He puts the scope in Dave's hand. Slowly, Dave raises it and looks. Lorimer can hear him breathe. Suddenly Dave pulls up the mike.

"Houston!" he says harshly. *"Sunbird* to Houston, *Sunbird* calling Houston. Houston, come in!"

Into the silence the speaker squeals, "They fired their engines—wait, she's calling!" And shuts up.

In *Sunbird*'s cabin nobody speaks. Lorimer stares at the twin stars ahead, impossible realities shifting around him as the minutes congeal. Bud's reflected face looks downwards, grin gone. Dave's beard moves silently; praying, Lorimer realises. Alone of the crew Dave is deeply religious; at Sunday meals he gives a short, dignified grace. A shocking pity for Dave rises in Lorimer; Dave is so deeply involved with his family, his four sons, always thinking about their training, taking them hunting, fishing, camping. And Doris his wife so incredibly active and sweet, going on their trips, cooking and doing things for the community. Driving Penny and Jenny to classes while Ginny was sick that time. Good people, the backbone. . . . This can't be, he thinks; Packard's voice is going to come through in a minute, the antenna's beamed right now. Six minutes now. This will all go away. *Before the year two thousand*—stop it, the language would have changed. Think of Doris. . . . She has that glow, feeding her five men; women with sons are different. But Ginny, but his dear woman, his *wife,* his *daughters*—grandmothers now? All dead and dust? *Quit that.* Dave is still praying. . . . Who knows what goes on inside those heads? Dave's cry. . . . Twelve minutes, it has to be all right. The second sweep is stuck, no, it's moving. Thirteen. It's all insane, a dream. Thirteen plus. . . . fourteen. The speaker hissing and clicking vacantly. Fifteen now. A dream. . . . Or are those women staying off, letting us see? Sixteen. . . .

At twenty Dave's hand moves, stops again. The seconds jitter by, space crackles. Thirty minutes coming up.

"Calling Major Davis in *Sunbird?*" It is the older woman, a gentle voice. "This is Luna Central. We are the service and communication facility for space flight now. We're sorry to have to tell you that there is no space center at Houston any more. Houston itself was abandoned when the shuttle base moved to White Sands, over two centuries ago."

A cool dust-colored light enfolds Lorimer's brain, isolating it. It will remain so a long time.

The woman is explaining it all again, offering help, asking if they were hurt. A nice dignified speech. Dave still sits immobile, gazing at Earth. Bud puts the mike in his hand.

"Tell them, Dave-o."

Dave looks at it, takes a deep breath, presses the send button.

"*Sunbird* to Luna Control," he says quite normally. (It's "Central," Lorimer thinks.) "We copy. Ah, negative on life support, we have no problems. We copy the course change suggestion and are proceeding to recompute. Your offer of computer assistance is appreciated. We suggest you transmit position data so we can get squared away. Ah, we are economising on transmission until we see how our accumulators have held up. *Sunbird* out."

And so it had begun.

Lorimer's mind floats back to himself now floating in *Gloria,* nearly a year, or three hundred years, later; watching and being watched by them. He still feels light, contented; the dread underneath has come no nearer. But it is so silent. He seems to have heard no voices for a long time. Or was it a long time? Maybe the drug is working on his time sense, maybe it was only a minute or two.

"I've been remembering," he says to the woman Connie, wanting her to speak.

She nods. "You have so much to remember. Oh, I'm sorry—that wasn't good to say." Her eyes speak sympathy.

"Never mind." It is all dreamlike now, his lost world and this other which he is just now seeing plain. "We must seem like very strange beasts to you."

"We're trying to understand," she says. "It's history, you learn the events but you don't really feel what the people were like, how it was for them. We hope you'll tell us."

The drug, Lorimer thinks, that's what they're trying. Tell them . . . how can he? Could a dinosaur tell how it was? A montage flows through his mind, dominated by random shots of Operations' north parking lot and Ginny's yellow kitchen telephone with the sickly ivy vines. . . . Women and vines. . . .

A burst of laughter distracts him. It's coming from the chamber they call the gym, Bud and the others must be playing ball in there. Bright idea, really, he muses: Using muscle power, sustained mild exercise. That's why they are all so fit. The gym is a glorified squirrel-wheel, when you climb or pedal up the walls it revolves and winds a gear train, which among other things rotates the sleeping drum. A real Woolagong. . . . Bud and Dave usually take their shifts together, scrambling the spinning gym like big pale apes. Lorimer prefers the easy rhythm of the women, and the cycle here fits him nicely. He usually puts in his shift with Connie, who doesn't talk much, and one of the Judys, who do.

No one is talking now, though. Remotely uneasy he looks around the big cylinder of the cabin, sees Dave and Lady Blue by the forward window. Judy Dakar is behind them, silent for once. They must be looking at Earth; it has been a beautiful expanding disk for some weeks now. Dave's beard is moving, he is praying again. He has taken to doing that, not ostentatiously, but so obviously sincere that Lorimer, a life atheist, can only sympathise.

The Judys have asked Dave what he whispers, of course. When Dave understood that they had no concept of prayer and had never seen a Christian Bible there had been a heavy silence.

"So you have lost all faith," he said finally.

"We have faith," Judy Paris protested.

"May I ask in what?"

"We have faith in ourselves, of course," she told him.

"Young lady, if you were my daughter I'd tan your britches," Dave said, not joking. The subject was not raised again.

But he came back so well after that first dreadful shock, Lorimer thinks. A personal god, a father-model, man needs that. Dave draws strength from it and we lean on him. Maybe leaders have to believe. Dave was so great; cheerful, unflappable, patiently working out alternatives, making his decisions on the inevitable discrepancies in the position readings in a way Lorimer couldn't do. A bitch. . . .

Memory takes him again; he is once again back in *Sunbird*, gritty-eyed, listening to the women's chatter, Dave's terse replies. God, how they chattered. But their computer work checks out. Lorimer is suffering also from a quirk of Dave's, his reluctance to transmit their exact thrust and fuel reserve. He keeps holding out a margin and making Lorimer compute it back in.

But the margins don't help; it is soon clear that they are in big trouble. Earth will pass too far ahead of them on her next orbit, they don't have the acceleration to catch up with her before they cross her path. They can

carry out an ullage manoeuver, they can kill enough velocity to let Earth catch them on the second go-by; but
that would take an extra year and their life-support
would be long gone. The grim question of whether they
have enough to enable a single man to wait it out
pushes into Lorimer's mind. He pushes it back; that one
is for Dave.

There is a final possibility: Venus will approach their
trajectory three months hence and they may be able to
gain velocity by swinging by it. They go to work on that.

Meanwhile Earth is steadily drawing away from them
and so is *Gloria,* closer toward the sun. They pick her
out of the solar interference and then lose her again.
They know her crew now: the man is Andy Kay, the
senior woman is Lady Blue Parks; they appear to do the
navigating. Then there is a Connie Morelos and the two
twins, Judy Paris and Judy Dakar, who run the communications. The chief Luna voices are women too, Margo
and Azella. The men can hear them talking to the *Escondita* which is now swinging in toward the far side of
the sun. Dave insists on monitoring and taping everything that comes through. It proves to be largely replays
of their exchanges with Luna and *Gloria,* mixed with a
variety of highly personal messages. As references to
cows, chickens and other livestock multiply Dave reluctantly gives up his idea that they are code. Bud counts a
total of five male voices.

"Big deal," he says. "There were more chick drivers
on the road when we left. Means space is safe now, the
girlies have taken over. Let them sweat their little asses
off." He chuckles. "When we get this bird down, the
stars ain't gonna study old Buddy no more, no ma'm. A
nice beach and about a zillion steaks and ale and all
those sweet things. Hey, we'll be living history, we can
charge admission."

Dave's face takes on the expression that means an
inappropriate topic has been breached. Much to Lorimer's impatience, Dave discourages all speculation as to
what may await them on this future Earth. He confines
their transmissions strictly to the problem in hand; when
Lorimer tries to get him at least to mention the

unchanged-language puzzle Dave only says firmly, "Later." Lorimer fumes; inconceivable that he is three centuries in the future, unable to learn a thing.

They do glean a few facts from the women's talk. There have been nine successful *Sunbird* missions after theirs and one other casualty. And the *Gloria* and her sister ship are on a long-planned fly-by of the two inner planets.

"We always go along in pairs," Judy says. "But those planets are no good. Still, it was worth seeing."

"For Pete's sake Dave, ask them how many planets have been visited," Lorimer pleads.

"Later."

But about the fifth meal-break Luna suddenly volunteers.

"Earth is making up a history for you, *Sunbird,*" the Margo voice says. "We know you don't want to waste power asking so we thought we'd send you a few main points right now." She laughs. "It's much harder than we thought, nobody here does history."

Lorimer nods to himself; he has been wondering what he could tell a man from 1690 who would want to know what happened to Cromwell—was Cromwell then?—and who had never heard of electricity, atoms or the U.S.A.

"Let's see, probably the most important is that there aren't as many people as you had, we're just over two million. There was a world epidemic not long after your time. It didn't kill people but it reduced the population. I mean there weren't any babies in most of the world. Ah, sterility. The country called Australia was affected least." Bud holds up a finger.

"And North Canada wasn't too bad. So the survivors all got together in the south part of the American states where they could grow food and the best communications and factories were. Nobody lives in the rest of the world but we travel there sometimes. Ah, we have five main activities, was industries the word? Food, that's farming and fishing. Communications, transport, and space—that's us. And the factories they need. We live a lot simpler than you did, I think. We see your things all over, we're very grateful to you. Oh, you'll be interested to know we use zeppelins just like you did, we have six big ones. And our fifth thing is the children. Babies. Does that help? I'm using a children's book we have here."

The men have frozen during this recital; Lorimer is holding a cooling bag of hash. Bud starts chewing again and chokes.

"Two million people and a space capability?" He coughs. "That's incredible."

Dave gazes reflectively at the speaker. "There's a lot they're not telling us."

"I gotta ask them," Bud says. "Okay?"

Dave nods. "Watch it."

"Thanks for the history, Luna," Bud says. "We really appreciate it. But we can't figure out how you maintain a space program with only a couple of million people. Can you tell us a little more on that?"

In the pause Lorimer tries to grasp the staggering figures. From eight billion to two million . . . Europe, Asia, Africa, South America, America itself—wiped out. *There weren't any more babies.* World sterility, from what? The Black Death, the famines of Asia—those had been decimations. This is magnitudes worse. No, it is all the same: beyond comprehension. An empty world, littered with junk.

"*Sunbird?*" says Margo, "Da, I should have thought you'd want to know about space. Well, we have only the four real spaceships and one building. You know the two here. Then there's *Indira* and *Pech,* they're on the Mars run now. Maybe the Mars dome was since your day. You had the satellite stations though, didn't you? And the old Luna dome, of course—I remember now, it was during the epidemic. They tried to set up colonies to, ah, breed children, but the epidemic got there too. They struggled terribly hard. We owe a lot to you really, you men I mean. The history has it all, how you worked out a minimal viable program and trained everybody and saved it from the crazies. It was a glorious achievement. Oh, the marker here has one of your names on it. Lorimer. We love to keep it all going and growing, we all love travelling. Man is a rover, that's one of our mottoes."

"Are you hearing what I'm hearing?" Bud asks, blinking comically.

Dave is still staring at the speaker. "Not one word about their government," he says slowly. "Not a word about economic conditions. We're talking to a bunch of monkeys."

"Should I ask them?"

"Wait a minute . . . Roger, ask the name of their chief of state and the head of the space program. And—no, that's all."

"President?" Margo echoes Bud's query. "You mean like queens and kings? Wait, here's Myda. She's been talking about you with Earth."

The older woman they hear occasionally says, *"Sunbird?* Da, we realise you had a very complex activity, your governments. With so few people we don't have that type of formal structure at all. People from the different activities meet periodically and our communications are good, everyone is kept informed. The people in each activity are in charge of doing it while they're there. We rotate, you see. Mostly in five-year hitches, for example Margo here was on the zeppelins and I've been on several factories and farms and of course the, well, the education, we all do that. I believe that's one big difference from you. And of course we all work. And things are basically far more stable now, I gather. We change slowly. Does that answer you? Of course you can always ask Registry, they keep track of us all. But we can't, ah, take you to our leader, if that's what you mean." She laughs, a genuine, jolly sound. "That's one of our old jokes. I must say," she goes on seriously, "it's been a joy to us that we can understand you so well. We make a big effort not to let the language drift, it would be tragic to lose touch with the past."

Dave takes the mike. "Thank you, Luna. You've given us something to think about. *Sunbird* out."

"How much of that is for real, Doc?" Bud rubs his curly head. "They're giving us one of your science fiction stories."

"The real story will come later," says Dave. "Our job is to get there."

"That's a point that doesn't look too good."

By the end of the session it looks worse. No Venus trajectory is any good. Lorimer reruns all the computations; same result.

"There doesn't seem to be any solution to this one, Dave," he says at last. "The parameters are just too tough. I think we've had it."

Dave massages his knuckles thoughtfully. Then he nods. "Roger. We'll fire the optimum sequence on the Earth heading."

"Tell them to wave if they see us go by," says Bud.

They are silent, contemplating the prospect of a slow death in space eighteen months hence. Lorimer wonders if he can raise the other question, the bad one. He is pretty sure what Dave will say. What will he himself decide, what will he have the guts to do?

"Hello, *Sunbird?*" the voice of *Gloria* breaks in. "Listen, we've been figuring. We think if you use all your fuel you could come back in close enough to our orbit so we could swing out and pick you up. You'd be using solar gravity that way. We have plenty of manoeuver but much less acceleration than you do. You have suits and some kind of propellants, don't you? I mean, you could fly across a few kays?"

The three men look at each other; Lorimer guesses he had not been the only one to speculate on that.

"That's a good thought, *Gloria,*" Dave says. "Let's hear what Luna says."

"Why?" asks Judy. "It's our business, we wouldn't endanger the ship. We'd only miss another look at Venus, who cares. We have plenty of water and food and if the air gets a little smelly we can stand it."

"Hey, the chicks are all right," Bud says. They wait.

The voice of Luna comes on. "We've been looking at that too, Judy. We're not sure you understand the risk. Ah, *Sunbird,* excuse me. Judy, if you manage to pick them up you'll have to spend nearly a year in the ship with these three male persons from a *very different culture.* Myda says you should remember history and it's a risk no matter what Connie says. *Sunbird,* I hate to be so rude. Over."

Bud is grinning broadly, they all are. "Cave men," he chuckles. "All the chicks land preggers."

"Margo, they're human beings," the Judy voice protests. "This isn't just Connie, we're all agreed. Andy and Lady Blue say it would be very interesting. If it works, that is. We can't let them go without trying."

"We feel that way too, of course," Luna replies. "But there's another problem. They could be carrying diseases. *Sunbird,* I know you've been isolated for fourteen months, but Murti says people in your day were immune to organisms that aren't around now. Maybe some of ours could harm you, too. You could all get mortally sick and lose the ship."

"We thought of that, Margo," Judy says impatiently. "Look, if you have contact with them at all somebody has to test, true? So we're ideal. By the time we get home you'll know. And how could we all get sick so fast we couldn't put *Gloria* in a stable orbit where you could get her later on?"

They wait. "Hey, what about that epidemic?" Bud pats his hair elaborately. "I don't know if I want a career in gay lib."

"You rather stay out here?" Dave asks.

"Crazies," says a different voice from Luna. *"Sunbird,* I'm Murti, the health person here. I think what we have to fear most is the meningitis-influenza complex, they mutate so readily. Does your Doctor Lorimer have any suggestions?"

"Roger, I'll put him on," says Dave. "But as to your first point, madam, I want to inform you that at time of takeoff the incidence of rape in the United States space cadre was zero point zero. I guarantee the conduct of my crew provided you can control yours. Here is Doctor Lorimer."

But Lorimer can not of course tell them anything useful. They discuss the men's polio shots, which luckily have used killed virus, and various childhood diseases which still seem to be around. He does not mention their epidemic.

"Luna, we're going to try it," Judy declares. "We couldn't live with ourselves. Now let's get the course figured before they get any farther away."

From there on there is no rest on *Sunbird* while they set up and refigure and rerun the computations for the envelope of possible intersecting trajectories. The *Gloria*'s drive, they learn, is indeed low-thrust, although capable of sustained operation. *Sunbird* will have to get most of the way to the rendez-vous on her own if they can cancel their outward velocity.

The tension breaks once during the long session, when Luna calls *Gloria* to warn Connie to be sure the female crew members wear concealing garments at all times if the men came aboard.

"Not suit-liners, Connie, they're much too tight." It is the older woman, Myda. Bud chuckles.

"Your light sleepers, I think. And when the men unsuit, your Andy is the only one who should help them. You others stay away. The same for all body functions and sleeping. This is very important, Connie, you'll have to watch it the whole way home. There are a great many complicated taboos. I'm putting an instruction list on the bleeper, is your receiver working?"

"Da, we used it for France's black hole paper."

"Good. Tell Judy to stand by. Now listen, Connie, listen carefully. Tell Andy he has to read it all. I repeat, *he* has to read every word. Did you hear that?"

"Ah, dinko," Connie answers. "I understand, Myda. He will."

"I think we just lost the ball game, fellas," Bud laments. "Old mother Myda took it all away."

Even Dave laughs. But later when the modulated squeal that is a whole text comes through the speaker, he frowns again. "There goes the good stuff."

The last factors are cranked in; the revised program spins, and Luna confirms them. "We have a pay-out, Dave," Lorimer reports. "It's tight but there are at least two viable options. Provided the main jets are fully functional."

"We're going EVA to check."

That is exhausting; they find a warp in the deflector

housing of the port engines and spend four sweating hours trying to wrestle it back. It is only Lorimer's third sight of open space but he is soon too tired to care.

"Best we can do," Dave pants finally. "We'll have to compensate in the psychic mode."

"You can do it, Dave-o," says Bud. "Hey, I gotta change those suit radios, don't let me forget."

In the psychic mode . . . Lorimer surfaces back to his real self, cocooned in *Gloria*'s big cluttered cabin, seeing Connie's living face. "It must be hours, how long has he been dreaming?"

"About two minutes," Connie smiles.

"I was thinking of the first time I saw you."

"Oh yes. We'll never forget that, ever."

Nor will he . . . He lets it unroll again in his head. The interminable hours after the first long burn, which has sent *Sunbird* yawing so they all have to gulp nausea pills. Judy's breathless voice reading down their approach: "Oh, very good, four hundred thousand . . . Oh great, *Sunbird,* you're almost three, you're going to break a hundred for sure—" Dave has done it, the big one.

Lorimer's probe is useless in the yaw, it isn't until they stabilise enough for the final burst that they can see the strange blip bloom and vanish in the slot. Converging, hopefully, on a theoretical near-intersection point.

"Here goes everything."

The final burn changes the yaw into a sickening tumble with the starfield looping past the glass. The pills are no more use and the fuel feed to the attitude jets goes sour. They are all vomiting before they manage to hand-pump the last of the fuel and slow the tumble.

"That's it, *Gloria.* Come and get us. Lights on, Bud. Let's get those suits up."

Fighting nausea they go through the laborious routine in the fouled cabin. Suddenly Judy's voice sings out, "We see you, *Sunbird!* We see your light! Can't you see us?"

"No time," Dave says. But Bud, half-suited, points at the window. "Fellas, oh, hey, look at that."

Lorimer stares, thinks he sees a faint spark between the whirling stars before he has to retch.

"Father, we thank you," says Dave quietly. "All right, move it on, Doc. Packs."

The effort of getting themselves plus the propulsion units and a couple of cargo nets out of the rolling ship drives everything else out of mind. It isn't until they are floating linked together and stabilised by Dave's hand jet that Lorimer has time to look.

The sun blanks out their left. A few meters below them *Sunbird* tumbles empty, looking absurdly small. Ahead of them, infinitely far away, is a point too blurred and yellow to be a star. It creeps: *Gloria,* on her approach tangent.

"Can you start, *Sunbird?*" says Judy in their helmets. "We don't want to brake any more on account of our exhaust. We estimate fifty kay in an hour, we're coming out on a line."

"Roger. Give me your jet, Doc."

"Goodbye, *Sunbird,*" says Bud. "Plenty of lead, Dave-o."

Lorimer finds it restful in a childish way, being towed across the abyss tied to the two big men. He has total confidence in Dave, he never considers the possibility that they will miss, sail by and be lost. Does Dave feel contempt? Lorimer wonders; that banked-up silence, is it partly contempt for those who can manipulate only symbols, who have no mastery of matter? . . . He concentrates on mastering his stomach.

It is a long, dark trip. *Sunbird* shrinks to a twinkling light, slowly accelerating on the spiral course that will end her ultimately in the sun with their precious records that are three hundred years obsolete. With, also, the packet of photos and letters that Lorimer has twice put in his suit-pouch and twice taken out. Now and then he catches sight of *Gloria,* growing from a blur to an incomprehensible tangle of lighted crescents.

"Woo-ee, it's big," Bud says. "No wonder they can't

accelerate, that thing is a flying trailer park. It'd break up."

"It's a space ship. Got those nets tight, Doc?"

Judy's voice suddenly fills their helmets. "I see your lights! Can you see me? Will you have enough left to brake at all?"

"Affirmative to both, *Gloria*," says Dave.

At that moment Lorimer is turned slowly forward again and he sees—will see it forever: the alien ship in the starfield and on its dark side the tiny lights that are women in the stars, waiting for them. Three—no, four; one suit-light is way out, moving. If that is a tether it must be over a kilometer.

"Hello, I'm Judy Dakar!" The voice is close. "Oh, mother, you're big! Are you all right? How's your air?"

"No problem."

They are in fact stale and steaming wet; too much adrenalin. Dave uses the jets again and suddenly she is growing, is coming right at them, a silvery spider on a trailing thread. Her suit looks trim and flexible; it is mirror-bright, and the pack is quite small. Marvels of the future, Lorimer thinks; Paragraph One.

"You made it, you made it! Here, tie in. Brake!"

"There ought to be some historic words," Bud murmurs. "If she gives us a chance."

"Hello, Judy," says Dave calmly. "Thanks for coming."

"Contact!" She blasts their ears. "Haul us in, Andy! Brake, brake—the exhaust is back there!"

And they are grabbed hard, deflected into a great arc toward the ship. Dave uses up the last jet. The line loops.

"Don't jerk it," Judy cries. "Oh, I'm *sorry*." She is clinging on them like a gibbon, Lorimer can see her eyes, her excited mouth. Incredible. "Watch out, it's slack."

"Teach me, honey," says Andy's baritone. Lorimer twists and sees him far back at the end of a heavy tether, hauling them smoothly in. Bud offers to help, is refused. "Just hang loose, please," a matronly voice tells them. It is obvious Andy has done this before.

They come in spinning slowly, like space fish. Lorimer finds he can no longer pick out the twinkle that is *Sunbird*. When he is swung back, *Gloria* has changed to a disorderly cluster of bulbs and spokes around a big central cylinder. He can see pods and miscellaneous equipment stowed all over her. Not like science fiction.

Andy is paying the line into a floating coil. Another figure floats beside him. They are both quite short, Lorimer realises as they near.

"Catch the cable," Andy tells them. There is a busy moment of shifting inertial drag.

"Welcome to *Gloria,* Major Davis, Captain Geirr, Doctor Lorimer. I'm Lady Blue Parks. I think you'll like to get inside as soon as possible. If you feel like climbing go right ahead, we'll pull all this in later."

"We appreciate it, Ma'm."

They start hand-over-hand along the catenary of the main tether. It has a good rough grip. Judy coasts up to peer at them, smiling broadly, towing the coil. A taller figure waits by the ship's open airlock.

"Hello, I'm Connie. I think we can cycle in two at a time. Will you come with me, Major Davis?"

It is like an emergency on a plane, Lorimer thinks as Dave follows her in. Being ordered about by supernaturally polite little girls.

"Space-going stews," Bud nudges him. "How 'bout that?" His face is sprouting sweat. Lorimer tells him to go next, his own LSP has less load.

Bud goes in with Andy. The woman named Lady Blue waits beside Lorimer while Judy scrambles on the hull securing their cargo nets. She doesn't seem to have magnetic soles; perhaps ferrous metals aren't used in space now. When Judy begins hauling in the main tether on a simple hand winch Lady Blue looks at it critically.

"I used to make those," she says to Lorimer. What he can see of her features looks compressed, her dark eyes twinkle. He has the impression she is part Black.

"I ought to get over and clean that aft antenna." Judy floats up. "Later," says Lady Blue. They both smile at Lorimer. Then the hatch opens and he and Lady Blue go in. When the toggles seat there comes a rising scream of air and Lorimer's suit collapses.

"Can I help you?" She has opened her faceplate, the voice is rich and live. Eagerly Lorimer catches the latches in his clumsy gloves and lets her lift the helmet off. His first breath surprises him, it takes an instant to identify the gas as fresh air. Then the inner hatch opens, letting in greenish light. She waves him through. He swims into a short tunnel. Voices are coming from around the corner ahead. His hand finds a grip and he stops, feeling his heart shudder in his chest.

When he turns that corner the world he knows will be dead. Gone, rolled up, blown away forever with *Sunbird*. He will be irrevocably in the future. A man from the past, a time traveller. In the future. . . .

He pulls himself around the bend.

The future is a vast bright cylinder, its whole inner surface festooned with unidentifiable objects, fronds of green. In front of him floats an odd tableau: Bud and Dave, helmets off, looking enormous in their bulky white suits and packs. A few meters away hang two bare-headed figures in shiny suits and a dark-haired girl in flowing pink pajamas.

They are all simply staring at the two men, their eyes and mouths open in identical expressions of pleased wonder. The face that has to be Andy's is grinning openmouthed like a kid at the zoo. He is a surprisingly young boy, Lorimer sees, in spite of his deep voice; blond, downy-cheeked, compactly muscular. Lorimer finds he can scarcely bear to look at the pink woman, can't tell if she really is surpassingly beautiful or plain. The taller suited woman has a shiny, ordinary face.

From overhead bursts an extraordinary sound which he finally recognises as a chicken cackling. Lady Blue pushes past him.

"All right, Andy, Connie, stop staring and help them get their suits off. Judy, Luna is just as eager to hear about this as we are."

The tableau jumps to life. Afterwards Lorimer can recall mostly eyes, bright curious eyes tugging his boots, smiling eyes upside-down over his pack—and always that light, ready laughter. Andy is left alone to help them peel down, blinking at the fittings which Lorimer still finds embarrassing. He seems easy and nimble in his own half-open suit. Lorimer struggles out of the last lacings, thinking, a boy! A boy and four women orbiting the sun, flying their big junky ships to Mars. Should he feel humiliated? He only feels grateful, accepting a short robe and a bulb of tea somebody—Connie?—gives him.

The suited Judy comes in with their nets. The men follow Andy along another passage, Bud and Dave clutching at the small robes. Andy stops by a hatch.

"This greenhouse is for you, it's your toilet. Three's a lot but you have full sun."

Inside is a brilliant jungle, foliage everywhere, glittering water droplets, rustling leaves. Something whirs away—a grasshopper.

"You crank that handle." Andy points to a seat on a large cross-duct. "The piston rams the gravel and waste into a compost process and it ends up in the soil core. That vetch is a heavy nitrogen user and a great oxidator. We pump CO_2 in and oxy out. It's a real Woolagong."

He watches critically while Bud tries out the facility.

"What's a Woolagong?" asks Lorimer dazedly.

"Oh, she's one of our inventors. Some of her stuff is weird. When we have a pluggy-looking thing that works we call it a Woolagong." He grins. "The chickens eat the seeds and the hoppers, see, and the hoppers and iguanas eat the leaves. When a greenhouse is going darkside we turn them in to harvest. With this much light I think we could keep a goat, don't you? You didn't have any life at all on your ship, true?"

"No," Lorimer says, "not a single iguana."

"They promised us a Shetland pony for Christmas," says Bud, rattling gravel. Andy joins perplexedly in the laugh.

Lorimer's head is foggy; it isn't only fatigue, the year in *Sunbird* has atrophied his ability to take in novelty. Numbly he uses the Woolagong and they go back out and forward to *Gloria*'s big control room, where Dave makes a neat short speech to Luna and is answered graciously.

"We have to finish changing course now," Lady Blue says. Lorimer's impression has been right, she is a small light part-Negro in late middle age. Connie is part something exotic too, he sees; the others are European types.

"I'll get you something to eat," Connie smiles warmly. "Then you probably want to rest. We saved all the cubbies for you." She says "syved"; their accents are all identical.

As they leave the control room Lorimer sees the withdrawn look in Dave's eyes and knows he must be feeling the reality of being a passenger in an alien ship; not in command, not deciding the course, the communications going on unheard.

That is Lorimer's last coherent observation, that and the taste of the strange, good food. And then being led aft through what he now knows is the gym, to the shaft of the sleeping drum. There are six irised ports like dog-doors; he pushes through his assigned port and finds himself facing a roomy mattress. Shelves and a desk are in the wall.

"For your excretions." Connie's arm comes through the iris, pointing at bags. "If you have a problem stick your head out and call. There's water."

Lorimer simply drifts toward the mattress, too sweated out to reply. His drifting ends in a curious heavy settling and his final astonishment: the drum is smoothly, silently starting to revolve. He sinks gratefully onto the pad, growing "heavier" as the minutes pass. About a tenth gee, maybe more, he thinks, it's still accelerating. And falls into the most restful sleep he has known in the long weary year.

It isn't till next day that he understands that Connie and two others have been on the rungs of the gym chamber, sending it around hour after hour without pause or effort and chatting as they went.

How they talk, he thinks again floating back to real present time. The bubbling irritant pours through his memory, the voices of Ginny and Jenny and Penny on the kitchen telephone, before that his mother's voice, his sister Amy's. Interminable. What do they always have to talk, talk, talk of?

"Why, everything," says the real voice of Connie beside him now, "it's natural to share."

"Natural. . . ." Like ants, he thinks. They twiddle their antennae together every time they meet. Where did you go, what did you do? Twiddle-twiddle. How do you *feel?* Oh, I feel this, I feel that, blah blah twiddle-twiddle. Total coordination of the hive. Women have no self-respect. Say anything, no sense of the strategy of words, the dark danger of naming. Can't hold in.

"Ants, bee-hives," Connie laughs, showing the bad tooth. "You truly see us as insects, don't you? Because they're females?"

"Was I talking aloud? I'm sorry." He blinks away dreams.

"Oh, please don't be. It's so sad to hear about your sister and your children and your, your wife. They must have been wonderful people. We think you're very brave."

But he has only thought of Ginny and them all for an instant—what has he been babbling? What is the drug doing to him?

"What are you doing to us?" he demands, lanced by real alarm now, almost angry.

"It's all right, truly." Her hand touches his, warm and somehow shy. "We all use it when we need to explore something. Usually it's pleasant. It's a laevonoramine compound, a disinhibitor, it doesn't dull you like alcohol. We'll be home so soon, you see. We have the responsibility to understand and you're so locked in." Her eyes melt at him. "You don't feel sick, do you? We have the antidote."

"No . . ." His alarm has already flowed away somewhere. Her explanation strikes him as reasonable enough. "We're not locked in," he says or tries to say. "We talk . . ." He gropes for a word to convey the judiciousness, the adult restraint. Objectivity, maybe? "We talk when we have something to say." Irrelevantly he thinks of a mission coordinator named Forrest, famous for his blue jokes. "Otherwise it would all break down," he tells her. "You'd fly right out of the system." That isn't quite what he means; let it pass.

The voices of Dave and Bud ring out suddenly from opposite ends of the cabin, awakening the foreboding of evil in his mind. They don't know us, he thinks. They should look out, stop this. But he is feeling too serene, he wants to think about his own new understanding, the pattern of them all he is seeing at last.

"I feel lucid," he manages to say, "I want to think."

She looks pleased. "We call that the ataraxia effect. It's so nice when it goes that way."

Ataraxia, philosophical calm. Yes. But there are monsters in the deep, he thinks or says. The night side. The night side of Orren Lorimer, a self hotly dark and complex, waiting in leash. They're so vulnerable. They don't know we can take them. Images rush up: a Judy spread-eagled on the gym rungs, pink pajamas gone, open to him. Flash sequence of the three of them taking over the ship, the women tied up, helpless, shrieking, raped and used. The team—get the satellite station, get a shuttle down to Earth. Hostages. Make them do anything, no defense whatever . . . Has Bud actually said that? But Bud doesn't know, he remembers. Dave knows they're hiding something, but he thinks it's socialism or sin. When they find out. . . .

How has he himself found out? Simply listening, really, all these months. He listens to their talk much more than the others; "fraternising," Dave calls it. . . . They all listened at first, of course. Listened and looked and reacted helplessly to the female bodies, the tender bulges so close under the thin, tantalising clothes, the magnetic mouths and eyes, the smell of them, their electric touch. Watching them touch each other, touch Andy, laughing, vanishing quietly into shared bunks. *What goes on? Can I? My need, my need—*

The power of them, the fierce resentment. . . . Bud muttered and groaned meaningfully despite Dave's warnings. He kept needling Andy until Dave banned all questions. Dave himself was noticeably tense and read his Bible a great deal. Lorimer found his own body pointing after them like a famished hound, hoping to Christ the cubicles are as they appeared to be, unwired.

All they learn is that Myda's instructions must have been ferocious. The atmosphere has been implacably antiseptic, the discretion impenetrable. Andy politely ignored every probe. No word or act has told them what, if anything, goes on; Lorimer was irresistibly reminded of the weekend he spent at Jenny's scout camp. The men's training came presently to their rescue, and they resigned themselves to finishing their mission on a super-*Sunbird*, weirdly attended by a troop of Boy and Girl Scouts.

In every other way their reception couldn't be more courteous. They have been given the run of the ship and their own dayroom in a cleaned-out gravel storage pod. They visit the control room as they wish. Lady Blue and Andy give them specs and manuals and show them every circuit and device of *Gloria*, inside and out. Luna has bleeped up a stream of science texts and the data on all their satellites and shuttles and the Mars and Luna dome colonies.

Dave and Bud plunged into an orgy of engineering. *Gloria* is, as they suspected, powered by a fission plant that uses a range of Lunar minerals. Her ion drive is only slightly advanced over the experimental models of their own day. The marvels of the future seem so far to consist mainly of ingenious modifications.

"It's primitive," Bud tells him. "What they've done is sacrifice everything to keep it simple and easy to maintain. Believe it, they can hand-feed fuel. And the back-ups, brother! They have redundant redundancy."

But Lorimer's technical interest soon flags. What he really wants is to be alone a while. He makes a desultory attempt to survey the apparently few new developments in his field, and finds he can't concentrate. What the hell, he tells himself, I stopped being a physicist three hundred years ago. Such a relief to be out of the cell of *Sunbird;* he has given himself up to drifting solitary through the warren of the ship, using their excellent 400 mm telescope, noting the odd life of the crew.

When he finds that Lady Blue likes chess they form a

routine of bi-weekly games. Her personality intrigues him; she has reserve and an aura of authority. But she quickly stops Bud when he calls her "Captain."

"No one here commands in your sense. I'm just the oldest." Bud goes back to "Ma'm."

She plays a solid positional game, somewhat more erratic than a man but with occasional elegant traps. Lorimer is astonished to find that there is only one new chess opening, an interesting queen-side gambit called the Dagmar. One new opening in three centuries? He mentions it to the others when they come back from helping Andy and Judy Paris overhaul a standby converter.

"They haven't done much anywhere," Dave says. "Most of your new stuff dates from the epidemic, Andy, if you'll pardon me. The program seems to be stagnating. You've been gearing up this Titan project for eighty years."

"We'll get there." Andy grins.

"C'mon Dave," says Bud. "Judy and me are taking on you two for the next chicken dinner, we'll get a bridge team here yet. Woo-ee, I can taste that chicken! Losers get the iguana."

The food is so good. Lorimer finds himself lingering around the kitchen end, helping whoever is cooking, munching on their various seeds and chewy roots as he listens to them talk. He even likes the iguana. He begins to put on weight, in fact they all do. Dave decrees double exercise shifts.

"You going to make us *climb* home, Dave-o?" Bud groans. But Lorimer enjoys it, pedalling or swinging easily along the rungs while the women chat and listen to tapes. Familiar music: he identifies a strange spectrum from Handel, Brahms, Sibelius, through Strauss to ballad tunes and intricate light jazz-rock. No lyrics. But plenty of informative texts doubtless selected for his benefit.

From the promised short history he finds out more about the epidemic. It seems to have been an air-borne quasi-virus escaped from Franco-Arab military labs, possibly potentiated by pollutants.

"It apparently damaged only the reproductive cells," he tells Dave and Bud. "There was little actual mortality, but almost universal sterility. Probably a molecular substitution in the gene code in the gametes. And the main effect seems to have been on the men. They mention a shortage of male births afterwards, which suggests that the damage was on the Y-chromosome where it would be selectively lethal to the male fetus."

"Is it still dangerous, Doc?" Dave asks. "What happens to us when we get back home?"

"They can't say. The birth-rate is normal now, about two percent and rising. But the present population may be resistant. They never achieved a vaccine."

"Only one way to tell," Bud says gravely. "I volunteer."

Dave merely glances at him. Extraordinary how he still commands, Lorimer thinks. Not submission, for Pete's sake. A team.

The history also mentions the riots and fighting which swept the world when humanity found itself sterile. Cities bombed, and burned, massacres, panics, mass rapes and kidnapping of women, marauding armies of biologically desperate men, bloody cults. The crazies. But it is all so briefly told, so long ago. Lists of honoured names. "We must always be grateful to the brave people who held the Denver Medical Laboratories—" And then on to the drama of building up the helium supply for the dirigibles.

In three centuries it's all dust, he thinks. What do I know of the hideous Thirty Years War that was three centuries back for me? *Fighting devastated Europe for two generations.* Not even names.

The description of their political and economic structure is even briefer. They seem to be, as Myda had said, almost ungoverned.

"It's a form of loose social credit system run by consensus," he says to Dave. "Somewhat like a permanent frontier period. They're building up slowly. Of course they don't need an army or airforce. I'm not sure if they even use cash money or recognise private ownership of land. I did notice one favorable reference to early

Chinese communalism," he adds, to see Dave's mouth set. "But they aren't tied to a community. They travel about. When I asked Lady Blue about their police and legal system she told me to wait and talk with real historians. This Registry seems to be just that, it's not a policy organ."

"We've run into a situation here, Lorimer," Dave says soberly. "Stay away from it. They're not telling the story."

"You notice they never talk about their husbands?" Bud laughs. "I asked a couple of them what their husbands did and I swear they had to think. And they all have kids. Believe me, it's a swinging scene down there, even if old Andy acts like he hasn't found out what it's for."

"I don't want any prying into their personal family lives while we're on this ship, Geirr. None whatsoever. That's an order."

"Maybe they don't have families. You ever hear 'em mention anybody getting married? That has to be the one thing on a chick's mind. Mark my words, there's been some changes made."

"The social mores are bound to have changed to some extent," Lorimer says. "Obviously you have women doing more work outside the home, for one thing. But they have family bonds; for instance Lady Blue has a sister in an aluminum mill and another in health. Andy's mother is on Mars and his sister works in Registry. Connie has a brother or brothers on the fishing fleet near Biloxi, and her sister is coming out to replace her here next trip, she's making yeast now."

"That's the top of the iceberg."

"I doubt the rest of the iceberg is very sinister, Dave."

But somewhere along the line the blandness begins to bother Lorimer too. So much is missing. Marriage, love-affairs, children's troubles, jealousy squabbles, status, possessions, money problems, sicknesses, funerals even—all the daily minutiae that occupied Ginny and her friends seems to have been edited out of these women's talk. *Edited.* . . . Can Dave be right, is some big, significant aspect being deliberately kept from them?

"I'm still surprised your language hasn't changed more," he says one day to Connie during their exertions in the gym.

"Oh, we're very careful about that." She climbs at an angle beside him, not using her hands. "It would be a dreadful loss if we couldn't understand the books. All the children are taught from the same original tapes, you see. Oh, there's faddy words we use for a while, but our communicators have to learn the old texts by heart, that keeps us together."

Judy Paris grunts from the pedicycle. "You, my dear children, will never know the oppression we suffered," she declaims mockingly.

"Judys talk too much," says Connie.

"We do, for a fact." They both laugh.

"So you still read our so-called great books, our fiction and poetry?" asks Lorimer. "Who do you read, H.G. Wells? Shakespeare? Dickens, ah, Balzac, Kipling, Brian?" He gropes; Brian had been a bestseller Ginny liked. When had he last looked at Shakespeare or the others?

"Oh, the historicals," Judy says. "It's interesting, I guess. Grim. They're not very realistic. I'm sure it was to you," she adds generously.

And they turn to discussing whether the laying hens are getting too much light, leaving Lorimer to wonder how what he supposes are the eternal verities of human nature can have faded from a world's reality. Love, conflict, heroism, tragedy—all "unrealistic"? Well, flight crews are never great readers; still, women read more. . . . Something *has* changed, he can sense it. Something basic enough to affect human nature. A physical development perhaps; a mutation? What is really under those floating clothes?

It is the Judys who give him part of it.

He is exercising alone with both of them, listening to them gossip about some legendary figure named Dagmar.

"The Dagmar who invented the chess opening?" he asks.

"Yes. She does anything, when she's good she's great."

"Was she bad sometimes?"

A Judy laughs. "The Dagmar problem, you can say. She has this tendency to organise everything. It's fine when it works but every so often it runs wild, she thinks she's queen or what. Then they have to get out the butterfly nets."

All in present tense—but Lady Blue has told him the Dagmar gambit is over a century old.

Longevity, he thinks; by god, that's what they're hiding. Say they've achieved a doubled or tripled life span, that would certainly change human psychology, affect their outlook on everything. Delayed maturity, perhaps? We were working on endocrine cell juvenescence when I left. How old are these girls, for instance?

He is framing a question when Judy Dakar says, "I was in the creche when she went pluggo. But she's good, I loved her later on."

Lorimer thinks she has said "crash" and then realises she means a communal nursery. "Is that the same Dagmar?" he asks. "She must be very old."

"Oh no, her sister."

"A sister a hundred years apart?"

"I mean, her daughter. Her, her *grand*-daughter." She starts pedalling fast.

"Judys," says her twin, behind them.

Sister again. Everybody he learns of seems to have an extraordinary number of sisters, Lorimer reflects. He hears Judy Paris saying to her twin, "I think I remember Dagmar at the Creche. She started uniforms for everybody. Colors and numbers."

"You couldn't have, you weren't born," Judy Dakar retorts.

There is a silence in the drum.

Lorimer turns on the rungs to look at them. Two flushed cheerful faces stare back warily, make identical head-dipping gestures to swing the black hair out of their eyes. Identical. . . . But isn't the Dakar girl on the cycle a shade more mature, her face more weathered?

"I thought you were supposed to be twins."

"Ah, Judys talk a lot," they say together—and grin guiltily.

"You aren't sisters," he tells them. "You're what we called clones."

Another silence.

"Well, yes," says Judy Dakar. "We call it sisters. Oh, mother! We weren't supposed to tell you, Myda said you would be frightfully upset. It was illegal in your day, true?"

"Yes. We considered it immoral and unethical, experimenting with human life. But it doesn't upset me personally."

"Oh, that's beautiful, that's great," they say together. "We think of you as different," Judy Paris blurts, "you're more hu—more like us. Please, you don't have to tell the others, do you? Oh, *please* don't."

"It was an accident there were two of us here," says Judy Dakar. "Myda *warned* us. Can't you wait a little while?" Two identical pairs of dark eyes beg him.

"Very well," he says slowly. "I won't tell my friends for the time being. But if I keep your secret you have to answer some questions. For instance, how many of your people are created artificially this way?"

He begins to realise he *is* somewhat upset. Dave is right, damn it, they are hiding things. Is this brave new world populated by subhuman slaves, run by master brains? Decorticate zombies, workers without stomachs or sex, human cortexes wired into machines, monstrous experiments rush through his mind. He has been naive again. These normal-looking women could be fronting for a hideous world.

"How many?"

"There's only about eleven thousand of us," Judy Dakar says. The two Judys look at each other, transparently confirming something. They're unschooled in deception, Lorimer thinks; is that good? And is diverted by Judy Paris exclaiming, "What we can't figure out is why did you think it was wrong?"

Lorimer tries to tell them, to convey the horror of manipulating human identity, creating abnormal life. The threat to individuality, the fearful power it would put in a dictator's hand.

"Dictator?" one of them echoes blankly. He looks at their faces and can only say, "Doing things to people without their consent. I think it's sad."

"But that's just what we think about you," the younger Judy bursts out. "How do you know who you *are*? Or who anybody is? All alone, no sisters to share with! You don't know what you can do, or what would be interesting to try. All you poor singletons, you—why, you just have to blunder along and die, all for nothing!"

Her voice trembles. Amazed, Lorimer sees both of them are misty-eyed.

"We better get this m-moving," the other Judy says.

They swing back into the rhythm and in bits and pieces Lorimer finds out how it is. Not bottled embryos, they tell him indignantly. Human mothers like everybody else, young mothers, the best kind. A somatic cell nucleus is inserted in an enucleated ovum and re-implanted in the womb. They have each borne two "sister" babies in their late teens and nursed them a while before moving on. The creches always have plenty of mothers.

His longevity notion is laughed at; nothing but some rules of healthy living have as yet been achieved. "We should make ninety in good shape," they assure him. "A hundred and eight, that was Judy Eagle, she's our record. But she was pretty blah at the end."

The clone-strains themselves are old, they date from the epidemic. They were part of the first effort to save the race when the babies stopped and they've continued ever since.

"It's so perfect," they tell him. "We each have a book, it's really a library. All the recorded messages. The Book of Judy Shapiro, that's us. Dakar and Paris are our personal names, we're doing cities now." They laugh, trying not to talk at once about how each Judy adds her individual memoir, her adventures and problems and discoveries in the genotype they all share.

"If you make a mistake it's useful for the others. Of course you try not to—or at least make a *new* one."

"Some of the old ones aren't so realistic," her other self puts in. "Things were so different, I guess. We make excerpts of the parts we like best.. And practical things, like Judys should watch out for skin cancer."

"But we have to read the whole thing every ten years," says the Judy called Dakar. "It's inspiring. As you get older you understand some of the ones you didn't before."

Bemused, Lorimer tries to think how it would be, hearing the voices of three hundred years of Orren Lorimers. Lorimers who were mathematicians or plumbers or artists or bums or criminals, maybe. The continuing exploration and completion of self. And a dozen living doubles; aged Lorimers, infant Lorimers. And other Lorimers' women and children . . . would he enjoy it or resent it? He doesn't know.

"Have you made your records yet?"

"Oh, we're too young. Just notes in case of accident."

"Will we be in them?"

"You can say!" They laugh merrily, then sober. "Truly you won't tell?" Judy Paris asks. "Lady Blue, we have to let her know what we did. Oof. But *truly* you won't tell your friends?"

He hadn't told on them, he thinks now, emerging back into his living self. Connie beside him is drinking cider from a bulb. He has a drink in his hand too, he finds. But he hasn't told.

"Judys will talk." Connie shakes her head, smiling. Lorimer realises he must have gabbled out the whole thing.

"It doesn't matter," he tells her. "I would have guessed soon anyhow. There were too many clues . . . Woolagongs invent, Mydas worry, Jans are brains, Billy Dees work so hard. I picked up six different stories of hydroelectric stations that were built or improved or are being run by one Lala Singh. Your whole way of life. I'm more interested in this sort of thing than a respectable physicist should be," he says wryly. "You're all clones, aren't you? Every one of you. What do Connies do?"

"You really do know." She gazes at him like a mother whose child has done something troublesome and bright. "Whew! Oh, well, Connies farm like mad, we grow things. Most of our names are plants. I'm Veronica, by the way. And of course the creches, that's our weakness. The runt mania. We tend to focus on anything smaller or weak."

Her warm eyes focus on Lorimer, who draws back involuntarily.

"We control it." She gives a hearty chuckle. "We aren't all that way. There's been engineering Connies, and we have two young sisters who love metallurgy. It's fascinating what the genotype can do if you try. The original Constantia Morelos was a chemist, she weighed ninety pounds and never saw a farm in her life." Connie looks down at her own muscular arms. "She was killed by the crazies, she fought with weapons. It's so hard to understand . . . And I had a sister Timothy who made dynamite and dug two canals and she wasn't even an andy."

"*An* andy," he says.

"Oh, dear."

"I guessed that too. Early androgen treatments."

She nods hesitantly. "Yes. We need the muscle-power for some jobs. A few. Kays are quite strong anyway. Whew!" She suddenly stretches her back, wriggles as if she'd been cramped. "Oh, I'm glad you know. It's been such a strain. We couldn't even sing."

"Why not?"

"Myda was sure we'd make mistakes, all the words we'd have had to change. We sing a lot." She softly hums a bar or two.

"What kinds of songs do you sing?"

"Oh, every kind. Adventure songs, work songs, mothering songs, roaming songs, mood songs, trouble songs, joke songs—everything."

"What about love songs?" he ventures. "Do you still have, well, love?"

"Of course, how could people not love?" But she looks at him doubtfully. "The love stories I've heard from your time are so, I don't know, so weird. Grim and pluggy. It doesn't seem like love. . . . Oh, yes, we have famous love songs. Some of them are partly sad too. Like Tamil and Alcmene O, they're fated together. Connies are fated too, a little." She grins bashfully. "We love to be with Ingrid Anders. It's more one-sided. I hope there'll be an Ingrid on my next hitch. She's so exciting, she's like a little diamond."

Implications are exploding all about him, sparkling with questions. But Lorimer wants to complete the darker pattern beyond.

"Eleven thousand genotypes, two million people: that averages two hundred of each of you alive now." She nods. "I suppose it varies? There's more of some?"

"Yes, some types aren't as viable. But we haven't lost any since early days. They tried to preserve all the genes they could, we have people from all the major races and a lot of small strains. Like me, I'm the Carib Blend. Of course we'll never know what was lost. But eleven thousand is a lot, really. We all try to know every one, it's a life hobby."

A chill penetrates his ataraxia. Eleven thousand, period. That is the true population of Earth now. He thinks of two hundred tall olive-skinned women named after plants, excited by two hundred little bright Ingrids; two hundred talkative Judys, two hundred self-possessed Lady Blues, two hundred Margos and Mydas and the rest. He shivers. The heirs, the happy pallbearers of the human race.

"So evolution ends," he says somberly.

"No, why? It's just slowed down. We do everything much slower than you did, I think. We like to experience things *fully*. We have time." She stretches again, smiling. "There's all the time."

"But you have no new genotypes. It is the end."

"Oh but there are, now. Last century they worked out the way to make haploid nuclei combine. We can make a stripped egg-cell function like pollen," she says proudly. "I mean sperm. It's tricky, some don't come out too well. But now we're finding both Xs viable we have over a hundred new types started. Of course it's hard for them, with no sisters. The donors try to help."

Over a hundred, he thinks. Well. Maybe. . . . But "both Xs viable," what does that mean? She must be referring to the epidemic. But he had figured it primarily affected the men. His mind goes happily to work on the new puzzle, ignoring a sound from somewhere that is trying to pierce his calm.

"It was a gene or genes on the X-chromosome that was injured," he guesses aloud. "Not the Y. And the lethal trait had to be recessive, right? Thus there would have been no births at all for a time, until some men recovered or were isolated long enough to manufacture undamaged X-bearing gametes. But women carry their lifetime supply of ova, they could never regenerate reproductively. When they mated with the recovered males only female babies would be produced, since the female carries two Xs and the mother's defective gene would be compensated by a normal X from the father. But the male is XY, he receives only the mother's defective X. Thus the lethal defect would be expressed, the male fetus would be finished. . . . A planet of girls and dying men. The few odd viables died off."

"You truly do understand," she says admiringly.

The sound is becoming urgent; he refuses to hear it, there is significance here.

"So we'll be perfectly all right on Earth. No problem. In theory we can marry again and have families, daughters anyway."

"Yes," she says. "In theory."

The sound suddenly broaches his defenses, becomes the loud voice of Bud Geirr raised in song. He sounds plain drunk now. It seems to be coming from the main garden pod, the one they use to grow vegetables, not sanitation. Lorimer feels the dread alive again, rising closer. Dave ought to keep an eye on him. But Dave seems to have vanished too, he recalls seeing him go towards Control with Lady Blue.

"OH, THE SUN SHINES BRIGHT ON PRETTY RED WI-I-ING," carols Bud.

Something should be done, Lorimer decides painfully. He stirs; it is an effort.

"Don't worry," Connie says. "Andy's with them."

"You don't know, you don't know what you've started." He pushes off toward the garden hatchway.

"—AS SHE LAY SLE-EEPING, A COWBOY CREE-E-EEPING—" General laughter from the hatchway. Lorimer coasts through into the green dazzle. Beyond the radial fence of snap-beans he sees Bud sailing in an exaggerated crouch after Judy Paris. Andy hangs by the iguana cages, laughing.

Bud catches one of Judy's ankles and stops them both with a flourish, making her yellow pajamas swirl. She giggles at him upside-down, making no effort to free herself.

"I don't like this," Lorimer whispers.

"Please don't interfere." Connie has hold of his arm, anchoring them both to the tool rack. Lorimer's alarm seems to have ebbed; he will watch, let serenity return. The others have not noticed them.

"Oh, there once was an Indian maid." Bud sings more restrainedly, "Who never was a-fraid, that some buckaroo would slip it up her, ahem, ahem," he coughs ostentatiously, laughing. "Hey, Andy, I hear them calling you."

"What?" says Judy, "I don't hear anything."

"They're calling you, lad. Out there."

"Who?" asks Andy, listening.

"*They* are, for Crissake." He lets go of Judy and kicks over to Andy. "Listen, you're a great kid. Can't you see me and Judy have some business to discuss in private?" He turns Andy gently around and pushes him at the bean-stakes. "It's New Year's Eve, dummy."

Andy floats passively away through the fence of vines, raising a hand at Lorimer and Connie. Bud is back with Judy.

"Happy New Year, kitten," he smiles.

"Happy New Year. Did you do special things on New Year?" she asks curiously.

"What we did on New Year's." He chuckles, taking her shoulders in his hands. "On New Year's Eve, yes

we did. Why don't I show you some of our primitive
Earth customs, h'mm?"

She nods, wide-eyed.

"Well, first we wish each other well, like this." He
draws her to him and lightly kisses her cheek. "Kee-rist,
what a dumb bitch," he says in a totally different voice.
"You can tell you've been out too long when the geeks
start looking good. Knockers, ahhh—" His hand plays
with her blouse. The man is unaware, Lorimer realises.
He doesn't know he's drugged, he's speaking his
thoughts. I must have done that. Oh, god. . . . He
takes shelter behind his crystal lens, an observer in the
protective light of eternity.

"And then we smooch a little." The friendly voice is
back, Bud holds the girl closer, caressing her back. "Fat
ass." He puts his mouth on hers; she doesn't resist. Lorimer watches Bud's arms tighten, his hands working on
her buttocks, going under her clothes. Safe in the lens
his own sex stirs. Judy's arms are waving aimlessly.

Bud breaks for breath, a hand at his zipper.

"Stop staring," he says hoarsely. "One fucking more
word, you'll find out what that big mouth is for. Oh,
man, a flagpole. Like steel. . . . Bitch, this is your
lucky day." He is baring her breasts now, big breasts.
Fondling them. "Two fucking years in the ass end of
noplace," he mutters, "shit on me will you? Can't wait,
watch it—titty-titty-titties—"

He kisses her again quickly and smiles down at her.
"Good?" he asks in his tender voice, and sinks his
mouth on her nipples, his hand seeking in her thighs.
She jerks and says something muffled. Lorimer's arteries are pounding with delight, with dread.

"I, I think this should stop," he makes himself say
falsely, hoping he isn't saying more. Through the pulsing tension he hears Connie whisper back, it sounds like
"Don't worry, Judy's very athletic." Terror stabs him,
they don't know. But he can't help.

"Cunt," Bud grunts, "you have to have a cunt in
there, is it froze up? You dumb cunt—" Judy's face appears briefly in her floating hair, a remote part of Lorimer's mind notes that she looks amused and uncomfort-

able. His being is riveted to the sight of Bud expertly controlling her body in midair, peeling down the yellow slacks. Oh god—her dark pubic mat, the thick white thighs—a perfectly normal woman, no mutation. Ohhh, god. . . . But there is suddenly a drifting shadow in the way: Andy again floating over them with something in his hands.

"You dinko, Jude?" the boy asks.

Bud's face comes up red and glaring. "Bug out, you!"

"Oh, I won't bother."

"Jee-sus Christ." Bud lunges up and grabs Andy's arm, his legs still hooked around Judy. "This is man's business, boy, do I have to spell it out?" He shifts his grip. "Shoo!"

In one swift motion he has jerked Andy close and back-handed his face hard, sending him sailing into the vines.

Bud gives a bark of laughter, bends back to Judy. Lorimer can see his erection poking through his fly. He wants to utter some warning, tell them their peril, but he can only ride the hot pleasure surging through him, melting his crystal shell. Go on, more—avidly he sees Bud mouth her breasts again and then suddenly flip her whole body over, holding her wrists behind her in one fist, his legs pinning hers. Her bare buttocks bulge up helplessly, enormous moons. "Ass-s-s," Bud groans. "Up you bitch, ahhh-hh—" He pulls her butt onto him.

Judy gives a cry, begins to struggle futilely. Lorimer's shell boils and bursts. Amid the turmoil ghosts outside are trying to rush in. And something *is* moving, a real ghost—to his dismay he sees it is Andy again, floating toward the joined bodies, holding a whirring thing. Oh, no—a camera. The fools.

"Get away!" he tries to call to the boy.

But Bud's head turns, he has seen. "You little pissass." His long arm shoots out and captures Andy's shirt, his legs still locked around Judy.

"I've had it with you." His fist slams into Andy's mouth, the camera goes spinning away. But this time Bud doesn't let him go, he is battering the boy, all of them rolling in a tangle in the air.

"Stop!" Lorimer hears himself shout, plunging at them through the beans. "Bud, stop it! You're hitting a woman."

The angry face comes around, squinting at him.

"Get lost Doc, you little fart. Get your own ass."

"Andy is a *woman*, Bud. You're hitting a girl. She's not a man."

"Huh?" Bud glances at Andy's bloody face. He shakes the shirt-front. "Where's the boobs?"

"She doesn't have breasts, but she's a woman. Her real name is Kay. They're all women. Let her go, Bud."

Bud stares at the androgyne, his legs still pinioning Judy, his penis poking the air. Andy puts up his/her hands in a vaguely combative way.

"A dyke?" says Bud slowly. "A goddam little bull dyke? This I gotta see."

He feints casually, thrusts a hand into Andy's crotch.

"No balls!" he roars, "No balls at all!" Convulsing with laughter he lets himself tip over in the air, releasing Andy, his legs letting Judy slip free. "Na-ah," he interrupts himself to grab her hair and goes on guffawing. "A dyke! Hey, dykey!" He takes hold of his hard-on, waggles it at Andy. "Eat your heart out, little dyke." Then he pulls up Judy's head. She has been watching unresisting all along.

"Take a good look, girlie. See what old Buddy has for you? Tha-a-at's what you want, say it. How long since you saw a real man, hey, dog-face?"

Maniacal laughter bubbles up in Lorimer's gut, farce too strong for fear. "She never saw a man in her life before, none of them has. You imbecile, don't you get it? There aren't any other men, they've all been dead three hundred years."

Bud slowly stops chuckling, twists around to peer at Lorimer.

"What'd I hear you say, Doc?"

"The men are all gone. They died off in the epidemic. There's nothing but women left alive on Earth."

"You mean there's, there's two million women down

there and no men?" His jaw gapes. "Only little bull dykes like Andy. . . . Wait a minute. Where do they get the kids?"

"They grow them artificially. They're all girls."

"Gawd. . . ." Bud's hand clasps his drooping penis, jiggles it absently. It stiffens. "Two million hot little cunts down there, waiting for old Buddy. Gawd. The last man on Earth. . . . You don't count, Doc. And old Dave, he's full of crap."

He begins to pump himself, still holding Judy by the hair. The motion sends them slowly backward. Lorimer sees that Andy—Kay—has the camera going again. There is a big star-shaped smear of blood on the boyish face; cut lip, probably. He himself feels globed in thick air, all action spent. Not lucid.

"Two million cunts," Bud repeats. "Nobody home, nothing but pussy everywhere. I can do anything I want, any time. No more shit." He pumps faster. "They'll be spread out for miles begging for it. Clawing each other for it. All for me, King Buddy. . . . I'll have strawberries and cunt for breakfast. Hot buttered boobies, man. 'N' head, there'll be a couple little twats licking whip cream off my cock all day long. . . . Hey, I'll have contests! Only the best for old Buddy now. Not you, cow." He jerks Judy's head. "Li'l teenies, tight li'l holes. I'll make the old broads hot 'em up while I watch." He frowns slightly, working on himself. In a clinical corner of his mind Lorimer guesses the drug is retarding ejaculation. He tells himself that he should be relieved by Bud's self-absorption, is instead obscurely terrified.

"King, I'll be their god," Bud is mumbling. "They'll make statues of me, my cock a mile high, all over. . . . His Majesty's sacred balls. They'll worship it. . . . Buddy Geirr, the last cock on Earth. Oh man, if old George could see that. When the boys hear that they'll really shit themselves, woo-ee!"

He frowns harder. "They can't all be gone." His eyes rove, find Lorimer. "Hey, Doc, there's some men left someplace, aren't there? Two or three, anyway?"

"No." Effortfully Lorimer shakes his head. "They're all dead, all of them."

"Balls." Bud twists around, peering at them. "There has to be some left. Say it." He pulls Judy's head up. *"Say it,* cunt."

"No, it's true," she says.

"No men," Andy/Kay echoes.

"You're lying." Bud scowls, frigs himself faster, thrusting his pelvis. "There has to be some men, sure there are. . . . They're hiding out in the hills, that's what it is. Hunting, living wild. . . . Old wild men, I knew it."

"Why do there have to be men?" Judy asks him, being jerked to and fro.

"Why, you stupid bitch." He doesn't look at her, thrusts furiously. "Because, dummy, otherwise nothing counts, that's why. . . . There's some men, some good old buckaroos—Buddy's a good old buckaroo—"

"Is he going to emit sperm now?" Connie whispers.

"Very likely," Lorimer says, or intends to say. The spectacle is of merely clinical interest, he tells himself, nothing to dread. One of Judy's hands clutches something: a small plastic bag. Her other hand is on her hair that Bud is yanking. It must be painful.

"Uhhh, ahh," Bud pants distressfully, "fuck away, fuck—" Suddenly he pushes Judy's head into his groin, Lorimer glimpses her nonplussed expression.

"You have a mouth, bitch, get working! . . . Take it for shit's sake, *take* it! Uh, uh—" A small oyster jets limply from him. Judy's arm goes after it with the bag as they roll over in the air.

"Geirr!"

Bewildered by the roar, Lorimer turns and sees Dave—Major Norman Davis—looming in the hatchway. His arms are out, holding back Lady Blue and the other Judy.

"Geirr! I said there would be no misconduct on this ship and I mean it. Get away from that woman!"

Bud's legs only move vaguely, he does not seem to have heard. Judy swims through them bagging the last drops.

"You, what the hell are you doing?"

In the silence Lorimer hears his own voice say, "Taking a sperm sample, I should think."

"Lorimer? Are you out of your perverted mind? Get Geirr to his quarters."

Bud slowly rotates upright. "Ah, the reverend Leroy," he says tonelessly.

"You're drunk, Geirr. Go to your quarters."

"I have news for you, Dave-o," Bud tells him in the same flat voice. "I bet you don't know we're the last men on Earth. Two million twats down there."

"I'm aware of that," Dave says furiously. "You're a drunken disgrace. Lorimer, get that man out of here."

But Lorimer feels no nerve of action stir. Dave's angry voice has pushed back the terror, created a strange hopeful stasis encapsulating them all.

"I don't have to take that any more. . ." Bud's head moves back and forth, silently saying no, no, as he drifts toward Lorimer. "Nothing counts any more. All gone. What for, friends?" His forehead puckers. "Old Dave, he's a man. I'll let him have some. The dummies. . . . Poor old Doc, you're a creep but you're better'n nothing, you can have some too. . . . We'll have places, see, big spreads. Hey, we can run drags, there has to be a million good old cars down there. We can go hunting. And then we find the wild men."

Andy, or Kay, is floating toward him, wiping off blood.

"Ah, no you don't!" Bud snarls and lunges for her. As his arm stretches out Judy claps him on the triceps.

Bud gives a yell that dopplers off, his limbs thrash— and then he is floating limply, his face suddenly serene. He is breathing, Lorimer sees, releasing his own breath, watching them carefully straighten out the big body. Judy plucks her pants out of the vines, and they start towing him out through the fence. She has the camera and the specimen bag.

"I put this in the freezer, dinko?" she says to Connie as they come by. Lorimer has to look away.

Connie nods. "Kay, how's your face?"

"I felt it!" Andy/Kay says excitedly through puffed

lips, "I felt physical anger, I wanted to hit him. Woo-ee!"

"Put that man in my wardroom," Dave orders as they pass. He has moved into the sunlight over the lettuce rows. Lady Blue and Judy Dakar are back by the wall, watching. Lorimer remembers what he wanted to ask.

"Dave, do you really know? Did you find out they're all women?"

Dave eyes him broodingly, floating erect with the sun on his chestnut beard and hair. The authentic features of man. Lorimer thinks of his own father, a small pale figure like himself. He feels better.

"I always knew they were trying to deceive us, Lorimer. Now that this woman has admitted the facts I understand the full extent of the tragedy."

It is his deep, mild Sunday voice. The women look at him interestedly.

"They are lost children. They have forgotten He who made them. For generations they have lived in darkness."

"They seem to be doing all right," Lorimer hears himself say. It sounds rather foolish.

"Women are not capable of running anything. You should know that, Lorimer. Look what they've done here, it's pathetic. Marking time, that's all. Poor souls." Dave sighs gravely. "It is not their fault. I recognise that. Nobody has given them any guidance for three hundred years. Like a chicken with its head off."

Lorimer recognises his own thought; the structure-less, chattering, trivial, two-million-celled protoplasmic lump.

"The head of the woman is the man," Dave says crisply. "Corinthians one eleven three. No discipline whatsoever." He stretches out his arm, holding up his crucifix as he drifts toward the wall of vines. "Mockery. Abominations." He touches the stakes and turns, framed in the green arbor.

"We were sent here, Lorimer. This is God's plan. I was sent here. Not you, you're as bad as they are. My middle name is Paul," he adds in a conversational tone. The sun gleams on the cross, on his uplifted face, a strong, pure, apostolic visage. Despite some intellectual reservations Lorimer feels a forgotten nerve respond.

"Oh Father, send me strength," Dave prays quietly, his eyes closed. "You have spared us from the void to bring Your light to this suffering world. I shall lead Thy erring daughters out of the darkness. I shall be a stern but merciful father to them in Thy name. Help me to teach the children Thy holy law and train them in the fear of Thy righteous wrath. Let the women learn in silence and all subjection; Timothy two eleven. They shall have sons to rule over them and glorify Thy name."

He could do it, Lorimer thinks, a man like that really could get life going again. Maybe there is some mystery, some plan. I was too ready to give up. No guts. . . . He becomes aware of women whispering.

"This tape is about through." It is Judy Dakar. "Isn't that enough? He's just repeating."

"Wait," murmurs Lady Blue.

"And she brought forth a man child to rule the nations with a rod of iron, Revelations twelve five," Dave says, louder. His eyes are open now, staring intently at the crucifix. *"For God so loved the world that he sent his only begotten son."*

Lady Blue nods; Judy pushes off toward Dave. Lorimer understands, protest rising in his throat. They mustn't do that to Dave, treating him like an animal for Christ's sake, a man—

"Dave! Look out, don't let her get near you!" he shouts.

"May I look, Major? It's beautiful, what is it?" Judy is coasting close, her hand out toward the crucifix.

"She's got a hypo, watch it!"

But Dave has already wheeled round. "Do not profane, woman!"

He thrusts the cross at her like a weapon, so menacing that she recoils in mid-air and shows the glinting needle in her hand.

"Serpent!" He kicks her shoulder away, sending himself upward. "Blasphemer. All right," he snaps in his ordinary voice, "there's going to be some order around here starting now. Get over by that wall, all of you."

Astounded, Lorimer sees that Dave actually has a weapon in his other hand, a small grey handgun. He must have had it since Houston. Hope and ataraxia shrivel away, he is shocked into desperate reality.

"Major Davis," Lady Blue is saying. She is floating right at him, they all are, right at the gun. Oh god, do they know what it is?

"Stop!" he shouts at them. "Do what he says, for god's sake. That's a ballistic weapon, it can kill you. It shoots metal slugs." He begins edging toward Dave along the vines.

"Stand back." Dave gestures with the gun. "I am taking command of this ship in the name of the United States of America under God."

"Dave, put that gun away. You don't want to shoot people."

Dave sees him, swings the gun around. "I warn you, Lorimer, get over there with them. Geirr's a man, when he sobers up." He looks at the women still drifting puzzledly toward him and understands. "All right, lesson one. Watch this."

He takes deliberate aim at the iguana cages and fires. There is a pinging crack. A lizard explodes bloodily, voices cry out. A loud mechanical warble starts up and overrides everything.

"A leak!" Two bodies go streaking toward the far end, everybody is moving. In the confusion Lorimer sees Dave calmly pulling himself back to the hatchway behind them, his gun ready. He pushes frantically across the tool rack to cut him off. A spray cannister comes loose in his grip, leaving him kicking in the air. The alarm warble dies.

"You will stay here until I decide to send for you," Dave announces. He has reached the hatch, is pulling the massive lock door around. It will seal off the pod, Lorimer realises.

"Don't do it, Dave! Listen to me, you're going to kill us all." Lorimer's own internal alarms are shaking him, he knows now what all that damned volleyball has been for and he is scared to death. "Dave, listen to me!"

"Shut up." The gun swings toward him. The door is moving. Lorimer gets a foot on solidity.

"Duck! It's a bomb!" With all his strength he hurls the massive cannister at Dave's head and launches himself after it.

"Look out!" And he is sailing helplessly in slow motion, hearing the gun go off again, voices yelling. Dave must have missed him, overhead shots are tough—and then he is doubling downwards, grabbing hair. A hard blow strikes his gut, it is Dave's leg kicking past him but he has his arm under the beard, the big man bucking like a bull, throwing him around.

"Get the gun, get it!" People are bumping him, getting hit. Just as his hold slips a hand snakes by him onto Dave's shoulder and they are colliding into the hatch door in a tangle. Dave's body is suddenly no longer at war.

Lorimer pushes free, sees Dave's contorted face tip slowly backward looking at him.

"Judas—"

The eyes close. It is over.

Lorimer looks around. Lady Blue is holding the gun, sighting down the barrel.

"Put that down," he gasps, winded. She goes on examining it.

"Hey, thanks!" Andy—Kay—grins lopsidedly at him, rubbing her jaw. They are all smiling, speaking warmly to him, feeling themselves, their torn clothes. Judy Dakar has a black eye starting, Connie holds a shattered iguana by the tail.

Beside him Dave drifts breathing stertorously, his blind face pointing at the sun. *Judas . . .* Lorimer feels the last shield break inside him, desolation flooding in. *On the deck my captain lies.*

Andy-who-is-not-a-man comes over and matter-of-factly zips up Dave's jacket, takes hold of it and begins to tow him out. Judy Dakar stops them long enough to wrap the crucifix chain around his hand. Somebody laughs, not unkindly, as they go by.

For an instant Lorimer is back in that Evanston toilet. But they are gone, all the little giggling girls. All gone forever, gone with the big boys waiting outside to jeer at him. Bud is right, he thinks. *Nothing counts any more.* Grief and anger hammer at him. He knows now what he has been dreading: not their vulnerability, his.

"They were good men," he says bitterly. "They aren't bad men. You don't know what bad means. You did it to them, you broke them down. You made them do crazy things. Was it interesting? Did you learn enough?" His voice is trying to shake. "Everybody has aggressive fantasies. They didn't act on them. Never. Until you poisoned them."

They gaze at him in silence. "But nobody does," Connie says finally. "I mean, the fantasies."

"They were good men," Lorimer repeats elegaically. He knows he is speaking for it all, for Dave's Father, for Bud's manhood, for himself, for Cro-Magnon, for the dinosaurs too, maybe. "I'm a man. By god yes, I'm angry. I have a right. We gave you all this, we made it all. We built your precious civilisation and your knowledge and comfort and medicines and your dreams. All of it. We protected you, we worked our balls off keeping you and your kids. It was hard. It was a fight, a bloody fight all the way. We're tough. We had to be, can't you understand? Can't you for Christ's sake understand that?"

Another silence.

"We're trying," Lady Blue sighs. "We are trying, Doctor Lorimer. Of course we enjoy your inventions and we do appreciate your evolutionary role. But you must see there's a problem. As I understand it, what you protected people from was largely other males, wasn't it? We've just had an extraordinary demonstration. You have brought history to life for us." Her wrinkled brown eyes smile at him; a small, tea-colored matron holding an obsolete artifact.

"But the fighting is long over. It ended when you did, I believe. We can hardly turn you loose on Earth, and we simply have no facilities for people with your emotional problems."

"Besides, we don't think you'd be very happy," Judy Dakar adds earnestly.

"We could clone them," says Connie. "I know there's people who would volunteer to mother. The young ones might be all right, we could try."

"We've been *over* all that." Judy Paris is drinking from the water tank. She rinses and spits into the soil bed, looking worriedly at Lorimer. "We ought to take care of that leak now, we can talk tomorrow. And tomorrow and tomorrow." She smiles at him, unselfconsciously rubbing her crotch. "I'm sure a lot of people will want to meet you."

"Put us on an island," Lorimer says wearily. "On three islands." That look; he knows that look of preoccupied compassion. His mother and sister had looked just like that the time the diseased kitten came in the yard. They had comforted it and fed it and tenderly taken it to the vet to be gassed.

An acute, complex longing for the women he has known grips him. Women to whom men were not simply—irrelevant. Ginny . . . dear god. His sister Amy. Poor Amy, she was good to him when they were kids. His mouth twists.

"Your problem is," he says, "if you take the risk of giving us equal rights, what could we possibly contribute?"

"Precisely," says Lady Blue. They all smile at him relievedly, not understanding that he isn't.

"I think I'll have that antidote now," he says.

Connie floats toward him, a big, warm-hearted, utterly alien woman. "I thought you'd like yours in a bulb." She smiles kindly.

"Thank you." He takes the small, pink bulb. "Just tell me," he says to Lady Blue, who is looking at the bullet gashes, "what do you call yourselves? Women's World? Liberation? Amazonia?"

"Why, we call ourselves human beings." Her eyes twinkle absently at him, go back to the bullet marks. "Humanity, mankind." She shrugs. "The human race."

The drink tastes cool going down, something like peace and freedom, he thinks. Or death.

The Psychologist Who Wouldn't Do Awful Things to Rats

He comes shyly hopeful into the lab. He is unable to suppress this childishness which has deviled him all his life, this tendency to wake up smiling, believing for an instant that today will be different.

But it isn't; is not.

He is walking into the converted cellars which are now called animal laboratories by this nationally respected university, this university which is still somehow unable to transmute its nationwide reputation into adequate funding for research. He squeezes past a pile of galvanized Skinner boxes and sees Smith at the sinks, engaged in cutting off the heads of infant rats. Piercing squeals; the headless body is flipped onto a wet furry pile on a hunk of newspaper. In the holding cage beside Smith the baby rats shiver in a heap, occasionally thrusting up a delicate muzzle and then burrowing convulsively under their friends, seeking to shut out Smith. They have previously been selectively shocked, starved, subjected to air blasts and plunged in ice water; Smith is about to search the corpses for appropriate neuroglandular effects of stress. He'll find them, undoubtedly.

Eeeeeeee—Ssskrick! Smith's knife grates, drinking life.

"Hello, Tilly."

"Hi." He hates his nickname, hates his whole stupid name: Tilman Lipsitz. He would go nameless through

227

the world if he could. If he even could have something simple, Moo or Urg—anything but the absurd high-pitched syllables that have followed him through life: Tilly Lipsitz. He has suffered from it.

Ah well. He makes his way around the pile of Purina Lab Chow bags, bracing for the fierce clamor of the rhesus. Their Primate Room is the ex-boiler room, really; these are tenements the university took over. The rhesus scream like sirens. Thud! Feces have hit the grill again; the stench is as strong as the sound. Lipsitz peers in reluctantly, mentally apologizing for being unable to like monkeys. Two of them are not screaming, huddled on the steel with puffy pink bald heads studded with electrode jacks. Why can't they house the creatures better, he wonders irritably for the nth time. In the trees they're clean. Well, cleaner, anyway, he amends, ducking around a stand of somebody's breadboard circuits awaiting solder.

On the far side is Jones, bending over a brightly lighted bench, two students watching mesmerized. He can see Jones's fingers tenderly roll the verniers that drive the probes down through the skull of the dog strapped underneath. Another of his terrifying stereotaxes. The aisle of cages is packed with animals with wasted fur and bloody heads. Jones swears they're all right, they eat; Lipsitz doubts this. He has tried to feed them tidbits as they lean or lie blear-eyed, jerking with wire terrors. The blood is because they rub their heads on the mesh; Jones, seeking a way to stop this, has put stiff plastic collars on several.

Lipsitz gets past them and has his eye rejoiced by the lovely hourglass-shaped ass of Sheila, the brilliant Israeli. Her back is turned. He observes with love the lily waist, the heart-lobed hips that radiate desire. But it's his desire, not hers; he knows that. Sheila, wicked Sheila; she desires only Jones, or perhaps Smith, or even Brown or White—the muscular large hairy ones bubbling with professionalism, with cheery shop talk. Lipsitz would gladly talk shop with her. But somehow his talk is different, uninteresting, is not in the mode. Yet he too believes in "the organism," believes in the miraculous wiring diagram of life; he is naïvely impressed by the complexity, the intricate interrelated delicacies of living matter. Why is he so reluctant to push metal into it, produce lesions with acids or shock? He has this unfashionable yearning to learn by appreciation, to tease out the secrets with only his eyes and mind. He has even the treasonable suspicion that such procedures might be more efficient, more instructive. But what holistic means are there? Probably none, he tells himself firmly. Grow up. Look at all they've discovered with the knife. The cryptic but potent centers of the amygdala, for example. The subtle limbic homeostats—would we ever have known about these? It is a great knowledge. Never mind that its main use seems to be to push more metal into human heads, my way is obsolete.

"Hi, Sheila."

"Hello, Tilly."

She does not turn from the hamsters she is efficiently shaving. He takes himself away around the mop stand to the coal-cellar dungeon where he keeps his rats— sorry, his experimental subjects. His experimental subjects are nocturnal rodents, evolved in friendly dark warm burrows. Lipsitz has sensed their misery, suspended in bright metal and plexiglas cubes in the glare. So he has salvaged and repaired for them a stack of big old rabbit cages and put them in this dark alcove nobody wanted, provoking mirth among his colleagues.

He has done worse than that, too. Grinning secretly, he approaches and observes what has been made of his latest offering. On the bottom row are the cages of parturient females, birthing what are expected to be his experimental and control groups. Yesterday those cages were bare wire mesh, when he distributed to them the classified section of the Sunday *Post*. Now he sees with amazement that they are solid cubic volumes of artfully crumpled and plastered paper strips. Fantastic, the labor! Nests; and all identical. Why has no one mentioned that rats as well as birds can build nests? How wrong, how painful it must have been, giving birth on the bare wire. The little mothers have worked all night, skillfully constructing complete environments beneficient to their needs.

A small white muzzle is pointing watchfully at him from a paper crevice; he fumbles in his pocket for a carrot chunk. He is, of course, unbalancing the treatment, his conscience remonstrates. But he has an answer; he has carrots for them all. Get down, conscience. Carefully he unlatches a cage. The white head stretches, bright-eyed, revealing sleek black shoulders. They are the hooded strain.

"Have a carrot," he says absurdly to the small being. And she does, so quickly that he can barely feel it, can barely feel also the tiny razor slash she has instantaneously, shyly given his thumb before she whisks back inside to her babies. He grins, rubbing the thumb, leaving carrots in the other cages. A mother's monitory bite, administered to an ogre thirty times her length. Vitamins, he thinks, enriched environments, that's the respectable word. Enriched? No, goddam it. What it is is something approaching sane unstressed animals—experimental subjects, I mean. Even if they're so genetically selected for tameness they can't survive in the feral state, they're still rats. He sees he must wrap something on his thumb; he is ridiculously full of blood.

Wrapping, he tries not to notice that his hands are criss-crossed with old bites. He is a steady patron of the antitetanus clinic. But he is sure that they don't really mean ill, that he is somehow accepted by them. His colleagues think so too, somewhat scornfully. In fact Smith often calls him to help get some agonized creature out and bring it to his electrodes. Judas-Lipsitz does, trying to convey by the warmth of his holding hands that somebody is sorry, is uselessly sorry. Smith explains that his particular strain of rats is bad. A bad rat is one that bites psychologists; there is a constant effort to breed out this trait.

Lipsitz has tried to explain to them about animals with curved incisors, that one must press the hand into the biter's teeth. "It can't let go," he tells them. "You're biting yourself on the rat. It's the same with cats' claws. Push, they'll let go. Wouldn't you if somebody pushed his hand in your mouth?"

For a while he thought Sheila at least had understood him, but it turned out she thought he was making a dirty joke.

He is giving a rotted Safeway apple to an old male named Snedecor whom he has salvaged from Smith when he hears them call.

"Li-i-ipsitz!"

"Tilly! R. D. wants to see you."

"Yo."

R. D. is Professor R. D. Welch, his department head and supervisor of his grant. He washes up, makes his way out and around to the front entrance stairs. A myriad guilts are swirling emptily inside him; he has violated some norm, there is something wrong with his funding, above all he is too slow, too slow. No results yet, no columns of data. Frail justifying sentences revolve in his head as he steps into the clean bright upper reaches of the department. Because he is, he feels sure, learning. Doing something, something appropriate to what he thinks of as science. But what? In this glare he (like his rats) cannot recall. Ah, maybe it's only another hassle about parking space, he thinks as he goes bravely in past R. D.'s high-status male secretary. I can give mine up. I'll never be able to afford that transmission job anyway.

But it is not about parking space.

Doctor Welch has a fat file folder on his desk in Exhibit A position. He taps it expressionlessly, staring at Lipsitz.

"You are doing a study of, ah, genetic influences on, ah, tolerance of perceptual novelty."

"Well, yes . . ." He decides not to insist on precision. "You remember, Doctor Welch, I'm going to work in a relation to emotionalism too."

Emotionalism, in rats, is (a) defecating and (b) biting psychologists. Professor Welch exhales troubledly through his lower teeth, which Lipsitz notes are slightly incurved. Mustn't pull back.

"It's so unspecific," he sighs. "It's not integrated with the overall department program."

"I know," Lipsitz says humbly. "But I do think it has relevance to problems of human learning. I mean, why some kids seem to shy away from new things." He jacks up his technical vocabulary. "The failure of the exploration motive."

"Motives don't *fail*, Lipsitz."

"I mean, conditions for low or high expression. Neophobia. Look, Doctor Welch. If one of the conditions turns out to be genetic we could spot kids who need help."

"Um'mmm."

"I could work in some real learning programs in the high tolerants, too," Lipsitz adds hopefully. "Contingent rewards, that sort of thing."

"Rat learning . . ." Welch lets his voice trail off. "If this sort of thing is to have any relevance it should involve primates. Your grant scarcely extends to that."

"Rats can learn quite a lot, sir. How about if I taught them word cues?"

"Doctor Lipsitz, rats do not acquire meaningful responses to words."

"Yes, sir." Lipsitz is forcibly preventing himself from bringing up the totally unqualified Scotswoman whose rat knew nine words.

"I do wish you'd go on with your brain studies," Welch says in his nice voice, giving Lipsitz a glowing scientific look. Am I biting myself on him? Lipsitz wonders. Involuntarily he feels himself empathize with the chairman's unknown problems. As he gazes back, Welch says encouragingly, "You could use Brown's preparations; they're perfectly viable with the kind of care you give."

Lipsitz shudders awake; he knows Brown's preparations. A "preparation" is an animal spread-eagled on a rack for vivisection, dosed with reserpine so it cannot cry or struggle but merely endures for days or weeks of pain. Guiltily he wonders if Brown knows who killed the bitch he had left half dissected and staring over Easter. Pull yourself together, Lipsitz.

"I am so deeply interested in working with the intact animal, the whole organism," he says earnestly. That is his magic phrase; he has discovered that "the whole organism" has some fetish quality for them, from some far-off line of work; very fashionable in the abstract.

"Yes." Balked, Welch wreathes his lips, revealing the teeth again. "Well. Doctor Lipsitz, I'll be blunt. When you came on board we felt you had a great deal of promise. *I* felt that, I really did. And your teaching seem to be going well, in the main. In the main. But your research; no. You seem to be frittering away your time and funds—and our space—on these irrelevancies. To put it succinctly, our laboratory is not a zoo."

"Oh, no, sir!" cries Lipsitz, horrified.

"What are you actually doing with those rats? I hear all kinds of idiotic rumors."

"Well, I'm working up the genetic strains, sir. The coefficient of homozygosity is still very low for meaningful results. I'm cutting it as fine as I can. What you're probably hearing about is that I am giving them a certain amount of enrichment. That's necessary so I can differentiate the lines." What I'm really doing is multiplying them, he thinks queasily; he hasn't had the heart to deprive any yet.

Welch sighs again; he *is* worried, Lipsitz thinks, and finding himself smiling sympathetically stops at once.

"How long before you wind this up? A week?"

"A week!" Lipsitz almost bleats, recovers his voice. "Sir, my test generation is just neonate. They have to be weaned, you know. I'm afraid it's more like a month."

"And what do you intend to do after this?"

"After this!" Lipsitz is suddenly fecklessly happy. So many, so wondrous are the things he wants to learn. "Well, to begin with I've seen a number of behaviors nobody seems to have done much with—I mean, watching my animals under more . . . more naturalistic conditions. They, ah, they emit very interesting responses. I'm struck by the species-specific aspect—I mean, as the Brelands said, we may be using quite unproductive situations. For example, there's an enormous difference between the way Rattus and Cricetus—that's hamsters—behave in the open field, and they're both *rodents*. Even as simple a thing as edge behavior—"

"*What* behavior?" Welch's tone should warn him, but he plunges on, unhappily aware that he has chosen an insignificant example. But he loves it.

"Edges. I mean the way the animal responds to edges and the shape of the environment. I mean it's basic to living and nobody seems to have explored it. They used to call it thigmotaxis. Here, I sketched a few." He pulls out a folded sheet,* pushes it at Welch. "Doesn't it raise interesting questions of arboreal descent?"

Welch barely glances at the drawings, pushes it away.

"Doctor Lipsitz. You don't appear to grasp the seriousness of this interview. All right. In words of one syllable, you will submit a major project outline that we can justify in terms of this department's program. If you can't come up with one such, regretfully we have no place for you here."

Lipsitz stares at him, appalled.

"A major project . . . I see. But . . ." And then something comes awake, something is rising in him. Yes. Yes, yes, of course there are bigger things he can tackle. Bigger questions—that means people. He's full of such questions. All it takes is courage.

"Yes, sir," he says slowly, "There are some major problems I have thought of investigating."

"Good," Welch says neutrally. "What are they?"

"Well, to start with . . ." And to his utter horror his mind has emptied itself, emptied itself of everything except the one fatal sentence which he now hears himself helplessly launched toward. "Take us here. I mean, it's a good principle to attack problems to which one has easy access, which are so to speak under our noses, right? So. For example, we're psychologists. Supposedly dedicated to some kind of understanding, helpful attitude toward the organism, toward life. And yet all of us down here—and in all the labs I've heard about—we seem to be doing such hostile and rather redundant work. Testing animals to destruction, that fellow at

*See illustration.

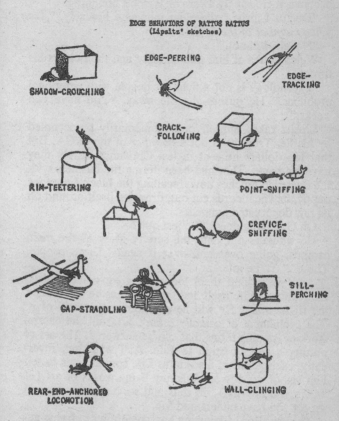

Appendix III, Figure 18.   Examples of Thigmotaxic Responses
Drawings by Raccoons. Sheldon

Princeton. Proving how damaged organisms are damaged, that kind of engineering thing. Letting students cut or shock or starve animals to replicate experiments that have been done umpteen times. What I'm trying to say is, why don't we look into why psychological research seems to involve so much cruelty—I mean, aggression? We might even . . . ."

He runs down then, and there is a silence in which he becomes increasingly aware of Welch's breathing.

"Doctor Lipsitz," the older man says hoarsely, *"Are you a member of the SPCA?"*

"No, sir, I'm not."

Welch stares at him unblinkingly and then clears his throat.

"Psychology is not a field for people with emotional problems." He pushes the file away. "You have two weeks."

Lipsitz takes himself out, momentarily preoccupied by his lie. True, he is not a *member* of the SPCA. But that ten dollars he sent in last Christmas, surely they have his name. That had been during the business with the dogs. He flinches now, recalling the black Labrador puppy, its vocal cords cut out, dragging itself around on its raw denervated haunches.

Oh God, why doesn't he just quit?

He wanders out onto the scruffy grass of the main campus, going over and over it again. These people. These . . . people.

And yet behind them loom the great golden mists, the reality of Life itself and the questions he has earned the right to ask. He will never outgrow the thrill of it. The excitement of *actually asking,* after all the careful work of framing terms that can be answered. The act of putting a real question to Life. And watching, reverently, excited out of his skin as Life condescends to tell him yes or no. My animals, my living works of art (of which you are one), do thus and so. Yes, in this small aspect you have understood Me.

The privilege of knowing how, painfully, to frame answerable questions, answers which will lead him to more, insights and better questions as far as his mind can manage and his own life lasts. It is what he wants more than anything in the world to do, always has.

And these people stand in his way. Somehow, some way, he must pacify them. He must frame a project they will buy.

He plods back toward the laboratory cellars, nodding absently at students, revolving various quasi-respectable schemes. What he really wants to do is too foggy to explain yet; he wants to explore the capacity of animals to *anticipate,* to gain some knowledge of the wave-front of expectations that they must build up, even in the tiniest heads. He thinks it might even be useful, might illuminate the labors of the human infant learning its world. But that will have to wait. Welch wouldn't tolerate the idea that animals have mental maps. Only old crazy Tolman had been allowed to think that, and he's dead.

He will have to think of something with Welch's favorite drive variables. What are they? And lots of statistics, he thinks, realizing he is grinning at a really pretty girl walking with that cow Polinski. Yes, why not use students? Something complicated with students—that doesn't cost much. And maybe sex differentials, say, in perception—or is that too far out?

A wailing sound alerts him to the fact that he has arrived at the areaway. A truck is offloading crates of cats, strays from the pound.

"Give a hand, Tilly! Hurry up!"

It's Sheila, holding the door for Jones and Smith. They want to get these out of sight quickly, he knows, before some student sees them. Those innocent in the rites of pain. He hauls a crate from the tailboard.

"There's a female in here giving birth," he tells Sheila. "Look." The female is at the bottom of a mess of twenty emaciated struggling brutes. One of them has a red collar.

"Hurry up, for Christ's sake." Sheila waves him on.

"But . . ."

When the crates have disappeared inside he does not follow the others in but leans on the railing, lighting a cigarette. The kittens have been eaten, there's nothing he can do. Funny, he always thought that females would be sympathetic to other females. Shows how much he knows about Life. Or is it that only certain types of people empathize? Or does it have to be trained in, or was it trained out of her? Mysteries, mysteries. Maybe she is really compassionate somewhere inside, toward something. He hopes so, resolutely putting away a fantasy of injecting Sheila with reserpine and applying experimental stimuli.

He becomes aware that the door has been locked from the inside; they have all left through the front. It's getting late. He moves away too, remembering that this is the long holiday weekend. Armistice Day. Would it were—he scoffs at himself for the bathos. But he frowns, too; long weekends usually mean nobody goes near the lab. Nothing gets fed or watered. Well, three days—not as bad as Christmas week.

Last Christmas week he had roused up from much-needed sleep beside a sky-high mound of term papers and hitchhiked into town to check the labs. It had been so bad, so needless. The poor brutes dying in their thirst and hunger, eating metal, each other. Great way to celebrate Christmas.

But he will have to stop that kind of thing, he knows. Stop it. Preferably starting now. He throws down the cigarette stub, quickens his stride to purposefulness. He will collect his briefcase of exam papers from the library where he keeps it to avoid the lab smell and get on home and get at it. The bus is bound to be jammed.

Home is an efficiency in a suburban high-rise. He roots in his moldy fridge, carries a sandwich and ale to the dinette that is his desk. He has eighty-one exams to grade; junior department members get the monster classes. It's a standard multiple-choice thing, and he has a help—a theatrically guarded manila template he can lay over the sheets with slots giving the correct response. By just running down them he sums an arithmetical grade. Good. Munching, he lays out the first mimeoed wad.

But as he starts to lay it on the top page he sees—oh, no!—somebody has scrawled instead of answering Number 6. It's that fat girl, that bright bum Polinsky. And she hasn't marked answers by 7 or 8 either. Damn her fat female glands; he squints at the infantile uncials: "I won't mark this because its smucky! Read it, Dr. Lipshitz." She even has his name wrong.

Cursing himself, he scrutinizes the question. "Fixed versus variable reinforcement is called a—" Oh yes, he remembers that one. Bad grammar on top of bad psychology. Why can't they dump these damn obsolete things? Because the office wants grade intercomparability for their records, that's why. Is Polinsky criticizing the language or the thought? Who knows. He leafs through the others, sees more scribbles. Oh, shit, they know I read them. They all know I don't mark them like I should. Sucker.

Grimly masticating the dry sandwich, he starts to read. At this rate he is working, he has figured out, for seventy-five cents an hour.

By midnight he isn't half through, but he knows he ought to break off and start serious thought about Welch's ultimatum. Next week all his classes start Statistical Methods; he won't have time to blow his nose, let alone think creatively.

He gets up for another ale, thinking, Statistical Methods, brrr. He respects them, he guesses. But he is incurably sloppy-minded, congenitally averse to ignoring any data that don't fit the curve. Factor analysis, multivariate techniques—all beautiful; why is he troubled by this primitive visceral suspicion that somehow it ends up proving what the experimenter wanted to show? No, not that, really. Something about qualities as opposed to quantities, maybe? That some statistically insignificant results *are* significant, and some significant ones . . . aren't? Or just basically that we don't know enough yet to use such ultraprecise weapons. That we should watch more, maybe. Watch and learn more and figure less. All right, call me St. Lipsitz.

Heating up a frozen egg roll, he jeers at himself for superstition. Face facts, Lipsitz. Deep down you don't really believe dice throws are independent. Psychology is not a field for people with personality problems.

Ignoring the TV yattering through the wall from next door, he sits down by the window to think. Do it, brain. Come up with the big one. Take some good testable hypothesis from somebody in the department, preferably something that involves electronic counting of food pellets, bar presses, latencies, defecations. And crank it all into printed score sheets with a good Fortran program.

But what the hell are they all working on? Reinforcement schedules, cerebral deficits, split brain, God knows only that it seems to produce a lot of dead animals. "The subjects were sacrificed." They insist on saying that. He had been given a lecture when he called it "killing." Sacrificed, like to a god. Lord of the Flies, maybe.

He stares out at the midnight streets, thinking of his small black-and-white friends, his cozy community in the alcove. Nursing their offspring, sniffing the monkeys, munching apples, dreaming ratly dreams. He likes rats, which surprises him. Even the feral form, Rattus rattus itself; he would like to work with wild ones. Rats are vicious, they say. But people know only starving rats. Anything starving is "vicious." Beloved beagle eats owner on fourth day.

And his rats are, he blushingly muses, affectionate. They nestle in his hands, teeteringly ride his shoulder, display humor. If only they had fluffy tails, he thinks. The tail is the problem. People think squirrels are cute. They're only overdressed rats. Maybe I could do something with the perceptual elements of "cuteness," carry on old Tinbergen's work?

Stop it.

He pulls himself up; this isn't getting anywhere. A terrible panorama unrolls before his inner eye. On the one hand the clean bright professional work he should be doing, he with those thousands of government dollars invested in his doctorate, his grant—and on the other, what he is really doing. His cluttered alcove full of irregular rodents, his tiny, doomed effort to . . . what? To live amicably and observantly with another species? To understand trivial behaviors? Crazy. Spending all his own money, saving everybody's cripples—God, half his cages aren't even experimentally justifiable!

His folly. Suddenly it sickens him. He stands up, thinking, It's a stage you go through. I'm a delayed adolescent. Wake up, grow up. They're only animals. Get with it.

Resolve starts to form in him. Opening another ale can, he lets it grow. This whole thing is no good, he knows that. So what if he does prove that animals learn better if they're treated differently—what earthly use is that? Don't we all know it anyway? Insane. Time I braced up. All right. Ale in hand, he lets the resolve bloom.

He will go down there and clean out the whole mess, right now.

Kill all his rats, wipe the whole thing off. Clear the decks. That done, he'll be able to think; he won't be locked into the past.

The department will be delighted, Doctor Welsh will be delighted. Nobody believed his thing was anything but a waste of time. All right, Lipsitz. Do it. Now, tonight.

Yes.

But first he will have something analgesic, strengthening. Not ale, not a toke. That bottle of—what is it, absinthe?—that crazy girl gave him last year. Yes, here it is back of the roach-killer he never used either. God knows what it's supposed to do, it's wormwood, something weird.

"Fix me," he tells it, sucking down a long liquorice-flavored draft. And goes out, bottle in pocket.

It has, he thinks, helped. He is striding across the campus now; all the long bus ride his resolve hasn't wavered. A quiet rain is falling. It must be two in the morning, but he's used to the spooky empty squares. He has often sneaked down here at odd hours to water and feed the brutes. The rain is moving strange sheens of shadow on the old tenement block, hissing echoes of the lives that swirled here once. At the cellar entrance he stops for another drink, finds the bottle clabbered with carrot chunks. Wormwood and Vitamin C, very good.

He dodges down and unlocks, bracing for the stench. The waste cans are full—cats that didn't make it, no doubt. Inside is a warm rustling reek.

When he finds the light, a monkey lets out one eerie whoop and all sounds stop. Sunrise at midnight; most of these experimental subjects are nocturnal.

He goes in past the crowded racks, his eye automatically checking levels in the hundreds of water bottles.

Okay, okay, all okay . . . What's this? He stops by Sheila's hamster tier. A bottle is full to the top. But there's a corpse by the wire, and the live ones look bedraggled. Why? He jerks up the bottle. Nothing comes out of the tube. It's blocked. Nobody has checked it for who knows how long. Perishing of thirst in there, with the bottle full.

He unblocks it, fishes out the dead, watches the little beasts crowd around. How does Sheila report this? Part of an experimental group was, uh, curtailed. On impulse he inserts some carrots too, inserts more absinthe into himself. He knows he is putting off what he has come here to do.

All right, get at it.

He stomps past a cage of baby rabbits with their eyes epoxyed shut, somebody's undergraduate demonstration of perceptual learning, and turns on the light over the sinks. All dirty with hanks of skin and dog offal. Why the hell can't they clean up after themselves? We are scientists. Too lofty. He whooshes with the power hose, which leaks. Nobody cares enough even to bring a washer. He will bring one. No, he won't! He's going to be doing something different from here on in.

But first of all he has to get rid of all this. Sacrifice his subjects. His ex-subjects. Where's my ether?

He finds it back of the mops, has another snort of the cloudy liquor to fortify himself while he sets up his killing jars. He has evolved what he thinks is the decentest way: an ether pad under a grill to keep their feet from being burned by the stuff.

The eight jars are in a row on the sink. He lifts down a cage of elderly females, the grandmothers of his present group. They cluster at the front, trustfully expectant. Oh God; he postpones murder long enough to give them some carrot, deals out more to every cage in the rack so they'll have time to eat. Tumult of rustling, hopping, munching.

All right. He goes back to the sink and pours in the ether, keeping the lids tight. Then he reaches in the holding cage and scoops up a soft female in each hand. Quick: He pops them both in one jar, rescrews the lid.

He has this fatuous belief that the companionship helps a little. They convulse frantically, are going limp before he has the next pair in theirs. Next. Next. Next . . . It takes five minutes to be sure of death.

This will be, he realizes, a long night.

He lifts down another cage, lifts up his bottle, leaning with his back to the jars to look at his rack, his little city of rats. My troops. My pathetic troops. An absinthe trip flashes through his head of himself leading his beasts against his colleagues, against the laughing pain-givers. Jones having his brain reamed by a Dachshund pup. A kitten in a surgical smock shaving Sheila, wow. Stop it!

His eye has been wandering over the bottom cages. The mothers have taken the goodies in to their young; interesting to see what goes on in there, maybe if he used infra-red—stop that, too. A lab is not a zoo. Down in one dark back cage he can see the carrot is still there. Where's Snedecor, the old brain-damaged male? Why hasn't he come for it? Is the light bothering him?

Lipsitz turns off the top lights, goes around to the side to check. Stooping, he peers into the gloom. Something funny down there—good grief, the damn cage is busted, it's rotted through the bottom. Where's old Sneddles?

The ancient cage rack has wheels. Lipsitz drags one end forward, revealing Stygian darkness behind. In prehistoric times there was a coal chute there. And there's something back here now, on the heap of bags by the old intake.

Lipsitz frowns, squints; the lab lights behind him seem to be growing dim and gaseous. The thing—the thing has black and white patches. Is it moving?

He retreats to the drainboard, finds his hand on the bottle. Yes. Another short one. What's wrong with the lights? The fluorescents have developed filmy ectoplasm, must be chow dust. This place is a powder keg. The monkeys are still as death too. That's unusual. In fact everything is dead quiet except for an odd kind of faint clicking, which he realizes is coming from the dark behind the rack. An animal. Some animal has got out and been living back there, that's all it is.

All right, Lipsitz: Go see.

But he delays, aware that the absinthe has replaced his limbs with vaguer, dreamlike extensions. The old females on the drainboard watch him alertly; the dead ones in the jars watch nothing. All his little city of rats has stopped moving, is watching him. Their priest of pain. This is a temple of pain, he thinks. A small shabby dirty one. Maybe its dirt and squalor are better so, more honest. A charnel house shouldn't look pretty, like a clean kitchen. All over the country, the world, the spotless knives are slicing, the trained minds devising casual torments in labs so bright and fair you could eat off their floors. Auschwitz, Belsen were neat. With flowers. Only the reek of pain going up to the sky, the empty sky. But people don't think animals' pain matters. They didn't think my people's pain mattered either, in the death camps a generation back. It's all the same, endless agonies going up unheard from helpless things. And all for what?

Maybe somewhere there is a reservoir of pain, he muses. Waiting to be filled. When it is full, will something rise from it? Something created and summoned by torment? Inhuman, an alien superthing . . . He knows he is indulging drunkenness. The clicking has grown louder.

Go and look at the animal, Lipsitz.

He goes, advances on the dark alcove, peering down, hearing the click-click-click. Suddenly he recognizes it: the tooth-click a rat makes in certain states of mind. Not threatening at all, it must be old Sneddles in there. Heartened, he pulls a dim light bulb forward on its string—and sees the thing plain, while the lab goes unreal around him.

What's lying back there among the Purina bags is an incredible whorl—a tangle of rat legs, rat heads, rat bodies, rat tails intertwined in a great wheellike formation, *joined* somehow abnormally rat to rat—a huge rat pie, heaving, pulsing, eyes reflecting stress and pain. Quite horrible, really; the shock of it is making him fight for breath. And it is not all laboratory animals; he can see the agouti coats of feral rats mixed in among it. Have wild rats come in here to help form this gruesome thing?

And at that moment, hanging to the light bulb, he knows what he is seeing. He has read in the old lore, the ancient grotesque legends of rat and man.

He is looking at a Rat King.

Medieval records were full of them, he recalls dimly. Was it Württemberg? *"They are monstrously Joynt, yet Living . . . It can by no way be Separated, and screamed much in the Fyre."* Apparitions that occurred at times of great attack on the rats. Some believed that the rat armies had each their king of this sort, who directed them. And they were sometimes connected to or confused with King Rats of still another kind: gigantic animals with eyes of fire and gold chains on their necks.

Lipsitz stares, swaying on the light cord. The tangled mass of the Rat King remains there clicking faintly, pulsing, ambiguously agonized among the sacks. His other hand seems to be holding the bottle; good. He takes a deep pull, his eyes rolling to fix the ghastliness, wondering what on earth he will do. "I can't," he mumbles aloud, meaning the whole thing, the whole bloody thing. *"I can't . . ."*

He can do his own little business, kill his animals, wind up his foolishness, get out. But he cannot—can not—be expected to cope with this, to abolish this revenant from time, this perhaps supernatural horror. For which he feels obscurely, hideously to blame. It's my fault, I . . .

He realizes he is weeping thinly, his eyes are running. Whether it's for the animals or himself he doesn't know; he knows only that he can't stand it, can't take any of it any more. And now *this.*

"No!" Meaning, really, the whole human world. Dizzily he blinks around at the jumbled darkness, trying to regain his wits, feeling himself a random mote of protesting life in an insignificant fool-killer. Slowly his eyes come back to the monstrous, pitiable rat pie. It seems to be weakening; the click has lost direction. His gaze drifts upward, into the dark shadows.

—And he is quite unsurprised, really, to meet eyes looking back. Two large round animal eyes deep in the darkness, at about the level of his waist, the tapetums reflecting pale vermilion fire.

He stares; the eyes shift right, left, calmly in silence, and then the head advances. He sees the long wise muzzle, the vibrissae, the tuned shells of the ears. Is there a gold collar? He can't tell; but he can make out the creature's forelimbs now, lightly palping the bodies or body of the Rat King. And the tangled thing is fading, shrinking away. It was perhaps its conjoined forces which strove and suffered to give birth to this other—the King himself.

"Hello," Lipsitz whispers idiotically, feeling no horror any more but emotion of a quite other kind. The big warm presence before him surveys him. Will he be found innocent? He licks his lips. They have come at last, he thinks. They have risen; they are going to wipe all this out. Me, too? But he does not care; a joy he can't possibly control rises in him as he sees gold glinting on the broad chest fur. He licks his dry lips again, swallows.

"Welcome. Your Majesty."

The Beast-King makes no response; the eyes leave him and go gravely toward the aisles beyond. Involuntarily Lipsitz backs aside. The King's vibrissae are fanning steadily, bringing the olfactory news, the quiet tooth-click starts. When the apparition comes forward a pace Lipsitz is deeply touched to see the typical halfhop, the ratly carriage. The King's coat is lustrous graybrown, feral pelage. Of course. It is a natural male, too; he smiles timidly, seeing that the giant body has the familiar long hump, the heavy rear-axle loading. Is old Snedecor translated into some particle of this wonder? The cellar is unbreathing, hushed except for the meditative click-click from the King.

"You, you are going to . . ." Lipsitz tries but is struck dumb by the sense of something happening all around him. Invisible, inaudible—but tangible as day.

An emergence, yes! In the rooms beyond they are emerging, coming out from the score upon score of cages, boxes, pens, racks, shackles and wires—all of them emerging, coming to the King. All of them, blinded rabbits, mutilated hamsters, damaged cats and rats and brain-holed rhesus quietly knuckling along, even the paralyzed dogs moving somehow, coming toward their King.

And at this moment Lipsitz realizes the King is turning too, the big brown body is wheeling, quite normally away from him, going away toward the deeper darkness in the end of the coal bay. They are leaving him!

"Wait!" He stumbles forward over the dead rat pie; he cannot bear to lose this. "Please . . ."

Daring all, he reaches out and touches the flank of the magical beast, expecting he knows not what. The flank is warm, is solid! The King glances briefly back at him, still moving away. Boldly Lipsitz strides closer, comes alongside, his hand now resting firmly on the withers as they go.

But they are headed straight at what he knows is only wall, though he can see nothing. The cellar ends there. No matter—he will not let go of the magic, no, and he steps out beside the moving King, thinking, I am an animal too! —And finds at the last instant that his averted, flinching head is moving through dark nothing, through a blacker emptiness where the King is leading—they are going, going out.

Perhaps an old sewer, he thinks, lurching along beside the big benign presence, remembering tales of forgotten tunnels under this old city, into which the new subway has bored. Yes, that's what it must be. He is finding he can see again in a pale ghostly way, can now walk upright. His left hand is tight on the shoulders of the calmly pacing beast, feeling the living muscles play beneath the fur, bringing him joy and healing. Where are the others?

He dares a quick look back and sees them. They are coming. The dim way behind is filled with quiet beasts, moving together rank on rank as far as he can sense, animals large and small. He can hear their peaceful rustling now. And they are not only the beasts of his miserable lab, he realizes, but a torrent of others—he has glimpsed goats, turtles, a cow, raccoons, skunks, an opossum and what appears as a small monkey riding on a limping spaniel. Even birds are there, hopping and fluttering above!

My God, it is everything, he thinks. It is Hamlin in reverse; all the abused ones, the gentle ones, are leaving the world. He risks another glance back and thinks he can see a human child too and maybe an old person among the throng, all measuredly, silently moving together in the dimness. An endless host going, going out at last, going away. And he is feeling their emanation, the gentleness of it, the unspeaking warmth. He is happier than he has been ever in his life.

"You're taking us away," he says to the King-Beast beside him. "The ones who can't cut it. We're all leaving for good, isn't that it?"

There is no verbal answer; only a big-stemmed ear swivels to him briefly as the King goes gravely on. Lipsitz needs no speech, no explanation. He simply walks alongside letting the joy rise in him. Why had it always been forbidden to be gentle? he wonders. Did they really see it as a threat, to have hated us so? But that is all over now, all over and gone, he is sure, although he has no slightest idea where this may be leading, this procession into chthonian infinity. For this moment it is enough to feel the silent communion, the reassurance rising through him from his hand on the flank of the great spirit-beast. The flank is totally solid; he can feel all the workings of life; it is the body of a real animal. But it is also friendship beyond imagining; he has never known anything as wonderful as this communion, not sex or sunsets or even the magic hour on his first bike. It is as if everything is all right now, will be all right forever—griefs he did not even know he carried are falling from him, leaving him light as smoke.

Crippled, he had been; crippled from the years of bearing it, not just the lab, the whole thing. Everything. He can hardly believe the relief. A vagrant thought brushes him: Who will remain? If there is anything to care for, to be comforted, who will care? He floats it away, concentrating on the comfort that emanates from the strange life at his side, the myth-beast ambling in the most ordinary way through this dark conduit, which is now winding down, or perhaps up and down, he cannot tell.

The paving under his feet looks quite commonplace, damp and cracked. Beside him the great rat's muscles bunch and stretch as each hind leg comes under; he glances back and smiles to see the King's long ring-scaled tail curve right, curve left, carried in the relaxed-alert mode. No need for fluffy fur now. He is, he realizes, going into mysteries. Inhuman mysteries, perhaps. He doesn't care. He is among his kind. Where they are going he will go. Even to inhumanity, even alone.

But he is not, he realizes as his eyes adapt more and more, alone after all! A human figure is behind him on the far side of the King, quietly threading its way forward, overtaking him. A girl—is it a girl? Yes. He can scarcely make her out, but as she comes closer still he sees with growing alarm that it is a familiar body—it could be, oh God, it is! Sheila.

Not *Sheila,* here! No, no.

But light-footed, she has reached him, is walking even with him, stretching out her hand, too, to touch the moving King.

And then to his immense, unspeakable relief he sees that she is of course not Sheila—how could it be? Not Sheila at all, only a girl of the same height, with the same dove-breasted close-coupled curves that speak to his desire, the same heavy dark mane. Her head turns toward him across the broad back of the King, and he sees that although her features are like Sheila's, the face is wholly different, open, informed with innocence. An Eve in this second morning of the world. Sheila's younger sister perhaps, he wonders dazedly, seeing that she is looking at him now, that her lips form a gentle smile.

"Hello," he cannot help whispering, fearful to break the spell, to inject harsh human sound into his progress. But the spell does not break; indeed, the girl's face comes clearer. She puts up a hand to push her hair back, the other firmly on the flank of the King.

"Hello." Her voice is very soft but in no way fragile. She is looking at him with the eyes of Sheila, but eyes so differently warmed and luminous that he wants only to gaze delighted as they pass to whatever destination; he is so overwhelmed to meet a vulnerable human soul in those lambent brown eyes. A soul? he thinks, feeling his unbodied feet step casually, firmly on the way to eternity, perhaps. What an unfashionable word. He is not religious, he does not believe there are any gods or souls, except as a shorthand term denoting—what?—compassion or responsibility, all that. And so much argument about it all, too; his mind is momentarily invaded by a spectral horde of old debating scholars, to whom he had paid less than no attention in his classroom days. But he is oddly prepared to hear the girl recite conversationally, "There is no error more powerful in leading feeble minds astray from the straight path of virtue than the supposition that the soul of brutes is of the same nature as our own."

"Descartes," he guesses.

She nods, smiling across the big brown shape between them. The King's great leaflike ears have flickered to their interchange, returned to forward hold.

"He started it all, didn't he?" Lipsitz says, or perhaps only thinks. "That they're robots, you can do anything to them. Their pain doesn't count. But we're animals too," he adds somberly, unwilling to let even a long-dead philosopher separate him from the flow of this joyous River. Or was it that? A faint disquiet flicks him, is abolished.

She nods again; the sweet earnest woman-face of her almost kills him with love. But as he stares the disquiet flutters again; is there beneath her smile a transparency, a failure of substance—even a sadness, as though she was moving to some inexorable loss. No; it is all right. It is.

"Where are we going, do you know?" he asks, against some better judgment. The King-Beast flicks an ear; but Lipsitz must know, now.

She smiles, unmistakably mischievous, considering him.

"To where all the lost things go," she says. "It's very beautiful. Only . . ." She falls silent.

"Only what?" He is uneasy again, seeing she has turned away, is walking with her small chin resolute. Dread grows in him, cannot be dislodged. The moments of simple joy are past now; he fears that he still has some burden. It is perhaps a choice? Whatever it is, it's looming around him or in him as they go—an impending significance he wishes desperately to avoid. It is not a thinning out nor an awakening; he clutches hard at the strong shoulders of the King, the magical leader, feels his reassuring warmth. All things are in the lotus . . . But loss impends.

"Only what?" he asks again, knowing he must and must not. Yes; he is still there, is moving with them to the final refuge. The bond holds. "The place where lost things go is very beautiful, only what?"

"Do you really want to know?" she asks him with the light of the world in her face.

It *is* a choice, he realizes, trembling now. It is not for free, it's not that simple. But can't I just stop this, just go on? Yes, he can—he knows it. Maybe. But he hears his human voice persist.

"Only *what?*"

"Only it isn't real," she says. And his heart breaks.

And suddenly it is all breaking too—a fearful thin wave of emptiness slides through him, sends him stumbling, his handhold lost. "No! Wait!" He reaches desperately; he can feel them still near him, feel their passage all around. "Wait . . ." He understands now, understands with searing grief that it really is the souls of things, and perhaps himself that are passing, going away forever. They have stood it as long as they can and now they are leaving. The pain has culminated in this, that they leave us—leave me, leave me behind in a clockwork Cartesian world in which nothing will mean anything forever.

"Oh, wait," he cries in dark nowhere, unable to bear the loss, the still-living comfort, passing away. *Only it isn't real,* what does that mean? Is it the choice, that the reality is that I must stay behind and try, and try?

He doesn't know, but can only cry, "No, please take me! Let me come too!" staggering after them through unreality, feeling them still there, still possible, ahead, around. It is wrong; he is terrified somewhere that he is failing, doing wrong. But his human heart can only yearn for the sweetness, for the great benevolent King-Beast so surely leading, to feel again their joy. "Please, I want to go with you—"

—And yes! For a last instant he has it; he touches again the warmth and life, sees the beautiful lost face that is and isn't Sheila—they are there! And he tries with all his force crazily to send himself after them, to burst from his skin, his life if need be—only to share again that gentleness. *"Take* me!"

But it is no good—he can't; they have vanished and he has fallen kneeling on dank concrete, nursing his head in empty shaking hands. It was in vain, and it was wrong. Or was it? his fading thought wonders as he feels himself black out. Did something of myself go too, fly to its selfish joy? He does not know.

. . . And will never know, as he returns to sodden consciousness, makes out that he is sprawled like a fool in the dirt behind his rat cages with the acid taste of wormwood sickly in his mouth and an odd dryness and lightness in his heart.

What the hell had he been playing at? That absinthe is a bummer, he thinks, picking himself up and slapping his clothes disgustedly. This filthy place, what a fool he'd been to think he could work here. And these filthy rats. There's something revolting back here on the floor, too. Leave it for posterity; he drags the rack back in place.

All right, get this over. Humming to himself, he turns the power hose on the messy floor, gives the stupid rats in their cages a blast too for good measure. There are his jars—but whatever had possessed him, trying to kill them individually like that? Hours it would take. He knows a simpler way if he can find a spare garbage can.

Good, here it is. He brings it over and starts pulling

out cage after cage, dumping them all in together. Nests, babies, carrots, crap and all. Shrieks, struggling. Tough tit, friends. The ether can is almost full; he pours the whole thing over the crying mess and jams on the lid, humming louder. The can walls reverberate with teeth. Not quite enough gas, no matter.

He sits down on it and notices that a baby rat has run away hiding behind his shoe. Mechanical mouse, a stupid automaton. He stamps on its back and kicks it neatly under Sheila's hamster rack, wondering why Descartes has popped into his thoughts. There is no error more powerful—Shit with old D., let's think about Sheila. There is no error more powerful than the belief that some cunt can't be had. Somehow he feels sure that he will find that particular pussy-patch wide open to him any day now. As soon as his project gets under way.

Because he has an idea. (That absinthe wasn't all bad.) Oh yes. An idea that'll pin old Welch's ears back. In fact it may be too much for old Welch, too, quotes, commercial. Well, fuck old Welch, this is one project somebody will buy, that's for sure. Does the Mafia have labs? Ho ho, far out.

And fuck students too, he thinks genially, wrestling the can to the entrance, ignoring sounds from within. No more Polinskis, no more shit, teaching is for suckers. My new project will take care of that. Will there be a problem getting subjects? No—look at all the old walking carcasses they sell for dogfood. And there's a slaughterhouse right by the freeway, no problem at all. But he *will* need a larger lab.

He locks up, and briskly humming the rock version of "Anitra's Dance," he goes out into the warm rainy dawnlight, reviewing in his head the new findings on the mid-brain determinants of motor intensity.

It should be no trick at all to seat some electrodes that will make an animal increase the intensity of whatever it's doing. Like say, *running*. Speed it right up to max, run like it never ran before regardless of broken legs or what. What a natural! Surprising someone else hasn't started already.

And just as a cute hypothesis, he's pretty sure he could seal the implants damn near invisibly; he has a smooth hand with flesh. Purely hypothetical, of course. But suppose you used synthetics with, say, acid-release. That would be hard to pick up on X rays. H'mmm.

Of course, he doesn't know much about horses, but he learns fast. Grinning, he breaks into a jog to catch the lucky bus that has appeared down the deserted street. He has just recalled a friend who has a farm not fifty miles away. Wouldn't it be neat to run the pilot project using surplus Shetland ponies?

She Waits for All Men Born

Pale, beyond porch and portal,
Crowned with calm leaves she stands
Who gathers all things mortal
With pale, immortal hands.
                              —Swinburne

*In the wastes of nonbeing it is born, flickers out, is born
again and holds together, swells and spreads. In lifelessness it lives, against the gray tide of entropy it strives,
improbably persists, gathering itself into ever richer
complexities until it grows as a swelling wave. As a wave
grows it grows indeed, for while its crest surges trium-
phant in the sunlight its every particle is down-falling
forever into dark, is blown away into nothing in the moment of its leap. It triumphs perishing, for it was not
born alone. Following it into being came its dark twin,
its Adversary, the shadow which ceaselessly devours it
from within. Pitilessly pursued, attacked in every vital,
the living wave foams upward, its billion momentary
crests blooming into the light above the pain and death
that claims them. Over uncounted aeons the mortal
substance strives, outreaches. Death-driven, it flees ever
more swiftly before its Enemy until it runs, leaps, soars
into flashing flight. But it cannot outrace the fire in its
flesh, for the limbs that bear it are Death, and Death is*

255

the wing it flies on. In the agony of its myriad members, victorious and dying, Life drives upon the indifferent air . . .

The burrow is dark. Pelicosaurus squats over her half-grown pups, her dim node of awareness holding only the sensation of their muzzles sucking the glandular skin of her belly among her not-quite hair. From outside comes a thunderous eructation, splashing. The burrow quakes. Pelicosaurus crouches, rigid; the huddled pups freeze. All but one—a large female pup has squirmed free, is nosing nervously toward the recesses of the burrow. She moves in a half-crawl, her body slung from the weak reptilian shoulder girdle.

More crashes outside. Earth showers down within the damp nest. The mother only crouches tighter, locked in reflexive stasis. The forgotten pup is now crawling away up a tunnel.

As she vanishes, the giant hadrosaur in the stream outside decides to clamber out. Twenty tons of reptile hit the soft bank. Earth, rocks and roots slam together, crushing Pelicosaurus and her pups and all other bank-dwellers into an earthy gel, a trough of destruction behind the departing one. Leather wings clap; pterosaurs are gathering to stab in the wreckage.

Farther up the bank beside a gymnosperm root, the lone pup wriggles free. She cowers, hearing the hoarse grunts of the scavengers. Then an obscure tropism rises in her, an undefined urge toward space, toward up. Awkwardly she grips the bole of the gymnosperm with her forelimbs. A grub moves on the bark. Automatically she seizes and eats it, her eyes blinking as she strives to focus beyond. Presently she begins to clamber higher, carrying, in the intricacy of her genes, the tiny anomaly which has saved her. In the egg from which she grew a molecule has imperceptibly shifted structure. From its aberrant program has unfolded a minute relaxation of the species-wide command to freeze, a small tendency to action under stress. The pup that is no longer wholly Pelicosaur feels her ill-adapted hindlimb slip upon the branch, scrabbles for purchase, falls, and crawls weakly from the graveyard of her kind.

. . . So the wave of Life mounts under the lash of Death, grows, gathers force in unbounded diversity. Ever-perishing, ever-resurgent, it foams to higher, more complex victories upon the avalanche of its corpses. As a wave swells, it surges, swarming, striving ever more strongly, achieving ever more intricate strategies of evasion, flinging itself in wilder trajectories to escape its pain. But it bears its Enemy within it, for Death is the power of its uprush. Dying in every member, yet every moment renewed, the multiple-hearted wave of Life crests into strangeness . . .

Yelling, the hairless creature runs swiftly, knuckles to earth, and screams again as a rock strikes him. He swerves and scuttles, limping now; he is unable to avoid the hail of missiles flung by those stronger, more freely jointed arms. His head is struck. He goes down. The bipeds close around him. Shouting in still wordless joy they fall upon their brother with thin jaws and sharpened stones.

. . . The living, dying tumult mounts, fountains into culminate light. Its billion tormented fragments take on intenser being; it leaps as a great beast above the ravenings of its Adversary. But it cannot shake free, for the force of its life is Death, and its strength is as the strength of the deaths that consume it, its every particle is propelled by the potency of the dark Assailant. In the measure of its dying, Life towers, triumphs, and rolls resistless across the planet that bore it . . .

Two horsemen move slowly across the plain under the cold autumn rain. The first is a young boy on a spotted pony; he is leading a black-eared roan on which his father is riding slumped, breathing open-mouthed above the rifle-ball in his chest. The man's hand holds a bow, but there are no arrows. The Kiowas' stores and supplies were lost at Palo Duro Canyon and the last arrows were fired in the slaughter at the Staked Plains three days back, where his wife and oldest son were killed.

As they pass a copse of willows the rain eases for a moment. Now they can see the white man's buildings ahead: Fort Sill with its gray stone corral. Into that corral their friends and relatives have vanished, family by family, surrendering to their merciless enemy. The boy halts his pony. He can see a column of soldiers riding out of the fort. Beside him his father makes a sound, tries to raise his bow. The boy licks his lips; he has not eaten for three days. Slowly he urges his pony forward again.

As they ride on, faint sounds of firing come to them on the wet wind, from a field west of the fort. The white men are shooting the Kiowas' horses, destroying the life of their life. For the Kiowas, this is the end. They were among the finest horsemen the world has ever known, and war was their sacred occupation. Three centuries before, they had come down out of the dark mountains, had acquired horses and a god and burst out in glory to rule a thousand miles of range. But they never understood the grim, unrelenting advance of the U.S. Cavalry. Now they are finished.

The Kiowas have been toughened by natural hardship, by millennia of death in the wilderness. But their death-strength is not enough. The pale soldiers before them are the survivors of more deadly centuries in the cauldrons of Europe; they drive upon the Indians with the might derived from uncountable generations of close-quarter murder in battle, deaths under merciless tyrannies, by famines and plagues. As has happened before and before and before, the gray-faced children of the greater death roll forward, conquer and spread out across the land.[1]

. . . *So the great Beast storms among the flames that devour it, the myriad lives of its being a crucible of always fiercer deaths and more ascendant life. And now its agonized onrush changes. What had been flight becomes battle. The Beast turns on the enemy that sav-*

ages it and strives to cast Death from its heart. Desperately it struggles; streaming from the wounds that are its life, it fights to save some fragment while Death slays whole members. For Death is the twin of its essence, growing as Life grows, and the fury of its attack mounts with the power that attacks it. Locked into intimate battle, the Beast and its Enemy are now nearing a consummating phase of pain. The struggle rages, breaches the norms of matter. Time accelerates . . .

As night comes over the Mediterranean the battered freighter limps warily past the enemy ears on Cyprus. Rain and darkness hide it; it creeps with all lights extinguished, every human sound quenched. Only the throbbing of its engines and the thrashing of its rusty screw remain to betray it to the blockaders. In its body is the precious cargo, the huddled silent sparks of life. The children. The living ones, the handfuls saved from the six million corpses of the death camps, saved from the twenty million killed by the Reich. In darkness and desperation it crawls on, leaking, the crew not daring to work the creaking pumps. Hidden by the night it steams mile by daring mile through the gauntlet of the blockade, carrying the children to Palestine.

While on the other side of the world, in the morning of that same night, a single bomber leaves its escort and bores steadily westward through the high cold air. The *Enola Gay* is on course to Hiroshima.

. . . Pain-driven, death-sinewed, the convulsed Beast strives against its Enemy. In ever-new torment it grows, rears itself to new brilliancy, achieves ever-greater victories over Death, and is in turn more fearfully attacked. The struggle flames unseen across the planet, intensifying until it breaks from the bounds of earth and flings portions of itself to space. But the Beast cannot escape, for it carries Death with it and fuels Death with its fire. The battle heightens, fills earth, sea and air. In supreme agony it fountains into a crest of living fire that is a darkness upon the world . . .

"Doctor, that was beautiful." The senior surgical nurse's whisper barely carries beyond her mask.

The surgeon's eyes are on the mirror where the hands of the suturist can be seen delicately manipulating the clamped-back layers. *Lub-dub, lub-dub;* the surgeon's eyes go briefly to the biofeedback display, check the plasma exchange levels, note the intent faces of the anesthesiology team under their headsets, go back vigilantly to the mirror. Vigilant—but it is over, really. A success, a massive success. The child's organs will function perfectly now, the dying one will live. Another impossibility achieved.

The senior nurse sighs again appreciatively, brushing away a thought that comes. The thought of the millions of children elsewhere now dying of famine and disease. Healthy children too, not birth-doomed like this one but perfectly functional; inexorably dying in their millions from lack of food and care. Don't think of it. Here we save lives. We do our utmost.

The operating room is sealed against the sounds of the city outside, which yet comes through as a faint, all-pervading drone. Absently, the nurse notices a new sound in the drone: an odd high warbling. Then she hears the interns behind her stirring. Someone whispers urgently. The surgeon's eyes do not waver, but his face above the mask turns rigid. She must protect him from distraction. Careful that her clothing does not rustle, she wheels on the offenders. There is a far burst of voices from the corridor.

"Be quiet!" She hisses with voiceless intensity, raking the interns with her gray gaze. As she does so, she recalls what that continuous warbling tone is. Air-attack warning. The twenty-minute alert, meaning that missiles are supposed to be on their way around the world from the alien land. But this cannot be serious. It must be some drill—very laudable, no doubt, but not to be allowed to disturb the operating room. The drill can be held another time; it will take more than twenty minutes to finish here.

"Quiet," she breathes again sternly. The interns are still. Satisfied, she turns back, holding herself proudly, ignoring fatigue, ignoring the shrill faint whining, ignoring at the end even the terrible flash that penetrates the seams of the ceiling far above.

—And the riven Beast crashes, bursts together with its Enemy into a billion boiling, dwindling fragments that form and re-form under the fires of a billion radiant deaths. Yet it is still one, still joined in torment and unending vitality. With its inmost plasm laid bare to the lethal energies Life struggles more intensely still, more fiercely attacks the Death that quenches its reborn momentary lives. The battle grows to total fury, until it invades the very substrata of being. Culminant paroxysm is reached; in ultimate agony the ultimate response is found. The Beast penetrates at last into its Adversary's essence and takes it to itself. In final transcendence. Life swallows Death, and forges the heart of its ancient Enemy to its own . . .

The infant between the dead thighs of its mother is very pale. Dismayed, the Healer frees it from the birth slime, holds it up. It is a female, and perfectly formed, he sees, despite the whiteness of its skin. It takes breath with a tiny choke, does not cry. He hands it to the midwife, who is covering the mother's corpse. Perhaps the pallor is natural, he thinks; all his tribe of Whites have heavy pale skins, though none so white as this.

"A beautiful baby girl," the midwife says, swabbing it. "Open your eyes, baby."

The baby squirms gently but its eyes remain closed. The Healer turns back one delicate eyelid. Beneath is a large, fully-formed eye. But the iris is snow-white around the black pupil. He passes his hand over it; the eye does not respond to light. Feeling an odd disquiet, he examines the other. It is the same.

"Blind."

"Oh, no. Such a sweet baby."

The Healer broods. The Whites are a civilized tribe, for all that they have lived near two great craters before they came here to the sea. He knows that his people's albinism is all too frequently coupled with optical defect. But the child seems healthy.

"I'll take her," says Marn, the midwife. "I still have milk, look."

They watch as the baby girl nuzzles Marn's breast and happily, normally, finds her food.

Weeks pass into months. The baby grows, smiles early, though her eyes remain closed. She is a peaceful baby; she babbles, chortles, produces a sound that is surely "Marn, Marn." Marn loves her fiercely and guiltily; her own children are all boys. She calls the pale baby "Snow."

When Snow begins to creep Marn watches anxiously, but the blind child moves with quiet skill, seeming to sense where things are. A happy child, she sings small songs to herself and soon pulls herself upright by Marn's leather trousers. She begins to totter alone and Marn's heart fears again. But Snow is cautious and adroit, she strikes few obstacles. It is hard to believe that she is blind. She laughs often, acquires only a few small bumps and abrasions which heal with amazing speed.

Though small and slight, she is a very healthy baby, welcoming new experience, new smells, sounds, tastes, touches, new words. She speaks in an unchildishly gentle voice. Her dark world does not seem to trouble her. Nor does she show the stigmata of blindness; her face is mobile, and when she smiles, the long white lashes tremble on her cheeks as if she is holding them closed in fun.

The Healer examines her yearly, finding himself ever more reluctant to confront that blank silver gaze. He knows he will have to decide if she should be allowed to breed, and he is dismayed to find her otherwise so thriving. It will be difficult. But in her third year the decision is taken from him. He feels very unwell at the time of her examination and shortly realizes that he has contracted the new wasting sickness which has been beyond his power to cure.

The daily life of the Whites goes on. They are a well-fed, Ingles-speaking, littoral people. Their year revolves around the massive catches of fish coming up from the sea-arm to spawn. Most of the fish are still recognizable as forms of trout and salmon. But each year the Whites check the first runs with their precious artifact, an ancient Geiger counter which is carefully recharged from their water-driven generator.

When the warm days come Snow goes with Marn and her sons to the beach where the first-caught will be ritually tested. The nets are downstream from the village, set in the canyon's mouth. The beaches open out to the sea-arm, surrounded by tall ice-capped crags. Fires burn merrily on the sands, there is music and children are playing while the adults watch the fishermen haul in the leaping, glittering nets. Snow runs and laughs, paddling in the icy stream edge.

"Fliers up there," the Netmaster says to Marn. She looks up at the cliffs where he points, searching for a flitting red shape. The Fliers have been getting bolder, perhaps from hunger. During the last winter they have sneaked into an outlying hut and stolen a child. No one knows exactly what they are. Some say they are big monkeys, some believe they are degenerated men. They are man-shaped, small but strong, with loose angry-looking folds of skin between their limbs on which they can make short glides. They utter cries which are not speech, and they are always hungry. At fish-drying times the Whites keep guards patrolling the fires day and night.

Suddenly there is shouting from the canyon.

"Fliers! They're heading to the town!"

Fishermen paddle swiftly back to shore, and a party of men go pounding upstream toward the village. But no sooner have they gone than a ring of reddish heads pops into sight on the near cliffs, and more Fliers are suddenly diving on the shore.

Marn snatches up a brand from a fire and runs to the attack, shouting at the children to stay back. Under the women's onslaught the Fliers scramble away. But they are desperate, returning again and again until many are killed. As the last attackers scramble away up the rocks

Marn realizes that the blind baby is not among the other children by the fires.

"Snow! Snow, where are you?"

Have the Fliers snatched her? Marn runs frantically along the beach, searching behind boulders, crying Snow's name. Beyond a rocky outcrop she sees a Flier's crumpled legs and runs to look.

Two Fliers lie there unmoving. And just beyond them is what she feared to find—a silver-pale small body in a spread of blood.

"Snow, my baby, oh, no—"

She runs, bends over Snow. One of the little girl's arms is hideously mangled, bitten nearly off. A Flier must have started to eat her before another attacked him. Marn crouches above the body, refusing to know that the child must be dead. She makes herself look at the horrible wound, suddenly stares closer. She is seeing something that makes her distraught eyes widen more wildly. A new scream begins to rise in her throat. Her gaze turns from the wound to the white, still face.

Her last sight is of the baby's long pale lashes lifting, opening to reveal the shining silver eyes.

Marn's oldest son finds them so; the two dead Fliers, the dead woman and the miraculously living, scarless child. It is generally agreed that Marn has perished saving Snow. The child cannot explain.

From that time little Snow the twice-orphaned is cared for among the children of the Netmaster.

She grows, though very slowly, into a graceful, beloved little girl. Despite her blindness she makes herself skilled and useful at many tasks; she is clever and patient with the endless work of mending nets and fish-drying and pressing oil. She can even pick berries, her small quick hands running through the thickets almost as expert as eyes. She patrols Marn's old gathering paths, bringing back roots, mushrooms, bird's eggs and the choicest camass bulbs.

The new Healer watches her troubledly, knowing he will have to make the decision his predecessor dreaded. How serious is her defect? The old Healer had thought that she must be interdicted, not allowed to breed lest the blindness spread. But he is troubled, looking at the bright, healthy child. There has been so much sickness in the tribe, this wasting which he cannot combat. Babies do not thrive. How can he interdict this little potential breeder, who is so active and vigorous? And yet— and yet the blindness must be heritable. And the child is not growing normally; year by year she does not mature. He becomes almost reassured, seeing that Snow is still a child while the Netmaker's baby son is attaining manhood and his own canoe. Perhaps she will never develop at all, he thinks. Perhaps there will be no need to decide.

But slowly, imperceptibly Snow's little body lengthens and rounds out, until when the ice melts one year he sees that small breasts have budded on her narrow ribs. The day before she had been still a child; today she is unmistakably a baby woman. The Healer sighs, studying her tender, animated face. It is hard to see her as defective; the lightly closed eyes seem so normal. But two of the dead-born infants have been very pale and white-eyed. Is this a lethal mutation? His problem is upon him. He cannot resolve it; he determines to call a council of the tribe.

But his plan is never to be put to action. Someone else has been studying Snow too. It is the Weatherwoman's youngest son, who follows her to the fern-root grove.

"This is the kind you eat," Snow tells him, holding up the yellow fiddle-heads. He stares down at her delicious little body. Impossible to remember or care that she is thrice his age.

"I want—I want to talk to you, Snow."

"Umm?" She smiles up at his voice. His heart pounds.

"Snow . . ."

"What, Byorg?" Listening so intently, the silvery lashes quivering as if they will lift and open to him. Yet they do not, and pity for her blindness chokes him. He touches her arm, she comes against him naturally. She is smiling, her breathing quickened. He holds her, thinking how she must feel his touch in her dark world, her helplessness. He must be gentle.

"Byorg?" she breathes. "Oh, Byorg——"

Trying to restrain himself he holds her more tightly to him, touching her, feeling her trembling. He is trembling too, caressing her beneath her light tunic, feeling her yielding, half trying to pull away, her breath hot on his neck.

"Oh, Snow——" Above the pounding of his blood he is vaguely conscious of a sound overhead, but he can think only of the body in his arms.

A harsh yowl breaks out behind him.

"Fliers!"

He whirls around too late—the red flapping figure has launched something at him, a spear—and he is staggering, grasping a bony shaft sunk in his own neck.

"Run, Snow!" he tries to shout. But she is there still, above him, trying to hold him as he falls. More Fliers pound past. As the world dims, he sees in last wonderment her huge eyes opening wide and white.

Silence.

Snow raises herself slowly, still open-eyed. She lets the dead boy's head down to the moss. Three dead Fliers sprawl around them. She listens, hears faintly the sound of screaming from the village. It is a major attack, she realizes. And Fliers have never used weapons before. Shivering, she strokes Byorg's hair. Her face is crumpled in grief but the eyes remain open, silver reflectors focused at infinity.

"No," she says brokenly. "No!" She jumps up, begins running toward the village, stumbling as she races open-eyed, as a blind person runs. Three Fliers swoop behind her. She screams and turns to face them. They drop in red, ragged heaps and she runs on, hearing the clamor of battle at the village walls.

The frantic villagers do not see her coming, they are struggling in a horde of Fliers who have infiltrated the side gate and broken loose among the huts. At the main gate the torches have started thatch fires; Fliers and Whites alike have fallen back. Suddenly there is redoubled shouting from the huts. Six Fliers are seen clumsily hopping and gliding from roof to roof. They carry stolen infants.

Men and women clamber fiercely after them, shouting imprecations. A Flier pauses to bite savagely into his victim's neck, leaps onward. The evil band outrace their pursuers and launch themselves onto the outer wall.

"Stop them!" a woman shrieks, but there is no one there.

But as the Fliers poise to leap, something does halt them. Instead of sailing they are tumbling limply with their captives, falling on the ground below the walls. And other Fliers have stopped yowling and striking, they are falling too.

The villagers pause uncertainly and become aware of a stillness spreading from a point beside the gates.

Then they see her, the girl Snow, in the blue evening light. A slender white shape with her back to them, surrounded by a red ruin of dead Fliers. She is leaning bent over, dragged down by a shaft sticking in her side. Blood is flooding down her thighs.

Painfully she tries to turn toward them. They see her pull feebly at the spear in her belly. As they watch aghast she pulls the weapon out and drops it. And still stands upright, blood pouring down.

The Healer is nearest. He knows it is too late, but he runs toward her across the rank bodies of the Fliers on the ground. In the dimness he can see a shining loop of intestine torn and hanging from her mortal wound. He slows, staring. Then he sees the blood-flow staunch and cease. She is dead—but she stands there still.

"Snow—"

She lifts her head blindly, smiles with a strange, timid composure.

"You're hurt," he says stupidly, puzzled because the gaping flesh of her wound seems somehow radiant in the fading light. Is it—moving? He stops, staring fearfully, not daring to go closer. As he stares, the rent in which he has seen viscera seems to be filming over, is drawing itself closed. The white body before him is bloodstained but becoming whole before his unbelieving gaze. His eyes start from their sockets, he trembles violently. She smiles more warmly and stands straighter, pushing back her hair.

Behind them a last Flier yowls as it is run down.

Has he had an hallucination? Surely so, he tells himself. He must say nothing.

But as he thinks this he hears an indrawn gasp behind him. Another, others have seen this too. Someone mutters sibilantly. He senses panic.

Those Fliers, he thinks confusedly, how did they die? They show no wounds. What killed them? When they came near her, did she—what did she—

A word is being hissed behind him now, a word the Whites have not heard for two hundred years. The muttered hissing is rising. And then it is broken with wails. Mothers have found that the saved children are lying too still among the Fliers who had captured them, are in fact not saved but dead.

"Witch! Witch! Witch!"

The crowd has become a menacing ring behind him, they are closing warily but with growing rage upon the white, still girl. Her blind face turns questioningly, still half smiling, not understanding what threatens. A stone whizzes past her, another strikes her shoulder.

"Witch! Killer witch!"

The Healer turns on them, holding up his arms.

"No! Don't! She's not—" But his voice is lost in the shouting. His voice will not obey him, he too is terrified. More stones fly by from the shadows. Behind him the girl Snow cries out in pain. Women trample forward, shoving him aside. A man jumps past him with uplifted spear.

"No!" the Healer shouts.

In full leap the man is suddenly slumping, is falling bonelessly upon the dead Fliers. And women beyond him are falling too. Screams mingle with the shouts. Hardly knowing what he does, the Healer bends to the downed man, encounters lifelessness. No breath, no wound; only death. And the woman beside him the same, and the next, and all around.

The Healer becomes aware of unnatural quiet

spreading through the twilight. He lifts his head. All about him the people of his village have fallen like scythed grain. Not one is standing. As he stares, a small boy runs from behind a hut, and is instantly struck down. Unable to grasp the enormity, the Healer sees his whole village lying dead.

Behind him where the girl Snow stands alone there is silence too, terror-filled. He knows she has not fallen; it is she who has done this thing. The Healer is a deeply brave man. Slowly he forces himself to turn and look.

She is there upright among the dead, a slight, childish form turned away from him, one hand pitifully clutching her shoulder. Her face in profile is contorted, whether from pain or anger he cannot tell. *Her eyes are open.* He sees one huge silver orb glinting wide, roving the silent village. As he stares, her head turns slowly around to where he stands. Her gaze reaches him.

He falls.

When the dawn fills the valley with gray light, a small, pale figure comes quietly from the huts. She is alone. In all the valley no breath sighs, no live thing stirs. The dawn gleams on her open silver eyes.

Moving composedly she fills her canteen from the well and places food in her simple backpack. Then she gazes for a last time on the tumbled bodies of her people, reaches out her hand and draws back again, her face without expression, her eyes blank and wide. She hoists her pack to her shoulders. Walking lightly, resiliently—for she is unwounded—she sets out on the path up the valley, toward where she knows another village lies.

The morning brightens around her. Her slight figure is tender with the promise of love, her face lifted to the morning breeze is sweet with life. In her heart is loneliness; she is of mankind and she goes in search of human companionship.

Her first journey will not be long. But it will be soon resumed, and resumed again, and again resumed and again, for she carries wasting in her aura, and Death in her open eyes. She will find and lose, and seek and find and lose again, and again seek. But she has time. She has all the time of forever, time to search the whole world over and over again, for she is immortal.

Of her own kind she will discover none. Whether any like her have been born elsewhere she will never know. None but she have survived.

Where she goes Death goes too, inexorably. She will wander forever, until she is the last human, is indeed Humanity itself. In her flesh the eternal promise, in her gaze the eternal doom, she will absorb all. In the end she will wander and wait alone through the slow centuries for whatever may come from the skies.

. . . And thus the Beast and its Death are at last at one, as when the fires of a world conflagration die away to leave at their heart one imperishable crystal shape. Forged of Life-in-Death, the final figure of humanity waits in perpetual stasis upon the spent, uncaring earth. Until, after unimaginable eons, strangers driven by their own agonies come from the stars to provide her unknown end. Perhaps she will call to them.

[1] The material on the Kiowa Indians here is due, with thanks, to N. Scott Momaday's beautiful elegy, *The Way to Rainy Mountain*, University of New Mexico Press, 1969, and Ballantine Books.